Echoing Ancestors

Leigh Gaitskill

LadyLake Press
Corte Madera, CA

This novel is a work of fiction. Any resemblance to real situations or to actual people, living or dead, is entirely coincidental.

FIRST EDITION

Published by
LadyLake Press
P.O. Box 376
Corte Madera, CA 94976

Library of Congress Catalog Card Number: 96-076742

ISBN: 0-9652624-2-1

Cover art: Michael Eller
Design: Solomon Faber

Dedicated to the memory of my grandmother, Jane Wilson Gallaher, whose wonderful storytelling inspired the character of Virginia.

and to

The Moody Blues, whose music served as my muse throughout the writing of this book.

Acknowledgements

Many thanks to those who read the book in its entirety and gave me comments: Ellen Margron, Gay Luce, Gay Goessling, Caroline Heck, Jan Jacobson, Jana Doherty, Joe Durepos, Don Girard and Sue Shanks.

Thanks especially to my writing group – John and Johnna Lambert, Joe Reif and Sue Shanks – for their inciteful reading and critiques and for putting up with my anxious questions meeting after meeting.

Virginia

Chapter One

I was up in the hayloft again. Mama didn't like me to be up there because young ladies aren't supposed to climb or get dirty. But my brothers go up there and jump down into the hay. They won't let me jump with them. Mama's been more worried since I fell out of the apple tree onto a canning jar and got a big gash in my leg. I told her the hayloft is much safer. Besides, I like to go up there when no one else is in the barn. I can have adventures like the boys do. There was no pile of hay to jump into that day, so I was dancing around and thinking and all of a sudden I was on the edge and I lost my balance and fell.

Mama says ladies should be quiet and demure and she tells me I'm too loud. I guess sometimes that can be a good thing because I screamed really loud when I fell out of the hayloft and Sarah heard me. There was a big ol' pitchfork lying on the floor of the barn and I landed on it and one of the tines poked into my neck. Blood started spurting straight out. Sarah came in and said, "Lord have mercy," and then she started screaming for help. Loud. "Somebody come help me. Help!" she yelled. At the same time she knelt down beside me and started pressing on my neck, hard, while she propped me up enough to slide her lap under me. The blood stopped spurting out but then it hurt something awful and I started crying so hard I was moving all around.

"Hold still, baby," she told me. "If you move I might let go and this is real important—I can't let go." It hurt where she pushed on my neck too. But I liked to have Sarah holding me. She didn't hold me as much now that I was 10. Mama said I was too big for hanging onto a mammy. I felt pretty lonely sometimes, not being able to climb in Sarah's lap any more and smell the starch in her dress and the soap on her skin. Seems like there's hardly anything it's okay for a young lady to do. If I had known what it was really like for a girl to grow up I wouldn't have gotten bigger. Now I suppose I won't be allowed to climb anything.

Clayton, who really runs the farm, came in with my brother, Charley, right away. Charley's 18 and almost finished with school. Mama's trying to figure out some way he can go to college. Jim is already there. Sarah told them to go find the doctor. "Miz Ginnie's open her jug'lar, I think," she told them and kept on pressing. They ran for the stable, hollering for Jake to help them saddle up two of the horses. After a while we heard the horses pounding out of the stableyard and out onto the road. As they faded into the distance, it sounded like they were going in the same direction. Doc Bingham gets around the county a lot, so I reckoned they'd have to split up if he wasn't at his office. I'd like to be able to gallop off like that, with the hooves crashing on the road like thunder and the horse's mane flying.

Soon after they rode out, Mama, wearing her washed out grey dress, came back from delivering eggs with Bobby and Tommy. Sarah called out and they came to the barn. Mama gasped and fell against the door when she saw us. "What's happened Sarah?"

"Miz Virginia fell out of the hayloft and that ol' pitchfork poked her neck open—blood was spurting out so's I think it might be her jug'lar," Sarah answered.

"Oh, my God." Mama swallowed, "Can I take over now?"

"I don't think I should let go, Miz 'Manda. We don't want her losin' no more blood," Sarah said and nodded to the pool that collected on the floor before she got there. Mama sucked in a big breath.

"What can I do?"

"Help me hold her still for now."

After Jake put away the horse and buggy, he came back and stood gaping at the door. He's Sarah's son and he's 12 and when no one else is looking, he's my best friend. Mama told him to go to the house for clean cloths and hot water and a blanket. Bobby and Tommy ran to the house with him. When they came back with a bucket of water and piles of rags and blankets, Mama soaked the cloths and cleaned up Sarah and me and covered me with a blanket. Mama doesn't like blood much even though I guess she saw plenty when my brothers were younger.

I felt pretty weak, so I couldn't do much, but after a while I got kind of tired of not moving. As soon as I wriggled a foot, though, Mama held me still. I could feel her hands trembling. When I opened my eyes, I could see through some spaces in the roof of the barn. Mama wanted to fix it up but since Papa left we don't have enough money. She worries a lot about money and it makes her face all scrinched up sometimes and she's more short-tempered than she used to be. There were grey clouds moving over, some pale, some dark and now and again the sun broke through and made slivers of light around the barn. I faded in and out of watching so the lights seemed to dance around, kind of slow and eerie. Sarah started humming one of the songs she used to sing to me, but her voice was higher than usual and she felt tense. It kind of scared me that Sarah and Mama were so upset. It took an hour for Clayton and Charley to get back with Doc Bingham. I didn't see, but he probably drove up in his gig. He always wears a black suit and a white shirt and a hat. He has brown curly hair that pokes out from under the hat every which way. Sarah never let go for a second that whole time. Doc told everybody she saved my life. I didn't know I was almost dead, but I sure was glad Sarah pushed on my neck till I thought I couldn't stand it.

Sarah's taller than Mama and kind of thin. She and Clayton came here with Mama after she got married. They all lived on the plantation that Grandmama's family left her and Grandpapa to run. Mama says there wasn't much left of the place after the war. Sarah raised me more than Mama did and I love her more than Mama, I think. I am the fifth child of the fifth wife. Mama was pretty busy with all the boys and, for a while, some of Papa's other children were here too. So I spent most of the time with Sarah and Jake. Jake and me are great friends, but Mama and Papa decided a while ago that I couldn't spend so much time with a colored boy, so we have to be careful no one sees when we play together. I know Sarah and Jake more than Mama and Papa and my brothers, and I love them so I don't understand. But Mama says coloreds are different and we can't be friends. That scares me a little, because they seem regular to me. If there's something wrong, it must be some sneaky, suspicious kind of thing. My brother Tommy told me about changelings and sometimes I hide and watch Jake to see if he changes into something but he never does.

Doc Bingham asked for some more hot water. He put a smelly cloth over my nose and after that I only know what they told me. He wouldn't let them move me out of the barn before he stitched me up, so he did it right there. Sarah helped. Then they carried me in to my bed. When I woke up later my neck hurt really bad and Mama said I had to stay in bed for a week. I didn't know how I could just lie around that long, although, right then, I didn't feel too much like pitching stones across the pond or anything. I asked Sarah to look after my garden for me. Mama let me have a small plot near the house and I'd planted all my favorite kinds of flowers. Then I remembered Papa. I hoped maybe he would hear I got hurt and come out to the house to visit. He hadn't come out since he left the year before. Maybe if I was laid up long enough he'd want to see if I was all right.

He and Mama fought a lot before he left. He came home really late sometimes and then he yelled and yelled at Mama. Sometimes I could hear crying. My brothers and I went out to the fields or the barn or stayed in our rooms when they were fighting. Mama seemed tense and sad all the time. If I asked about it, though, she just told me not to be a nosy Parker. Once I heard her scream that he had to stop drinking or else. Not long after that Papa left.

Mama was always telling me to drink my milk and we could always have water. After Papa left I tried not to drink any milk or water for a couple of days, so I wouldn't have to leave too. Sarah caught me pouring my milk out and when I told her why I couldn't drink it, she laughed and laughed and told me Mama was mad because Daddy was drinking something else. She also told me not to tell Mama we had that talk. Mama always said Papa just wanted to be closer to his law office and the courthouse. Still, I worried sometimes that Mama would send me away too if I did something she didn't like and it seemed like no matter how hard I tried to please her I was always doing something she didn't like.

One time Mama got me and my brothers dressed up like Sunday and Clayton drove us into town to have dinner at Papa's house. He lives right in Columbia, on a street lined with big old trees. It was right after the magnolias had bloomed and petals still covered the yard of his house so that it was all pink and white and fluffy. My bloomers were stiff and rubbed against my legs and Sarah pinned a big bow in my hair and the pins poked my head. She made me wear my prettiest white dress with ribbons that matched the one in my hair and she fixed my hair in ringlets. I like it better in braids.

Sis was there and a couple of my other half brothers and sisters were coming. They're all old and I don't know them much. Papa didn't come out when we got there. We sat in the parlor. It's at the front of the house and looks out toward the street. The chairs are really stiff and hard, but we were pretty still for a while. The smell of ham and cloves floated out from the kitchen. Mama always said ladies and gentlemen do not fidget and we wanted Papa to be glad to see us, so we tried hard. But it was kind of boring and we were hungry. After a while the boys starting pulling on their collars and wriggling around till the chairs creaked. Tommy got up and went over to a cabinet with little figurines in it. I didn't think it would hurt anything to just look, so I slipped over and stood next to him. They were little wooden soldiers. Tommy and me loved playing soldiers. Well, when our older brothers were out in the fields, he liked to play soldiers with me.

I opened the cabinet and picked one up. Then Tommy picked one up. Next thing, we had them all out on the floor, lined up for a battle. Charley was still sitting in his chair. "Y'all are gonna get in trouble," he warned. "Why don't you just put those away and sit down?"

Tommy and me looked at one another and started the war. I was England and Tommy was the Colonies. We never played War Between the States because nobody would be the Yankees. We used strategy and moved our armies around pretty good. And we got madder and madder. Tommy liked to make up rules while we played so every time I cornered a battalion or pressed the cavalry forward he'd try to put in some rule about how I couldn't do that because it violated the codes of war. Before long I started yelling and throwing soldiers at him.

Bob finally couldn't stand it and jumped in and started fighting too. Charley kept telling us to stop. After a while we heard a roar from down the hall. A couple doors opened and shut and Sis came scurrying in, kind of scared looking.

"Oh, Ginnie, just look at you. You come with me. You boys put those soldiers away and behave yourselves. Papa's trying to work." The boys started whining, like they always do, that I started it and they shouldn't have to clean up.

"Never mind that, just pick up before Papa sees it and then tuck your shirts in and straighten your hair," Sis told them as she dragged me off to her room. "Look at yourself," she said and pointed me at the mirror. My bow was all crooked and my sash was twisted and loose and one sock was down and my curls were tangled. I kind of felt better but I knew Papa wouldn't like it so I tried to sit still while she combed and tied and fussed. Sis was 22 and she was always a little nervous and kind of tired. She must have looked like her Mama because she sure didn't look anything like Papa. I don't look like him either. We both have dark brown hair, though. She wears hers pulled back in a bun at the nape of her neck.

"Now, I have to go check on dinner, so you come with me to the kitchen where you'll be out of trouble." I always like a chance to be in a kitchen while cooking is going on and I can sneak tastes of things, so I hopped alongside her. Sis and Papa's cook got to worrying over the custards and I started making my way around, touching things and hoping to get my fingers in something good. The big old fireplace still took up most of one wall but since they had a big new stove, there was no fire. It looked to me like a good place to go sit but when I bent down just to see, Sis told me to get away from there. Then I spied a bunch of apples, piled high. I was pretty hungry and I love apples, so I went over, keeping an eye on Sis and Cook, naturally, and reached up to take an apple off the top. When I pulled it off, the whole pile started falling and rolling around the kitchen floor. They spread all over in nothing flat. When Cook turned to look, she stepped on one and whirled around the other way and crashed into the sink. The custard in the dish she was holding flew out onto the floor. I hoped they made extras so that I could still have one.

I picked up apples and stacked 'em back up as fast as I could go, while Cook caught her breath and Sis got some rags to clean up the custard. Cook was muttering something about the devil. Sis was trying not to laugh. Times like that I miss when she used to live with us and we shared a room before she went away to school. She rolled her eyes toward the door so I knew to skedaddle back to the parlor.

Bob and Tommy were playing marbles in the corner. The boys all look like Papa or Mama's papa. Charley was reading and trying not to look anxious. He had known Papa the longest, so maybe it was the hardest for him not to see Papa any more. He'd won a prize in school and he was about to bust wanting to tell Papa and see him proud. I just sat and twiddled my thumbs so's not to get in any more trouble.

Finally the dinner bell rang and we stood up and waited for Papa. We heard the study door open and Papa's slow walk down the hall. He stood in the door and surveyed all of us. His hair is bushy and mostly all white and he always wears a nice suit. He's tall and thin and looks very dignified, I think. He came to me first and gave me a kiss on the cheek. "How's my little girl?" His breath had that funny smell it always had when he'd been closeted in his study working. It was nice to smell it again. Dinner was pretty good, but kind of stiff. We were all pretty anxious to please Papa and we don't know our other brothers and sisters much. I don't even talk to my brothers very much cause they're older and they just think I'm a stupid girl.

"I have some news, Papa," Charley finally said.

"Yes, what is it?"

"I won the award for highest achievement at the school this year," Charley told him and waited anxiously. He was hoping that the prize would make Papa realize that he should go to college.

"Well, that's just fine, Charley. That's very fine," Papa beamed. But then he didn't say anything else. He never was much of a talker. If I had some money I'd give it to Charley even if he does pull my braids and call me "little bit".

When we left, Papa didn't say anything about seeing us again. Charley slumped down in the corner of the buggy and stared out at the darkness.

After I'd been laid up a couple of days, I asked Mama if Papa knew I'd been hurt. She said she was sure he did. The next day Sis came out and brought a package with some books she said Papa sent. They were just what I like: a mystery and one about a boy named Huck Finn having adventures on a river—it was written the year I was born—and a periodical about decorating houses. Mama gave Sis a funny look when Sis said Papa got me the books. Papa never came to visit me that week.

Chapter Two

"Not like that, Ginnie, like this," Grandmama grabbed the spoon from me with one hand and boxed me on the ear with the other. My eyes watered, my ear started ringing, and pains went zinging from one side of my head to the other. When I could see straight again, she was beating the egg whites herself. I couldn't see how she did it so differently. As soon as I turned 12 I had to start learning about cooking and needlework and lady things. None of my brothers had to take those lessons. "A well-trained lady must know all aspects of creating meals in order to manage a well-run kitchen," Mama'd say when I asked why the cook couldn't just do it. Grandmama taught me a lot of it. She's a very good cook. But she's a kind of mean teacher. While I watched the clear liquid in the bowl turning white and frothy and growing bigger, I asked Grandmama to tell me again about the parties they used to have.

"Oh, Ginnie, the dresses were so lovely. Full skirts with giant hoops and the prettiest petticoats." She loved to tell stories about life before the war. I could always turn her up sweet by asking for a story about it. "And the boys were so handsome in their suits. Very dashing. We'd fill the ballroom with flowers and hire an orchestra and the dancing would go on into the night." She smiled softly as she told the story and, for just a minute, she didn't look so old and tired. Her hair was always put up and all white, like the angel hair on the Christmas tree.

I watched how perfectly straight her back stayed as she finished whipping up the egg whites and let me fold in the ingredients she had me measure out earlier. Folding was part of the lesson for today. I held my breath and went pretty slow. I don't like being cuffed on the ear and I especially don't like having both ears done in one day. Grandmama kept smiling dreamily and when I asked her about putting the meringues on the baking sheet, she didn't seem all there. The egg kisses looked frail and defenseless on that sheet. We made a bunch of them. I love egg kisses. If Grandmama was still in a good mood when they finished baking, she might let me have one with some ice cream on it. We'd already made the chocolate ice cream and packed it away in some ice.

After the kisses were in the oven, I sat and looked around. This little house didn't have any ballroom in it. The kitchen was crowded, but cozy, somehow. Most all the furniture that the Yankees hadn't ruined was in that house. They said the old house was kind of barren by the time they left, but there was a little too much furniture for this space. And those fine old pieces sometimes looked a little embarrassed to be in this ordinary little house, I thought. I closed my eyes and tried to picture the ballroom, all decorated with flowers and loads of people in their party clothes, whirling around the room to beautiful music.

The ballroom was in the house where Grandmama grew up. When she was 17, she married Grandpapa. He was a professor of Greek and Latin at a fine university in the north, so he'd been away from home for a long time, but he came back to visit and met Grandmama at one of her first parties. They fell in love right away. He courted her all through his visit and then they wrote letters for a while before they got married.

"Ginnie, stop air dreaming and help me clean up these things so we can start the dinner." I jumped up and got to work on washing up. Mama and my brothers were coming to eat my first whole dinner later on. The kisses could be put aside while we fixed everything else. We had lessons on planning the timing too. Mama had Bobby kill a chicken for me to bring over. Grandpapa took it out to pluck it for me, while Grandmama wasn't looking. Just then he brought it back in. His hair was getting a little long, hanging in white clumps around his head and he seemed to grow more stooped all the time. Grandmama and her mama never had to pluck their own chickens before the war.

"Jason did you pluck that chicken for her? How am I going to teach her how to do it properly if you do her job for her? I declare, I have no idea how you and Amanda expect she's going to learn anything when you both spoil her so. "

I tried to figure out how it was that Mama ever spoiled me and wondered why my rich future husband would make me pluck chickens. Grandpapa looked a little sheepish but said, "Now, Lily, I like to do it and I thought it would just help you all get everything done a little faster." He added, softly, "I don't think the child is spoilt."

Grandmama grabbed the bird out of his hand and slammed it on the table. "Ginnie, get over here and help me start dressing this bird." I wiped off the last dish and dried my hands quick. "Hurry up you lazy child," she snapped just as I got there. While I started helping to smear butter on the chicken, I said, "Grandpapa, Grandmama was just telling me about the dances you all used to have." I looked up under my lids and let out my breath as her face relaxed a bit.

Grandpapa's eyes twinkled. He knew what I was up to. Mama's eyes and mine are the same color as his: grayish blue.

****

I used to climb into Grandpapa's lap and beg for stories about teaching. First, I always had him tell me how he could stand working up there in the North and having to talk to all those Yankees. He'd say, "The students were from the North and the South, Ginnie. And when you're teaching, all students are just young minds to fill with knowledge. I never thought of them as being from one place or another." Then he'd tell me a story like the one about the god who kidnapped a woman with a pretty name and made her live in hell. When he finished, he seemed like he was some far away place.

"Do you miss teaching, Grandpapa?"

"Yes, Ginnie, I suppose sometimes I do," he told me. "You know, there's no work more important, to my way of thinking, than filling young minds with knowledge."

"Why is it so important?"

"Well, knowledge enables people to make informed decisions. The more a person knows, the more he's able to see the possibilities and to know the probable outcomes of different choices. Then he can evaluate important decisions in his life. And I think it's especially important in a democracy for a man to have as much knowledge as possible so that every vote is based on understanding the issues."

"What's a democracy?" I asked him.

"It's a country where the people are allowed to vote for their government officials instead of being subjected to tyranny."

"Do I need to learn so that I can vote when I grow up?"

Grandpapa looked at me for a minute before he said slowly, "No, Ginnie, ladies don't vote. But that doesn't mean that there isn't a great deal of value to an education for you anyway. The more any person knows in life, the better the quality of that life can be."

I loved when we talked like that. And I worked really hard at my lessons so he'd be proud of me and pretty often he told me he was. Seemed like my teacher and Grandpapa were the only people who thought I was good.

****

I started scrubbing the vegetables while Grandmama put the last touches on the chicken. This time she told the story of the final party before the war started. Everyone was tense, knowing that the war would begin any time. But the ladies flirted more than ever and she said the young men seemed to grow more strong and dashing before their eyes. Most of them never came back.

"Watch what you're doing there, you need to cut those more uniform," Grandmama said from between her teeth. The last party never put her in a good mood. Mostly, except when she reminisced about the times before the war, she alternated between being sad and cranky. Her cheekbones were high and her face was kind of uppity when she wasn't smiling. She didn't have pretty gowns any more. And she sold all her jewelry so they could buy this house near us. Grandmama sniffed and called it a cabin, but it's really a house. Her parents and Grandpapa exchanged all their money for Confederate money so there was nothing left after the war but the house and land and those went before long.

"Do you know that those barbarians actually put their swords through all our lovely pictures? They have no appreciation for art. They broke porcelains and fine crystal. They burned our barns and they threw Daddy down and kicked him." Her eyes filled with tears. Sarah told me about how the women hid when the Yankees came into the area, but they could hear. Mama was eight then. Grandpapa was in Nashville on Confederate business. Grandmama's parents both died during the war. Broken hearted, she always said. She was left alone with Mama and Sarah and Clayton and their parents. All the rest of the coloreds had run off. She did more work than three people, they said, trying to save the place. One picture the Yankees didn't ruin hung in the parlor. I loved to look at it. It was an oil of Grandmama in one of her party dresses, her hair arranged in lovely ringlets, and she was laughing till even her eyes smiled.

I hate those Yankees. If it weren't for them, we'd all have pretty dresses and dance at parties instead of gathering eggs and killing and cooking chickens. I started massacring the carrots and got my other ear boxed. I hate her when she does that. It makes my head all achy. Grandpapa rustled around kind of nervous and poured some whiskey. She got mad at him when they talked about the war. Sometimes it seemed like she blamed him for all she lost. "I had no idea the day would come when I'd wish I'd been practical about choosing a husband," she'd mutter darkly. "Living in an ivory tower...." Grandpapa said she was never the same after the war. Before, she was lovely and charming and very gay. Sometimes when she told me about a party or a picnic or riding with her friends, I could see how she used to be. But mostly she was drawn and bitter. Once Sarah told me that even before the war she wasn't so charming if you crossed her. She said Mama was the one who changed the most because she had been quiet and sweet but as life got harder she developed a tough streak.

"Does it make you sad, Grandmama, that the war changed everything?"

"I don't have time to fool around with being sad," she snapped. "In this life, there isn't time to waste on pining over things that used to be. You pick yourself up and carry on."

"I'm sad sometimes that Papa left," I mentioned.

"All the more reason for you to pay attention to your cooking and sewing. With your Papa gone it's even more important that you be prepared to find a good husband, because you'll get no help from that man. So my advice to you, young lady, is that you don't waste your time with moping around when there's so much you need to do to take care of yourself. Put a good face on it and go on, that's what I say."

Grandpapa drank his whiskey and stared into his glass for a while, then said, "I went over and did some patching on the outhouse," and tried to hide his smile. Last week, when my friends came to visit, my brothers followed us out there and put sticks through the spaces in the wood and poked our bottoms. Lizzie and Bella said they didn't know if their Mamas would let them come back to a place with such unruly boys and flounced off in a huff. We ate lunch together at school the next day and giggled over how scared the boys were that we might tell on them. I don't know how Grandpapa found out but I'm glad he fixed it because I've been getting poked a lot and sometimes it hurts to sit down.

Pretty soon we had everything cooking and Grandmama went off to take a nap. My head ached a little. Grandpapa and I had one of our talks. I loved to be alone with him like that. Pretty soon, though, we heard whoops a ways off and some scolding and in a couple of minutes Mama and Tommy and Bob and Charley came in. By all rights, Charley should have been off at school these last two years, but Papa wouldn't help. He insisted on giving the schooling to Jim and got him apprenticed to a lawyer in Nashville. Jim wanted to be a farmer. Charley wanted to be a lawyer like Papa, instead of working the farm. Nobody seems to get to do what they want to when they grow up.

"We tried to have a snack first in case your food stinks," announced Tommy, "but she wouldn't let us, so this had better be good." He and Bob snickered and muttered about having to eat poison. They got Grandpapa to start telling stories about the times he was out at the camps near battlefields to meet with the officers.

Grandmama got up and came into the kitchen and we started serving the plates. Her cook, Sarah's mama, had the night off to go visit with Jake and Sarah and Clayton. Mama came in to help us finish. "Hello Mama," she said and brushed her lips by the side of Grandmama's cheek. "What can I do?"

"You could stop spoiling this child and make sure that she learns better than you did how to keep a husband."

Mama blinked and swallowed. Her nostrils flared a little so I knew she was angry but she wouldn't dare talk back to Grandmama. "I think she's been learning very well," was all she said. I was pretty surprised to hear it because she surely never told me that. I'd have liked to hear her say that I was doing well sometimes, especially if she said it to me instead of just picking apart everything I did.

While they talked, I grabbed the pepper and sprinkled lots of pepper on Bob's and Tommy's chicken. Then I slipped the pepper back and took their plates. We were all supposed to practice at being at a formal dinner. The boys had to get up and help us with our chairs once we served all the plates. Then we were supposed to use all the right silverware and carry on company conversation. Nobody talked at first.

Finally, Grandpapa said, "Charley, is that rascal of a father of yours making any effort to help you go to school?"

Charley turned red. Grandpapa knew he should have been off to school long since, but Papa was insisting that Charley was needed on the farm and wouldn't help pay for it. Charley had been pretty moody ever since the year for him to begin college had passed. "No, Grandpapa. We're hoping that if we can get the extra crops in for the next year or two there will be enough to pay for my schooling."

Tommy took his first bite of chicken at the same time as Bob . They sneezed and got all watery-eyed and started out to complain but everyone else said the food was delicious and told them to stop teasing me or they'd get a whipping. I have an idea that nobody threatens to whip the dinner guests at a real formal party. I thought I'd bust, trying not to smile while they struggled to eat the chicken without gagging. One of the rules is that we have to eat everything whether we like it or not. After dinner they sidled over and told me they'd get me at the outhouse when I was least expecting it. I just laughed.

Chapter Three

"Straight back, Ginnie," Mama instructed. I thought I was as straight as I could be while I tried to see my needlework. I never could figure out how you could do it without bending at all, but I knew she'd threaten to get a board out and make me sit strapped to it if I didn't keep my back straight.

"Why is it so important, Mama?"

"Because ladies always stand straight and tall. Gentlemen will notice your carriage first of all and you want to make a good first impression." She told me that before, but I hoped one day she'd give me a better answer.

"Why do I have to please gentlemen?" I sure wasn't interested in pleasing my brothers or their friends and older men didn't pay any attention to me at all.

"When you finish with school you will want to marry. And of course you will want to marry a gentleman who's very well off, so you must be pleasing." Her voice was getting a little irritated, so I didn't ask again why I wanted to marry a rich man. "It will be particularly important for you to be well behaved and biddable," she continued, as usual not explaining why I had to be especially careful.

Mama had me stitching a sampler. I could see the blue sky and hear the birds singing. Tommy and some friends were out by the pond skipping stones and roughhousing. Bob and Charley got to be out ploughing in the south forty. Of course, Charley wanted to be in school instead of out in the field, so I supposed he didn't feel much happier than I did. I had to stay inside trying to make my stitches neat and even enough to suit Mama. Seems like there get to be more rules and more lessons to learn about growing up to be a lady all the time. I've learned about arranging flowers, greeting guests, how to be charming and carry on a Polite Conversation and other things we never seem to have an occasion to use.

Mama looked mighty tired. Her face was a lot like Grandmama's except somehow Mama never appeared as haughty. I tried to imagine what she would have looked like if she'd gotten to have the come-out and the pretty dresses and all they thought she'd have when she was little. Sarah told me how they talked about her coming out party and how she planned to wear a white dress with pink ribbons. Instead she lived in a boardinghouse with her parents and when her party would have been, Grandmama set up her marriage to my Papa. He's a lot older than Mama, but he had a big law practice and Grandmama said that after the war a girl was lucky to find a marriageable man alive and in one piece and it was a windfall if he had some money. When they thought I wasn't listening, some people shook their heads and said what a shame it had been to marry such a pretty thing to an old devil who'd already buried four wives. I think Papa was a good catch anyway. I guess if I have to do all these things to get a husband, I'd like to have one who wouldn't go off with his money and live some place else, though.

"Keep stitching, Ginnie," Mama said. I didn't realize I'd stopped. It seemed I never got to be out running or climbing or anything fun any more. If I wasn't stitching something or doing my lessons I was helping Sarah prepare a meal. None of the other girls liked to play outside any more. I didn't tell them I still went out to climb up in the hayloft when nobody was looking. I didn't dance up there any more. The scar on my neck doesn't show too bad, I think. With the girls I talked about dresses and how to put your hair up and who would be courted by a beau first. All the boys were friends with my brothers and I couldn't imagine being courted by some boy who used to poke my bottom in the outhouse and pull my braids at school.

Grandmama died last summer so I didn't go over there for cooking lessons any more. I'd learned it pretty well before she died anyway, but I kept going because I could take that long walk on the path through the fields and spend time with Grandpapa. I think Grandmama liked teaching me too. Those last months she got dreamier and dreamier. I wished I knew her when she was happy. I figure she's in heaven in a real pretty ball dress and dancing with those boys who never came home from the war.

Grandmama set beautiful stitches. Mama brought out napkins and table-cloths that she stitched designs on and told me I had to learn to be that good. Mama fingered some of the old pieces that were spread around us. Some of them her grand-mama tatted or embroidered. Fine old pieces covered all the tables and chairs in the parlor. The furniture was old and stiff and the wood parts were carved all over. Some of it came from Grandmama's old house. The upholstery was a little threadbare in a few places but it was still pretty. The room was always a little dark because Mama tried to protect the furniture by keeping the shades partly drawn to keep out the sun. I could still see what a pretty day it was, though. My fingers were sore and I felt fid-gety. I noticed Mama's eyes misting up. "Mama," I said, "why don't I go over and see if Grandpapa wants to come over here for dinner? And I could fix up Jim's bed so he could stay till morning."

She looked up absently and said, "Of course." I asked if she wanted me to help put all the things away before I went. She shook her head and started folding a tablecloth. Everybody says I look just like her. We have the same straight nose and high cheekbones Grandmama had, but I didn't seem to be getting as tall as Mama. I hope I never get to looking as old and tired as them.

We ask Grandpapa to dinner a lot lately. We don't know why she did it, but instead of leaving the house to him or to Mama, Grandmama left it to some distant cousins in Kentucky that she didn't even know. Of course, Grandpapa was so much older, she probably never figured he'd outlive her. But Mama could have used the money from it. After a few months those cousins showed up to take over the house. They let Grandpapa stay, but he hated it. They were noisy and rude and they ruined some of his books. It was hard to believe they were any relation to my Grandmama with all her lady ways. Grandpapa couldn't get any peace. Mama told him he could come live with us, but he kept dragging his feet about leaving all Grandmama's things with those people. None of the children came to the school and I didn't like to be around them much because they played rough and mean and they were hard to understand with their mountain talk.

I ran out the door and just stood there for a minute to feel the sun on my face and decide which way to go. One of the ways to the path went past the pond. I went that way. I could still hear Tommy and his friends hollering and laughing. They only had a year of school left and sometimes I thought they played harder now than ever, like they wanted to take the last chance before they had to be grown up. I ran down there with my arms out so I could feel the air all over me. They were wrastling around when I came up. Tommy saw me and jumped up, "Oh ho. There's Ginnie. Bet she can't beat the new record." The others rolled around laughing, "That's no bet. Of course she can't."

"Bet I can," I said. Tommy and I bet whoever lost would do the other's chores for a week. Nathan and Zeke said they wouldn't bet because it wouldn't be sporting.

"What's the new record?" I asked, a little too late.

"Three skips." Tommy puffed out his chest and strutted around.

I drew in my breath. The most I'd ever gotten was two. "What happens if I equal the new record?"

"Hm," Tommy stroked his chin and thought for a minute. "We'll be even," he finally said and I let out my breath.

I pushed up my sleeves and studied all the stones around me to pick the best one I could find. You want your stone to be the best shape. They poked one another and joked that I was killing time 'cause I knew I'd lose. I didn't let 'em ruffle me. I knew they wanted me to just pick up any old stone. Finally I found a good one and picked it up.

"Now y'all back off and keep quiet," I told 'em. They moved back a little and didn't talk but they did poke one another with their elbows. I stood near the pond and turned the stone in my hand, getting the feel of it. Finally I got it in my palm just right, turned a little bit to the side, flipped my wrist and put the best twist on it I knew how. It sailed out a little then hit the water and bounced, skimmed a little farther and bounced again. I could hear the boys counting in the background. I could hardly stand to keep my eyes open to see what it would do next. It seemed to stop in the air for a second, like it was going to go on down. Then it moved on over and bounced one more time before it sank. Tommy groaned and I hopped up and down and whooped. The boys all started slamming stones in the water so it splashed up on me.

I ran on over to the path and shouted that I would get them for this. If Mama saw me all wet like that she'd figure I'd played with the boys and she'd be hopping mad about unladylike behavior. I started whirling down the path so the wind could help me dry off. Then I tried to think up something Grandpapa and I could do to give me time. I knew he'd help me. I asked him once why she got so angry with me all the time.

He shook his head. "Well," he said, "of course I can't know for sure what's going on in another person's head. But your mama has seen some mighty hard times you know. She was a pretty little thing." He smiled and remembered for a minute. "Always a little quiet, not as spunky as her mother. After the war, times were hard. Your grandmama and mama weren't raised to have to work the way they did. It turned Lily bitter and she was pretty hard on Amanda. I don't know, I think your mama is mighty anxious to set you up so that you have it easier than she did and maybe it just makes her push harder."

"Why doesn't she push the boys then, so they won't have a hard time?"

"Well, boys are tougher. She doesn't worry so much about them, maybe."

"My stomach feels all tight and my heart pounds and my head starts to aching when she's really mad at me, Grandpapa."

"I know, honey," he said. "You know you can always come to me when you're upset and I'll help you out," he told me and reached out to touch my cheek.

With my dress all wet as I walked along, I figured I was heading for the right person. After a while, I could see something big in the path up ahead. As I got closer, I realized that it was a person, lying face down. I stopped for a second to see if the person was moving and then I ran the rest of the way. When I got up next to him my heart started pounding 'cause I recognized Grandpapa's clothes. I called to him while I knelt down and started shaking his shoulder. He didn't move. I turned him over on his back and felt surprised at how light and fragile he seemed. A little blood trickled down his forehead where it hit a small rock in the path. I kept shaking and yelling louder but he didn't move or answer me. A big, heavy carpetbag was next to him.

I jumped up and ran back down the path screaming, "Help me ... somebody help me! It's Grandpapa." When I came close to the pond, the boys just stood there. Nathan said, "Sure, Ginnie, you're gonna get us now, huh?" Then I got close enough for Tommy to see my face.

"Something really is wrong with Grandpapa?" he asked and looked scared. Then I quit screaming and started to cry.

"Go get the doctor. He's lying in the path and I can't get him to move."

Tommy and the boys ran for the stable. We'd heard that in the cities people were starting to drive horseless carriages, but we'd never seen one and we couldn't imagine it was real. Tommy set up a shout for Clayton. A minute later Tommy and Zeke galloped off to find Doc and shortly after Clayton drove out in the farm cart with Nathan up next to him. They picked me up and I told Clayton where Grandpapa was. The path was just wide enough to take the cart. When we got there they jumped down and lifted Grandpapa and his bag up into the back of the cart. I held his head in my lap and told him over and over that he was going to be okay.

Back at the house they hauled Grandpapa down. Mama and Sarah heard the commotion earlier and were out waiting for us. They hustled ahead to open doors. Clayton and Nathan put Grandpapa in Charley's room on Jim's old bed. The room was very plain, especially since Jim left and took his things. There wasn't much sign of Charley in there, like he didn't acknowledge he still lived on the farm. After Mama and Sarah looked at Grandpapa and held his wrist, they exchanged a look and sent me out to the kitchen to slow down the dinner. Mama seemed kind of pokered up and scared.

"Mama, if Doc Bingham gets here soon enough, Grandpapa will be okay won't he?" I asked as I turned to go. Sarah patted me on the shoulder and tried to smile but no one answered. I don't even remember what I did to keep dinner, but I know I stayed busy in the kitchen until I heard the horses clattering. Tommy and Zeke rode in ahead of the Doc's gig and jumped down and waited so they could take his horse.

I shouted to Mama and opened the door. Sarah bustled in and led Doc Bingham back to the room. I tried to follow but Sarah told me to stay in the kitchen. Tommy came on in and said the boys had to go home because they were already late. I told him we couldn't go back to Charley's room. He wandered around the kitchen looking in all the pots. After a while Bob came in from the field he'd been working in and wanted to know why Doc's gig was out there. I explained and told him maybe he should wash up now so he'd be all ready for dinner. He went out to the pump and we heard the water, then Charley's voice joining him. Just as they finished and came in, Doc Bingham walked in all slow and solemn, with his head down a little. His hat was off and his hair seemed more wild and unruly than ever. Sarah followed on his heels with tears pouring down her cheeks.

"What about Grandpapa?" we asked together, still hoping.

"He's dead," Sarah sobbed, while Doc said, "I'm sorry, it's too late."

I crept back into Charley's room. Mama sat rigid and still, holding Grandpapa's hand in hers. Grandpapa's white hair fanned out around him on the pillow. His face was all pale and that made his nose look pretty red. He had that far away look on his face, like he'd been thinking of one of his old lectures.

Mama whispered, "He'd packed his things up in that bag. He finally couldn't stand it over there any more and he tried to come home." Her voice caught then and she cried quietly. I wanted to cry and crawl up next to Grandpapa, but I knew Mama wouldn't like such a display, so I swallowed hard and felt like my neck was swelling up from all it had to hold down. I didn't know how I could stand it without Grandpapa to help me and talk to me.

I spent all my time stitching the next couple of days and never tried to go outside. Mama helped when she could. Sarah could hardly stop crying and I even surprised Clayton wiping tears off his cheeks a couple of times. They knew Grandpapa all their lives. "He 'uz one of the finest, kindest gentlemen I ever knew," Sarah kept saying. Her mama came to live in the cabin with them.

Jim came to the funeral but Papa didn't. Jake was off working on another farm but he came back and helped out. He seemed to be uncomfortable about talking to me much any more. All my friends said girls had to be careful about talking to colored boys anyway so I guess it was just as well, but I'd have kind of liked to talk with him about Grandpapa.

We told the Kentucky cousins they killed Grandpapa and asked them not to come to the funeral. They called him an old drunk and none of us ever talked again. They kept all Grandmama's pretty things. Everybody thought the embroidered cloth over the casket was lovely and I thought maybe it was a good thing I knew how to stitch.

Chapter Four

All the way to Hamilton's Ladies' College, Mama explained to me again that I needed to be educated in the finer points of being a lady as well as learning from books like Grandpapa taught me and that this school could give me both. I don't know why she didn't think I'd heard her the first million times she said it. I'd learn French and music and watercolors and literature. I needed these things, she told me, so I could make a good marriage. I began to feel the pinpricks behind my eyes that meant one of my headaches was coming on.

"Ginnie, we lost our land. This little scrap of a farm has to go to your brothers. If you marry well you can get some land again. As long as you have land you can always survive." If Grandmama said that once she said it a hundred times. I didn't remember Mama saying it before Grandmama died. Then it seemed like she never stopped. I had a funny feeling there was something more to this single-minded pursuit of a marriage for me but no one ever talked about anything else.

I nodded from the corner of the carriage and tried to remember if Mama ever talked to me about anything but the things I needed to do to marry. I couldn't call anything else to mind. We'd never just talked with one another and I only knew her as this critical, overbearing woman whose life seemed to be devoted to the single-minded pursuit of making me feel small and miserable. All these years of cooking and stitching and learning to sit still instead of running in the wind with my brothers, she'd told me I needed to prepare to take my rightful place in society. One day I meant to ask her what good she thought all that had done her.

We were invited sometimes to join the parties given by the wealthier families around Columbia, but since we were no longer wealthy and especially because Papa had left us we were not really part of the circle. Mama fascinated me at parties or when she ran into her acquaintances. She was warm and charming to everyone, laughing and chatting, in a quiet sort of way. She didn't talk to any of us that way. I guessed that was how Grandmama taught her to socialize. Sometimes I wondered why they didn't learn to act that way with their families.

Papa died last year. He left a little money to each of his children and, since they were still married, Mama inherited the farm and the house in town. Most of the money from selling the house went into improvements for the farm, which Jim came back to manage, but some she added to what she'd put aside for my education and now I was able to go to a better school than she'd hoped. We never did see Papa for more than an occasional, stiff dinner at his house. After a while we never even talked about him and the invitations to dinner came as a surprise. Sis got married and after that I never had as much fun going to his house.

The part of my inheritance that Mama let me have bought me some new dresses. The rest, she said, was for my dowry. Mama and the seamstress managed to stretch the money as far as they could so that I could take fashionable clothes to school and all the trimmings. I had a number of new dresses with elegant bustles making folds that cascaded to the floor behind me. Even though I couldn't see it, I could feel the flow of fabric swishing and swaying. I felt a little better then about the school. I had been afraid that I'd be the only one who didn't have trunks of pretty dresses. Actually, a lot of the girls turned out to be from families that weren't as well off after the war, trying to restore their positions in society through meeting the right people.

Riding along toward Nashville with Mama that day, though, I felt trapped and sad. It was hard to say good bye to Sarah. Jake was gone. He left to look for work in the north and we hadn't heard much from him since. Sis came out to see us off and made me promise to write. Tommy had used his money to go to school, even though he didn't have enough to finish and Robert had gone off to work for the railroad. Charley was apprenticed with some old lawyer friends of Papa's in Knoxville. So, only Jim was at the carriage to say good bye and he slipped a packet into my cloakbag. "This is for when you're feeling lonely those first couple weeks, Little Bit," he whispered and gave me a kiss on the cheek.

****

I'd never been to a city so big before and I was afraid. I couldn't imagine living in a place where buildings were everywhere. Even Columbia seemed bustling and noisy compared to home. And now I'd have to use all the things Grandmama and Mama taught me to pretend to be a lady all the time. I did look forward to seeing a horseless carriage though. One day, when I was sitting on the hayloft, just dangling my legs and leaning against a beam, worrying about how I could stand the school, Jim came in and saw me and climbed the old ladder up to the hayloft and sat next to me. We could look out ahead of us and see the sun shining on the yard outside or turn to the side and see the late afternoon sky, cornflower blue, hovering over the south forty, brown and barren after the late summer harvest.

"Hey, Little Bit, you look mighty glum," he said. "What's the matter?"

I smiled at him, "You haven't called me Little Bit in a long time."

"Well, you aren't quite such a little bit any more. Although you're never gonna be very big either," he answered, "but right now, you look like a scared little girl again."

I had stopped growing at five feet, a little shorter even than Mama or Grandmama. The boys were all tall like Papa. "Well, I guess you're right, I'm not likely to get any bigger," I told him. Then I went back to swinging my legs and staring at my feet. Jim and I never talked much and I felt a little strange about telling him how I was so afraid. Mama snapped my head off every time I mentioned anything about being scared.

"You scared about going off by yourself?" he asked with such kindness and understanding in his voice that my eyes filled with tears and I could only nod. He reached out a hand and rubbed up and down my back. "What is it that scares you so?"

Suddenly I started telling him everything that no one had allowed me to say, starting off with my fears about a city as big as Nashville and being there all alone.

"I know what you mean, Little Bit. When I first went there to apprentice, I thought it was the biggest, noisiest place that ever was. Those fellows in the law firm seemed awfully sophisticated and I felt out of place until I got the hang of it. But you know what, it's gonna be different for you."

"Why will it be different for me?"

"Well, because you're going to school. You'll meet all kinds of friends through the school and the school will look out for you. You'll go to parties and dinners and ... Mama won't be there to criticize you about everything you do." He said the last part softly, as if he couldn't quite believe he was saying it out loud. "She was never as hard on us as she was on you. I don't know why... ." He shook his head and contemplated the issue almost as if I weren't there.

I looked around at him and just stared, I was so surprised that anyone noticed how hard she was on me. I'd decided long ago that I must be an especially inept learner, with little talent for being a well-bred lady. He just gave me an "I know" nod and, since he looked terribly uneasy, I changed the subject. "How am I going to be invited to parties when I don't know anyone there?"

"From what Mama tells me, the school sees to it that the students are introduced into the local society to some extent. And they give permission for the girls to go to parties that they're invited to as long as at least one other girl goes as well. I, uh, wrote to a few people that I met when I lived there and told them you'd be at the school. And I think Mama contacted some old family friends. Don't you tell her I told you though."

I threw my arms around his neck. And he hugged me for a second. "You feel better?" he asked and pulled back a little.

I let him go and nodded my head, "Yes, Jim, thank you."

****

As I leaned against the side of the buggy, I reached out to my bag to give it a pat and listen for the crackle of the paper around Jim's present. Then I realized I'd been daydreaming and came back to hear Mama still droning on about how I needed to take advantage of this opportunity to make good connections. My head ached and it seemed hard to breathe. Clayton was maneuvering into the city streets. There were other horses and buggies, but all around us were the motorcars that we'd heard so much about. Mama and I stared in wonder while Clayton fought the horses to keep them from bolting with fright. What a noise those contraptions made! The din was unbelievable, between the cars and all the horses, and all the people walking, running, talking, shouting.

The school, when we arrived, turned out to have some land around it and it was a little more quiet by the time we'd pulled up the drive to the door. I began to think maybe a person could get some sleep. The school was one, big, red brick building with lots of white-shuttered windows in gay contrast with the stern-looking turrets at the top. Clayton unloaded my baggage while Mama and I went up the steps and through the big double doors into the school. Butterflies danced in my stomach at such a pace I almost forgot that my head pounded. A pretty older woman came down the hall toward us, wearing a very neat high-necked gown with a white bodice and black skirt. Her hair, dull brown with a sprinkling of grey at the temples, was pulled up in a twist. "Hello, I'm Mrs. Meacham. And which of our new ladies have we here?" she said in a voice so gentle I could hardly believe she was the headmistress. She didn't sound anything like Mama.

"I'm Amanda Johnson, and this is my daughter, Virginia." Mama smiled her company smile and put out her hand. "I'm very glad to meet you in person at last."

Mrs. Meacham clasped Mama's hand, then put her hand toward me. Mama gave me a push on the back so that I lurched forward to squeeze the outstretched fingers and drop a slight curtsy. "Nice to meet you Miz Meacham." For a moment I thought she flashed a slightly angry look at Mama before smiling warmly at me, "Ginnie, I'm so glad to have you here. I'm sure we're going to be great friends. Can I offer you all something cool to drink?"

"That would be lovely, Mrs. Meacham," Mama answered. "Although I must head back to Columbia today, so that I cannot tarry long."

"Fine, then. Do you have someone to help you get your things to your room?"

"Yes ma'am."

"Why don't you bring him in and I'll get one of the staff to come help him and then I'll lead all of you to your room. I'll have some cold drinks brought up—oh, you can send your man to the kitchen in the back, if you like, so that he can have something too—and then I'll show Virginia around later and tell her our rules."

I ran to get Clayton, giving him the news that he could have a cold drink and advising him to slip back there between trips, and he came in with the first of my bags. We came back in and Mrs. Meacham led us to number 24. "Now, Frederica Wilkes is your roommate. She came in earlier but has gone out to do a little shopping and she'll be having dinner with her family."

Once in the room, Mama started bustling around and hurrying Clayton. I sank into a chair on the side of the room that had been left for me and watched the commotion. One part of me wanted to tell Mama to let me go home with her and to tell her I didn't know how to find a husband, but I knew that she'd just plant her lips together and flare her nostrils and tell me through clenched teeth that I should feel grateful to have this opportunity to assure my position in life. When she asked me what was wrong I just told her I had the headache. She found my pills and had me swallow one. Another part of me was attracted to the softness of Mrs. Meacham and the warmth in her eyes.

"Ginnie, we need to leave now. Mind your manners and keep up with your studies," Mama announced and gave me a peck on the cheek before she turned to go. Clayton stood turning his hat in his hands as she passed by him and out the door. I got up and walked over to him. I wanted to hug him, but that would make Mama mad and Clayton would catch it all the way home. My eyes burned and my chin quivered a little. Finally, he stuck out a tentative hand and said, "You take care, Miz Virginia." I couldn't speak a word, but I clasped his hand in both of mine and then watched him follow Mama down the hall.

The hall was busy as other girls were arriving and having their bags brought up. I didn't feel ready to meet them, so I went back into my room and sat down again. For a little while I closed my eyes and waited for the medicine to take. Then I opened them and looked around me. Two plain beds with matching flowered coverlets, a little faded. Two old wooden bureaus on opposite sides of the wall and two small desks with chairs as well as two velvet covered parlor chairs near the windows. Gas lights on the wall over each bed and each desk. We only had lanterns and candles at home. I was a little afraid those lamps would catch on fire, but still, it was exciting to think of having so much light so easily. Suddenly I remembered Jim's package. I'd pushed the cloakbag out of Mama's way so that she would not unpack it. Now I reached in and retrieved the gift, pulling the ribbon open and unfolding the paper. A whole box of chocolates.

I'd just put the lid back on when the door burst open and a blonde vision bounced into the room, carrying a number of parcels. Fair ringlets, big brown eyes, dimples and the most enchanting smile I thought I'd ever seen. "Oh, you must be Virginia," she exclaimed, depositing her bundles on her bed, "I'm Frederica, but everyone, absolutely everyone, calls me Freddie. Mrs. Meacham said she's going to come in in a minute and tell us the rules. I hope there aren't too many rules, don't you? I want to have some fun. Well, we'll just have to break some of them, if there are. You look worn out. Was it a hard journey?"

She paused for my reply, but it took me a moment to contemplate which question to answer. "Well, the trip wasn't too bad, but my head ached when I got here. It's getting better now."

Mrs. Meacham knocked just then and came in to explain some of the rules and to tell us where the lavatories were and the cafeteria and the meeting room that we were to be in at eight o'clock the next morning. "Breakfast is at seven o'clock every morning and classes always begin at eight. You'll receive your schedules tomorrow morning at the meeting. All ladies are to be in bed by eleven o'clock every night, unless there is an off-campus party on the weekend and permission to stay out until eleven, in which case midnight is bedtime. Someone will come around to check the rooms every night. Ladies are not to leave the campus without permission and there must always be at least one other student accompanying in order for permission to be given. Men are not allowed above the first floor. Unchaperoned visits with gentlemen are not allowed at any time or any place."

While Mrs. Meacham went on to explain the rules about parties, Freddie gazed at her with a rapt expression on her face, but every time Mrs. Meacham turned to me, Freddie shot me a look of devilment until I was struggling to keep a straight face. Finally Mrs. Meacham asked us if we needed anything else and told me that there would be a light supper served in an hour. Freddie had apparently come back to change before the dinner with her parents and began to bustle about as Mrs. Meacham closed the door, talking all the while.

"Well, it's not as bad as it could be, I suppose. We'll have to figure out how to get past the bedchecks and have after hours parties, don't you think? I'm going to find the washroom and splash some water on my face, do you want to come with me?" Happy to follow this amazing creature anywhere, I walked out into the hall in her wake. We halloed some of the other girls and came to the washroom. I didn't want to appear unsophisticated, but once over the threshold I could only turn and stare. A few houses in Columbia had indoor bathrooms that I had seen, but this enormous one with a line of sinks was new and astonishing to me. "Do you still have an outhouse too?" Freddie asked merrily. "Do you have brothers?" As I began to nod and say yes, she continued, "oh, did yours find ways to poke your bottom from the outside?" We both went into whoops. Just then, some of the other girls came in and we all introduced ourselves. Freddie told them what we were laughing about. They joined in with their own stories and I had some new friends to go to supper with by the time we went back to our room.

Freddie never stopped chatting while she whisked off her dress and slipped on a gown and then she was gone in a flash. In her wake, the quiet of the room was almost overwhelming. I sat back for a minute to take stock of how I felt to be there. Fear definitely still gripped my stomach as I faced new people, places and classes, but, I had to admit, the outlook was definitely growing brighter. As I changed for supper I noticed that my head didn't ache any more.

Chapter Five

Thanks, in large part, to Freddie, that year at Hamilton's became the best year I'd ever spent. We quickly became ringleaders among the girls, organizing regular late night visits in various rooms and raids on the kitchen to add snacks to the treats we brought in when we shopped, among other minor violations. We were very good at taking tiny amounts of each item so that rarely was anything missed. Freddie, with her angelic fairness, seemed never to fall under suspicion and, either because I was an excellent student or because I was her bosom friend, I rarely came under scrutiny either.

At first I felt nervous—after all those years I'd spent with Mama and Grandmama watching my every move, I was sure we were being observed. Soon, though, I relished our escapades and the fact that we could enjoy such high spirits without fear of the kind of repercussions I suffered at home. I could throw myself into the fun and adventure I'd longed for. My whole body seemed to expand with the freedom and my head didn't ache so often. At the same time, I was so truly fond of Mrs. Meacham that I always made sure we never crossed any line that I knew she could not accept. Every now and then she invited me into her apartments for tea. She told me all about how her husband had died when she was very young, and fortunately, since he was not able to leave her very much money, she had been trained as a teacher. She taught at this school and gradually worked her way up to the headmistress position. Her rooms were bright and cheerful, decorated in light colors and she had some lovely pieces of furniture. I particularly liked her empire style sofa with flowers carved across the wood at the top. I talked with her about how I wanted to be a teacher.

"Well, Virginia, you're certainly more than smart enough. Perhaps you would rather be at a teacher's college?"

"Mama won't let me," I told her wistfully. "She wants me to be at this kind of school, so that I can, well, make connections and, uh..."

"Marry well," Mrs. Meacham nodded understandingly. "Well, that's what most all of our girls are here for. A teacher's life, you know, is often not that easy. I was very fortunate to get a position in a quiet, genteel school like this where the staff is treated with respect."

"I couldn't see that Mama's life with Papa was so terribly easy, either." I had no idea how that popped out of my mouth and looked up in horror at Mrs. Meacham. She just smiled though. She seemed never to get mad.

"That's true, Virginia. I've known many women to have a very hard time in marriage. I loved my husband and had such a happy few years that I forget that sometimes."

"I don't know if Mama would let me marry someone I loved. And I would so like to teach out west where there'd be some excitement and adventure."

"I'm sorry Virginia, that your dreams and your Mama's plans are at such cross purposes. Perhaps she knows best, though." She said it a bit doubtfully, as if she felt it was her duty to back Mama up, but didn't really believe what she was saying. "Would you like some more tea or another macaroon?"

Sometimes Mrs. Meacham and I discussed Greek myths or literature over our tea. We were both a little sad, I think, that neither of us would ever teach at a university like Grandpapa did.

****

A large dance and reception was held for us the first weekend of school at one of the big hotels. A committee of prominent citizens put this event on every year and so began our introductions into society. The hotel was very grand and the ballroom was elegant. Three of the biggest crystal chandeliers I ever saw hung in a row from the frescoed ceiling.   From then on, the number of invitations grew. Jim's and Mama's friends introduced us at their parties, Freddie was instantly deluged with would be beaus and I received my share of attention as well. I was so much smaller and darker than she that I liked to think we made a complementary set, though I had no delusions about being as pretty as Freddie.

Between the two of us we were invited to events all over town and always went together. Freddie had a sweetheart back home so she did not intend anything serious, but she surely liked to flirt. She found more ways to get news to some of the fellows whenever the art teacher took us on a field trip to paint watercolors in a park. A few showed up every time and bought everyone ices, even the art instructor, who was young and pretty herself.

At one of the first parties, I looked up and noticed the most handsome man I had ever seen across the room. His hair was even fairer than Freddie's and his eyes were the deepest blue, like the sky just after the sun has set. He looked at me and then I saw him speak to our hostess. She brought him over in a minute and introduced him.

"Virginia, this is Adrian Knight. Adrian, Virginia Johnson." I almost giggled as I held out my hand—I'd just been thinking he looked like the knight in a romance story. He asked me to dance and soon we swirled around the room. My heart pounded while I concentrated on my steps—I'd seldom danced with anyone but my brothers. This was very different. He danced very gracefully and lightly, yet under my hand the muscles in his shoulder were strong. I'd never had such a powerful feeling on first meeting someone. He seemed familiar. I felt more at home in his arms than I'd ever felt before and at the same time my stomach fluttered as I wondered what he was feeling. We were soon laughing and talking as if we'd met somewhere long before. I was promised to dance with several others, so we periodically separated, but he took me for refreshments.

Over supper, he turned those dark eyes on me and pressed me to tell him all about my life and my family. I started out with just the basics, "Well, I grew up on a farm outside Columbia with my four older brothers."

He wasn't satisfied with an outline, though. He wanted to know what the farm was like and how I got on with my brothers, whether the war had changed things for my family. I found myself pouring out everything and especially how I'd felt. Words came spilling from my mouth, one tumbling over another, sometimes so fast that they landed in a sentence in the wrong order. It was as if he'd reached down into some recessed and well-blockaded cavity in my being where I'd shoved all my thoughts and feelings and then he pressed the magic latch that set them free. I couldn't remember when anyone had listened to me like that, except maybe Sarah, when I was little. And he seemed to understand.

"My grandmother was pretty angry about all she lost in the war too and she was pretty hard on my mama. It used to make me angry to watch the hurt in Mama's eyes when my grandmother lit into her or my sister—Cecy, we call her, but her name's really Cecilia. I don't think it hit Cecy so hard, since my parents weren't like that with her, but Mama's a little nervous and unsure of herself sometimes, like she's waiting to be told she's wrong."

"I feel like that all the time," I told him, entranced by the comprehension and sympathy in his eyes. Then I began to draw him out. As he spoke I watched his face, so animated and alive. His eyes subtly reflected the mood of whatever story he told and never strayed from me.

His family had been one of the most prominent families in Tennessee before the war. They didn't lose everything, but they weren't left with very much either. He was a gentleman from head to toe and there had been enough money to educate him well and give him a good start in business, but he was not wealthy yet. His lack of fortune didn't bother me and I hoped that his family's prominence would weigh with Mama, if at some future point her permission were needed.

Suddenly we realized that virtually all the guests had gone back to the ballroom and we returned and danced several more dances together. From then on, Adrian appeared at most parties I went to. We exchanged little notes to tell one another which invitations we each received and which we wanted to accept.

"Virginia, I declare, you're spending more and more time with Adrian and you all look cow's eyes at each other. You haven't gone and lost your heart in the first month of school have you?" Freddie asked roguishly.

For a moment I felt trapped and was too afraid to answer. Then, I looked at those disarming dimples and nodded. "Yes, I think maybe I have."

"Why are you lookin' so glum, then?"

"Well, I don't know if Mama will like it."

"You know, Ginnie, sometimes your Mama sounds mean as a snake! There couldn't be a more charming or well-bred man in the south than Adrian. Except for my Sonny, of course. Oh," she paused as realization dawned, "he's not rich enough? I declare, a person would think you're for sale to the highest bidder or something."

"Well, of course not," I answered with what I hoped was real conviction, "she just wants to be sure I'm comfortable—more comfortable than she was, I guess." We had these talks often, dressed in our nightgowns and curled up on our beds after lights out. I looked forward to it all day long. I'd had Bella and Lizzie and some of the other girls for friends back in Columbia, but Freddie was more, somehow.

I loved dancing in Adrian's arms at the parties, but I think my favorite times were at the park, when the two of us could take a little walk—as long as we stayed in sight of the chaperone—and talk about our dreams. Adrian didn't want to stay in business, a fact I decided I would never tell Mama.

"I have another book idea, Ginnie," he'd tell me.

"Oh, you do? Tell me, please," I'd answer.

"It's about a fellow who goes out west to find more space and some land. He faces harder times than he expected, but he gets a little farm going after a series of trials and tribulations."

"Oh, that sounds lovely, Adrian."

He grinned mischievously, "And then he meets the lovely local school-teacher, a tiny little thing with pretty grayish blue eyes." I'd told him about how I wanted to be a teacher out west. He thought it would be splendid for the two of us to be out there, me teaching about reading and writing and him writing his books. So did I.

For all he looked so very ethereal, Adrian rode and played with an intrepid spirit and was full of fun. We loved to try to top one another with stories of our pranks. He and his brother and sister thought up some grand ones. Once they went down a busy Memphis street and let all the horses loose from the hitching posts.

One day when we attended a country party at a nearby farm, Adrian and I gathered a few people and headed off for the pond to hold a stone skipping contest. Adrian didn't believe I could get three skips, so I had issued a challenge a while back, to be waged at the first opportunity. None of the other contestants were serious contenders and the battle soon came down to the two of us. We wound up tied at three skips each. My brothers would have been sulky about not actually winning, but Adrian shouted with laughter and glowed with pride that I could match him. "Isn't she amazing?" he asked of anyone within earshot.

"You two are wonderfully well suited," Freddie told me later.

"Why do you say so?" It pleased me to hear her confirmation of my own feelings.

"Well, to begin with, most girls I know would have let him win. And I know that never occurred to you. And most men I know would have been miffed that you really challenged them and sulky at not winning. But Adrian couldn't have been more pleased that you were able to keep up with him. You both so genuinely pull for one another. And you both want to grab so much from life. Well, I don't know how to say it. It just seems like you all belong together."

There was an older man who came to many of the parties we went to and always asked me to dance. Jack Wrigley was a fine figure of a man, tall and powerful, with grey hair around the temples and peppered through the rest of his hair, and 50 if he was a day. He loved to hear stories of my escapades with Freddie. He'd throw back his head and laugh and laugh. Sometimes he told me about tricks he and his friends pulled when he was in school. Mostly things about frogs in beds and the kinds of tomfoolery boys like to do. Not much to interest Freddie and me, mostly, but every now and then he'd give me an idea that was kind of fun—like sneaking downstairs in the night and switching the salt and sugar.

Jack treated me like some kind of hot house flower, fragile and delicate. Sometimes I liked it. Especially when I had the headache. He was very solicitous. Sometimes I felt a little impatient with his avuncular behavior, but he didn't come to all the affairs and even when he did, I spent far more time with Adrian, my kindred spirit. Once, I mentioned to Jack that I 'd like to be a schoolteacher, and he looked astounded and said, "Oh, Virginia, I hope you'll never have to do that," as if he, like Mama, found the idea to be more a nightmare than a dream. Times like that I was especially grateful for Adrian's and Mrs. Meacham's understanding of my vision.

The months whirled by so quickly that I could hardly believe it when Freddie turned to me one day and said, "Well, Ginnie our year together is almost over. I can hardly believe you won't be back next year with me. I declare I don't know what I'll do without you."

I was shocked. Life at Hamilton's had turned out to be so deliciously happy that I got caught up in it as if it were going to go on endlessly, like a carrousel of flower-bedecked ponies gaily turning to music with the switch stuck on. Adrian, Freddie and Mrs. Meacham were the dearest friends I'd ever known and I had scores of other lovely friends among my schoolmates and those I regularly encountered at parties. Freddie was coming back for a second year, but no amount of begging in notes and on vacations availed to convince Mama that the rest of my inheritance should be used to finance another year at the school. I had finally mentioned Adrian to her, telling her I'd met someone of whom I was very fond. Later she told me that she heard he was a nicely behaved young man.

Although our conversations assumed a future together, Adrian and I had not discussed our plans formally and I didn't know how soon he might be prepared for marriage. As far as I knew, no one else would consider asking for my hand since everyone took for granted that Adrian and I would marry. After my year of exquisite freedom, the idea of living with Mama again was insupportable.

Soon after realizing that the end of the year loomed before me, I attended a small dinner party at which Adrian and Jack were both guests. The hostess coyly seated Adrian and I together and we worked valiantly at conversing with the guests around us instead of only with one another. After dinner, one of Adrian's friends drew him aside for a moment and Jack asked if he might speak to me. He drew me out onto the porch and after chattering inconsequentially for a few minutes, announced that he had been to see my mother.

"What?" I burst out, startled, "Why on earth... ."

"I sought her out to ask her permission for your hand in marriage, Virginia," he said formally.

I began to stammer. I had no idea what to say. Adrian had done nothing official so far as I knew and, for all our plans and assumptions about the future, he certainly had not formally proposed to me so that I dared not say that I was already promised. I abruptly threw a hand to my head and announced that my head ached and I couldn't give him an answer just then. I was too embarrassed to tell Adrian what had happened, but asked him to find Freddie for me so that we could leave.

Over the next several weeks, Jack occasionally had flowers delivered to me at the school, but he did not press me for an answer. In the meantime, about a week after Jack's proposal, Adrian suddenly stopped appearing at any function that I attended and only stared miserably and refused to talk if we did run into one another. Then he disappeared altogether. I soon heard that he had quit his job in business and headed out west. I don't know how I kept up with my schoolwork in that period. My belief in Adrian's feelings for me had been as deep and unshakeable as bedrock and now my devastation seemed to penetrate to greater depths. I questioned whether I could trust anyone I had ever believed in. Even Freddie had difficulty drawing a smile from me. For some reason I never talked to her about Adrian. Mama sent notes asking when I planned to announce my engagement.

"Well, Virginia, I'm as stunned as you are that Jack suddenly proposed, but with Adrian gone, maybe it would be all right. He's so-o-o old, though." She wrinkled her pretty nose and thought a minute. "I don't suppose you'd be willing to find out where Adrian went and just hop on a train and go after him?"

"I don't have any money unless I ask Mama," I reminded her. What I didn't say was that the pranks I pulled on my brothers or with Freddie were one thing, but that sort of scandalous behavior was another. It would never be forgiven by my family or most of the social circle I'd built in Nashville. I just shook my head while the tears began to flow again.

"Well, darlin', then it's Jack or your Mama, isn't it?" she asked rhetorically.

At last, I contacted Jack and told him that I would accept his proposal. I had no idea what possessed him to decide to marry me after our slight acquaintance, but with Adrian gone and no teaching credentials, not to mention the specter of Mama drawing nearer, marrying Jack seemed the least of the evils. So, we set a date for our wedding in the early fall.

****

For a few weeks after school finished, I went home. Mama took over the wedding preparations because I didn't care how it was put together. With new routines for housework that didn't include me, Mama told me that I could just rest. She said I looked a little pale.

At first I didn't have the heart for anything, but then I decided to enjoy my little period of freedom. I danced around in the hayloft and pitched stones across the pond. I ran along the path to my grandparents' house, under the cathedral arch of the trees, and sat in the place where I'd found Grandpapa, trying to feel something left of him, some imprint on the path or the stones or a faint song that whispered him on the leaves. I couldn't find him. Those weeks, it seemed the sky was bluer, the leaves greener and the plants bigger than any time since I was a little girl. The spirit of summer permeated the landscape and I felt awake inside again. When it was time for me to join in the wedding preparations the cold returned to my heart. On the way back to Nashville, I noticed the leaves beginning to turn. I wished we'd set the wedding later, so that the leaves would be down and the season would feel more suitable to the occasion.

Everyone said the wedding was very pretty, but I honestly don't remember anything about it, except that all my family and friends from Columbia and Hamilton's and Nashville came; all but Adrian. My school year and my dreams ended and I married a rich man, just the way Mama always dreamed.

Chapter Six

After the wedding, I moved into Jack's house in Nashville. It was a huge place that his first wife had decorated with expensive furniture and rugs and paintings. I guess the artists must have been busy after the war when all the artwork hung in tatters on the walls of broken homes. Jack told me I could do some redecorating. I picked lighter curtains and softer, cheerier wallpapers for a few rooms, but, even though they were a little dark and forbidding to my eye, I couldn't imagine spending the money for all new furniture when the other Mrs. Wrigley had filled every room with such fine, quality pieces.

Jack's housekeepers and maid and cook all knew their jobs and kept the house running just fine. Technically I was in charge and I did check on things and ordered some new menus and occasionally made a change. But by and large I didn't have to do all the housework that I'd spent my girlhood indoors learning. Mama never told me about the duties I had to perform at night. Jack was very gentle with me but sex didn't turn out to be very exciting. Freddie had always hinted that it was supposed to be grand, but I supposed she would be disappointed when she actually tried it too. Sometimes I wondered if Mama was wrong about teaching careers along with everything else.

I noticed that life at the farm underwent a number of improvements that first year. An indoor bathroom was added to the house and the latest farm equipment was purchased. Mama bought her parents' farm from the Kentucky cousins and Jim married and moved in with his new bride. Tommy finished school after all. I imagined Jack had something to do with this sudden good fortune but no one breathed a word to me and I asked no questions.

****

With little to do around the house, life seemed pretty dull. I spent a lot of time stitching hems and embroidering decorative tablecloths and tatting doilies. At one point I tried to stitch a tableau of Persephone, but my drawing wasn't quite good enough to make a suitable pattern and I gave it up. Freddie was back at Hamilton's and Mrs. Meacham gave special permission for her to come to my house for tea or dinner or just a cozy afternoon without bringing another of the girls, so we occasionally had a chance to talk.

"Virginia, you're still looking a little pale and thin. Is Jack treating you well?" she demanded to know one day.

"Yes, he's always kind," I told her morosely. "I just don't have all that much to do."

She looked up with a twinkle and said, "Wait till you have a baby."

I'd imagined the angelic children that Adrian and I would have many times, but it had never occurred to me that Jack and I would have a child. He was so old. I supposed that loving a baby would fill the empty spaces but I couldn't feature it.

"Has anyone had news of Adrian?" I asked.

"Someone at a party recently told me that they'd seen a byline with his name on a story in a periodical out west, but you know I can't remember even what state it was, if they told me." She paused for a moment and looked closely at me, then said quietly, "What would you do if you knew where he was, Ginnie?"

Initially my mind was blank, but then I remembered that Adrian left to avoid marrying me and I knew that I would do nothing. I just shrugged in answer.

Often Freddie and I went to the ice cream parlor or the park or, in the season, to the skating rink. I could take the carriage and pick her up after class and we'd go off on a lark. She still always had strings of admirers around and she'd put out the word that we were going to the skating rink or the ice cream parlor and a few fellows would show up. Sometimes they flirted with me too and I enjoyed the sensation of toying with scandal.

I think my favorite days were the ones when Freddie and I went to the skating rink in a small park. There was only a short period when it was cold enough in Nashville to make a rink and we made sure to enjoy it. I loved it because I could fly across the ice with the wind rushing by like a bird when it holds its wings out motionless and soars through the air. One day at the rink, one of Freddie's beaus arrived with a friend named Miles who was visiting from out of town. They were older, but not so much as Jack.

When they came up, Freddie and I had been facing one another, holding hands and twirling. We laughed so hard we almost couldn't stop and careened around when we let go. Miles arrived just in time to grab me and stop me from falling. When I looked up at him he had the strangest expression on his face; sort of a mix of delight and disapproval. Miles was tall and handsome and quite shy. He didn't skate, so they invited us to sit with them and drink hot chocolate. Freddie and Ben became so involved in flirting that we were left on our own. It was difficult for a while, because Miles contributed little to the conversation, but eventually I began telling him stories about my brothers, like the time I peppered the chicken, and he laughed and laughed. It was one of our loveliest afternoons.

****

Mrs. Meacham invited me for tea occasionally. We still discussed books. She was becoming interested in political issues and considering whether women should vote. She loaned me some books on political affairs and economics which I began reading with great curiosity as I had never been exposed to these ideas before.

"I don't know, Virginia. I'm beginning to feel that men should not be allowed to make every decision that affects our lives while we have no say. I earn a living, support myself and pay sales taxes and yet the local politicians can choose to make changes around this city or state or to raise taxes on things that I buy and I may not participate. And yet, the old way seems to serve well enough and I don't know that I am in favor of overturning the order of society."

I'd never thought about such things at all. Someone had always made my decisions for me and I couldn't imagine it any other way. "I don't know, Mrs. Meacham, it frightens me a little to think of having the responsibility for voting. Maybe as I read more of the materials you've given me I will come to understand the political process better."

And, over time, I suppose I did. Having digested a certain amount of information on the theories of politics, I began to read the papers with more interest and to try to follow some of the local political issues. Freddie, who just wanted to marry Sonny, run a household, and belong to the social scene, said she was glad the men had to bother with these boring matters, but I began to have some strong opinions about decisions that were being made. Occasionally I brought one of them up to Jack. Rarely, he felt I had made a good point. More often he laughed and told me not to be silly. Finally, at a dinner party one evening, where, as usual, I was by far the youngest guest, I was seated next to a local councilman about whom I'd read in the papers and I began to question him about his intended vote on an expansion of the city borders.

"Well, no question, Virginia, the city must grow and develop. I have every intention of voting in favor of the expansion."

"But, do you not feel that there is also value in preserving the countryside, not to mention the farmers' contributions to the economy?" One man with a handlebar mustache who was seated farther down the table abruptly dropped his fork. Several of the haughty grey-haired ladies began to stare quellingly at me.

The councilman laughed uneasily but spoke forcefully. "Now, Virginia, the land is worth far more in development, everyone knows." He pulled his chin tight so his beard stuck straight out. There were increasing signs of discomfort and disapproval on the faces poised over fine china but I didn't care.

"I think that there will come a time when we are sorry that we have allowed our farmland to be destroyed," I maintained. Jack cut into the conversation at that point and steered it another direction. He scolded me all the way home and told me never to put myself forward in that way again.

"I never thought I could feel so embarrassed by you, Ginnie. How could you presume to talk to the councilman that way?"

"I just raised some questions about the issues involved in the expansion vote," I began, only to be interrupted.

"Virginia, I am telling you not to do it," he hollered. He had never raised his voice to me before and I was shocked. I had carried the illusion that I never need fear the unexpected attacks and ready repercussions from Jack that had haunted me at home. Although I could not say that I was deliriously happy with him, it was a great source of comfort to me to feel safe. From that moment, a bit of fear always lurked in my mind that anything I tried to do might possibly cause him to erupt like that again and I became more careful, the way I was with Mama, to avoid things that I thought might set him off. I quit reading books on political matters and tried to keep Mrs. Meacham from drawing me into discussions. She was becoming so obsessed with the suffrage, though, that it was hard to keep her from bringing it up and I began to go less and less frequently to have tea with her. I felt her absence keenly as there was no one else with whom I could share books and interesting ideas about the world.

Sometimes Jack and I did have fun. He bought a motorcar not long after we were married. Once he had mastered driving it, I begged him to teach me how and a number of sunny Sundays he drove out into the country and struggled to teach me about clutch and brake and steering. It was clearly not a natural talent with me and we lurched down country lanes, came to crashing halts and spent as much time driving along the sides of the roads as on them for a while, but I was determined, and eventually I could accelerate smoothly, hold steady on the road and come to a stop without pitching Jack forward. We took picnic lunches out and found lovely open meadows where we could stop. They were nice days.

The summer after Jack and I married, Freddie returned home to be married at last to her childhood sweetheart. We attended the wedding and I was her matron of honor, but we didn't have a chance to spend much time alone and then it was over and we left her behind. I missed her dreadfully, but I did have many engagements by that point and kept pretty busy. Occasionally her husband came to town on business and Freddie came along to shop. On quiet days, I still got out my embroidery and tatting. Time seemed to meander along a little slowly, but it passed pleasantly enough I suppose. The preparation for marriage had been so long and arduous and Mama's determination to achieve this so fierce, that I expected to feel special somehow. I had no idea that I'd feel just as trapped as ever or so bored. Still, even though I did not enjoy married life much, the shock when Jack suddenly died at the end of our third year of marriage was enormous.

In three years I grew accustomed to the slow rhythm of our marriage and the faint feeling of boredom and came to depend on his almost unfailing kindness, solicitousness and generosity. I missed the cycles of planting and the sounds of the animals, but no one boxed my ears or complained that I was slow or clumsy and, with the servants to keep the house running, in some ways I enjoyed a measure of freedom beyond anything I'd known since I was a small child. And I was able to indulge in the love for reading that Grandpapa instilled in me. If I could have taken my books out to the hayloft, I would have been pretty happy, I think. As it was, Jack built a lovely gazebo out back and I spent many pleasant hours directing a gardener in planting hyacinths and heliotropes and lavender and roses to scent the air and please the eye before spending many tranquil hours reading in the midst of sweet aromas.

I lost weight and became listless, having headaches more often and difficulty sleeping. After a while I grew better and began to make plans. Now I was wealthy, or so the lawyers told me, and on my own. I wanted to take the teaching courses and go out west to teach on a reservation or in a small town. But when I announced my plan, Mama said, no, I was too young to be out there on my own and she brought the lawyer by to convince me I didn't know enough to handle the money Jack left me. Left without my husband's protection, I still could not find it in myself to defy Mama and gave in. Then I didn't know what on earth to do with myself. I think I never felt such despair, not even when Adrian left. Immediately I lost my appetite again and began declining in health. Everyone assumed I mourned Jack and I let them. Mama decided that I needed a change of scene.

****

I looked over at Mama, dozing next to me while the scenery flashed by at a pace I found astonishing. The last time we traveled together was the trip to Hamilton's. While Mama's grey head bobbed lightly to the movement of the train, I leaned close to the window, fascinated at the sight of houses and pastures that appeared to be moving at a great rate while we sat still and determined to enjoy my first train ride to the fullest. I'd never seen an ocean or even a big lake and, even though they said the train didn't run near the water, I hoped to catch my first glimpse of the Gulf. I didn't expect Florida to be so dry and barren. When we came to Fort Meyers, we finally saw rows of palm trees and lush tropical flowers.

Jack meant for us to travel together, but business kept him close to home and sometimes working long hours. I tried to decide if I'd have felt freer travelling with him than with Mama. I wasn't sure. But I wished I knew what it felt like to travel with my husband instead.

The hotel was lovely and we could walk to the beach. For days I spent hours in a chair planted in the sand under an umbrella and watched the waves move in their infinite patterns. Oh, and the sunsets. Billowy clouds bathed in pink and lavender floated on the horizon and a path of orange light moved out across the water from the sun to the beach where I sat. Mama seemed more peaceful than I'd ever known her to be. Actually, it was the only time she'd ever had a chance to stop working in my memory. She'd worked hard before Papa left, but nothing to the constant pace she kept after he left, developing her egg business and pitching in on the farm, trying to make ends meet. Something about the beauty and tranquillity around me gradually lulled me into a sense of well being. At last it seemed possible that something might work out for my life, even if I still had no idea what it might be.

When Mama visited with Jack and I, she didn't tell me what to do other than occasionally offering advice on household matters or something I might do to make Jack more comfortable. She left decisions about my life in Jack's hands. Her approach was softer this time, but, when a week had brought some color back into my cheeks and improved my appetite, Mama broached the subject of my future—as she had decided it must be. I needed another husband, being too young to be respectably set up on my own, even as a widow.

Now she mentioned that she chose this place for my recuperation because she had been asking questions and discovered that this was a place where one might encounter eligible Southern gentlemen. With sinking heart, I realized I should have guessed an underlying agenda in her anxiety to hustle me away from Nashville, however genuine her concern may have been.

She did not seem to have developed a plan for how a lady might meet one of these gentlemen in a place where there were no friends to supply introductions nor invitations to parties. I made no comment on the situation, content to sit under my canopy by the beach and stroll about the town. As I strolled one day, I became aware of someone's scrutiny and looked up into a familiar but almost forgotten face.

"Mrs. Wrigley?" he queried.

"Why, yes ... Miles," I replied. "How lovely to see you again. Are you visiting here?"

He stayed in the same hotel, in fact. He no longer worked for the railroad and was realizing his dream to own and race thoroughbreds. With a partner, he bought his first horse not long after I met him and built enough of a business racing and breeding that he could leave his employment. He had been at Hialeah to watch one of his horses run and now, having won, he planned to take a short rest. After I pried this information out of him, he mentioned that he'd heard about Jack from Freddie's friend Ben and offered condolences.

"Are you here alone, Mrs. Wrigley?"

I told him I'd come with Mama. He invited us to join him for dinner in the hotel dining room the next night. I accepted, sure that Mama would be pleased. She was very pleased. I managed to imply that Miles's business was larger than I imagined it really was, counting on his reticent nature to leave Mama that illusion.

Miles rose to my expectations quite nicely, merely naming his business and offering no further information as to its success or size. He also treated Mama with such flattering courtesy that she became almost flirtatious. I blanched when Mama began to question him about his family and whether they had suffered losses in the war. I had no idea whether they'd had anything to lose and, even though it had always been one of her favorite topics, I knew what she was up to.

"My father's family had most of their assets tied up in slaves, so they lost everything but the land. They managed to keep the farm going and, with some new crop rotations and experimental farming, they brought it back. My mother's family owned several business in a little town that was named after them and they barely managed to hold on, but they were able to keep a couple of the businesses afloat."

"I guess we all have had to work harder than we ever thought we would to keep from losing everything," she sighed.

"Yes ma'am, I believe that's been true. My parents began life surrounded by comfort and wound up toiling to get by. But they managed to give my brother and I a good education and we have had it a little easier."

Mama was pleased. I enjoyed watching his ability to tell her exactly what she wanted to hear, in that deep authoritative voice of his. I liked his quiet strength and the air of stability about him. He did not have the romance or passion of Adrian, but perhaps that was just as well. I didn't know that I wanted to feel that deeply for someone again even if it were possible to love another as I loved Adrian. I gathered that he was about 10 years older than I—just enough older to have established an air of self-confidence and certainty but not as much older as Jack, who was closer to my father in age.

In the ensuing days, Miles frequently lunched or dined with us, or walked along the beach with me. He never did talk a lot, but he seemed to enjoy my stories about life on the farm and my escapades with Freddie. I enjoyed watching his ordinarily serious, determined expression dissolve into laughter and the enthusiasm with which he talked about the Kentucky Blue Grass. I'd never felt quite this way about a man before. It was a feeling somewhere in between the unquestioning love I'd felt for Adrian and the warm friendliness I felt for Jack. When it was time for Miles to leave, I felt Fort Meyers was going to be rather dull and nervously wondered if I'd see him again.

"Ginnie, I'd like to write to you, if that would be acceptable," he began.

"Oh, yes."

"And, uh, perhaps I could call on you in Nashville the next time I come through on business?"

I floated through the remaining days in Fort Meyers. Mama and I even got along well enough. She didn't lecture much except to tell me to keep looking my best in case there were further opportunities. "After all, Miles hasn't stated his intentions, darlin'."

Chapter Seven

We had written several letters back and forth when Miles reappeared in Nashville. He spent so much time with me that I couldn't fathom how he was getting his business done. In fact, he never did tell me what aspect of his business brought him to Nashville. One day we walked in the park where we'd ice skated that winter. The trees were lush and green and roses and lilies and hyacinths gently perfumed the pathway. We bought ices at the little shop where we had had hot chocolate and sipped them while looking at the park.

"You've never been to Kentucky?" he asked.

"No. I never was out of Tennessee until that trip to Florida with Mama."

"It's beautiful country. All rolling hills and meadows with horses prancing and playing. When the wind blows across and the sun is at just the right angle, the grass really is blue."

"Sounds lovely." I'd never heard Miles so eloquent. His enthusiasm for his adopted home was palpable.

"Most of the farms have white fences that wind over hills and valleys. It's very striking. And along the roadways, there are interesting stone fences. Irish immigrants put them together. Small stones are just fitted together, no mortar," he shook his head in wonder as I tried to picture these foreign fences.

"My, I'd like to see such interesting things," was all I could think of to say.

"Well, uh, Ginnie... I thought, uh... I hoped... Well, Ginnie, if you would marry me, then you'd come live there with me," he began and rushed on, "Right now I just rent a house, but soon I hope to buy a farm. You know, quit boarding my horses, expand the operation."

"Yes, Miles, I'll marry you and live in Kentucky." I wasn't sure which made me happier, the proposal or the fact that my status as widow meant that he could properly address me instead of Mama and that, for the first time ever, I could provide my own answer to a question that affected the course of my life. Whatever the reason, I beamed over my strawberry ice and allowed him to squeeze my hand.

Miles went back to Lexington to oversee the training of one of his horses. We planned to be married in six months, which let Miles get through the main racing season and gave me a chance to prepare the wedding and the sale of Jack's home. It also gave me time to worry about how to tell Miles about my teeth.

I'd been plagued by ear infections off and on and, during my marriage to Jack, I started having problems with my hearing. A doctor in Nashville finally decided that my teeth were the problem and sent me to the dentist to have all my teeth pulled. I began wearing false teeth shortly before Jack's death. At the time, I didn't think very much about it. Jack, as always, was very kind through the whole process and I didn't worry much about how I looked to him. But now I dreaded taking them out at night when Miles could see.

I tried to write it in a letter, but that didn't seem like the way. He only came to visit twice, very briefly. I knew that I should say something, but we had such a short time... . Suddenly the wedding was upon us and he still didn't know. Mama and all my brothers were coming.

Freddie arrived several days early and brought her husband and child. She was my matron of honor and still blonde and beautiful and full of the devil. We were sitting in the little dressing room I had decorated. It was the only room in the house where I turned out the first Mrs. Wrigley's furniture. I'd picked a wallpaper with roses and pretty little chairs with rose velvet upholstery and a carpet that matched the dark green leaves in the wallpaper. The color seemed to bring out the bloom in Freddie's cheeks. In marriage she'd become even more ravishing, or so it seemed to me.

"Oh, Ginnie," she was saying, "he's quite debonair, I declare. Now, you can tell little ol' me, does he have enough money to suit your Mama?"

I chuckled, "I'm not sure how much he has. He's obviously not poor. But I let Mama think he has a whole string of horses and a big breeding operation." I bit my lower lip and waited to see how she reacted.

"Ginnie, aren't you the smart one," she giggled conspiratorially. "Jack left you plenty of money; I don't know why you need to marry another rich one. Didn't Jack pull your family out of trouble?"

"I guessed that he did, but no one ever talked to me." I shrugged.

"Forgive me, Ginnie, but your family is peculiar sometimes, I swear. Of course in our families a man's position would have mattered any time and after the war, goodness knows it was crucial. But I knew all along that I needed to marry well. Thank the good lord Sonny's rich because I don't know what I'd have done if I could-n't have married him. And there was never any secret that he made a big settlement on my family. But you, your Mama spends your life training you for sale to the high-est bidder so you could save those brothers of yours and no one ever talked to you about what they were really doing?"

"Well, I knew I was to marry well. But you're right, I didn't know that Mama planned to restore the whole family through me. As for bidders, Jack turned out to be the only one who offered... ."

Freddie interrupted, astonished, "No he wasn't darlin'. What about Adrian?"

"Adrian never talked to Mama," I began.

"You mean she never told you?" Freddie broke in.

"Never told me what?" My stomach began to tighten and my head felt light.

"Adrian spoke to your Mama and she told him you weren't interested and even if you were she wouldn't give her permission to him because she'd already given it to Jack." She watched my face grow frozen in horror. "Oh my lord. She never told you? Didn't Adrian ever say anything to you? He swore me to secrecy but I told him he had to talk to you. And I just assumed you knew from your Mama. Oh why didn't I say something? You knew nothing?"

"No. No one told me. I thought all these years Adrian just wasn't as fond of me as I was of him."

"He was devastated. That's why he disappeared so quickly."

"I did everything Mama ever asked of me. Freddie, how could she have done this?" I looked up hopefully, as if there really might be a reasonable explanation, but she just shook her head sadly.

I confronted Mama later that night. For a moment she looked embarrassed but then she just drew herself up and said, "I don't see what you have to complain about. Thanks to me, you're a wealthy young woman and you're about to marry a very eligible man."

"Mama, I loved Adrian and you just sent him away without asking me what I wanted? How could you?"

"I could because I'm your mother and I knew what was best. Now, Adrian was a very appealing young man but he was not wealthy and he was a dreamer. He never could have made you happy." I stared into her face and realized that she honestly believed that there was no reason for me to be angry. I didn't know if I'd ever get over the feeling of betrayal.

****

The next day, I had arranged a family luncheon, just for Mama and my brothers and Jim's and Charley's wives. The cook made a lovely soup and some lamb and green beans cooked with country ham. As we lingered over custards, Charley talked about his law practice.

"I'm getting to have a pretty full client list now. I've been winning quite a few cases and some of the businessmen I've represented have been recommending me to their friends."

Shirley, his wife, chimed in, "He's really being modest. He's doing very very well and says that he may take on another lawyer."

"Oh my," we all nodded our pleasure for him.

"Isn't it fortunate that you were finally able to go to law school?" I asked quietly.

"Yes. I'm so grateful to Mama for finding the money for me to go."

I cast an indignant look at Mama, but she just smiled benignly at Charley and ignored me. "And Jim, haven't you been pleased that you were able to buy our grandparents' place?"

"Absolutely. I've done so well with that property that I've been able to buy up quite a bit more acreage."

"Oh, he's becoming quite the gentleman farmer," Tommy grinned.

"How about you, Tommy?" I questioned. "You got that degree in business. Tell me, has it brought you what you wanted?"

"Well, I have a good position at the bank and, with the degree, I have hopes of being able to wind up with a vice presidency at least. I guess I can say I'm doing pretty well."

"Hm," I frowned down at my uneaten custard. "It's interesting how the money for buying land and going to school suddenly turned up shortly after I married Jack." A stunned silence fell over the room. My brothers looked uneasily from me to Mama while their wives looked merely bewildered.

"Now Ginnie," said Jim, "after Mama scraped and saved so that we could get ahead, I don't think it's right for you to imply that Jack had something to do with it. I'm sure it was just a coincidence of timing." He ended on an uneasy note and glanced at Mama as if waiting for corroboration. She just sat there like a thundercloud.

"Well, Mama," I invited her to chime in. "Do tell us. How did you contrive all at once to come up with thousands and thousands of dollars after there had never been any extra for years and years? What price did Jack pay so that he could own me?"

"Ginnie!" Charley gasped.

"Don't tell me not one of you ever suspected for a minute that Jack paid some kind of settlement," I shot back. "Or was it just easier on you all to pretend that Mama gave it to you than to admit that you got what you wanted by letting your sister be sold?"

"Ginnie, that's enough!" Mama commanded.

"No, Mama, it's not nearly enough," I shouted. "Tell them what you did to me." She sat rigidly silent. "Tell them," I screamed.

"You know I did what I thought was best for you."

"What was best for me? You did what was best for the boys and you didn't care what happened to me." By then I was crying and shouting at once.

"Mama, what is she talking about?" demanded Jim.

"Yes, Mama. What is it that happened?" Bob and Charley and Tommy asked together. Mama just sat with her head bowed, glaring at the custard dish.

"All right, I'll tell them. Did you know I was in love? I know I told you a little about Adrian. Didn't any of you know that I loved him? That we wanted to be married?"

"I vaguely remember something about him, yes," said Tommy uneasily.

"Didn't she ever tell you that Adrian went to her and asked her permission to marry me? But he didn't have as much money as Jack so she turned him down and told him that I didn't love him. She sent away the love of my life and married me to Jack so that you all could have all that money to go to school and buy land and all. She married me off to an old man so that she could get that money. Now what I want to know, Mama, was how much did he pay for me?" I was screaming through my sobs by the end.

Mama threw her napkin on the table and stood up. "He made a very handsome settlement." She looked defiantly around the table at my brothers. "And yes, that was the money that sent you all to school and bought land for Bob and Jim. And you, Ginnie. You haven't ever had to hunt for eggs in a hen house or spend hours every day in the kitchen or scrub down a whole house since the day you left home. And you never will. That's because I knew how to fix you up with what you needed. I spent hours teaching you everything you needed to know and I found Hamilton's... .

"But that's all in the past now. We're here for your wedding to Miles. I don't know why you're throwing all this up now. You do want to marry Miles don't you? No one is standing in your way." With that she marched from the room. My brothers and their wives sat around uncomfortably for a minute or two before excusing themselves and leaving me alone in the dining room.

I tossed and turned and paced the room that night. I packed a bag and got ready to head out on the first train to New Mexico to find Adrian. I thought about Miles and tried to decide whether I loved him as much as I loved Adrian. I realized that I didn't know how much he loved me and I wondered whether he'd feel just as lost and hurt if I ran away as I had felt when Adrian vanished. What I still wanted more than anything was to be with Adrian but Miles didn't deserve to be hurt and I didn't see how I could waltz off and leave him stranded in the midst of guests and wedding preparations. And, after all, Adrian was the one who left me. I had to face the probability that he would not be glad to see me. I unpacked the bag and returned to lying sleeplessly on my bed.

****

Having decided that I did want to marry Miles, I pulled myself together and put on my most charming smile while I blindly walked through the many social events leading up to the wedding. Fortunately, Miles didn't seem to notice the tell-tale circles under my eyes. Freddie kept telling me how awful she felt for revealing the news just when I should be happy.

In a way, I was actually glad. Any vestige of sadness about leaving my home and family and moving to a strange new place was gone. Mama had betrayed me and my brothers let me be sacrificed. I couldn't believe that none of them had ever guessed that Jack made a handsome settlement. Even when the news came out they didn't thank me. Tommy did come up to me the next day and told me that he was sorry and he should have realized, but that he'd never thought about it. After that he stayed clear of me as much as possible. Jake hadn't been heard from in a couple of years and we had nothing in common any more anyway. Miles was my new life and I would trust him to care for me.

I held the wedding out at the gazebo Jack built for me. I didn't think he would mind this final enjoyment of the place he built to give me pleasure and I couldn't think of a lovelier setting. The wedding went smoothly and everyone enjoyed the garden party I arranged afterward. I avoided Mama as much as I could through all the festivities.

****

Miles arranged for us to travel to Savannah for a honeymoon. We left on a train right after the wedding. Miles still didn't know about my teeth. I kept them in until after he was asleep. Then I got up and took them out and cleaned them and left them to soak, making sure I got up before he did and put them back in before he woke up. Somehow once I'd begun, it became easy to continue and I let more and more time go by without telling him.

Freddie told me that making love with Sonny was everything she had thought it would be, so I looked forward to the possibility that I would finally enjoy it with Miles. It was worse though. Jack at least spent a lot of time caressing me and holding me. Miles just pushed up my nightgown, climbed on top of me, grunted for a couple of minutes while he moved urgently inside me and then he rolled over. I daydreamed about how it might have been with Adrian, but of course I couldn't tell Miles I wanted it to be different.

Savannah was charming. I so enjoyed seeing the lovely homes and gardens. Looking at them I understood more about the life my grandparents lost than I ever had—the graciousness, the elegance. I couldn't understand why the Yankees were so determined to destroy such a refined culture. Miles and I took long walks around the town, past rows of stately townhouses. Azaleas of every hue grew large and bold and festive everywhere.

We talked at length about the stories our grandparents told us about the war and how their lives had changed. How our parents began with certain expectations of wealth and education and social position and suddenly found themselves having to learn to survive when the only skills they knew had become useless. I told him I thought Mama had been very embittered by it all but I didn't know anything about how Papa was affected. Miles said his mother just sort of gave up and went through the motions of living while his father struggled silently to keep the family going. He knew early on that he had to learn how to make his way in the world.

I didn't tell Miles about Mama and Adrian. I didn't know how to tell him that I had loved someone else—someone to whom I would now be happily married but for Mama's intervention. In all the lessons on being a wife, she never taught me how to talk to a husband about anything important. I don't think I ever saw her have a major conversation with my father while he still lived with us. Miles and I already talked more than they, but that subject seemed best left alone. Mama and I were never demonstrably close, so he didn't notice that I seldom spoke of her.

As we rambled about the town and chatted, Miles began to reveal to me more of the lifestyle involved in his business. I hadn't realized that he traveled around so much, following his horses to racetracks around the country and Canada and attending the sales at Saratoga. My stomach fluttered at the thought that I would be left alone for months at a time in the strange new city to which he was taking me. Then he made it clear that he expected me to accompany him and my spirits soared in anticipation of exciting travels and adventures.

Lovely as Savannah was, the week began to drag on a bit, I thought. I became rather worn out with the effort of overcoming Miles's lack of conversational skills. Fleetingly, it crossed my mind that we had actually spent little time in one another's company over the year of our renewed acquaintance. I had assumed that his reticence to speak grew from initial shyness, but I began to realize that his was a taciturn nature. Occasionally some topic sparked him to converse at length, or even with some animation. Such occasions had led me to infer that in time he would speak more readily. By the end of our honeymoon I began to realize that I'd better not hold my breath waiting for him to wax eloquent.

****

Over dinner one night, soon after we arrived in Lexington, Miles broached the subject of Jack's money. "I think his accounts should be moved to banks closer to us. And, of course, I'll oversee the money." He went on about husbands owning wives' property and the like, but he kept muttering uncomfortably and I didn't have enough interest to ask him to repeat himself.

Finally, I just said, "Miles, you know I don't know the first thing about taking care of money. Jack's executors have handled everything for me. I'm sure you will do just as well." I felt slightly relieved. I assumed that he would continue to give me a regular income for expenses as Jack's executors had. When the time came to sign the necessary papers I never even read them, just allowing Miles to take charge.

Not many months later, we bought a farm. I thought it was going to take longer than that for Miles to afford it but I was pleased. We had 500 acres, which, at least to me, seemed a substantial property. The house was small but appealing, a two-story white clapboard with black shutters. We had considerable remodelling done before we moved in, adding a study and a big porch downstairs, upgrading the bathrooms and modernizing the kitchen. I created gardens around the exterior while the workmen created a new interior. When the work was complete, I was sure there was no sweeter house in Lexington.

I had shipped a few of my favorite pieces from Jack's house and they looked as if they'd always been meant for our new home. Miles put me on an awfully tight budget for purchasing the rest of the furnishings we needed, but I was pleased with what I was able to do, especially the empire sofa like Mrs. Meacham's that I found for a good price.

The countryside was even prettier than I imagined. Miles's description of the mechanics of the stone fences had not done justice to their charm. The gentle rolling hills, the miles of white board fences, the expanse of farms all soothed me. I'd forgotten the tranquillity of a place where you can hear the rustle of the trees or a soft horse's whinny. Of course, automobiles intruded upon the silence even in the country by that time, but they didn't pass too often, and peace generally prevailed.

The horsey set, on the other hand, was a pretty wild crowd. They were rich and sophisticated and lived harder and faster than any people I ever saw. They downed bourbon at an astonishing rate, threw parties incessantly, drove fast, smoked cigarettes one after another and bantered endlessly about trainers and jockeys and the myriad cast of characters from around the globe that populated the world of thoroughbred racing. I was grateful for my social experience at Hamilton's, which served me well though the scene there was a bit more formal than amongst this nonchalant group.

At first I felt a little countrified in the midst of these wealthy gypsies, but I slowly began to find my way and made some lovely friends. Most of them were related to the "horse people", but, somewhat to Miles's chagrin, generally my dearest friends were not inclined to participate in that set. I got along well enough to attend the functions Miles felt were necessary and soon had sufficient acquaintances to enjoy myself. Miles tended to gravitate to a few other serious horsemen and talk business through the evening, and relied upon me to socialize and create more connections. Though I met many amusing people, the act of chatting with them because I was expected to do it reminded me of Mama and was distasteful to me.

Chapter Eight

Miles and I had been traveling nonstop for years, it seemed. In fact, we had traveled through 12 racing seasons, but we did actually go home for many months out of the year. His horses ran at major tracks all over—Florida, New York, California, Canada, Illinois, Maryland.... We sometimes spent a week or two in one place, while Miles fussed over the training of some horse or if he had horses entered in several races.

That form of ranging around the country had not proved to be quite the romantic adventure I'd hoped for. Miles seemed to want me along mainly so I could take care of his packing and see that his laundry was done and provide companionship when he chose to dine "at home" or to come home early enough to actually chat for a while. Of course I often attended the races and there were always parties, but it seemed I spent an eternity sitting in strange hotel rooms. The first couple of years it was more exciting because all the cities were new to me and I did a lot of sightseeing. But, however much one might wish them to be magically transported to other settings, the tracks remained immutably in the same places and Miles refused to arrange for any side excursions in our journeys so that my new horizons ceased expanding rather quickly. Still, we crisscrossed the country, past every imaginable terrain and I developed a cosmopolitan familiarity with the cities we frequented.

I didn't enjoy going to the North as much as other places. I found Yankees to be as lacking in social graces as Grandmama would have predicted. They were inclined to laugh at Southerners though I had no idea what amused the stupid things so. Northern cities seemed so dirty, with big ugly grey buildings that stretched for miles. I was taken by California. The mountains were mildly intimidating, so much larger than our gentle Kentucky hills, but so magnificent as well. The lifestyle seemed odd, but people were friendly and everything seemed lighter and brighter somehow.

Even the Great War didn't affect our comings and goings. Miles was beyond the age for the military. The sport of kings continued unabashedly, seemingly unaware of the cataclysm across the sea and so our caravan kept moving.

While influenza swept across the country, a note from Freddie managed to reach me. I didn't recognize her handwriting at first. It was shaky and the letters malformed.

"Dearest Ginnie," she wrote. "I'm hoping this letter will find its way to you in your travels. This influenza that seems to be everywhere has found its way to me. The doctor seems hopeful and Sonny is taking such good care of me. But the fever burns and I feel so weak. My babies aren't allowed to come in my room and I'm not able to do anything to care for them. It's so lonely here. I know it's a lot to ask, but I'm hoping that you can find a way to visit. It would cheer me so to see your eyes twinkle and tell some jokes with you. Please see if you can talk Miles into letting you go. I'm sorry to be so brief, but I'm too tired to write any more. With much love, Freddie."

"Miles, Freddie sounds dreadfully ill. Really, I think that I should go to her."

"Nonsense. She's just feeling sorry for herself because she's ill. Your place is with me."

"That's not fair Miles. People are dying of this influenza. She's my dearest friend and I think I should go to her. Now, please give me the money for train fare."

"You can send her a telegram." I started to protest but he raised a hand. "That's the end of it."

I sent a long telegram and then I kept sending little notes, but I never knew whether she received them. The letter Sonny sent to inform me that Freddie died didn't reach me for several months as it bounced from Lexington to various places we'd been and back again. I felt terrible to think of Sonny's distress at receiving all those notes after Freddie was gone.

Freddie and I had corresponded regularly through all the years and managed to see one another occasionally when I insisted on stopping the journey any time we went near Freddie's home, rejoining Miles after a couple of days of fun and heart to heart talks. No friend but Adrian had ever been so dear and I felt bereft of all support.

I begged Miles to let me go home, but he kept saying I was too upset and shouldn't be at home alone. I didn't want to be with people, though, so he left me alone in the hotel day after day, staring out the window at the brown brick wall and cheerless windows of the building across the way and grieving. The grieving lessened and then largely disappeared over the next few years. But in my heart there lived a sparkly-eyed, laughing, tender-hearted blonde nymph whose memory brought tears to my eyes.

****

Not very many of the wives my age travelled with their husbands because most were home with children. Clara Wilson and I sent one another schedules so we'd know when we would be in the same place. We usually managed a few weeks together during each season and we had combed the shops and restaurants in all the cities on the circuit until we knew just where to find anything we wanted and which shops we wanted to browse through every time we were in town. One of the last times we met, our husbands had horses running at Del Mar in California.

Clara and I decided to go to a motion picture at the nearby Bijou one evening when the men were all still at the track. It seemed every city we visited had a "Bijou"—I'd have thought they could have dreamed up some more imaginative names. That night we ate first in the hotel restaurant. I was feeling restless and it was good to talk to Clara.

"At first when Miles talked about our lives, travelling all over together, I thought it seemed so exciting. But I'm getting so bored, Clara. One hotel after another. Miles is too busy to spend much time with me. I've embroidered enough table wear to make dowries for a dozen girls, I think."

"Bless your heart, Ginnie. I know exactly what you mean. Sometimes I think I'll scream if I have to go to one more party where all the talk is about some jockey or trainer and the bloodlines of some horse." She shook her head and looked ruefully across the table at me. "What would you do if you stayed home?"

"Well, over the years, I've met some lovely friends. A lot of them are teachers, women from fine families. We talk about books and they tell stories about their students and it's very entertaining and interesting." I hesitated before going on to tell her what I was really thinking about. "And I think I'd like to have children."

Clara's jaw dropped. "My lord, I don't believe my ears. I never thought you two would decide to have a family."

"Well, we haven't exactly decided. I've just been thinking about it."

"You haven't talked to Miles? Bless my soul, wouldn't I just love to hear that conversation. But Ginnie, aren't you worried that y'all are, well, you know, a little too old? Aren't you more than 35?"

"Yes, and if I wait longer it will be too late. But my father was over 50 when I was born and my mother was over 30. So it doesn't seem strange to me or anything."

"What do you think Miles will say?"

"Who ever knows with Miles? You know he doesn't talk much about anything." I didn't mention that in my mind the question was not when I would talk to Miles but *if*.

"I know—prying a conversation out of that man is like pullin' teeth." She stopped and then chortled, "I'm sorry, Ginnie."

Clara knew I hadn't told Miles about my teeth for some years. Then one day when Miles and I were eating apples after dinner, I sank my teeth in and, when I bit down and pulled the apple out, my teeth flew out and landed on the table, still holding a big white, juicy piece of fruit. Miles was thunderstruck. He didn't say a word though. He didn't seem to know that I should be taking them out at night, so I still preserved my vanity. Every time it came up, Clara and I got the giggles. We were still laughing when the waiter brought the bill. I took it and told Clara that I wanted to treat her.

"Well, thank you, Ginnie," she said and looked mischievous. "Does this mean you've talked Miles into letting you have more money?"

"Not much," I answered. Clara was one of the few people who knew that Miles kept me on a strict allowance and that I chafed under the restriction. He didn't allow me as much as Jack's conservative business manager had. I felt that I earned that money and the idea that I had to beg or browbeat to have the use of it set my teeth on edge—so to speak. When Clara and I last met, I was preparing to battle for more money every month. He didn't give me as much as I wanted, but I did get more. However, that night I planned to put our dinner on the room charge and make him pay for it.

After I'd signed for dinner, we walked outside and dawdled along window shopping because we were a little early. A young man tried to chat with us outside the theater. We didn't encourage him but said we had to go and hurried to buy our tickets. Inside the theater we couldn't keep from smiling. It was still fun to be flirted with. We chatted for a few minutes in our seats. Just before the lights dimmed, someone sat down next to me. I recognized the fellow who had been outside.

For a while we all just watched the movie, caught up in the flickering light and the organ playing up front. Then I felt something on my knee and moved slightly. A minute later, I felt something again and moved. I don't know what possessed me, but I surreptitiously raised a hand to my hat and slipped out one of my hatpins, then put my hand down with the pin wrapped firmly in it. After I felt something brush me a couple more times, I looked down and realized that the man had reached out his hand and put it on my knee. I grabbed my hatpin firmly between my thumb and forefinger, the point sticking out and, instead of moving away from his hand, I put my hand down and jabbed him in the leg as hard as I could with the pin. He howled and swore, then jumped up and ran out. Clara whispered, "What happened?" My shoulders shook as I tried not to laugh. I muttered under my breath, "Stabbed him with my hat pin" and began to giggle. Then Clara started. People shushed us, but we couldn't stop. In a few minutes, an usher appeared and asked us to leave. I'd never been thrown out of a place in my life and I was embarrassed but I could not stop laughing to save my soul.

Outside the theater, we fell into one another, still in whoops. We laughed until tears rolled down our cheeks and our sides ached. Passersby gave us a wide berth and that set us off even more. Finally we settled down enough to walk, arm in arm, back to the hotel. Our husbands had not returned and we sat in the lobby for a while. The chairs and couches were covered in burgundy velvet and the background of the carpeting was the same shade with ornate gold designs across it.

"When do you all go back to Lexington?"

"Next week. When are you all going to Charlottesville?"

"Not for a month or so. Richard promises that he'll squire me around more these last stops and leave the trainer to take care of things. It should be fun. A number of our friends are going to be in town and there are some lovely parties planned."

I smiled and thought about how nice that would have sounded a few years before. But by that time I was growing so weary of hotels and restaurants and parties where all the talk was horses that I shuddered at the idea of a whole month left on the road.

Clara stared at me for a moment and commented, "You really are tired of all this aren't you, Ginnie?"

I nodded. "I thought you were too."

"Well, it wears me out sometimes and sometimes I think I can't stand it, but I'm accustomed to it and Richard isn't likely to come home and settle down... ." She didn't have to add that it was easier to put a good face on it. I knew Miles would not leave his business in the hands of his employees either. Nor was I sure life would be better if we spent more time together. If I had a child, though, I was sure that Miles would leave me at home. And surely I could figure out how to raise a child.

Miles and Richard sauntered into the lobby before we could carry our musings further. As usual, I felt a surge of warmth and pride at the fine figure Miles cut. At the same time, I was sorry I hadn't gotten upstairs and into my dressing gown. Miles always liked to have cocktails when he got home and, unless I was ready for bed, he insisted that I join him even though I don't like the taste of liquor. He and Richard shepherded Clara and I into a private parlor off the lobby and produced their secret flasks. The hotel conveniently supplied teacups, which served as a good camouflage in those days of prohibition. I sipped one drink as slowly as possible while the others had several. Miles and I needed to pack early in the morning and catch a train so we excused ourselves early, but not before plans were made for them to stay with us when they came to Lexington for the spring meet.

****

A week later we were finally at home. Once there, Miles stayed busy with the breeding side of his business and with working out schedules and strategies for the next year's racing season, so I didn't see him much more than I did when we travelled. But home was so comfortable and familiar. We had a new car and Miles let me keep the old one, so I could drive into town for visits with my friends whenever I liked. What a switch from my girlhood when I had to walk everywhere or rely on Clayton and the buggy!

Several of my friends and I liked to meet once a week for lunch. Since some of the ladies taught during the week, we met on Saturdays. Often we went to the Lafayette Hotel, where the atmosphere was elegant, the food was excellent and the service outstanding. All the waiters were colored and wore uniforms of starched white jackets and black trousers. Fine white linen cloths covered every table and the silver was very tasteful. Even the coffee pots and creamers were sterling. Our first Saturday meeting after I got back, I picked Georgie up on the way to the Hotel, which was just a short distance from her house.

Over lunch, I kept looking around the table at my friends and feeling tremendous pleasure at being home. We chatted about some of the books we had been reading. The reactions to Mr. Lawrence were decidedly mixed and several of us had tried one of Henry James's later novels and found it rather obscure (although the struggle through it filled a number of hours in hotels for me). They caught me up on the latest local news and gossip. By the end of lunch I had grown quite determined to make sure that I stayed home.

Georgie invited me in for iced tea when I drove her back. Stephen, a professor at the university, was in his study. We took our tea into the garden out back. Their house was right near downtown and walls surrounded the garden. I looked around at the scarlet, gold and orange leaves decorating the trees and noticed that a few late mums still bloomed. We wouldn't have too many more days left that would be warm enough to sit out like that. "Georgie, I don't want to keep going out on the road for months out of the year."

"Have you told Miles that you'd rather stay home?"

"Years ago, I tried once to stay home. Miles just refused to allow it. I don't know why it's so important to him because I scarcely see him. Except, of course, that I take care of his clothes and oversee the luggage."

"How are you going to change his mind now?"

"Well, I've been thinking that I'd like to have a child." I was afraid to look at Georgie, but having gotten the idea past Clara, I wanted to see how Georgie would react.

"Oh my," she said. "I just assumed after all these years that you all never would have children. But I suppose you would have to stay home. What does Miles think?" I shrugged. "You have talked to him? ... Oh, I see."

Georgie had a quick understanding and had become a dear friend. The best I'd had in my life aside from Freddie. She was barely taller than I was and seemed all angles, from her face to her feet, though the kindness of her eyes saved her face from harshness. She had a restless energy that seemed to propel her into constant motion. Hands fluttering, she went on to tell me of the trip she and Stephen had taken to Italy in July. They travelled to such interesting places every summer. All over the house she had fascinating porcelains and blown glass objects that she brought back from other countries. And books from everywhere. She often loaned me things to read and then we'd discuss them. Stephen was considerably older than she, but they shared a passion for travel and for learning that had kept their marriage strong and happy. Sometimes I couldn't help thinking that Adrian and I would have been that way.

****

I never found a way to bring the subject of fatherhood up to Miles. But I kept track of my schedule and made sure that I was available to him at the right time. It wasn't any more pleasurable than it had ever been. For a while, in the beginning, I pretended that it was Adrian with me. Then I decided that it was not fair to Adrian since I was sure he would never have been so thoughtless toward me. At any rate, before it was time for the spring meet here, I was pregnant. Usually we left after the meet for our travels. I was undecided whether I wanted to go with Miles one more time or to use my condition as an excuse to stay home. I'd known for a couple of weeks before I found the courage to tell him at breakfast one day.

"Miles, I need to talk to you. Could you put the paper down for a minute?" He always went through the Racing Form at breakfast.

"Yes, what is it?" He put the paper down with some annoyance.

"Well, I, uh, went to the doctor. And ... I'm going to have a baby in the fall."

Miles appeared dumbfounded. "There's no question?" he finally managed to say.

"No, it's certain. We're going to be parents. I'm very pleased about this. I mean, it's a surprise, of course, but, a baby. It will be lovely. Don't you think so?"

Miles blinked and, after a long pause, said, "Yes. Very nice. Yes, quite a surprise." He gazed searchingly at me, but seemed to draw no conclusion to whatever his question was and raised the *Racing Form* again.

"Do you think I should go with you this time? When you go out with the horses?"

"Of course, why not?" he asked over the top of his paper, then thought for a moment before he continued, "unless you won't be well enough or something? What does the doctor say?"

"Well, I definitely should be at home the last few months. And he said I shouldn't travel so much. But at the beginning, I could go with you for a while."

"Then come with me and we'll decide when you should come back." He returned to his paper and snapped it so decisively that I knew the conversation was over.

Miles never entered into any preparations for the baby and, by and large, he behaved as if nothing had changed. He was out of town looking at a horse when she was born. On his arrival, he insisted upon naming her after a horse of his that had won a number of races over the summer: Hunter.

Chapter Nine

Mama died long before Hunter was born. Sarah, widowed for some time, had moved to wherever Jake lived, so no one arrived to give advice or assist in the birth or babyhood of my first child. I'd seldom been in touch with Mama since the day I married Miles and I'd never forgiven her. I hadn't kept up with my brothers except Tommy. He wrote occasionally and thus I knew that Sis was gravely ill. I wasn't able to make arrangements to get away and see her before she died. The world of my girlhood seemed to belong to some other woman, far removed from me.

Once Hunter came along, my life changed remarkably. Although Miles was more charmed by fatherhood than either of us had expected him to be, he knew very little about babies and clearly had even less interest in learning. Crying got on his nerves and he wanted nothing to do with messy jobs like feeding or diapering. I stayed home year around. To my amazement, Miles began organizing his schedule so that he came back to Lexington for a few days here and there through the racing season. His taciturn nature had never changed. The mysteries I once thought must live behind the silence never came to light. His immersion in horses was often so total that I wondered what he had ever wanted with a wife. Then he would do something like the sudden schedule change and I'd wonder if I knew him at all. When I announced that we'd be having a second child, he reacted without surprise or enthusiasm.

By that time, Hunter was crawling and standing. She was already the most willful child I had ever seen. She howled furiously until she got what she wanted, her face red and puffy, her little fists beating at her sides. Sometimes she reminded me of Grandmama. Her moods were mercurial and alternated largely between glee and anger. I found it remarkable that so much anger already existed in a child so young. When Lily was born, Hunter became a regular little devil. She was two years old and jealous of her sister from the first day. Hunter slapped and scratched at Lily whenever she had a chance. One day I found her dangling at the side of the crib, and hopping up and down, trying to tip it. She looked so absurd it was hard not to laugh, but I was frightened too. That was when I started setting a schedule of supervision so that Lily was protected.

I was no longer able to see my friends as often as I wished. Most of them were spinsters and not accustomed to having babies around, so they rarely invited me to bring the children to visit. Of course I couldn't take the children to a restaurant, so, aside from the Saturdays when I arranged for the housekeeper or the farm manager's wife to stay with them, I didn't see them regularly. Georgie, however, had always wanted to have children and wasn't able, so she invited us often or came out to the house and we had such fun talking together and playing with my girls. Stephen had died before Lily was born and Georgie kept saying that she didn't know what she would do without us. I was grateful for Georgie's help and support as I struggled with demands far beyond what I expected when I decided to become a mother.

Miles belonged to the City Country Club. In warm weather, I took the children to the Club to use the wading pools and started becoming better acquainted with some of the women I'd met through Miles's work. The ones with small children came to the wading pool as well. We began taking turns; one mother would supervise the children while the rest of us chatted over iced tea and glanced over the golf greens beyond the pool. Often we all had lunch in the dining room. It was sunny and looked out across the green hills. The food was always delicious. Among the horse set, everybody belonged to one or more of the clubs. As my circle of friends widened, I began to circulate to other clubs as well. We'd sponsor one another as guests and get a change of scenery. These women weren't as interesting, in some ways, as my teacher friends, who were well read and well informed on all the issues of the day. Most of my new friends were considerably younger than I. But we all had small children and husbands who were in the horse business so that we found plenty to talk about. When Miles was in town, I enjoyed the parties we attended more than I had because I moved around talking with people who were genuinely my friends.

****

Hunter was really the one who made it difficult. Lily was a quiet baby. In contrast to Hunter's constant noise and demands, Lily was dreamy and easy going. She was as frail as Hunter was hardy. Sometimes I'd just stand over her crib and watch her sleeping. Tiny white fingers curled slightly, wispy brown hair barely covered her head, long lashes fluttered against pale cheeks tinged ever so slightly with pink, and her breath came so gently I worried sometimes that it had stopped. She rarely insisted upon anything except when it came to food. She absolutely refused to eat food that she didn't like and fussed to get the things she did want. Lord, the fights we had.

One day, I'd had the cook mash up some of the fresh green beans from the garden that we were cooking for dinner. Miles was out on the road. I gave Hunter her plate and sat down next to Lily's chair, the dish of mashed beans in my hand. I dipped the spoon in and said, "Open wide," while I flew the spoon toward her mouth. She opened and the spoon went in. She closed her mouth around it, then, as I withdrew the spoon, her face screwed up and she spat the whole mouthful out onto the tray across her chair. I slapped her hand, filled the spoon again and aimed for her mouth. This time she clamped her jaws shut. I pressed the spoon into her lips but she just turned her head to the side so that some of the beans smeared from her mouth across to her cheek. I added some more onto the spoon and as I pushed it toward her she reached out an arm and swatted the spoon. The green mush flew off the spoon and landed on Hunter's head. Hunter looked so stunned, I wished I could have had a picture of her face. Not thinking, I put the bowl down on the tray in front of Lily and grabbed a towel to wipe Hunter's head. As soon as I turned, Lily scooped a handful of mush and threw it at me, hitting the side of my face and shoulder—and Hunter's face. Hunter began screaming and Lily laughed and clapped her hands. I burst out laughing even though I was mad as fire at Lily. It was fun to see her give Hunter a taste of her own medicine.

It wasn't always quite so lively, but I often fought to get food in her mouth. Miles threatened to force her mouth open and shove the food down her throat. I managed to keep the peace and eventually I found which foods she would eat and arranged to keep them on hand. Other than that she was blissfully easy to deal with.

Hunter, on the other hand, was a scamp. Sometimes I felt I spent my life pulling her down from where she'd climbed up, taking her off furniture, retrieving her from places she'd wedged herself into, snatching things out of her hands and responding to her incessant demands. She caught her head between the balusters on the staircase. She fell off the top of the porch railing and into my peonies, coming up with a flower upside down on her head and looking for all the world like some demented elf. I never saw a child who needed to be the center of attention as much as Hunter.

    ****

Hunter had a great fascination with Miles. When he was home, she followed him all over, even out to the stables sometimes when she managed to slip out the door behind him. Miles was so oblivious, he didn't realize she toddled behind him until the stable hands started laughing and asking who his new trainer was. If he tried to send her back to the house with one of the men she'd set up a squall that we could hear from the house. I learned early on that if I ran out to retrieve her, Miles instantly announced that she could stay. I hated to leave her. She could charm a snake when she wanted to, so they always made a big fuss over her when she got out there. But then they'd get to talking business and forget her. I was afraid she'd wind up getting kicked in the head by one of the horses or something. The worst that happened was a fall into a pile of manure. If I ignored her cries, Miles would have someone bring her back to the house where I could deal with her shrieking.

When Hunter was five and Lily three, Miles decided we must all go out with him for a few weeks in the midst of the racing season. We were to go with him to Chicago, where, at that time, shootings seemed to be common in every street. He just laughed when I told him I was afraid to take the children there. And the amount of work involved in traipsing around with children that small never crossed his mind—it was just one more thing for me to take care of.

Shortly after the train pulled out he wandered off to the club car and left me alone with the children in our compartment. Lily was happy to sit in a corner drawing her own little fantasy world, but Hunter grew bored in short order and began whining to go out for a walk. I distracted her for a while with looking out the window and counting cows, but before long she demanded to go look around. A tantrum was clearly brewing, so I got Lily and her doll and took all of them into the corridor to walk up and down. Then Hunter wanted to go into the next car, where all the people seated in rows fascinated her. There were some empty seats in the back, so I sat down with Lily and let Hunter walk up and down. In no time, Lily was in the midst of some magic realm with her doll and Hunter was busily chatting with highly amused passengers.

I turned to gaze out the window, but soon felt someone's presence in the aisle next to us. As I turned to look up, a vaguely familiar voice asked, "Virginia, Ginnie, is that you?"

I stared a moment before I could recognize Adrian's face. It was slightly more careworn than when I'd last seen it, the fair hair thinning a bit on top, but it was essentially the same face that I had adored so long ago. The eyes were still as pure and clear and honest as ever. "Adrian? Well, I never!" was all I could say. Mentally I reviewed my clothing, from a lavender travelling suit to a new hat, and decided I was presentable.

"May I sit with you for a moment?" he asked and waved to the seat facing mine.

"Of course." I pulled myself together. "Adrian, how have you been? I can't tell you how many times I wondered what had become of you. Well, of course, I've seen your books, but, I mean... ." I floundered helplessly and hoped he wouldn't ask me if I'd read them. I read the first, but when Miles saw it was miffed. Somehow Miles knew about Adrian, through some of his Nashville acquaintances, I supposed. The tiny blue-eyed schoolteacher was in it—I'd heard she was in the first four or five. His writing displayed the zest for life and unsinkable optimism that so defined Adrian. I moped around for days after finishing that book.

Chivalrous as ever, Adrian gracefully stepped into the silence. "Oh, I've done well. I settled in Santa Fe after moving around for a while writing stories for various newspapers and publications. It was some years before I had any interest in women," he mentioned, significantly, "but eventually I got married and we had a son. He's in high school now. You've heard about my career—I'm on a speaking tour now. I was in Atlanta." I asked him quite a few questions about his writing and Santa Fe, hungry for a picture of the life I wished I had shared. He told me some amazing anecdotes about the hair raising situations in which he found himself during the years that he traveled the west alone. Plenty of material for his books came from his life.

"How about you, Ginnie? Have you ever gotten to teach or find adventure?"

"No. You know, I married Jack. And then after he died, Mama pressed me to marry again and I found Miles."

"Poor Ginnie, always trying to please everyone but yourself. Has no one ever tried to give you what you wanted?"

I shook my head gently. "No. I don't suppose anyone has." I swallowed before adding, "Except you, I guess. I always thought you wanted to give me the life I wanted."

We fell silent. I wondered whether it was all best left in the past or whether it was better to reveal Mama's treachery so that Adrian would know the truth. It wasn't so much that I wanted to protect Mama as that I didn't want people to know what my own mother did to me. Finally, I decided that I wanted to clear the air. Some people at the other end of the car were playing a game with Hunter and I sent Lily to join her. "Adrian, I want to tell you something. I suppose in a way it doesn't matter any more, but I want to tell you anyway."

"You can tell me anything, Ginnie. I hope you've always known that."

"It's about the time right before you left all those years ago. When I was still at Hamilton's."

He stiffened slightly, but nodded for me to go on.

"Mama didn't tell me that you asked for permission to marry me. And I had never really talked to her very much about you."

A frown crossed his brow and he drew in a deep breath, staring fixedly into my face, but he was speechless.

"I thought you didn't love me and that you left to avoid proposing. I went ahead and married Jack because my only other option was to go home and I knew I couldn't live with Mama any more. It wasn't until a few years later, right before I married Miles, that Freddie told me. She thought I knew what Mama had told you and that you had talked to me. But I didn't know. Adrian, I didn't want to marry Jack.

When he first spoke to me after he'd talked to Mama, I told him that I couldn't give him an answer right away because I wanted to wait for you. Then you just disappeared... ."

"Ginnie, your Mama told me you'd said you wouldn't marry me because of Jack. I was reeling. I thought you'd just led me along all that time, knowing that you had plans for a richer catch. I don't even know how I left my job and gathered my belongings to leave town. I just wanted to get as far away as I could."

He grabbed my hand and raised it to his lips, then held it absently as we stared at one another in disbelief, the full realization overtaking us both that if only we'd talked to one another that one time the way we had talked about everything else under the sun, we would have been married to one another all these years. It's funny, when Freddie told me about Adrian's proposal, I was so angry at Mama that I never really took it in that Adrian really loved me and we really could have spent our lives together—I might have taught school and lived in the wilds of New Mexico. Staring full into his eyes I saw all the tenderness and love for me that I had always seen there and knew that the same look was reflected back at him from mine. It occurred to me that neither Jack nor Miles had ever looked at me that way.

As we sat, my mind wandered through the past, something I rarely allowed myself to do. I seemed always to have had someone stronger willed than I telling me that I couldn't do what I wanted to do because something else would be best. I had finally learned to get some things I wanted by keeping silent about my wishes and merely moving ahead with my plan. But now I saw that I had never forged ahead with the things I wanted most.

I married Miles by omitting facts that might have led Mama to refuse to allow it, but getting married was still Mama's plan. Although I wanted the children, I had to admit that I'd wanted them more as a means of escape from the constant motion of Miles's life than because I really wanted to be a mother. I remembered rising to my brothers' challenges, competing against them in various sports, climbing trees and thinking up pranks. I couldn't reconcile how that spirited little girl became so paralyzed in the face of determined people who insisted upon exercising authority over her. Mama curtailed my tomboyishness, refused to consider allowing me to teach, then handed me to Jack, who wanted an entertaining companion but balked at a wife who expressed strong opinions. From Jack she handed me to Miles, who took control of the money that could have given me my freedom and expected me to lead the life he had chosen.

As trees and barns and telephone lines flew by on my left, I gazed into the face across from me and felt for the first time the price I paid for my willingness to obey the dictates of those I had been taught to respect. I wondered numbly how and when I came to the conclusion that Mama and my husbands had the right to control my decisions. Such reflections were rare in my life. Mostly I just lived along the way people expected and didn't give too much thought to what might have been or why things were one way instead of another. In that moment, I was overwhelmed by understanding so deep that I wondered how anyone could stand to ask those kinds of questions.

I glanced down the aisle at my daughters. Motherhood had proved to be harder and more annoying than I had imagined, but I loved them and would not disrupt their lives. The love I felt for Miles had more to do with shared years and experiences than with the kind of heart connection I felt for Adrian, but I would not want to hurt him either. Gazing back at Adrian, I knew that he would say the same things about his family.

"It's too late for us Ginnie," he said softly. He said it as a regrettable fact, not a question, and I could only shake my head in reply, swallowing tears as I registered the sadness in his eyes.

"Mother, I'm hungry." Hunter shook my arm, calling me back from the special world I inhabited with Adrian. "I'M HUNGRY. Why is that man holding your hand?" Regretfully, Adrian released my hand.

"I'm sorry, Adrian, I must feed the children. I have a lunch in our compartment." I hesitated a moment before asking if he'd care to join us. He declined and shook my hand, not letting go of it as he spoke.

"Ginnie, I'm glad to know, at last. Even though it doesn't change anything, it changes everything."

I knew. Oh, I knew. I watched him walk slowly away and decided there and then not to let myself think of it again.

Chapter Ten

Sometimes as I watched my girls growing up, I reviewed the changes I'd seen in the world and wondered what on earth life would be like when they grew up and had children. Horses were rarely seen on the road any more and cars were everywhere. It seemed they introduced more models and features all the time. Airplanes were used in the Great War, and then people started using them for travel. Our house had electric lights, a telephone and indoor plumbing. All the women wore dresses above their ankles and long, slim skirts with no bustles or long flowing folds. So many changes. The stock market fell and terrible times were upon us. Thousands of people lost everything. Horse racing continued much as before, and, other than reducing the stable staff, we lived much as we had. I constantly feared that we would suddenly lose everything. I couldn't get Miles to tell me how Jack's money had fared. He said it was his business to take care of it and that I shouldn't worry about it. He was irritable, but he insisted that we were fine. As I watched the grey of his hair become slowly silver and the lines on his face grow more deeply etched, I doubted his veracity but I let it go. Just as I had ultimately capitulated to Mama, I had given Miles the reins and long since abandoned any illusion that I had power relative to him.

I turned my attention to the children, both of whom concerned me aside from conditions in the wider world. Hunter continued to be willful and occasionally out of control while retaining her capacity to charm anyone she chose. She could sweet talk the hands into being organized into teams to do extra work before Miles came home or coordinate the schoolchildren in some project the teacher wanted done.

One day when a big storm was brewing, threatening a tornado, the school called to tell me they were keeping all the children until the storm passed over unless their parents wanted to come get them. I waited until the storm moved on and then drove out to pick them up. Hunter's teacher sent me to Lily's room. There was Hunter, telling a story and making shadow puppets on the wall while the younger children sat enthralled. Lily's teacher told me that Hunter had gone in to check on her little sister and, when she saw that the younger children were frightened, she stayed and helped out. I racked my brain to decide what we could do to channel her skills for leadership and action more into that kind of activity, but she remained at least as likely to employ them in some prank.

Such as the day when I thought Miles would finally wring her neck. Mrs. Amber, the mother of a man with whom he was negotiating some breeding contracts, came to visit. We sat in the living room chatting and drinking iced tea with fresh sprigs of mint from the garden. A tall big-boned woman with a stern face and grey hair pulled tightly into a neat bun, she chose to sit in the large upholstered rocking chair that was Miles's favorite. Hunter came bounding in carrying Miles's big black umbrella. It was all folded up and she'd been using it, as she often did, as a gun, stalking enemies out between the house and the barns. The sweet little yellow dress in which she'd gone out had streaks of dirt and grass stains on it. Her dark eyes gleamed defiantly, the set of her mouth portending trouble, so, under the circumstances I ignored the condition of her clothes. I tenuously prompted her to say hello and how do you do to Mrs. Amber, which she did begrudgingly.

The woman, who was rather self-important in my opinion, didn't seem to notice, but smiled and gushed, "Oh, what a darlin' little girl." Smiling seemed to require a great effort to force the corners of her lips upward from their natural down-turn and into a position rather more in a straight line. It didn't seem genuine and I glanced nervously at Hunter to see how she might react.

Hunter smiled and I relaxed, thinking that she'd chosen to charm my guest. Then she let out a whoop and ran toward the rocking chair with the umbrella held out in front of her, aimed at Mrs. Amber's head. In the end, the point missed Mrs. Amber and instead rammed into the chair with such force that it flew over backwards so far I was sure it had to tip. Mrs. Amber still wore the long, full skirts of her era and yards of black fabric flew up in the air, revealing numerous lace petticoats. The chair stopped for a moment mid-air, her feet in their ankle-high lace-ups pointed toward the ceiling. I held my breath as I sat in horror across the room and waited for the fall. Suddenly the chair lurched forward again and snapped back to the floor. Her skirts flew back down. As the chair continued to rock wildly for a moment, I saw that she gripped the arms of the chair so hard her knuckles were white and standing out so I half expected to see the bones burst through the skin. Nearby, Hunter laughed until she could hardly stand. I was too distressed to see any humor in the situation. I jumped to my feet and ran to Mrs. Amber.

"Oh my lord, are you all right?"

She sat for a moment in a daze and then began to pat tentatively at her hair and then her skirt as if her dignity would be restored if only everything proved to be in place. I handed her her iced tea as she told me faintly that she thought she was all right. Then I grabbed Hunter and swatted her on the behind while I thrust her toward the stairs and told her to get up to her room and stay there. She announced that she'd prefer to be there and stomped up the stairs in a fury.

After her door slammed, I turned to Mrs. Amber and said, "I have no idea what possessed her to do such a thing. I am so sorry. Really. I can't tell you how sorry I am." She really seemed to take it remarkably well, assuring me she'd merely been startled and telling an amusing anecdote about one of her son's early escapades. It reminded me of the pranks I used to pull with or on my brothers. But it seemed to me that our pranks were played in fun where Hunter's stunts were too often hostile and mean-spirited. Oftentimes she brought Grandmama to mind, but Grandmama had plenty of reason to be so irascible—I couldn't fathom why Hunter should be bitter.

When I told Miles that night what had happened, he was ready to get her out of bed and tan her hide. Since I'd taken care of that after our hapless visitor left, I talked him out of it. Then, all of a sudden the sight of those skirts floating in mid-air and those old-fashioned shoes thrusting upward came vividly to mind and I began to giggle.

"There is nothing funny about this, Ginnie," Miles assured me angrily. His spine was still stiff and straight and he pulled himself to his fullest, most imposing height. Rage spread slowly across his face, replacing its usual sternness with a more fiendish quality. Usually I desisted when I saw that look, inwardly cringing as if Mama were there, but I was too tickled to stop.

"Oh, but Miles, you should have seen her," I chuckled. "You know how stuffy she is." I broke off giggling again before I could go on, sputtering. "The chair flew back so fast her skirts flew up straight up so her slips were showing. It stopped for a second and her feet were just stuck up there, toward the ceiling... ." I started laughing so hard I couldn't keep talking. Miles continued glaring at me at first, but then the corners of his mouth began to twitch and he began to chortle, his shoulders shaking as he still tried to hold it in. Finally he let out a shout and the two of us were in stitches. We hadn't laughed that way together since we courted.

****

I watched over the girls' progress at school very carefully. I told them over and over that nothing is more important than a good education. I wanted them to have the freedom to make choices for their lives and never to feel pressure to marry a certain sort of man—or to marry at all. However, Lily, who was bright as could be, was not very interested in school. She drew and painted all the time. Her pictures were quite remarkable for her age, in fact. But she certainly couldn't be an artist. I wouldn't have her associating with all those peculiar people who live in the midst of scandal. And I understood it was a very uncertain living. When she wasn't drawing, she was lost in her own world, surrounded by her dolls and imaginary people. I let her have her paints and pastels and all and I hoped that she would have changed her mind by the time we'd have to seriously discuss her wish to attend art school.

Hunter lacked aptitude as well as inclination toward school. She was very sharp in some respects, but in academics she would never be on top. She didn't even try to achieve the best she could do. Her mind was filled with horses and she had this wild idea that she would follow in her father's footsteps and take over his business, just as if she were a boy. I suggested all sorts of other possibilities but she didn't even act as if she heard me.

Miles and I did not agree on the subject of their education. "Please talk to them about doing their schoolwork."

"Why does it make such a difference, Ginnie?" he asked with the most bewildered look on his face.

"Because education is important, Miles. Everyone should get the best education available, in my opinion."

"But they're girls. What difference is it going to make?" A shade of impatience slipped into his voice and I knew I was courting one of his temper flares, especially since he was just fixing his third vodka martini.

"Because knowledge is always worth having for its own sake. And because an education can give them more choices."

"Ha!" he broke in. "You want them to be old spinster schoolteachers like those old gals you're always gallivanting with. When are you going to give up on this schoolteacher fantasy? Some nonsense your granddaddy put in your head when you were a child... . Forget about it!"

"I never said I wanted them to teach. I want them to be informed, to have good minds... . And what about Hunter? She wants to get involved in your business. Don't you think she should know something?"

"Don't be ridiculous, Virginia. She's a child, indulging in a silly fantasy. Of course she won't be involved in my business."

I started to argue with him and then I decided to break off before mentioning choices again, for he looked as if he were about to have an apoplexy.

****

It was just after Christmas when Miles suffered a stroke. He came home after a few weeks in the hospital, but we had to have a nurse with him every day because he couldn't walk. We set him up in his study on the first floor. The children were nervous and unnaturally quiet in the funereal atmosphere. The household revolved around his convalescence. The preparation of the special foods he needed to eat took priority over our meals, although the need to feed the nurses as well basically just kept the kitchen in continuous operation.

Occasionally he signalled that he wanted one or more of his employees to come in to see him. The doctors said that that was all right as long as no meeting ever lasted more than half an hour. Miles's speech was quite impaired for a while, but he could convey quite a bit between his tortured words and a series of hand gestures we developed. The business out at the stables seemed to keep going without him, to my surprise and relief. As spring approached, the horses were shipped as usual, the trainers and manager accompanying them on the circuit.

He found the children's visits quite wearing, but they were anxious to be able to see him regularly and reassure themselves that he was all right. Hunter especially searched for every sign of improvement and would come to me each time she saw him to report in detail on her observations and beg me to tell her it meant that he would be fine. I did my best. And, for a while, he did improve and we felt quite hopeful.

I spent many hours with him, sometimes reading to him, often just sitting. His desk was pushed up against one of the book-lined walls. It was a huge mahogany piece that suited his size. I surveyed the desk and recalled the thousand times I'd brought him a cup of coffee or a snack. He'd be sitting with his head bowed, totally absorbed in his papers. Aside from whatever he was working on at the moment, the desk was always clear and neat. Once he was ill, the desk became strewn with papers, lined with bottles of medicine and occasionally piled with dishes of half eaten food. Miles was unable to move enough to express the disarray his life had become, but his desk seemed to have sympathetically arranged itself to express it for him.

Sometimes I examined the books, reading titles, exploring for patterns in the apparently random array of yellows, reds, greens, blues, purples and blacks. One day it occurred to me that it was interesting a man who never seemed to read owned so many books. I started to ask him about that, but then decided better of it. With more that probably should have been discussed between us than we had ever had, we actually talked even less than usual. I did buck up the courage one day to ask, "Is there any thing I should know about our business affairs?"

"I took care of everything with my lawyer. There's nothing you need to worry about," was all he would say.

Weakened though he was, he never broke down and allowed himself to reveal his inner life. Sometimes I watched him while he dozed and wondered how I could have lived with him so many years and still feel that I knew so little about him.

Occasionally I gazed at his hollow cheeks and sunken chest and felt a wave of tenderness for the man with whom I'd spent a significant portion of my life or experienced a sense of sadness at the idea of living without him. Other times he seemed like a stranger and I stirred up angry memories of his coldness and restrictive control over my life, repining over years that seemed wasted.

I had no idea what would be of real comfort to him and so busied myself with the usual pillow plumping, back rubbing, food serving sorts of things I assumed one did for a sick person. He never asked for anything else. On some days he reached for my hand and seemed to derive comfort from my presence and on others he was just as content to have the nurse in attendance.

In the spring, he began to move a bit more and the doctors began to speak of therapy to help him walk again. We were making plans to bring in a wheelchair so that he could be more mobile, when he developed a slight cold. It moved with startling rapidity into his lungs. He coughed and wheezed and struggled for breath. The doctor said it was pneumonia. I sat by his side for hours as he fought for air. After a few days, he had declined so rapidly that he rarely opened his eyes. Afraid to leave him, I was napping fitfully in the chair next to his bed one night while the nurse got some rest on the living room sofa. Suddenly he gasped loudly. Instantly awake, I bolted up in time to watch him striving to raise his head, one arm lifting slightly toward me. Before I could reach his hand, he sank back and was still. I called for the nurse. Grimly she felt his pulse and went out to call the doctor. She seemed loathe to pronounce him dead without the doctor's verdict. I knew the doctor could do no more for him, but I let her carry out the pretense that he could. Recovery had appeared to be imminent only days before and I cried with shock as much as sadness.

Georgie came out to stay and helped me make funeral arrangements, as I had for her when Stephen died. Hunter was inconsolable and Lily seemed just to withdraw further. I was dazed. There had long been a faint question in my mind whether my marriage to Miles had been a good decision but we had been married 25 years and my life was bound up in his so closely that it was difficult to face separation anyway. With the Depression still a grim reality, I panicked about what might become of us and how I would manage the farm and the money.

The shock of Miles's death was nothing compared to the shock of hearing his will read. I took Georgie with me. The lawyer's office was enormous, with big, dark pieces of furniture and an oriental rug that must have cost a fortune. An associate joined Miles's attorney. They told us that Miles actually increased Jack's estate somewhat over the years—in fact, in better economic times, they said the growth would have been substantial. But Miles put everything in trust for the children, allowing me to receive only the income for my life. When the lawyer finished reading he looked expectantly at me. I stared back in stunned disbelief.

"I don't think I can have understood you properly," I said, at last, deliberately.

"The bulk of the estate is to be held in trust for your daughters and you will have the income for your life."

I jumped to my feet, raised my voice and insisted, "He can't do this to me! I brought that money to the marriage. How can he tie it up like that? I won't allow it. What can be done?"

"That money legally belonged to Miles. This is a solid will, Miz Harrison. I'm afraid there isn't anything you can do."

Georgie reached up and tugged my arm downward, causing me to sit down again. "I can't believe this," I told them, my eyes filling with tears. "I gave up the love of my life for that money and then spent years arguing with Miles over how much of my money he would let me have. Do you mean to tell me that he managed to keep control of it even in death?"

Both men were clearing their throats and pulling at their collars in discomfort, but they assured me that that was what had happened and told me they were sorry that I was so distressed. "Your income will be very comfortable, though, very comfortable," they told me.

Georgie had to lead me out and take over the driving. I was crying and blustering at the same time. "This is intolerable! There must be something I can do to overturn this." She just let me rant on.

For days, never minding that I'd been frightened about handling the money myself, I fumed and raged and mourned until I thought I might go mad. In the midst of my fury, I suddenly thought of Grandmama one day and how everything was taken from her. As angry as I was at merely losing control over a fortune, I couldn't imagine the wrath she must have felt as her home, her land and most of her possessions as well as her wealth were stripped from her. Her bitterness, in that instant of comprehension, seemed perfectly understandable—what I began to admire was the fact that she survived at all.

****

When school let out, I packed up the girls and took them to California, where we rented a small furnished house near the beach. It was tiny and the furniture had seen better days, but it was clean and livable. Hunter was surly and even less patient with Lily than she had ever been. She had always been on better behavior when Miles was around than at any other time and made it her business to keep him charmed. With him gone, she seemed to go out of control. There were periodic outbursts and once she accused me of killing Miles. Fortunately she made friends with some of the local children and disappeared for hours on end, because I was not up to dealing with her. I had my suspicions some of the time that they were up to no good, but as long as no irate citizens knocked on my door, I preferred not to know what she did when she was away from me. Lily could hardly bear to let me out of her sight. She did spend a lot of time out sketching the ocean, but she always stayed on the part of the beach that could be seen from the house.

Georgie worked at cheering us up long distance by sending us the most charming letters. She'd found a series of drawings of a little dog much like her "Tip" and the letters were written as if Tip were telling us the goings on back in Lexington with the pictures pasted in to illustrate certain points. She dipped his paws in the ink and placed paw prints all over them. Lily was enchanted and even Hunter enjoyed them, I think, though she pretended indifference. Sometimes I thought she'd be better off with at least a modicum of Lily's sense of magic. At the same time, I wished that Lily were a little tougher or had a bit of Hunter's knack for dealing with people around her. Hunter was a natural leader while Lily shied away from people. Lily always had a fondness for Georgie, though, and she began writing little notes to her for me to enclose in my letters.

I sat and gazed at the ocean for hours—much as I had after my first widowhood so many years before. Sometimes I conjured up memories of Miles and his quiet strength and stubbornness. He was so much taller and more solid than I that I'd often lived in an illusion of protection as we strolled together. Other times I brooded over all I had suffered and lost for the sake of that money and how it seemed everyone around me but me had gained from it. My brothers, Miles, and now Hunter and Lily would have the money to do what they wanted. I imagined that I saw Adrian on the horizon, drifting farther and farther out to sea, followed by a little western schoolhouse.

Then I began to wonder if I should rethink my opinions about the girls' dreams. I always tried to provide the possibility of wider horizons for them, yet it occurred to me that I discouraged both of them from doing the things they told me they wanted to do, just as my mother had done to me. I'd come to understand her better over my years of wrestling with motherhood. The burden of responsibility to guide them past all pitfalls led me to try to control them just as she controlled me. It was too late when I finally realized that she really did try to do what she thought would give me a better life. I didn't want things to end the same way with my children.

With Miles gone, I didn't know how Hunter would achieve her goal, though. I'd always thought it questionable that Miles would consent to teaching her the business and leaving it to her as she assumed he would. I couldn't imagine that some other man of my acquaintance would take on the task. But Lily was a different story. I could help her go to art school. Georgie thought she was tremendously talented and had argued with me more than once about the need to encourage her. I decided that I wouldn't tell her that yet so that I could see what she might do. But if she still wanted to pursue it when she was older, I concluded that I would not stand in her way.

I was pleased at my decision about Lily, but my musings otherwise brought me small comfort. By the end of the summer, my hair had turned completely white and I weighed 65 pounds. I hadn't really noticed the change, but Georgie took one look at me when she picked us up at the train and called a friend to arrange for me to be placed in a special nursing home in Maryland. We made quick arrangements to enroll the girls in a very lovely boarding school near Lexington. Hunter was livid, and, when we pulled up in front of the school, she jumped from the car and marched up the steps without a backward glance. Then when the car started to leave after we'd set Lily up, Hunter came screaming down the driveway and grabbed the door, dragging alongside for a few yards before she let go and collapsed on the ground in tears. It was the saddest sight I ever saw and I wanted to stop and go back, but Georgie insisted that I'd be more use to them in the long run if I pulled myself together. I knew that I could barely take care of myself any more, let alone the children, but I felt as if I had betrayed them.

The place Georgie put me into was quite nice, with little bungalows for the patients scattered across the grounds. I'd expected some dingy old brick institution in spite of Georgie's assurances to the contrary, so that came as a pleasant surprise. They were very concerned about my eating and made special meals for me every day. A nurse would stay and insist that I eat each one. The doctors convinced me that what

Miles had done was perfectly normal and that I should not be so upset about the trust. They asked me all sorts of questions about my marriage and encouraged me to think only of happy times with Miles. After a while I didn't seem to find any sadness any more. I didn't feel much of anything else either.

By Christmas I was able to go back home. Lily and Hunter spent the holidays with me. Through the months I'd been away, I'd received several letters from the school about my children. Hunter quickly became a ringleader in devilment and the school considered her a disciplinary problem. Lily took no interest in her schoolwork but spent inordinate amounts of time drawing elaborate pictures instead. After a while the headmistress took her art supplies away from her. I wrote that I thought that was cruel when that was the child's only comfort and she had been deprived of both her parents. I was informed that I must allow the school to be the best judge. I didn't like it, but I was in no position to fight the decision. Georgie told me she argued with them also, to no avail. It was funny, Hunter wrote to tell me about what they did to Lily and was clearly outraged, but Lily never breathed a word.

I bought Lily a whole new set of art supplies when I got back to town and gave them to her right away. She thanked me, but I noticed that she didn't draw as much as she used to. She was more silent and afraid than ever and sat in her room reading for hours on end. Hunter was still mad at me, but she wanted new clothes and a few other things so she chose to manipulate me into taking her shopping instead of being hostile. Her timing was good because I felt tired and remote and preferred to allow myself to be manipulated rather than have to handle one of Hunter's tantrums. She refused to discuss her activities at the school, though, and insisted that since she had done nothing wrong, there was no need for her to change her behavior in the next term. I let that drop too. The school would probably ask her to leave at the end of the year, but I didn't intend to enroll them there again anyway.

I sent them back to the school after New Year's. The doctors had told me that I still needed to rest and I had a lot of arrangements to make. At least I could now see them on the weekends. The horses had been sold according to instructions Miles put in his will. I had long meetings with the trustees and soon was in a whirlwind of activity. I gave notice to those of Miles's employees who had not already left. The trustees helped me find a suitable tenant for the farm and, with Georgie's help, I located a nice house for rent in Lexington.

As a child, I never thought I'd choose to leave a life in the country for one in the city, but I'd become accustomed to noise and bustle in my traveling years with Miles and I did not want the responsibility for running a farm. By the time school let out for summer I had moved the furniture into our new home and set up lovely rooms for Lily and Hunter. I loved our house on Harrison Farm more than any place I ever lived and when the movers left I sat immobilized for a while, looking in through the windows at emptiness and finding the once-inviting white facade stark and cold.

Hunter

Chapter Eleven

Daddy had a stroke after Christmas. He had to sleep in his study downstairs and there were fusty ol' nurses around all the time, telling us to shush. They didn't let me go in to see him very often because they said I was too rambunctious for him. I thought he'd feel better if it wasn't so quiet and gloomy.

Mother ran things all the time then. She was a tiny little thing—I was almost 12 and nearly as tall as her—but she could get people hustling. We had had trouble pretty often because I didn't want to listen to all her silly "lady" stuff, but she didn't have time for as much of that, so that was one good thing about Daddy's being sick. Usually when Daddy was around I didn't have so much of a problem with her. When he was away at the races, though, Mother and I had some pretty good fights.

The last time Daddy was out on the road Mother and I fought about riding. Mother was being silly just because I fell off my horse and I wasn't gonna let her stop me. Mr. Lawrence, my riding teacher, always said, "You've got to get right back up and keep riding." I got right back on even though I landed on my tail bone and it hurt pretty much. I've got to be tough to be like Daddy. And I had to ride the next day because Daddy was coming home soon from the races and I wanted to show him how much I could do. My stupid sister Lily didn't like to ride, so he'd be the most proud of me.

My daddy owned a lot of fast race horses. They won all the time and we had lots of silver trophies in our house. In the summer his horses raced all over the place and Daddy went to the tracks with them. When he was home, I went everywhere I could with him and listened to everything he and his men said about horses because I'm gonna be important and exciting like him when I grow up. Mother says ladies don't get to run things but I don't think she knows anything much.

Daddy was really mad at me before he left the last time just because I hit the rocking chair when that ol' Mrs. Amber was in it and it tipped over a little. I was on maneuvers and I had to make sure the enemy wasn't behind the chair. Besides she's a fussy old lady and she talks to me in a stupid voice. Daddy said that sometimes you have to be nice to people because it's good for your business even if you don't really like 'em. I figured when Daddy got back and I showed him that I could take my jumps, he'd forget about being mad.

After I got Mother to say I could go riding the next day, I went out to the stables to see who I could talk to. Nobody much was around right then. But I saw Lily sitting out under a tree playing with those dumb dolls of hers. So I went over and grabbed one and ran with it over to the place behind the stable where Mother can't see from the house. She slowed down when she saw I'd gone there. I held up her doll and pretended like I was gonna pull the head off if she didn't come closer. She screamed and ran over, of course, and, before I gave her her doll back, I punched her in the stomach like I always do. Mother heard her scream and when she came out Lily was crying and holding her stomach.

"Hunter, how many times do I have to tell you not to hit your sister?" Mother asked and grabbed me by the arm and swatted me on the bottom, hard. That Lily was always getting me in trouble like that. While Mother kept shaking me by the arm and giving me a spank every now and then all the way back to the house, I started figuring how to get Lily back. I was afraid Mother'd change her mind about riding, but she left that alone. I just had to stay in my room until dinner. She told me to do some school-work but I got out Daddy's umbrella that I hid under the bed and practiced sword fighting like we saw them do it at the matinee.

****

Sometimes Daddy took us with him for a couple of weeks when he was out travelling. Daddy was very tall and handsome, even though his hair was grey and he looked a little tired a lot of times. Mother barely came up to his chest. I thought Daddy seemed older than the other children's fathers. But one of his horses beat Black Gold at Latonia. When I was with Daddy, I tried to behave like a lady, like Mother was always harping about, and I didn't pull pranks. Daddy had a terrible temper and I hated it when he was mad at me. If he was really mad, he wouldn't take me with him when he went to the track or the horse sales.

One time we took the train to Chicago. Daddy went off somewhere and wouldn't take me with him. I talked to all kinds of people on the train and told them about Daddy and how I'm gonna have great horses like his. Lots of people gave me some candy. I gave a couple of pieces to Lily, but she doesn't like candy much.

In Chicago, I stayed on the lookout for gangsters because I wanted to see them shoot somebody. Mother kept telling me to thank my stars we didn't see any such thing. Sometimes I think she and Lily are a lot alike. Daddy took me to the track with him and I got to meet all the jockeys and stableboys. They showed me all the best horses and explained to me all about how to look at the points or something. I can tell a good horse sometimes.

I learned some good words too. "Shit!"

Daddy chuckled and said, "You'd better not let your mother hear you say that."

"You mean you're not supposed to let me pick up bad language, right Daddy?" I grinned up at him.

"Right."

"Let's look at the Racing Form now. Can I make a bet?" Daddy let me see the field and make my pick for the winner in two races and he made the bets for me. Lily wasn't very interested in horses and she was afraid of the jockeys and stableboys so Daddy hardly ever brought her and that was just fine with me. There was a filly named Huntress running. She was the daughter of one of Daddy's horses. I bet on her. She was a little slow out of the starting gate, but she began to pick up after the first turn.

"Go Huntress," I yelled. She started moving up. "Go!" I screamed. I started hopping up and down next to Daddy.

He gripped his paper tight in his hand and under his breath I heard him say, "Come on Huntress."

Around the final turn she moved up to third and on the final stretch she started flying up to the front of the pack. I screamed and screamed and jumped up and down. When she won Daddy threw me up on his shoulder. Then I got to go to the winner's circle with him. That was one of the best days I ever had.

One day when I had to stay with Mother, she took Lily and me to Marshall

Field's. It was the biggest store I ever saw. The candy department had cases and cases of every kind of candy. Lily wanted to go look at dolls, but I took my time by the candy, trying to decide the best ones to buy with the money I won at the track the day before. Finally, Mother told me to think about it while we went to see the dolls. Lily's eyes were big as saucers at all the dolls. Every color of hair and size you could imagine, and babies, and ladies in beautiful dresses. I had to admit there were some good ones, even though I don't much like dolls.

Then we had to go try on dresses. Mother made us buy matching ones again. I can't stand having to wear the same thing as Lily, but Mother thinks it's sweet. Then she goes on about how she never got to have a sister except a grown-up half one named Sis and we should be glad to have one another. I figured she didn't know how good she had it, but I didn't say anything because I didn't want her getting teary and going on about family and how you should be loyal and treat your family with care. Mushy stuff. She had them wrap up our old clothes and made us wear the new dresses. I tried to stay far away from them so no one could see how silly we looked. That made Lily cry because she loved the dress, so Mother took her to look at art supplies. She always got her way like that.

I got farther and farther behind. Finally, when Lily had Mother eyeing some pastels, I turned and headed back down to the candy counter. I made some wrong turns I guess and finally I had to smile real nice at a lady in the jewelry department and she said she'd take me. Being nice to people when you need them for your business works pretty well. She wanted to know if I was alone and I told her where Mother and Lily were. She left me at the candy counter, trying to decide if I was going to get lemon gumdrops or orange slices, peanut brittle or chocolate raisins. I'd just gotten around to the divinity all piled up like little white pillows when a man in a uniform came up and asked me if I was Hunter Harrison. When I said yes, he grabbed me by the hand and started pulling me along after him, saying, "Your mother is frantic, little lady. You come on to the office with me."

I'd only bought two kinds of candy. I could sure see what Mother meant when she went on about Yankees. No one ever dragged me around back at The Bon Mot in Lexington. Old Mr. Haslett, the owner, did make me wait for Mother to come get me the time I tried out a new umbrella and broke a case in the scarves department, but he just told me I was a hellion and he hoped Mother would give me what I deserved, he didn't drag me anywhere.

"Oh, Hunter, where on earth have you been? What possessed you to go off like that?" Mother squealed when the man brought me in, and grabbed me in a hug and then shook me. Lily just sat there with her new pastels, running her fingers over all those colors.

"I didn't want to waste time with all that art stuff, so I went on down to buy my candy. I was coming back," I told her.

"Well, young lady, don't you ever wander off from me without asking. Never! Do you hear me?" She thanked the store people and pulled me out by my ear.
****

Mother got very excited over silly things. That's why I especially didn't like having Daddy sick. She was more nervous than ever. But she paid so much attention to Daddy that I could go out and talk to the stableboys and learn more words that she didn't want me to know or drag Lily behind the barn more often and not get in any trouble. I'd been able to do it pretty often anyway because Mother spent so much time with her friends and cleaning house and stuff. It wasn't quite as much fun, somehow, after Daddy got sick. Sometimes I sneaked into his room when no one was looking and told him some of the new words I'd learned out in the barn. He really laughed at that, but not as hard as he used to.

Mother kept on bothering me about school even then. "Hunter a good education is more valuable than you know," she'd say.

"I just need to know about how to check a horse's points or to follow the bloodlines so's I can pick a winner at the sales" I'd tell her, just like Daddy always talked. "They don't teach any of that at that stupid school, so how is it going to help?"

"Well, you're going to need to be able to read, for starters, to check the *Racing Form*. And you might want to do something else by the time you grow up. The more you know, the more choices you'll have."

"I'll never want to do anything but race horses," I told her. "Daddy will teach me everything I need to know."

"I wouldn't count on your father to favor this plan," she answered.

But I asked Daddy to teach me about it and he always told me things and he laughed and laughed every time I said I'd be like him when I grew up, so I knew he wanted me to do it. I didn't want to be like Mother and have to hang around cooking and talking to ladies about books.

One day Lily and I came home after school and the doctor was there. Our ride let us off and we ran in. Mother was sitting in the living room with a handkerchief all squeezed up in her hand. Lily ran over and asked, "What's happened to Daddy?"

"He's having a lot of trouble breathing, girls, but I'm sure the doctor will be able to help." The doctor came out of the spare room just then and Mother sent us upstairs to change out of our school clothes. We stayed in the hall near the bannister and tried to hear what he said, but we couldn't hear anything until he got to the door and said he'd send nurses to stay with Daddy round the clock.

Ladies in stiff uniforms seemed to be all around the place all the time after that. Mother wouldn't let us go in to see Daddy any more. I wanted to tell him about how well I was doing with my jumping. And how I made captain of the girls' softball team. Lily drew more pictures than ever. She went out to the paddock and drew each one of Daddy's best horses. She usually had fairies and elves and dumb stuff like that hanging around in her pictures, but, thank goodness, I didn't see any flying around those horses. Except for the fairies, her pictures were really beautiful. Mother took the drawings in and said Daddy liked them and she told me he was glad about my jumping.

Mother never did like that I was learning to take my fences, but she laughed about softball and said she used to play all the games the boys played. I can't imagine anyone as prim as her playing any kind of game. I asked her what boys she played with.

"Why, my brothers, of course," she said.

I never knew she had any brothers. "Does that mean I have uncles?" I asked.

"Well, yes, of course it does," she said, kind of testy.

"Am I going to meet them?" I wanted to know.

"Probably not," she snapped. I knew better than to ask any more questions when she sounded like that.

Other times I asked some questions and found out all my grandparents died before I was born. Sometimes Mother told us about her grandmother and grandfather and how they lost their plantation in the Civil War. She got to see them all the time and I think she really liked her grandfather. He was a classics professor at some university and told her stories about myths and read books with her. I guessed that was why she went on about school all the time.

I told her I wished I knew my grandparents. She just said my grandfather probably wouldn't have paid any attention to me even if he were alive. I'd have made him, though. She wouldn't say anything at all about her mother and she just got mad if we asked. Sometimes Lily and I tried to figure out why most all the other children seemed to have grandparents and we didn't have any. Daddy just said it was because he was so old when we were born that his parents had died already.

Not long after the doctor came to visit, we woke up in the night and heard voices. Lily and I both sneaked out of our rooms at the same time. The doctor was downstairs and Mother and the nurses were crying. We crept down the stairs in our nighties even though Mother always said we must never let anyone see us unless we were fully dressed. She didn't seem to notice us, though, so we went on past to the room Daddy stayed in. The nurse's cheeks were all wet and she was packing some things up. Daddy was just lying there. I called to him, but he didn't answer.

"He can't hear you, honey," the nurse told me.

"DADDY," I said louder, so he could hear. Lily shook him by the shoulder. He didn't move.

The nurse came over and took our hands and told us we should go out to Mother. When we got there, she was crying so hard she couldn't talk. The doctor took us a little way off from her and told us Daddy was dead and said he was real sorry. Lily started crying. I went back where Daddy was and told him he couldn't go yet because he hadn't taught me enough about horses and I needed him to help keep Mother from bothering me all the time. He didn't move still and I just turned my back on him and walked upstairs.

Aunt Georgie came out to stay for a few days and helped Mother with the funeral and spent time with us. Lily likes Georgie a lot and I guess she's all right, but she kind of bores on about things, I think. She took us out to get black dresses. By that time I was so much taller than Lily that no one tried to make us wear the same things any more. Lily and Mother cried and cried at the funeral but I was a good soldier and kept a stiff upper lip like Daddy.

Chapter Twelve

It was still hot and humid at nine o'clock that May night. I was 16 and I was supposed to be home in half an hour. But my friends and I had been following the principal for a few days, preparing our big plan for that night and I wasn't going to miss it. Besides, I'd organized it and I wasn't sure the others would have the gumption to carry it out without me.

I liked to organize people and lead them through big pranks. School was so boring. All that sitting around looking at books. Sometimes I could hardly sit still I wanted to run around so bad and I'd start feeling like I was gonna burst. So I had to do something. I had led the kids a few times when I was little. But I got really good after Daddy died and Mother pretended to be sick so she could dump us in that school and go off on a vacation. After Daddy died we went out to California for the summer. We were near the beach and there were lots of kids my age and we could swim and play ball and run around making as much noise as we wanted to. The beach went on for miles and the mountains dwarfed our Kentucky hills. Everything was bigger. Mother just sat around and didn't pay too much attention so I did what I wanted to, pretty much. After we went back to Lexington, the next thing I knew Mother popped us in the school and breezed out of town.

I didn't want to talk to her the day she dropped us off. When we drove up I got out of the car and went into the school before Georgie even finished parking and told the headmistress, Mrs. O'Toole, who I was and that I wanted to be shown to my room right away. Her cheeks were puffed out so her eyes were slits and she looked shifty to me.

"Isn't your mother with you, dear?" she asked.

"Her friend is parking the car. My sister is still with them. I'd just like to go to my room now."

She gave me a funny look, but finally said, "This must be a hard time for you girls." She signalled to an assistant and asked her to show me my room. There was another girl already in there. I saw thin black hair and big black eyes, a turned up nose and a thin mouth. Pretty, but a little too sweet looking, I thought. She turned and smiled right away and said her name was Mimi.

"This is my first year at the school, but I know a couple of the girls," she told me. "It isn't too bad here, I guess. Mrs. O'Toole is pretty strict I hear but it's not too hard to sneak around her." She smiled mischievously and I realized she might be more fun than I thought at first glance.

"I don't want to see my mother before she leaves," I told her. "Is there some place we can go for a while where they won't look for us?"

Mimi grinned and led me to one of her friends who lived down the hall. Her name was Jean and she had a really pretty bedspread with flowers on it that she'd brought from home. I stayed there for a while, and then I got to thinking how we weren't going to see Daddy any more and I ran downstairs to say good bye to Mother.

Most of the girls at the school were prissy, but it wasn't too hard to get together a crowd who'd follow me. Lily never came along because she just sat in her room drawing and crying all the time like the big sissy she always was. Mimi always helped me though.

One of our big raids was to steal this hideous bust of Socrates or some old Greek that Mrs. O'Toole kept on a pedestal in her office. She was a silly thing with grey frizzy hair and black glasses and lots of fool ideas about the possibilities of broader horizons for educated ladies—the kind of junk that Mother and her old cronies liked to gab about all the time. She liked to point to this Greek guy and babble about inspiration in education. I had some of the girls keep a watch around the office and we figured out Mrs. O'Toole had a copy of her office key in one of the secretary's desks. After bed check, five of us met in my room.

We sneaked downstairs and fanned out through the halls to be sure the staff had gone to bed. Then two girls stood guard at the ends of the main halls while three of us went to the secretary's desk. After we got the key, one stayed on watch there while Mimi and I went into the office and picked up the bust. Mrs. O'Toole had taken away Lily's art supplies and I wanted to take them back since I figured the old bat had no business taking them away even if Lily's pictures were silly. But I knew she'd finger me then, because I'd already asked her to please give my sister back her things, so I left them. Then we edged to the front door. Again, two girls stayed at the halls that emptied into the entryway; one worked the locks on the door open and Mimi and I slipped out with the bust and put it upside down in a flower pot by the entry.

At assembly the next day Mrs. O'Toole pitched a fit. She was such a sight that it would have been worth it even if we'd been found out. Her hair was frizzier and wilder even than usual. She kept stabbing a finger out in the air and jerking her head down for emphasis so that her glasses flapped up and down on her face. She didn't have enough nose at the top to hold the glasses up too well anyway. She was suspicious of me but no one came forward with any evidence. No one would have dared. I thought one of my gang was going to bust out laughing and give us away but I stamped down on her instep and she wasn't so amused any more.
****

That was small potatoes compared to the scheme we'd been hatching that May. Mr. Beecham, the principal, kept his eye on me from the beginning—the transfer papers from the second boarding school noted the reason I wasn't there any more and he called me in right away to tell me he wasn't going to put up with any shenanigans from me. He called me in over every prank anyone pulled and by spring I was getting pretty fired up about being harassed all the time.

At the second boarding school I went to, I dared the girls to join me in a big prank and they took me up on it. Mother rented a house in town that we moved into after the school year at the first boarding school ended. It was pretty crowded and boring. Sometimes I could see my old friends from when we lived on the farm. Then I went to Morton Junior High. It was a pretty red brick building with lots of trees all around. And I made some good friends. But I couldn't see any point to the school because I needed to figure out how to get someone to teach me about Daddy's business since he couldn't help me any more. My grades were worse than usual that year and Mother had hysterics practically and enrolled me in this Catholic boarding school where the nuns were supposed to be strict and the education tough. I hoped at first that they'd tell her Episcopalians weren't allowed in there, but no such luck.

She finally just about had me. Those nuns were some pieces of work, let me tell you. Grim and stiff and dressed from head to toe in black. The material must have been scratchy because it made this little grating sound where the headpieces brushed against their backs and where the folds of their skirts moved together. They had us scheduled from early in the morning until night with classes and schoolwork and activities. And you never saw such people for rapping knuckles, standing people in corners, boxing ears and other punishments for every little thing. Even Mother looked pretty calm and easy compared to those old biddies.

For a while I couldn't figure out how to get around them. But I recruited girls to watch out for schedules and patterns and after a while we figured out how to get past bed check and how to raid the kitchen. Those old apparitions wandered even at night though, so it wasn't easy even to do little stuff like that. After a while I couldn't stand it any more and I dared some of the girls to help me set the Mother Superior's office on fire in the night. We just set the wastepaper basket on fire and that time I made sure to leave a clue that it was me. I needed something bad enough that they wouldn't just rap my knuckles for the millionth time and it worked. I was expelled right away.

Mother was hopping mad. She lectured for days. "Our family has a position to maintain. Your behavior is disgraceful. Your father and I have brought you every possibility of spending your life with the right sort of people if you can behave yourself. But scandal is not acceptable behavior and if you don't watch out you'll go too far one day and find yourself ostracized." Golly, she could go on.

I didn't bother to explain to her that another good reason for leaving the nunnery was that almost none of the girls were from families in the horse business so I figured they couldn't do me any good. As far as I could tell the top of the top in Lexington was the horse people and they had been at the top practically forever. After Daddy died, Mother was no help because she didn't keep up as much with all the parties and events Daddy took her to. She liked those brainy spinsters better. They might have been from good families like she said, but what good did they do?

****

I promised I'd do my schoolwork if I could go to Carter's, a private day school in the city. Most all the students were from families that were in the horse business. Lily didn't want to go, which was probably just as well because Mother complained all the time about money and how we had to be careful. Besides, I didn't want to have to fool around with her and all her gawky ways. She went to Henry Clay High where she could be a quiet little mouse.

I did do my schoolwork; enough to keep Mother off my back anyway. And I had five beaus at once. We'd go for malts and hold hands at the movies. Sometimes we went to dances, but even though Lily practiced with me I couldn't dance as well as her. Put some music on near Lily and all of a sudden she turned into this graceful bird. Really. You'd never figure it to see her any other time, but, holy Moses, my sister could dance.

Lots of the boys in my school had cars so we could go all over the place. We went horseback riding at my friends' farms where we could go cross country. I wouldn't want to get a reputation for being too dull or soft, but it was kind of nice not to have Mother or some school official breathing down my neck all the time.

My best friend was Mimi, the one who had been my roommate back at Mrs. O'Toole's Torture Palace. Then we met up at Carter's. We had all the same classes. I thought she kind of looked up to me. But she didn't fawn. I like to be a leader and have people look up to me, but not to just say yes to everything I say. Before long, I got her to help me with my homework. She had the fairest skin and I tried using the same soap so mine would be as nice, but it didn't do anything. She got good grades and always buttered up the teachers. But she was still game for a good lark and I could always count on her to join when I had a good idea.

I came up with a lot of the ideas and my crowd pulled some pretty good pranks—like replacing a farmer's scarecrow with a mop wearing an evening dress with cantaloupes for bosoms. But we had been pretty quiet for a while because ol' Beecham threatened to speak to Mother if he caught me at anything and I was afraid she'd take me out of the school if he did. Then one day I saw an article in the newspaper about hooligans in Boston who turned over a streetcar. Right away I wanted to figure out how you could get a hold of one. And I wanted to take one with passengers on it.

"Hunter, I won't do something where people could get hurt," Mimi insisted.

"But it would be so much more fun. Joey?"

"No, I'm with Mimi. Nobody gets hurt. Including us. So I don't think we should do anything with a streetcar."

"Come on, I dare y'all."

"No, Hunter," they all said.

I thought it over and mulled about whether I should try to persuade them. Then I had it. "Hey!" I announced. "How about this? We scope out Beecham and figure out someplace he leaves his car where we can move it without being seen."

"If we got caught in a stolen car... ."

"So we just drive it around a few minutes and then leave it a couple blocks away, so he can't find it."

For a few weeks the guys took turns following Mr. Beecham around until they figured out that he visited the same house every Friday night and parked his car on a quiet street around the corner. Joey hung around at his uncle's garage and asked the mechanics questions until he figured out how he could get the car started.

It went like clockwork! We were all scattered around the area, hiding behind trees and fences when Mr. Beecham arrived at seven o'clock, right on schedule. We waited until no one was around and then I gave the signal. Joey sneaked up to the car and started it up, then the rest of us ran over one at a time and got in. We drove down Main Street and then took the car back and parked it on the other side of the block from where Mr. Beecham left it. Then we scattered to our hiding places to watch him come out.

He walked around the corner and stopped dead in his tracks. He rubbed his hand over his bald head and muttered, "Oh my goodness! Oh my goodness!" He raced farther down the block, looking around and then stopped and rubbed his head again. Finally he scurried back to the house and knocked on the door. A little old white haired lady answered and he shrieked that his car was missing. We were about to bust. As soon as he went inside we took off.

We had sodas afterward and then went home. Mother was waiting in the living room, sitting on the old empire sofa that we'd had forever. She was too cheap to buy new things. She looked at me hard.

"What have you been up to?" she asked.

"What do you mean? Just out with the gang."

She kept staring at me. "You just look like you've been up to no good. Do you realize what time it is?"

I figured I must be way past my curfew but I pretended not to know what she meant. I told her we'd just been out and started to go upstairs. Just then the doorbell rang. Mother opened it and a policeman was standing there. His uniform was all stiff and formal and he had red curly hair that showed under his hat.

"Miz Harrison?"

"Yes. Is something wrong?"

"Uh, there was a car taken tonight, ma'am, and, uh, someone has named your daughter, Hunter, as one of the young people involved... ."

"A car taken? What do you mean?"

"Well, ma'am, it belongs to Mr. Beecham, the headmaster. His car was taken while he was visiting his mother. It was left nearby, so there's not much harm done, but one of the neighbors reported seeing Hunter get in the car."

I saw that ramrod back of Mother's stiffen before she turned to where I'd stopped on the stairs. Her face was grim. "Hunter, come down here," she ordered. I moved down the stairs as slowly as I could. "Were you there?"

"Well, I guess maybe I was near there," I said cautiously. She stared right in my eyes and then turned back to the officer.

"This is a crime isn't it officer?" she asked.

He seemed surprised. "Yes, ma'am, it is."

"Well, I guess you'd better take her to jail then," she said.

He stared at her for a moment, then said real slowly, "Yes, ma'am, that's what we'll have to do."

"Mother!"

"I'm sorry, Hunter. There's nothing I can do if you've broken the law. You don't have any choice but to take her down to the jail, DO you officer?"

"Huh? Uh, no ma'am," he said and pushed his hat back a little on his head, "I'm afraid I'll have to run her in for this."

"Mother, please do something."

"What's going on?" Lily was at the top of the stairs in her pajamas and yawning.

"Mother."

"It's so late. I suppose I won't be able to get a lawyer until tomorrow. Will she have to stay there all night, then?"

Lily asked again, "What is going on?" But none of us paid attention.

"Jail? All night? This isn't funny, Mother," I shouted at the same time the officer said,

"I'm afraid so unless you might have enough money for bail around?"

"No, I'll have to wait until I can go to the bank on Monday morning. Should I pack a few things for her?"

"No ma'am, she won't be allowed to take anything in. We'll give her a prison uniform, of course." I thought his eyes were twinkling, but then he reached out a hand and said, "We'll have to go now, Hunter." He took my arm and turned to lead me out.

I dug my heels in and grabbed for Mother, but he pulled me out on the porch.

"Don't worry, it won't be such a bad night," he assured me.

"There must be some other way," I cried, "I can't spend the night in jail."

"You're going to send her to jail?" Lily asked. I thought she sounded pleased.

Mother finally stepped in. "Are you sure there's nothing else that can be done?"

"Well," he said, holding his chin in his hand, "sometimes, when it's a first offense like this, we can let a child off if she promises never to do it again and takes some friends out to clean up one of the parks. And you might have to bring her down and see about paying a fine."

"I could do that," I jumped in. "I won't ever move a car again. And we could clean up in the park."

"I don't know, Miz Harrison, do you think she'll do it again?"

"Oh, no," Mother said from between her teeth, "believe me she won't do it again."

"Well, maybe we can let her stay at home tonight," he said. "Someone from the station will call you if you need to bring her in tomorrow."

"Thank you very much, officer," Mother said.

"Not at all, ma'am," he said as he turned and waved a hand on the way down the porch steps.

By the time the old shrew finished lecturing and listing punishments I thought maybe I should have just gone with the officer. That was nothing compared to the yelling after she had to talk Mr. Beecham into letting me come back to school the next year. Then she invited him to dinner. He actually turned out to be kind of interesting and I told him I wouldn't cause any more trouble.

Chapter Thirteen

"Hunter, would you come into my office, please?" Mike Madigan, the publisher and editor-in-chief of the *Journal of Thoroughbred Racing*, had never asked me to come into his office before and I was afraid he was going to fire me for mouthing off to my supervisor, Sam Jackson.

"Yes, Mr. Madigan, what is it?" I asked as I poked my head in.

"Close the door and sit down, please." He stood and waved a hand toward a chair on the other side of the desk, then sat down right after I did. The leather furniture in his office was a little worse for the wear. I knew he was rich, so I wondered why he didn't get some new things. But I liked the leathery smell in there.

I remembered how Mother always talked about maintaining dignity and I took a deep breath, put my chin up and pretended my knees weren't shaking on the way to the chair. I sat down and pulled my back up as straight as it would go and looked him right in the eye.

"Hunter, you've been with us about a year now, haven't you?"

"Yes, sir."

"And you've done a pretty good job on the fact checking and proofreading. I have to admit I wasn't sure, with your academic record, whether you could do the job and, frankly, if it hadn't been for my fondness for your mother, I don't know that I'd have agreed to hire you."

He paused and I blinked. Mother had let most of her connections to the people in Daddy's world slide after he died. She just dragged around with those old lady friends of hers. I was furious with her while I went through college the way she pushed me to, because she wasn't going to be able to give me the connections to help me get started in the horse business and she said there was absolutely no possibility that she could help me with the money to get started either. I knew she could have gotten me started so I'd have been out working with my own horses by then but she wouldn't lift a finger. She was too busy making sure she "preserved the principal". I never knew Mother had anything to do with me getting my job.

He continued, "But, aside from a little too much spirit on occasion and, an ambition that exceeds your current skills and experience, I think you have potential. I think it's time to give you a chance on a story."

I had to swallow a gasp and I could only hope my eyes kept looking cool and professional instead of as excited as they felt.

"Sam told me about the idea you pitched him yesterday."

Uh oh. That was when I lost my temper and told Sam this fusty old rag was going to go under if no one accepted a new idea. Sam probably ran to Mike to complain about my insubordination and not to tell him I'd come up with a good idea. I noticed Mike's eyes were twinkling. He had these brown eyes that always seemed to smile and then just sparkled whenever he was really tickled about something. He was in his late forties and the lines around his eyes turned upward just the way his eyes crinkled up when he laughed. His hair was dark with just a bit of grey barely noticeable around the temples and he was tall and very sturdy. For all he seemed so good-humored, there was a certain no nonsense sort of something about Mike. I knew I'd never want to push him too far. After I met Mike, the boys my own age seemed sort of immature and uninteresting. Mike's wife left him years before and ran off to Italy with a sculptor. In college I had been engaged to be engaged to Johnny Kott, but he went off to the war and married some Frenchwoman. No one else interested me much until Mike and he interested me more than anyone ever had.

"I like your idea. Stories about the major players from a more personal angle with coverage of the big parties after the races and such is how I see it. It would broaden our horizons from straight horse business news to something that might appeal to a wider audience. I like it. Been wanting to expand circulation and build the business and this might help. Now, I'm going to give you a chance here, Hunter. You lack the experience for what I'm going to offer you and that worries me. And your writing skills don't seem to be that good. But you have a background that no one else here can claim. Plenty of folks still remember your daddy and his fine horses and plenty still know your mama. You can probably get into places that lots of others can't. So here's the deal. You're coming to Maryland with me for the round of pre- and post-race parties scheduled next month and you're going to get as close to the Prescotts and the Van Devlins as possible. Now, I want you to work with Sam on the stories so you have to cooperate with giving him all the information you've gotten and he'll do the actual writing."

I was dumbstruck. All year long I'd smiled and beamed and pretended to be pleased to check every stupid fact in other people's articles and I'd only slipped and let Sam know my frustration a few times. But I'd been starting to think I'd never get a chance to go anywhere. Now it was turning out that Daddy helped me after all and I'd be making all the connections Mother wouldn't give me. Immediately I began to figure how to tell Mother about this trip. I couldn't imagine she'd like me going off with Mike.

"Oh, and Hunter, I spoke to your mother already and told her I'd look out for you."

"You talked to Mother?"

"Well, yes. I've known her a long time and I don't want her to worry. In her day ladies your age didn't go traipsing off on their own with a man."

"Of course. Will anyone else from the staff go with us?" I tried to sound nonchalant and not to let him know my heart sank down to my heels when he sounded like some old uncle taking care of his little niece. If he was bringing more people with us I figured that would be a bad sign.

"No, this first time out, we'll go alone and arrange for one of the photographers to meet us later."

For months I'd worn slightly tight sweaters and really high heels—the kind that gave my calves that pretty curve and made my hips swing when I walked. It was a good thing he was tall, because I took after Daddy in size and was almost as tall as Mike with the heels on. I watched him to see if there was any sign that my efforts had brought me this assignment and this trip for just the two of us, but he seemed as businesslike as ever. I planned to make good use of our week in Virginia.

****

"Mimi, what do you think of this one?" I was trying on dresses so Mimi could help me pick the ones that were flattering and made me look sophisticated.

"You look like a floozy in that one. I can't believe your Mother knows you even have it."

"Good, now we're getting somewhere."

"I don't think a man Mike's age is going to like that kind of dress."

"Oh, maybe you're right." I slipped it off and tried another. "Besides the clothes, though, help me figure this out. What should I do to get him to my room?"

"Your room? Hunter, couldn't you just get him to invite you to dinner?" Mimi was so easily shocked.

"Well, I suppose we'll eat a lot of meals together since we're staying in the same hotel and all. That's just business again. How can I let him know over dinner that he can have more?"

"Hunter, really." Mimi tittered uncomfortably.

In the end, I didn't really have a plan except to keep a watch for any opening.

****

Actually, Mike insisted on being a total gentleman in spite of all my flirting, so I had to just concentrate on doing the best job of my life so that I could land the assignment permanently. We ate most of our meals together, sometimes joined by others, sometimes at social functions, and we talked about everything. I found myself telling him about Daddy and how I'd wanted to take over his business and still planned to make my mark in the horse world. Mike knew Daddy slightly and very kindly told me some of his memories and said how much everyone had admired Daddy. I told him about boarding school and the tricks we used to pull. His eyes always twinkled the whole time we talked, but he never touched me and for the first time in my life I couldn't tell that my flirting had any effect at all. The more I knew of him the crazier about him I became.

His family was one of the old Lexington families and he grew up in the midst of everyone who was anyone in the horse business—that was how he knew Mother and Daddy. But instead of just settling into his family's huge operation, he took the money he came into after college and invested in the *Journal*, which at that time was a tiny, local magazine about to gasp its last breath, and had slowly built it until he developed a national circulation among the horse people. It was rumored that there were plans afoot to go international. I loved that strength in him that drove him to create his own success and made him want to keep it growing. Daddy was like that too. Mike was doing with the magazine what I wanted to do in horse racing—creating an empire.

"Mike, have you ever been sorry you didn't go to work for your father?"

"Oh, I suppose I've wondered now and again how it might have been. But only out of curiosity, never because I was dissatisfied."

"Aren't you interested in horses?"

"No, I love the horse business. That's why I chose this particular magazine. I just love the publishing business as well and this way I've been able to pursue both. The magazine keeps me in the midst of the people and the world I've known all my life. I believe people should be able to work at what they love."

"I don't think I could ever get tired of the parties and the races and all. Have you—ever gotten tired of it, I mean?"

He thought for a moment and shook his head, "No, in all these years, I've never been bored. Everything about the racing business and the people involved in it has always fascinated me."

"Me too. As long as I can remember."

I didn't know what he thought about me, but I was in love with him by the time we returned to Lexington. At first, Sam and I were closeted all hours of the day and night, turning the material I'd collected into a story for the next issue. I let Sam run the show and answered his questions carefully. I had to admit he was awfully good. He said that we'd talk before my next assignment and he'd give me some things to ask about in my interviews. And he liked some of my ideas. I wanted to be sure the stories were terrific, not only for landing the assignment, but in order to impress Mike.

After the stories were turned in, Mike called me into his office again. "Hunter, I'm very pleased with this first story. So, I'm going to give you another assignment for the next issue. If the response to your story is as good as I expect it to be, we'll make it a regular feature and the assignment will be yours. What do you think?"

"Oh, Mr. Madigan, I couldn't be more delighted. Really, I'm so pleased." I tried not to gush. "Where will the next assignment be?" What I really wanted to know was whether we would travel together again.

No such luck. He wanted me to interview the Trevors, a prominent Lexington family. There was a party, though, that he told me I should cover as part of the story. As it happened, he was going also and suggested that he could pick me up and, if I liked, we could have dinner first. That was how it started. For the next few months he was my escort for one function after another that I needed to cover for my stories. During that time he never asked me to do anything else with him and he never touched me unless he was helping me with my coat or guiding me around a puddle. Long, friendly dinners together once a week or so became the norm. He kept it clear that my stories had to be up to snuff and he mentioned my improved relations with Sam in tones that let me know I'd better keep on getting along. Besides, I knew I couldn't write like Sam so I needed his part of the teamwork.

****

Lily got married after her first year of college. With her gone, Mother pestered me even more, always wanting to know what I was doing. Even though I kept dating some of my old beaus during the time when Mike and I were not officially courting, Mother began to ask questions.

"Mike seems to be picking you up and taking you out awfully regularly. Is this always for work?"

"I don't know what business it is of yours, but, yes, he takes me to parties where he wants me to talk to people for stories," I told her.

"Don't get uppity Hunter. I just asked a question. And several people have called and mentioned that the two of you are showing up all over town together."

"Don't you and your old biddy friends have anything better to do than stick your noses in my business?"

"I declare, I have no idea what possesses you to be so nasty!" She actually had the nerve to get exasperated with me when she was the one who was being unreasonable.

"Well, why don't you go pester Lily and that poor excuse of a husband she married?"

"Blaine is a perfectly fine young man. I don't know why you can't be more kind."

"Blaine is a dead bore. And a preacher's son. God, the chances Lily could have had if she'd just pulled herself together to get out there and meet the right people."

"She met Blaine. He's as smart as he can be and very ambitious. I'm sure he'll do very well."

"Oh, Mother, he's a clod. No amount of money will give that man polish."

"Fitting in at those snooty parties you're so crazy about is not the most important thing in life."

She was an idiot. I just shook my head and rolled my eyes up to where I could see the crack in the ceiling one more time. She and Lily both said silly things like that constantly. Mike wouldn't have been attractive without his polish and the air of success and affluence he wore as easily as his favorite overcoat. Really, if you can't move with the top people, what's the point?

****

Finally, after I'd begun to wonder if the man just had no feelings or something, one night Mike invited me to dinner when there wasn't a party I needed to attend. He was a little nervous all through dinner, pulling occasionally on his tie and downing more bourbon than usual. Finally, when the plates had been cleared, he reached across the table and took my hand. I squeezed my fingers right around his and prayed he'd finally tell me he wanted me.

"Hunter, I suppose I'm just a foolish old man, but I've been falling in love with you for a long time now and I want to know whether you could even think of me that way or if I'm too old for you to consider... ." his voice trailed off and the anxiety in his face took all the sparkle out of his eyes.

"Oh, Mike, I've been trying to get you to notice me since I started at the Journal, practically. I've never loved anyone the way I love you." He asked me to marry him then and that night when we got to my door he took me in his arms and kissed me like I'd never been kissed—right up until Mother started flashing lights in the house. She always loved to chase my boyfriends away by coming out to the porch or flipping the lights like that. Mike said he wanted to come in with me to tell her, so I opened the door and led him in, calling to Mother, "Mike and I want to talk to you. Can you come in here please?" She'd gone back upstairs, pretending she hadn't been down there working the lights.

"I'm not dressed Hunter."

"Put on your robe, Mother." As if she didn't already have it on. Of course she didn't like a man to see her in her robe either. After a minute she came down the stairs with a long robe wrapped around her so her pajamas were completely covered, one hand hitching it up nervously at the neck like it would be shocking if he even saw her Adam's apple.

"Hello, Mike. How are you darlin'?" she smiled as if she were really pleased to see him and put out a hand.

"Just fine, Miz Harrison. So sorry to bring you down like this. How are you ma'am?" Mike answered.

"I'm fine, thank you, Mike. How's your mother? The last time I spoke to her she was under the weather."

"She's doing pretty well now. Up and down, you know, at her age. But pretty well. She always speaks so fondly of you."

"Well, shall we go in here and sit down?" She waved toward the living room and started in that direction, still talking. "Can I fix you all anything? There's a nice pitcher of iced tea in the ice box."

"Mother, let me fix him a bourbon," I began, but Mike interrupted. "I don't need a thing Miz Harrison. The iced tea sounds lovely but really I don't need a thing."

Finally we all sat down in the living room and Mike cleared his throat to begin. "Well, Miz Harrison, you know Hunter has been working for me close to two years now. And I've gotten to know her pretty well in that time. Tonight I asked her to marry me and she accepted." I could tell he was nervous because he rushed through it. "I just wanted us to tell you together."

Mother just sat there with the most peculiar expression on her face for an endless moment and then she smiled faintly and said, "Isn't that just lovely? Well, I'm delighted, children." I'm not sure how I'd have described her face but delighted was not a word that came to mind.

We chitchatted for a while before Mike left. After I'd shown him out, I came back to the living room, where Mother still sat, with a little frown on her brow. She looked up at me for a second as if she didn't know who I was. Then she stared at her hands and twisted at her wedding ring before she started talking.

"Hunter, did I ever say anything to make you feel that you needed to marry someone wealthy?"

"Mother I don't recall that you ever made me feel that you wanted me to get married at all. I thought you wanted me to be an old spinster schoolteacher."

"Oh for heavens sake. I never wished for that." She paused a moment. "Mike's considerably older than you, Hunter. Are you really sure you want to marry a man that much older?"

"He's the only man I want to marry, Mother," I told her.

"You're sure you've never felt any pressure to marry someone rich?" She paused and then went on disjointedly, "Older men sometimes have a lot of control over their wives... ." She seemed so genuinely distressed that I tried not to get mad at her, but I didn't have the faintest idea what bothered her so. Daddy wasn't that much older than she was. She'd known Mike almost all his life and she always liked him. When I got the job, in fact, she kept exclaiming how lovely it was that I'd be working for such a nice man. "As long as I know you're sure you'll be happy," she said and wandered sadly upstairs.

Chapter Fourteen

Mike and I had such fun together. I kept the same job at the magazine, technically speaking, and the two of us attended every major social event held by the horse people in this country and occasionally Europe as well as countless dinners and cocktail parties. Business was conducted at those events all the time so my short interviews with people were not obtrusive. Scotch and bourbon were the main drinks of choice and Mike started me drinking bourbon with him. I got so I knew everybody and stayed on top of all the gossip and late breaking stories, so I always had a story to tell and I knew how to keep people having fun. I think Mike was proud of how people always surrounded me. A couple of times when I drank a little too much and got more attention than he thought was seemly, Mike got mad and told me I'd made a spectacle of myself.

With Mike, there was no getting away with the kind of tomfoolery I'd always pulled on Mother and at school—kind of like it had been with Daddy. I didn't mind knowing that there were boundaries with Mike because I wanted to please him and he didn't have a go-to-pieces over stupid little things like Mother did. Mike discussed his business dealings with me, telling me what he needed to do to prepare for a meeting and deciphering the ins and outs of the proceedings afterwards. It was just like the way I dreamed Daddy would have taught me if he'd been alive.

Mike was the oldest son and he inherited the share of the land with the family's home on it when his mother died shortly after our wedding. It was one of the big old Lexington homes, built in 1825; not a nothing little place like ours. Big white columns stood in a row across the front, like sentinels protecting the sweep of porch behind them. The whole place was white with dark shutters. Gorgeous oriental rugs and fine mahogany antiques filled the rooms. I brought in a decorator to appraise the furniture and weed out the lesser pieces and to brighten up the colors. I launched a kitchen remodeling project right away. I'd forgotten how quiet it was out in the country and I rather enjoyed being back.

Mother helped me to pick out china and silver so that we could set a particularly fine table and we began to have our own dinners and cocktail parties. After a few years I tried out a big party during Derby week. It was a big success and we began holding one every year. I always felt so proud standing next to Mike at the door and watching him charm every person who came in. He had a knack for remembering people and a lot of details about them so he could say something personal to each one. I started then to work harder at pretending to be interested in other people so that everyone would be fond of me the way they were of Mike.

Lily got pregnant a few times and then miscarried. She didn't seem to me to be all that anxious to be a mother. I knew I didn't want any children so I made sure there was no pregnancy. Mike and I hadn't really talked about it, but I loved the way we traveled and came and went as we pleased and I had no interest in turning my life upside down with some snotty-nosed kid making me stay home like Mother had to. I planned to move ahead and, in fact, I made sure I knew all the people on Mike's board and all the editors so that my move upward would be easier to accomplish. My first aim was for a management position but that would just be a stepping stone on my way to a seat on the board.

I asked Mike all kinds of questions and had a lot of input because Mike talked over big decisions with me before implementing changes or bringing ideas before the board. He made his move into international circulation and bought another small magazine and I followed all his negotiations and decisions. His eyes always held their dancing lights, but he was brusque and strong and the twinkle turned into more of a glitter when things were tough. He never said a word more than he had to but what he did say was straightforward and honest. I watched everything he did and learned, like I would have done with my father if he'd lived. For five years I kept the same job. It didn't seem that long, though, I enjoyed my life with him so much.

About the time Lily was pregnant again the last time, Mike suddenly put me up to fill a seat on the board. He said I'd learned the business more than well enough and it was less awkward to put his wife on the board than to promote her on the magazine production side. I never even actually told him of that ambition—at least not specifically. He knew me pretty well, though.

****

Chloe was born not long after I'd been promoted. She looked like a little wriggly worm at first, bald and wrinkled and pink. I had to admit she became awfully cute in the next few months, especially since I only had to see her now and then. She was sort of sparkly and bright. Mike was very enthusiastic about her and, while he agreed that Lily's insipidity was tiresome and that Blaine's stiff-backed morality was a bore, he loved to see Chloe. He also thought Lily was a nice little thing even if her faint voice and mousiness were wearing and he could charm her into being more talkative than usual. When she relaxed and chatted like that I noticed that she always kept a nervous eye on Blaine. I swear the man disapproved of too much laughing.

Mother was dotty over the child. It was hard to get her to talk about much else. She was pleased about my seat on the board, but never as interested in news of my work as she was in the next step in Chloe's progress. By the time Chloe walked and talked she adored Mother too and the two of them could play silly games for hours. Chloe beamed like a little star with everyone paying attention to her. She laughed and sang little songs and talked to everyone she saw. It was hard to see how that dreary pair produced such a child. I actually found her perkiness rather tiresome and sometimes developed a headache after Mike and Mother had her laughing and squealing for too long. I rather imagined she'd be a great success with my set later on if Lily managed to teach her anything about how to behave.

Mother was ecstatic that Chloe learned everything earlier than usual. She already recognized some written words when she was two or so and Blaine had her working on the alphabet and counting to ten when she was three. I guess Mother finally had the smart child she'd always wanted one of us to be. Somewhere along the way Chloe seemed to me to become awfully withdrawn and nervous for a child her age. Once she changed, she rarely laughed or sang and she became afraid of strangers. Actually, she became just like Lily. She was so crazy about Mike and Mother that she still bubbled over with them. But the rest of the time I swore she was almost dull. Growing up with Lily, what did I expect? The others were all so thrilled at all she learned, they didn't seem to notice any change.

It was a sight to see Mother chasing around with Chloe. Her hair was all white and she wore it rolled back with combs holding it in place. One or two of the combs fell out every time and wisps of white hair stuck out so she looked wild. And she'd laugh, big loud belly laughs. I'd never seen her tousled nor heard her laugh so unrestrainedly. I don't think she ever had fun with us in the same way—it seemed like she was always scolding or lecturing.

****

Once I took my place on the board, life in many ways stayed the same. I no longer had to go to all the parties and balls, but Mike and I were invited to all of them and attended most. My duties as a board member were not extensive beyond our regular meetings and keeping up generally with the company's progress, but I worked alongside Mike in everything. He was looking more tired all the time and I tried to take on as much as I could. I asked him to go to the doctor but he kept putting it off.

Finally I talked him into taking a long vacation with me. I booked us a suite in a big old hotel near Tampa. It took a few days to get Mike to wind down, but eventually we relaxed and just enjoyed sleeping late, walking on the beach, having drinks on the balcony and sampling lobster, grouper, crab and snapper. In all our years together, we hadn't ever really just taken time to relax and enjoy being together like that.

The nights were the best part. After dinner, Mike would move near and slowly bend over to kiss my neck or my ear. Then he'd wrap me in his arms and kiss me while his hands reached to my back and slowly unzipped my dress. One at a time, he removed my clothes and let his fingers gently roam my body. I'd return the favor and then we'd make long, slow, hot love for hours. We'd always had good sex, but that was the best ever.

I sat one day on the beach while he took a short swim. There weren't too many people out and the sun beamed across the bright sand so it sparkled. The light was so strong that the sky seemed pale. As Mike walked back to me, I noticed how strong and lean he still was. His hair had gone totally grey and his face was far more lined but he was still one good looking man. Even with the relaxation of the trip, though, his face wore a more strained expression than it ever had, belying those eyes that seemed lit by a permanent gleam of amusement. He sank down in the lounge next to mine and placed a wet hand on my leg while he sat companionably, gazing out at the waves.

"You know, Hunter," he said after a while, "when Marianne left me I thought I'd never marry again. Never risk letting anyone get that close again." He shook his head dreamily and looked off in the distance. "You were so young when I met you. I was sure you wouldn't be interested or that you'd get bored and run off too."

I grabbed the hand on my leg and squeezed it and started to speak, but he held up his other hand. "That's why it took me so long to let myself pay attention to all those tight sweaters," he chuckled. I had to laugh. I'd decided long ago that the sweaters had been fruitless. "But, Hunter, I thank my stars I finally gave in, because these have been the happiest years of my life."

I didn't know what to say. It was lovely of him to tell me those things, of course, but he never talked like that and I wasn't used to it. So I just squeezed his hand even harder and told him I was glad. For the rest of the trip, he fussed over me more than he ever had, touching me and muttering sweet nonsense. I'd never loved him more.

All too soon, we were back in Lexington and busy again with work. Mike was acquiring another small magazine and I handled a lot of the negotiating for him. He looked across at me during lunch one day and said, "You know, I don't think I've really told you what a contribution you've made here at the magazine. Your ability to put together a plan of action and inspire everyone to carry it out is remarkable and has helped me tremendously."

"Oh, Mike, everyone gives the extra effort because they think so much of you," I protested.

"Well, they may have some loyalty to me, but you have been able to bring a measure of ease to the implementation of projects that is a great talent." He paused for a moment, then said, almost to himself, "If you can control the tendency toward grandiose schemes... ."

"What, Mike? I'm not sure I heard you," I interrupted, puzzled as to what he was talking about. His sudden penchant for disclosure, combined with the continued look of strain on his face, made me uneasy.

He recalled himself with a shake of the head. "Oh, I was just thinking that you've really learned enough and developed enough skills that you could run the magazine without me. I hope you wouldn't overstep yourself."

"Well, Mike, why would I want to run it without you?" I questioned.

"No reason, I was just thinking," he replied vaguely.

Less than a month after we got back I came into the bedroom one morning after my shower and found Mike lying on the floor gasping for breath and barely conscious. I called for an ambulance and then sank to my knees by his side.

"Mike, help will be here soon," I told him while I squeezed his hand. He tried to smile and made an effort to squeeze back though he didn't seem to have the strength to use his hand.

"Hunter," he whispered and winced with pain.

"Please, Mike, just be still till someone comes."

"Love you, Hunter," he murmured and closed his eyes. I put my head to his chest and felt that he was still breathing. "Okay, you keep breathing, Mike." I nearly choked, trying not to cry. It felt like hours before I heard the siren and all the while I held his hand and willed him to live.

But in spite of all my prayers and whispered exhortations, by the time the ambulance got him to the hospital he was dead. Just like that. I thought back over the unusual conversations we'd been having and realized that he knew.

Mother helped me to arrange the funeral. We had it at the big Episcopalian Church downtown. Mike and I hadn't attended often but we knew the pastor and most of the congregation. We used to laugh and say it was the best place in town to catch up on the latest gossip. Lily and Blaine came home with Chloe although they said she was too young to come to the funeral. The church overflowed that day. People really loved Mike and I felt so proud that he chose to spend his life with me.

Those first days, there were so many people bustling around that I felt like I just kept on my party face and manners all the time. Periodically I looked around to see why Mike wasn't by my side as always. After people stopped dropping by to visit and bring country ham and beaten biscuits, I finally felt the pain. Mother found me crying.

"Oh, I'm so sorry," she murmured and patted me on the back.

I buried my face in her lap and wept. "I wish I knew what to tell you, Hunter," she said, stroking my hair. "But I've buried two husbands and I still don't know what to say. Especially since this was so sudden and unexpected." It was enough for me that she was there.

Mike was so much older, I should have prepared myself for the inevitability of widowhood, I supposed, but I had never expected it to come so soon. I had no plans that didn't include Mike. We spent all day every day together throughout our marriage. Everything that got done was completed through our joint efforts and suddenly I wasn't sure I knew how to accomplish a lot of things without him. I felt so anchored with him. We had so much fun and kept so busy that I didn't feel that overwhelming sense of malaise that used to drive me to crazy pranks. I always knew where the limits were and it was kind of safe. A few days after I was finally alone I began to cry again and couldn't stop. I sobbed in the shower and the kitchen and into my pillow in the guest room. I wept in the office, scarcely able to see while I cleaned his desk on a ghostly Sunday at the magazine. I drove with tears sliding relentlessly down my cheeks and onto my clothes. After a while I thought it was a shame we couldn't store up all that water in a reservoir someplace in case we had a drought.

****

Mike left me everything, including the magazines and instructions that I was to run the business. "Hunter, I'm not sure that this is enough to satisfy your ambition, but I know you'll take it from here," he wrote in a note that he gave his lawyer for me. At first, I was frightened at the thought of running the business without Mike. I'd handled a lot on my own and I'd watched him do everything but it was always his business, his show.

My first day back, a few weeks after Mike's funeral, I put on my most business-like suit and my best smile and marched into the office with a take charge attitude. I was touched that the staff all rallied around to give me a vote of confidence. As each one came up to chat I came to realize that everyone thought I'd played an important role while Mike was alive. It became easier every day after that. It didn't take long before I enjoyed the rush of power that came with each decision I made on my own. I figured I'd just settle in for a while before I launched any new expansion of the business. Instead I began to consult with the man who'd been managing Mike's horse operations at the farm. With his help I bought my first couple of horses and began studying the breeding side of the business more thoroughly than I ever had before. I was finally in the horse business.

****

Blaine got a job in Wisconsin a couple of years before Mike died and moved Lily and Chloe up there with him. Mother was pretty lonely without Chloe around and she fretted that the Yankee influence would ruin her. I refrained from mentioning that I thought Blaine and Lily would do that just fine without any help from our enemies to the North.

Mike's death really threw Mother. She'd always been crazy about him and losing him after Chloe and Lily left shook her up. She cried and cried at the funeral. Then she just didn't seem to be doing well. She complained more often than usual about headaches and forgot things. I began to worry about her being on her own. She lived alone in the little brick ranch house she bought after Lily got married. A house-keeper came in every day during the week and cleaned and cooked for her. But I was-n't sure she should be on her own.

"Mother," I finally told her, "I want you to move in with me out at the farm."

"Well, Hunter, I have a house and I like it just fine."

"You're not well enough any more to stay on your own. Really."

"I'm perfectly healthy and I don't want to give up my house." She could be very stubborn.

"Well, then, come stay at the farm for a couple of months and then we'll see whether you want to stay on or go back home."

"Who is going to take care of my house? I can't just go off and leave every-thing sitting there... ."

I had a lot of persuading to do, but eventually I convinced her that the trial was a good idea. Her housekeeper, Flo, came along too and we sent her to clean Mother's house every week or so. By the end of two months, I'd convinced her to sell the house. She insisted on bringing most of that old furniture from our farm that she'd been dragging around ever since we left. We put most of it in her rooms where I hoped nobody much would see it. I tried to get her to invest the money from the house in the magazine but she wouldn't do it. She refused to tell me what she did but I imagine it went to Chloe. It's a good thing Daddy set up that trust because every-thing would land in that child's hands otherwise.

I'd forgotten over the years how demanding Mother could be, always having to have everything just so... . But it was nice to have some company at breakfast and on the nights I stayed home for dinner. Unfortunately, with her in my house, I had to put up with Blaine, Lily and Chloe when they came to town. Mother just lived for those visits like I wasn't the one doing everything for her. She told them to come any time and they'd arrange it with her without even consulting me. They kept her occu-pied at least and I didn't have her nose in my business all the time. The place wasn't empty any more.

****

Chloe was withdrawn and quiet and lacked social skills. From what little she said, she missed Mother and Mike and she was having a hard time adjusting to the North. I told her over and over that she'd never get anywhere unless she learned to talk with people and quit being so quiet all the time. She just stared at me the way her mother always did. I couldn't get her to laugh the way Mike used to. I even took her out to the track to watch one of my horses race and introduced her to my jockey and trainer. She hardly said a word and I couldn't tell that she enjoyed it at all although she thanked me politely.

Sometimes it seemed unfair that I should be the only one who knew how to get on in life and that I had to look out for them all the time. I really wanted them to be happy, but I didn't have time to fool with their helplessness and inability to pull themselves together.

I had settled in at the magazine and I was lining up the board to back my plans for expanding the business. I wanted to head a big corporation. It was just the kind of outlet I'd always been looking for. Plenty to do, numerous places to put my attention and lots of power. I'd worked the board members at cocktail parties and dinners for years, keeping relations smooth and friendly to help Mike. Left on my own, I found those relationships very useful for pulling together whatever backing I needed. I didn't know that I'd bother wasting much time on Chloe when she visited. It was too bad, because if she'd shown any promise, I'd have groomed her to take over the business one day.

Chapter Fifteen

"Miz Madigan, you can't keep changing your mind about big issues like this. Nobody knows whether they're coming or going and the staff can barely work on anything concerning the next issue for all the moving from one desk to another and one department to another." My editor-in-chief pressed his lips together and glared at me.

"This is my magazine, Bill, and I'll make any changes I want to," I told him in no uncertain terms. Then I thought about what he'd said and asked, "What do you mean about all the moving around?"

He looked at me as if I'd lost my mind. "You've reassigned everyone on the staff twice this month and this is also the second time you've completely reorganized several departments."

I just sat there. For the life of me I couldn't remember making so many changes, though I remembered reassigning the staff once. "Well, all right, don't carry out this new memo. Now get out of here and get this magazine out." He marched out the door, still looking grim. I poured another bourbon and stared out the window. The board had been blocking every attempt I made at expanding the company. Every time, they said it wasn't a wise move and came up with some fool list of reasons. Several board members had actually had the nerve to ask me to lunch or dinner so that they could mention to me that I was drinking too much. I told them to keep their noses out of my personal life.

I couldn't figure out what was getting into everyone. Everybody around here went to cocktail parties and had drinks with lunch and dinner. It was expected. Mother had been after me for years, telling me I drank too much. She even brought it up a couple of times about Mike and I, while he was still alive. Well, I wasn't going to stop. I was bored. I built the company and then that got tiresome. I had lots of dates, of course, but no man really interested me after Mike. Besides, it seemed to me most men were afraid of me because I ran the company. In the end, men just leave you anyway. What else would I do?

* * * *

I tried and tried to straighten Chloe out so that she'd have a chance at living well. Before she went to college she came down and spent a couple of months every summer with us. I introduced her to the sons and daughters of my friends and held parties for her so she could meet the right people. She did make friends with one girl, Maggie, who lived on the next farm, and the two of them got together almost every day. After the parties, though, I'd ask her about the other children.

"They were pretty nice, I guess," she'd say so I could barely hear her.

"Did you talk to them?"

"Some. I don't really know any of them," she'd whine.

"You get to know people by talking to them, Chloe. I don't know how you expect to get ahead in this world if you won't take advantage of opportunities when they're offered to you. Those were the sons and daughters of the people at the top around here and they'll be the next ones who run things. I'm giving you the chance that Mother couldn't bother to give me to start out life with the best people and you just throw it away. I'm just going to wash my hands of you one of these days."

She sat there staring at me with those big, sad eyes like Lily's misting up and whispered, "I'm sorry. Can I go now?" She raced off to Mother's rooms and I didn't bother to follow where Mother would just tell me to leave the child alone. I never knew why Mother would not make a push to launch anyone in society. I guess it all came so easily in her family that she didn't understand that you've got to get out there and make things happen if you want to get anywhere.

I always sent Flo to supervise the parties for Chloe. If I questioned her enough afterwards she would eventually admit that, as far as she could see, Chloe didn't spend much time with the other children except Maggie. Flo said she didn't want me to ask her about Chloe like that because it made her feel like a spy, but I couldn't take the time to go out there myself, so I needed Flo to tell me what went on.

When Chloe was in high school, I took her to a party at the Huntsman's Club that gave her the chance to meet the cream of society. I had to try to corner Hal Durham to get him to agree to a story about him for the magazine so I couldn't be bothered with her. I told her to mingle and then got myself a bourbon, chatting with various acquaintances and maneuvering my way to Hal. By the time I cornered him my drink was getting low and I looked around for a waiter to refresh it. There was Chloe, looking like a post, standing on one foot and then the other. As soon as I sweet talked Hal into an agreement, I moved over to her. "Circulate. Move around and talk to these people," I told her.

She whined, "I don't know any of these people. And everyone's talking about horses. I don't know anything about horses."

"If you'd listened to me you'd be able to talk to some of them. Now, I want you to stop standing here looking pained and go talk to people." I gave her a push on the shoulder and watched her shuffle away. I swear she was impossible. If anyone had given me a chance like that I'd have chatted up everyone in the room.

Then she got out of college and it still didn't look like she was going to do anything. She used to yammer about music or some such fool thing. In college she started looking like a ragamuffin and spouting nonsense about the power elite. Who did she think we were? By then she was sullen as well as withdrawn—so unappealing. Even Mother, who never found fault with Chloe, was mildly distressed. I offered to fix her up with some nice young man, but she just laughed and said she had a boyfriend, then pulled out a picture of the scruffiest, hairiest looking thing I ever did see. I blinked, ordered another bourbon and advised her never to show it to Mother.

"We should choose some china and silver for you, Chloe. You can't really entertain properly without having those," I told her one day.

She laughed. "You're kidding, right?"

"No. You talk about the dinners you give and the parties you have and I'm glad you're getting out more and meeting people, but, really you need to do it right or you'll be out of the social scene in no time."

She laughed again and shook her head. "Hunter, I don't think that lasagne really needs to be served on fine china. And believe me none of my friends give a sh....., a damn about china. In fact, they'd think I was weird if I had it."

"Well, if you're hanging around with people who don't care about having lovely things around them and doing things properly, then all I can say is, you've fallen in with the wrong people," I told her. "You serve lasagne?" She just pressed her lips together like Blaine and said nothing, like her mother.

****

I poured another drink and gazed out my window. I'd moved our offices into a brand new office tower—one of the first in Lexington. I could look out over the top of the old Lafayette Hotel. It had been turned into offices long since. It's funny, it was the same old building, but after the change it looked more boring. I remembered when Mother used to dress us up in our frilly dresses and mary janes and take us to lunch there. She and her lady friends all wore hats and white gloves and we had to learn to use the nice china and silver elegantly and make polite conversation. Lily always adored Georgie and asked her all kinds of questions about all the places she had traveled and books she had read, and Georgie loved Lily and her pictures. I wasn't too interested in Mother's friends, but Georgie had gone some interesting places and I liked lunching in a fine restaurant. Mother never stopped lamenting the loss of the Lafayette.

Now I just waited. The board was meeting to decide on a new expansion plan I'd proposed. I wondered if I had made a mistake in deviating from Mike's methods. He had been sole owner of the company and created a board of businessmen he respected for various areas of expertise mostly because he wanted good advice. But he did give them the power of a board. They pretty much always voted for Mike's proposals or convinced him to drop them before they came to a vote. I had taken the company public. Several of the board members had been buying up blocks of stock and could put their votes together to block me after they voted to amend the by-laws and changed the percentage required to constitute a majority. I hadn't looked to the board for advice for a long time. Nor did I stay involved enough in putting people up for the board to have any sense of them as a group of trusted advisors. I seemed to be locked in battle all the time as I kept trying to change and expand the business and the board kept vetoing my plans.

The business had never really been as much fun as it was when Mike and I worked side by side. It was pretty exciting those first years when I took control after his death and learned to run the whole operation on my own. I liked the control and the realization that I had the power to make all those employees jump or to make a decision that involved millions of dollars. When Mike was alive, though, I enjoyed everything more even if it wasn't quite as exciting. The longer I spent without him the more I appreciated his brilliance in handling people, including me. He managed to create for me nearly everything I asked for and the freedom for me to do what I wanted and at the same time he really ran the show. Before him I'd never met anyone but Daddy who could stop me from doing anything. Without him life seemed to spin slowly but steadily out of control.

My years with him were the best I ever had with my family. Mother loved him and the two of them could sit and laugh over stories about their families for hours. He charmed Lily out of her shyness and humored Blaine enough to keep him from moralizing. Somehow in the middle of all that good will I got along better with them. And Chloe, he used to say, was the only child who ever made him sorry that he'd never wanted children. When I tried to correct her or teach her about how to behave, he'd say, "Now, Hunter, this child's a delight the way she is. You leave her alone." Mike's family pretty much let him do what he wanted to do and just stepped in when he seemed about to be in trouble. Of course, he was extraordinary, so I don't think he understood how much molding and shaping you need to do with children. In those days, though, she liked to do things with me.

Later, we didn't get along that well. When she was 8 or 10 she was visiting and talked about her father like he was some kind of hero. I finally informed her, "Your father is a dead bore nothing who never should have been allowed to get near your mother... ." I would have gone on, but Chloe jumped up with tears in her eyes and shouted, "Stop it, you can't talk that way about my father! When Uncle Mike was here you never used to talk to us like this." I didn't even know she remembered him.

Mother and I started bickering again. I still tried to light a fire under Lily every now and then but she just seemed to disappear more with time and I got tired of trying. Blaine let me know he found my lifestyle insupportable and I let him know I thought he was trash. Chloe stuck close to Mother when she was here and avoided doing anything alone with me... .

I found myself still staring out over the Lafayette and waiting, tilting my glass from side to side and listening to the clanking of the ice. Finally there was a knock and Bill came back in. I wondered what he wanted. "Hunter, the board has passed a number of resolutions this afternoon. And, uh, they asked me to come talk to you about them."

I figured I'd need another drink for this one. Bill, who'd known me through all the years with Mike, wasn't afraid of me and when anyone needed to give me bad news they passed it to me through Bill. Nobody seemed to think I knew. I offered him a drink, expecting the usual impatient shake of his head, but this time he said, "Yes, please ma'am." I went for my doubles glasses and fixed two, forgetting that I already had one. He gulped half of it right away. Clearly the board had not accepted my proposal, but that was nothing new. I couldn't imagine why Bill was so nervous about telling me. I watched him, big funny old thing that he was. I decorated the office in antiques and he sat in one of the delicate Chippendales, looking completely out of place. His suit was rumpled, as always, the first button of his shirt open and his tie loosened. He kept pulling at the tie anyway, as if it were choking him. After he'd stared into his glass for a moment, I decided to begin.

"Bill, I should have given you tea so you could read the leaves," I joked. He smiled painfully, and I went on, "I take it the board chose not to let me acquire another business?"

"No, ma'am. They feel the business is overstretched now and it's not a good time to invest in expansion." He paused and his face grew more miserable.

"I gather there is more. Did they have another item on the agenda that concerns me?"

"Yes, ma'am. Actually, several."

"Several?" Well, let's have it." I took another swallow, watching him grip that bourbon and search for words.

"Well, they've actually decided to make some other changes instead."

"Changes? Such as?"

"They're going to sell the advertising agency and those last two small magazines you bought."

I slammed my glass down. "They're going to what? I'll see about this. They'll sell pieces of my company over my dead body. Who do they think they are? It is still my company."

"Well, in a sense it is," he began.

"In every sense it is," I informed him in no uncertain terms.

"Not any more Miz Madigan, it's not yours any more," he blurted out.

"What do you mean, it's not mine any more? Mike left it to me, of course it's mine." I shouted.

"Yes, he did leave it to you and then it was a privately held corporation. But, you may recall," he said sarcastically, "you insisted on making a public offering a few years ago so you could play with the big boys."

I decided to ignore his barb, but I was grim. "Of course I remember. That move made plenty of money too. And I made sure that I held the majority of shares."

"You had a majority then," he said. "But the board has offered more shares a couple of times." He took a deep breath. "Several board members have been purchasing every common share that came up for sale for quite a while now. You already knew they had enough to prevent you from getting a vote through if they wanted to. Well, recently they've acquired enough to account for a majority of common shares among them. I think they've been planning this for a while and figuring what they would do when they got enough." He paused and fiddled with his empty glass. I reached for it and poured him another.

"So, they're going to sell off some pieces of the company and I can't stop them... . Well, I don't like it but I suppose I can learn to live with it. I'm furious, but I won't take it out on you. You didn't have to be so nervous."

He muttered, "When have you ever hesitated to take it out on anyone you damn well pleased," and swept on, "That isn't all Miz Madigan."

"Not all. What on earth else?"

"They, uh, voted to remove you as CEO."

"What?" I tried not to screech but did anyway. I threw my glass across the room. "This they can't do. This is my magazine. Mike clearly left me in charge."

"He did. But the structure has changed with your innovations. They consulted with their attorneys and, in fact, the attorneys gave presentations at the meeting on the legality of a vote to replace you and assured them that it is well within their rights under a number of provisions in the by-laws and corporate papers."

I couldn't even speak and he continued, "The board would like to meet with you next week, after you have had a chance to consult your attorney, to discuss a smooth transition... ."

"I can't think about that now," I told him. "Please leave me alone."

He set his glass down with deliberation and started walking slowly out. At the door, he turned around and said sadly, "I'm glad Mike isn't here to see what you've become. He left you a fortune and a great little company. In the beginning you had everyone in the place in the palm of your hand. You showed you could run the place like Mike did and everyone here was behind you. Why was it never enough?"

I stared at the back of the door and asked myself the same question. Just like I went wild after Daddy died and Mother couldn't seem to stop me, I'd gone out of control without Mike. I kept getting bored and wanting to have more and be more and do more to try to fill the empty spaces. I kept wondering how I could have been so foolish as to let it happen. Bill didn't understand one thing. If Mike had been here he wouldn't have seen this because it never would have happened. My hope was that, wherever he went when he died, he couldn't see what I had done to his company since then.

Chapter Sixteen

Mother planted an extensive garden after she moved out to the farm. Yellow roses tinged with pink, anemones and daffodils, bluebells and sunny twinkles—so many colors and sizes and scents. The gardeners did most of the work to keep it up, but she went out most days and did some pruning and weeding when she was out for her walk. Her gait was slow and careful and I realized one day that she had become very frail without my noticing it. She'd always been tiny, but there seemed to be no meat on her. Her skin was pale, almost translucent and moved loosely over her bones as though nothing interposed itself between.

She had complained of various aches and pains for years. When her final illness came, it worked slowly. The doctors never did seem to find one specific thing wrong with her. She'd taken so many pills for so many ailments over the years you needed a scorecard. In the end it seemed the whole conglomeration just converged to drain away the last traces of life in every part of her.

She was ill for months before she died. The doctors thought it would be quick, at first, and Chloe came in from Boston to be with her, though she was only able to stay for a couple of days. Lily and Blaine had moved back and Lily came out to stay at the farm for a while, for all the good she did. I swear, the woman was like a spook, creeping around in an old robe all the time and lying around for hours staring at the ceiling. And I think she was sneaking liquor out of my cabinet. Everything was up to me, as usual. I took Mother in and gave her a place to live when she was too old to live alone and then helped every time she was ill or something. I was the one who had to find nurses and see to it that the trustees coughed up the money to pay for it. Mother said Lily made her nervous, just sitting around staring at her. After a couple of weeks Lily said she had to go back to Blaine and we breathed a sigh of relief. She just came out several days a week after that.

Chloe came down off and on for a weekend all through that time. She and Mother would stay closeted talking for hours. I kept telling her that Mother was weak and she should leave her alone, but she insisted that Mother asked her to stay in there and seemed to have a lot of things on her mind. I questioned Mother several times about it but Mother just said she had some things she wanted to tell Chloe and she wouldn't listen to me when I told her she should rest instead. After the way Chloe pressured everyone into letting Mother risk her life in cataract surgery I thought she had some nerve pretending all that concern at the end. I wondered whether no one ever told her that Mother couldn't leave her anything.

* * * *

I never told Mother the whole story behind my leaving the magazine. I felt like she always figured I'd fail one day and I didn't want to hear her tell me it was my own fault. I ultimately talked to my lawyer, who confirmed that the board acted within its authority and reminded me that he advised me against making a public offering. For a while it seemed everyone in the company had to find a way to say "I told you so" about some piece of advice they gave me. Nobody was saying it when I was building the company into something bigger and more profitable than it had ever been. When I met with the board, they told me that they had made no announcements and sworn Bill to secrecy and that if I would like to break the news of my resignation they felt it would be best for the company's interest and my comfort. I was pleased at the chance to leave with the appearance that it was my choice although I gave them no indication that I liked anything about their mutiny. They also offered me a seat on the board again, but I told them thanks but no thanks. I reminded them that I still owned enough shares of stock to have plenty of influence and left.

If Mother was surprised at my early resignation she never said much. I told her I wanted to finally throw myself into raising horses and that I intended to come up with a Derby winner. She just said, "That'll be lovely darlin'. Another trophy in the library." All Daddy's silver trays and urns from races were displayed in the library. Lily asked Mother a couple of times about taking a couple of them and when I got wind of it I gave them both a piece of my mind. If I didn't watch her she'd waltz off with everything. The idea that she'd have the right to take any of Daddy's trophies. I'm sure Blaine, from that nothing family of his, would have loved to get his hands on them.

I did launch an expansion of my stable and the racing schedule, although Franklin, who'd been managing everything since shortly before Mike died, really took care of a lot. I attended the major sales around the country and bought a few more horses. I made plans to get more involved in the breeding side but somehow my participation remained limited except that I worked the connections at parties to put together syndicates and stay on top of the business.

I was free to get back into the social swing. After I took over the business, I didn't accept nearly as many invitations as Mike and I had although I had to attend enough functions to keep up the connections I needed for the magazine. Suddenly I could accept all the luncheon engagements and fashion showings and picnics as well as the dinners and cocktail parties.

After a while, Mother started nagging me again about drinking too much. She never liked to drink and I actually remembered that she complained occasionally that Daddy drank too much, so I didn't take her too seriously.

"Mother, you worry too much," I told her.

"Really, Hunter, since you left the magazine you've been drinking all day long."

"What, are you following me around counting drinks now? I can't tell you how sick I am of having you spying on me. You've done it all my life."

"I haven't needed to spy on you. You've always been in so much blatant trouble," she shook her head and raised a hand to stop me when I started to protest, "Oh, don't say it. I know. Nothing has ever been your fault. It was Lily, it was the other girls at school, it was Joey, it was me."

"If that isn't just like you, Mother. Blame everything on me and Lily gets to be the saint. What has she ever done for you? Who's been taking care of you all these years?"

"I didn't need to be taken care of," she said and walked out of the room.

Chloe was never grateful either. All the chances I gave her and she never made use of them. After she finished college I offered her a job in the copy center at the magazine but she didn't want to take it. I offered several times to take her on vacation with me but she always found some excuse not to go. After all I did for her she almost never called me.

    ****

Finally one morning after months of nurses and worry, Mother just didn't wake up. Chloe came in from Boston for the funeral. Neither she nor her parents really cared about Mother. Not one of them shed a tear or gave any sign that it made a difference. Chloe was stiffer even than usual. She didn't talk the whole time she was here. I don't know why she bothered to show up.

I couldn't stop crying for weeks. I'd fought with Mother all my life and she got on my nerves more than anyone but Lily, but she'd always been there. Since Mike died it felt good to know she'd be home when I got there. We fixed breakfast together every morning and if she was still up I went into her room to check in before I went to bed at night. Of course, half the time she said something infuriating. But other times, she had all these funny insights into the people around Lexington and we laughed together over the latest word on the grapevine. After a few weeks I'd have been happy even to hear her nag me about drinking.

    ****

Chloe and Lily went through a lot of her personal things and sorted them out before Chloe left. Later, I went through more of her papers. I examined her check register and found out what I'd always suspected: she'd sent Chloe a check for every birthday and Christmas. That kid had been bleeding her for years. But that wasn't the worst. The lawyers announced that Mother set up a trust for Chloe more than 20 years before. All the money that Mother didn't spend should have gone to Lily and to me. And if Daddy had known I'd have to take care of Mother for 20 years I'm sure he'd have given me more than half. That greedy Lily never even thought of offering me something extra to pay me back. The idea that on top of all that there was money held out for Chloe was really just too much.

I talked to Lily about it, figuring she'd be mad too. "Can you believe Mother set up that trust for Chloe and put our money in it?"

"It wasn't our money, Hunter. The income was Mother's to use as she pleased for life."

"If she had thousands of dollars extra, it would have come to us. I can't believe she tried to cut us out like this."

"For lord's sake, we got the whole estate Daddy left. You inherited millions of dollars from Mike. Mother wanted a chance to do something for Chloe. They were very close, in case you hadn't noticed. She set this up to give Chloe more independence. Why do you have to begrudge her an account that isn't all that significant compared to what you have?"

"Did you know about this?"

"She told me when she set up the trust, and I've been adding to it when I could."

"You added... ." They were two peas in a pod.

    ****

When Chloe turned 30 and got the money from the trust she suddenly quit her job and enrolled in some music school, of all things. Not that she'd had much of a job to begin with. Why she didn't just study music in the first place if that's what she wanted to do, I didn't know. I couldn't imagine what she thought she would do with the training once she had it. But that was Chloe all over—spoiled and determined to do whatever she wanted to do. I thought she took a lot of lessons when she was a child, but I didn't remember hearing her play or sing. Of course, after she got tired of that, she dropped out and then started in on therapy.

That fad for being so self-centered annoyed me. We didn't have time for that self indulgent hog wash in my day and I figured the world would make some sense when people stopped all that mewling and whining. I told her I didn't hold with all that therapy. People didn't need to be wandering around worrying about how they were feeling all the time. In my day, we had to get out and work. There was a depression and a war and there wasn't time to be so selfish. I thought Chloe just wanted attention—it seemed to me she'd had more than her share all her life. But she was going to fritter her money away getting someone to pay attention to her.

Her mother didn't seem to notice what she was doing. Lily did finally come to her senses and dump Blaine, so I didn't have to see that prissy face or listen to him prosing on and on any more. She got a nice little place here and bought herself some new furniture and things were settling down when she went crazy and bought a house down on Sanibel Island. I went down to check on her and be sure she hadn't been cheated. It was a pretty enough place, though I wouldn't want to live in anything so small. And everyone was so casual down there. No one really looked elegant. As usual, Lily found herself some very ordinary friends. If Sanibel had any residents who really amounted to anything, I never saw them.

Lily set up a room with an easel and pastels and watercolors and such and took up art again. Mostly she seemed to draw or paint outside, but she kept everything in the room and finished the pictures in there. The room was lined three deep in pictures of sunsets over the Gulf.

"Lily haven't you done enough sunsets?"

"No, it looks different every time. And there are some particular aspects of light and color that I keep trying to capture. I'll do it at least until I get the effect I want."

"At least these pictures don't have any fairies or leprechauns in them," I thought to myself. Then I started looking closer and realized that some had tiny creatures with wings and translucent colors tucked in a cloud or hovering over the water. I guessed she'd finally lost her mind. But I supposed she was harmless enough. I tried to get Chloe to help me talk Lily into putting her money in a trust, but Chloe wouldn't do it. Probably she figured she could get more out of her mother if all the money was available.

With Mother gone, Lily and I didn't see one another much. Once Lily headed down to Florida, I rarely talked with her. I could have helped her with her investments and introduced her to some nice eligible men, but she showed no interest in coming back to Lexington for more than a few months a year. I kept thinking one day she would realize that I was right all along about how to live, but she said she liked her friends and her life on that island.

****

Until I saw Lily's place, I'd thought about moving into a smaller place in town. But I couldn't really see myself in a small space like that. Mike's house had rooms that were 20 feet by 15 feet with 12 foot ceilings. I felt I had plenty of room to breathe. And there was something so elegant about those big old rooms. The floors were all beautiful hard woods and in the living room there was an inlaid border all the way around. The mantel, doors, window frames and moldings were all imported mahogany.

It was a fabulous setting for my parties. On the nights of really big parties, I set all the lights blazing so that people were dazzled as they came up the drive to the house. Parking attendants took their cars to a field I'd had cleared off to the back. The dining room was large enough for a huge buffet to be set up and waiters circulated with big silver trays of food. Hundreds of people moved through the big old rooms on the first floor. I didn't think I would like living in a place where I couldn't entertain that way.

At one time, I left the place to Chloe in my will, but later I assumed she cared nothing about it. If she had it she'd probably run it into the ground or give it to some of those nuts she ran around with. She never understood what it means to preserve a tradition and had no intention of continuing what I began here. Besides, I worked hard for my money and she shouldn't get to walk off with it. Mike's brother had some children and grandchildren and I thought maybe I would let the farm go back into his family. Mike wasn't especially close to his brother and didn't really know the offspring but I figured he'd be pleased to have the family place stay with his family.

I tried to get Lily to sell me her half of Daddy's farm, but she wouldn't do it. She said she was going to see to it that Chloe got some land. Mother used to go on about the importance of having land. I never realized that Lily had taken it so to heart. I was sickened by the image of a do-nothing like Chloe taking over the farm that represented everything Daddy achieved. Mother tried to talk to me about how she wanted Chloe to have it once, but I don't think Mother ever really appreciated Daddy and his work as much as she should have. When I changed my will I saw to it that Chloe would only get Lily's interest in the farm, but I'd have liked to keep her away from it altogether.

As time passed after Mother's death, in some ways I missed her more. She seemed so intrusive while she was there, but at least I knew someone cared what happened to me. Some days I felt so completely alone. Chloe and Lily rarely bothered to be in touch even though I always loved them and tried to do my best for them. They never troubled to ask much about what happened at the company so they didn't even know what those people did to me. When one of my horses finally won the Derby, Mother and Daddy and Mike were dead and Lily was so far away she hadn't even come to the race. Chloe didn't even watch it on T.V. and when I called her the next week she didn't know my horse had won. I thought Mother would have liked the trophy. Daddy and Mike would have been so proud of me.

Lily

Chapter Seventeen

"Lily, Mr. Wheeler's here with the ice," Mother called.

I grabbed up the picture I had finished and my sketchbook and pencil and ran downstairs and into the kitchen. Mr. Wheeler was just shutting the ice box that he'd loaded with ice.

"Lily! Hello darlin', how you doin' today?" he boomed. I liked Mr. Wheeler. He was just as nice as his voice was big. Lots of times he took Hunter and me up with him and drove us down the pike to the Jot 'Em Down Store, where Hunter could buy lots of candy and I could have a Coca Cola and a chat with Miz Beamish, who owned the place, and her boy Jimmy, who helped her. Jimmy had a boy too, who was there sometimes and he liked to see my sketches. Hunter said I shouldn't spend so much time talking to nobodies, but I liked them and to me they looked as much like somebodies as we did.

Last time, Mr. Wheeler came early and, since he was ahead of schedule, he stayed for a little while and let me draw Mike, his horse, and the wagon. Mama said soon no one would deliver with a horse and wagon any more. I put in the colors later. Mike was a bay, my favorite color of horse. Such a nice dark brown with a mane and tail like midnight on a starless night. His legs were stout and sturdy, not all fragile like Daddy's horses. I brought the picture down to him. I had a little trouble getting that rosy light that was all around the horse. Mother said there was no rose light, but I saw it. I didn't do all the fairies and elves that stayed around Mike because it was too much work to do all those tiny figures but I put one by his ear.

"Oh, Lily, this is beautiful. Mike looks like he's from heaven or somethin'." he told me with a big happy smile. "Isn't that funny. My youngest is always jabberin' about pink around Mike and here you went and put that in your picture. Thank you, Lily. This is just fine. Now Miz Harrison, Miz Beamish was askin' after Lily, wanting her to come draw something. If Lily wants to and it's all right with you, I'll take her up there with me and leave her and pick her up later after I make some more deliveries." I nodded yes and could hardly stand still to see if Mother gave permission.

"That would be fine, Mr. Wheeler," she said. "Lily you mind your manners and don't get in the way at the store. Have a good time darlin'," she called as I climbed up next to Mr. Wheeler. Mike flicked his tail and kept trying to look back over his shoulder. Mr. Wheeler said it meant he was pleased to see me.

I liked going with Mr. Wheeler the best when Hunter wasn't around to come too. Mr. Wheeler would stop at the side of the road and let me draw. Lots of forest nymphs and fairies lived all along there. Everything looked different on different days and different times so I could make lots of drawings and none of them were really the same. That day the leaves were just turning orange and rust and red and gold and I was able to color fall in pastels for the first time.

Mother bought the pastels for me at a huge store called Feeds or something when we went to Chicago with Daddy in the summer. I'd never been in a place so big before. There were chandeliers and cases that were so clear you could see the lights, like everything sparkled. In the middle was a place where the ceiling was floors and floors above the ground. Mother said at Christmas they brought in a giant Christmas tree that stood in that place and went up to the third floor. I watched everywhere we went on the first floor and I couldn't see where they could bring it in or how they could get it past all those glass cases without knocking them all over and breaking all the glass. I wanted to come back at Christmas and draw the tree. I could just imagine it covered with bows and balls, tinsel and angel hair, popcorn and twinkling lights. What a drawing that would be. I made a few the way I figured it must look but that wasn't the same as drawing from the real thing. Mother said maybe we'd go sometime.

While I sketched, sometimes Mr. Wheeler talked to me and sometimes he took a nap and asked me to check his watch and wake him in 10 minutes. He slept while I drew my autumn picture. He just stretched back so his head rested on the top of the seat and pushed his hat forward to cover his face. I sketched him into my picture with his arms folded across his stomach. He snored a little and the front of the cap moved up slightly every time he breathed out. I couldn't figure out how to draw that too well. Mike just stood there chewing on grass. You sure couldn't do that with Daddy's horses. They ran everywhere they went it seemed to me.

I took a couple minutes longer than 10, I thought, to finish what I needed. Then I called to Mr. Wheeler. He sat right up, pushed his cap back and grabbed the reins up. All he had to do was make a clicking noise with his tongue and Mike started walking. I loved the sound his hooves made on the pavement. Sometimes a car went by, but not often. Mike never even seemed to notice.

Mrs. Beamish sat behind the counter by the door. She looked up and smiled when we came in. "Lily. How are you darlin'? Tom, you brought her pretty quick. How are you today? It's warm don't you think? I always like this time of year when it's warm and the colors are so pretty."

Mr. Wheeler started bringing in her ice while she kept talking. She could go on sometimes, but she never noticed if you went on doing whatever you needed to. I stayed there listening but looked around the store. It was a bitsy place but Jimmy managed to pile and stack and organize so they fit in a little bit of just about everything. Cans of beans and corn next to Junket and tapioca and then bread then nails. Everything.

"Lily, I was so crazy about that drawing you showed me of your house, I was thinkin' how nice it would be to have one of the store. You always said you'd draw me something if I wanted it. Will you do it?"

"Sure. I brought my sketch book and Mother said I can stay while Mr. Wheeler delivers more ice. So I can do it now. Then I'll put the colors in at home and bring it back the next ice day."

"Well, that'll be just fine, honey," she said. "We're gonna hang it right here on the wall by the door."

When Hunter came, I usually didn't bring my sketchbook. She got mad if I even asked to stop. She always made fun of my pictures and sometimes she grabbed my sketchbook and tore out pictures and crinkled them. Once she stuffed one in my mouth and tried to make me swallow it. I hated it when she yelled at me and all. Mother hardly did anything to make her stop. Mother and Daddy had pretty bad tempers too, so I tried to stay out of the way and be really quiet so no one would notice me.

****

Mother seemed to get a kick out of Hunter and she laughed at some of the things Hunter did. I was too quiet, like Hunter said, so Mother didn't think I was as much fun. Daddy loved Hunter too. She loved horses and talked to him all the time about training and races and stuff. He took her to the track and the sales and everything. He did stand up for me about school. Mother and the teachers all said I was very smart and that I didn't try hard enough in school. I didn't like school. I just wanted to be left alone and to draw. When Mother started in on me about studying more and doing well in school so I could go to college, Daddy said, "Oh, leave her alone, Ginnie. She doesn't need to stuff her head with all those facts and figures. With those pretty brown eyes of hers she'll catch herself some fella and get married and she won't need all that learning."

Mother sent us upstairs before Daddy had his drinks, and sometimes I could hear them fighting after that. I never liked to be around when people were fighting and being mean. A few times, though, I sneaked out by the bannister to listen. Hunter never came out. She said Daddy didn't drink and punched me in the stomach for saying he did. I know she was wrong, though. He mixed drinks for himself and Mother every night. Mother didn't seem to like it too much. After he had his drinks he sounded funny, like he had a string tied around his tongue. And he was more bad-tempered than usual. That's when he and Mother would fight about how much education we needed and whether we would just get married.

That was all before Daddy got sick, not long after Christmas when I was nine. Mother put him in the spare room and wouldn't let us go in to see him hardly. I never saw him too much anyway so I didn't mind so much, but Hunter fussed and fumed and fought with Mother about it. Even though it was really cold, I went out to the stable and drew a few of Daddy's best horses. Daddy said there were no fairies so I pretended not to see them and just drew the horses. Mother said he was pleased. Hunter asked if I would draw a picture of her favorite horse. I figured she'd do something weird with it, but she asked Mother for a frame and hung it in her room.

After a while, Daddy died in the night one night. We got new black dresses for the funeral—not alike though. I used to think it was fun to have the same dresses, but not by then. I didn't want to have anyone think I was like Hunter. Sometimes I thought that she was the meanest thing that ever was. Everyone said how sweet we looked and clucked their tongues over us. I stayed close to Aunt Georgie as much as I could.

I loved Aunt Georgie. Mother said she wasn't really our aunt but we could call her that because we're at least as close as real family. Sometimes we went to visit at Aunt Georgie's house. She had a big back yard that was all walled in. The walls were old dark red bricks with bougainvillea and wisteria climbing over them. The garden was filled with colors that changed slowly from spring to summer to fall. Lavender lilacs, roses the shade of Mother's rouge, daffodils in a yellow so delicate it was almost not a color, purple English lavender, white wisps of baby's breath, golden mums. Fairies loved that garden and came out to dance around when I was there. Hunter pretended that she couldn't see them but I knew she could.

Aunt Georgie let me draw as much as I wanted and sat and talked to me while I worked. She said art was important and it was a wonderful thing that I had the talent. I wished Mother and Daddy thought so. Inside, Aunt Georgie had knick knacks from all around the world. She told exciting stories about them and I tried to draw each piece with the story in the picture. Some of the things from China had shades of blue and orange and green that I couldn't quite get from my watercolors or pastels, but sometimes I came pretty close.

Aunt Georgie came out to stay with us until after the funeral. She helped Mother pack and as soon as school let out Mother, Hunter and I got on a train and went to California. I'd never been so far before and I was pretty tired of the train by the time we got there. We went too fast for me to draw. I read some but the train shook so much I couldn't read for very long. Hunter had all the porters waiting on her in no time.

****

Mother got thinner and thinner all summer and her hair turned all white. Her headaches were worse than ever. Hunter made friends with a bunch of kids and spent all day every day out prowling around on the beach with them, playing games and thinking up devilment. I thought they were kind of tough and I didn't want to find out what Hunter could get them to do to me, so I stayed pretty close to the house we rented and drew my pictures of the ocean from a place right in sight of it. I knew Mother was just lying on the bed or the sofa and not watching, but I felt safer knowing that if I screamed she could see.

The sun shone every day in California. Sometimes it seemed too bright for my eyes. The sun on the water certain days was so dazzling it was like being in another world—the one I used to figure the fairies went to when I couldn't see them. I never drew anything quite like it before. Or the mountains. Every day I could make a picture of something I hadn't tried before.

Hunter pretty much did whatever she wanted to. She was meaner than ever and snarled at Mother and me all the time. "I don't know why you act like you're so unhappy that Daddy's gone," she said to Mother one day. "You never wanted to listen to him and you were always complaining. I bet he died just to get away from you."

Mother looked stunned for a minute and before she could say anything, Hunter turned to me. "And you. You just couldn't bother to take any interest in Daddy's horses, to pay attention to him. No. I was the only one who tried to help Daddy, so don't you two pretend to care now!"

"GET OUT!" Hunter and I both turned to Mother, who had pulled herself up to her fullest height—which by then meant she was just a little taller than Hunter. She spoke quietly but with more anger than I'd ever heard from her. "Get out of here I said."

Hunter got up and stood looking at her.

"Get out and don't come back in my sight until you're ready to apologize."

Hunter turned on her heel and stormed out. Mother sank back in her chair. We had lots of days like that. I kept hoping one day someone would come tell us that a wave had carried Hunter out to sea and they couldn't find her but I guess she was too ornery for a wave to want her.

I tried one night to make egg kisses. Mother loved them. She had our cook make them once a week and served them with chocolate ice cream over the top. They didn't come out as good as Cook's, but Mother said she loved them and it took her back to her girlhood to have me learning to make egg kisses. "You'll grow up to be a fine wife," she told me. Then she told a story about the time she and her grandmama made dinner for the family. Hunter jumped up and said she had to get to her ball game as soon as Mother started. After Mother told the story and we finished laughing, I asked her why I didn't have any grandparents. She said they all died before I was born. She wouldn't answer any questions about her mother and father, except that her father was a lawyer and her mother was the daughter of a professor who married a plantation owner's daughter.

Aunt Georgie sent us some wonderful letters. She found pictures of a dog like her dog, Tip. Tip wrote all the news and the pictures illustrated Tip's adventures. Aunt Georgie knew about magic. Hunter said the letters were silly. Mother let me save them. I liked hearing from home. California's mountains were too big, not like the friendly hills that rolled around Lexington. And it was not very green. Our hills were covered with grass. Mostly it was dark green, but when the sun was just right and the breeze rippled through, a blue tint spread across the pastures. Before we went out West I'd been trying to paint the blue and to show how the sunlight reflected off the leaves of the trees so when the wind blew every branch became like a sparkler, flashing light everywhere. I did think the practice I got on the light on water at the ocean would be helpful.

*****

At the end of the summer, we finally got to go home. Mother was thin as a rail and had giant circles under her eyes. She hardly ever laughed. When Aunt Georgie picked us up at the train, she took one look at Mother and announced that something had to be done. When we got home the two of them were closeted for a long time. Georgie stayed with us for a couple of days and they were busy as could be the whole time. Finally at dinner one night they made the announcement. Mother was being admitted to some hospital in another state and Hunter and I were going to live at a school near Lexington.

"You just don't want to be bothered with us," Hunter shouted. "There's nothing wrong with you." Georgie told her to hush.

I was too scared to talk. When Daddy started having to have doctors and nurses all the time he was too sick to be saved. Now Mother had to be taken care of the same way and this time she wouldn't even be near us. I was sure we'd never see her again. I hadn't even gotten used to Daddy not being with us. We'd never been away from home without Mother and Daddy. I didn't want to go to some place filled with strangers.

It seemed like no time till Mother and Georgie took us out to the school with our trunks and helped unpack our things. Since I was younger, I shared a room with a girl my age named Josie. Hunter roomed with Mimi. Mimi seemed like a nice girl and I thought it was too bad she had to room with Hunter. Josie was from up near Cincinnati but Mimi was from Lexington and Mother turned out to know her parents. Josie was kind of plump and had light brown hair and sort of pale brown eyes. Her folks were farmers and she wasn't all uppity like Hunter and her friends. Hunter kept telling me I could do better, but Josie was kind and I could talk to her.

I hated that school. Hunter and some of the older girls made fun of me all the time at first. Then one day one of the girls grabbed one of my pictures away from me and wouldn't give it back.

All of a sudden, Hunter whirled around to her and said, "Here, that's enough."

The girl looked surprised but kept laughing. "C'mon Hunter. All those fairies. Like she's a big baby."

"I said that's enough, Lucy." Hunter said fiercely. "You leave my sister's drawings alone." I just stared at her, wondering what had happened to my real sister. All of a sudden I realized that, as much as she picked on me when it was just the two of us at home, she'd stood up for me pretty often when we were at school or with other kids. I didn't know what to think.

Lucy held the picture up, still giggling but watching nervously as Hunter clenched her fists. When Hunter began to advance on her she flung the picture at me and took off. The other girls quit teasing me after that.

"Don't think this means we're best buddies or anything," Hunter said.

The art teacher told me I couldn't put fairies in my pictures and she didn't like the way I tried to paint the light. In class I tried to paint the stuff she wanted. Like she wanted us to copy this picture of a blue jay. It was a plain old picture of a bird. I imagined the bird in a tree with the sky all around and the light playing off the leaves and the clouds, creating light and shadow around the bird. She was really mad and wanted to know why I couldn't just do the assignment she gave me. So, whenever I could, I worked on sketches and pastels in my room.

After a while Mrs. O'Toole took away my sketchbook and pastels and water-colors. "You're spending too much time on these silly pictures—which, by the way, are far too childish for a girl your age—and ignoring your school work, so I'm afraid I must insist that you stop and I'm going to take these things away from you so that you'll mind your school work."

Hunter came in a while after Mrs. O'Toole left and found me crying. "Lily, really, you've got to stop hanging around being all weepy all the time," she said insistently.

I swallowed and tried not to cry as I told her, "Mrs. O'Toole just took away all my art supplies."

"What do you mean, 'took them away'?" Hunter demanded.

"Just what I said," I told her angrily. "She said I'm not paying enough attention to my school work and so I can't draw any more." I tried not to start sobbing again but I couldn't help it.

"Well, that old biddy! She can't do that to you and I'm going to tell her so," announced Hunter and marched off in a fury. I don't know what happened with Mrs. O'Toole, but I didn't get my things back.

Aunt Georgie came out to take us for lunch sometimes and she was hopping mad when I told her I couldn't draw any more but when Georgie tried to change her mind, Mrs. O'Toole said that as headmistress she had to be able to do what she felt was best for the progress of the students. Georgie said she would tell Mother to intervene. I guess it didn't work. Josie said my pictures were beautiful and that she wanted to give Mrs. O'Toole a piece of her mind. I told her not to get in trouble over it. Mrs. O'Toole never let anyone question her on any decision and I figured since she couldn't punish Georgie, she might take it out on Josie.

I read pretty much after that, but I didn't really feel like doing much any more. It just seemed like my whole life had gone topsy turvy and I couldn't see how to make anything right again. When I sketched and painted, I always felt like I knew who I was and what to do and how to do it. I didn't feel that way the rest of the time, so without my sketchbook I just felt like nobody.

Mother got well and came back after all. She made us stay at the school, though, for the rest of the year. She said she had a lot to do and it would be easier if we stayed there. She found some people to rent the farm and she rented a house in town. She moved all our furniture and set everything up before school let out so we never got to go back to our house before we had to go to the new place. Since Daddy died nothing stayed the same. I knew I'd never get to see Mr. Wheeler or Mrs. Beamish or Jimmy or to go out to sketch the blue grass in the pasture. I asked Mother why everything had to change so much but she didn't answer me.

Chapter Eighteen

I enrolled at UK in the fall after high school graduation—Mother browbeat me into it. I always loved to read but I never did like school. I didn't draw much any more and I wasn't sure what I would do but I didn't want to go to college. Hunter went off to the North two years before. Mother pressed for this university up there that she said her grandfather had something to do with. Hunter was anxious to get away and, between raising her grades and Mother pulling some strings, she got in. I had so much more fun with Mother when she wasn't around, I wished I could just stay home for a while.

Mother and I had some lovely long chats about books. Hunter was very impatient with book conversations and, when she was around, always found some reason Mother had to stop and do something for her. I savored our freedom to discuss without interruption. When I finished *The Ambassadors*, Mother told me that it had been the topic of discussion at one of her lunches many years before.

"It's very tedious, of course, and most of the ladies found it simply too difficult to enjoy."

"His language is so exquisite though. I didn't need to be wrapped up in the story."

"Oh my, I was very involved in the basic theme of a son whose family forced him to give up the love of his life because they had a different plan for him. But, even so, I did get bogged down in all the descriptive detail."

"Oh, but the descriptions painted such beautiful pictures. I felt that I moved from one lovely picture to another as he captured the play of light and colors—like Impressionist paintings. Do you really think that woman was the love of his life?"

"Yes, I was sure of it. Those things happened much more at that time, I think, than they do now," she said vaguely.

"Those things?"

"You know, parents marrying their children off to suit some silly notion of position and family pride."

"That used to happen a lot? Did you know anyone it happened to?"

"Why, yes, I did," she replied, suddenly becoming brusque. "Well, that was a long time ago."

"That was a good story," I owned, "but I still like the way he paints pictures with words."

We often noticed different things in books and it was so interesting to explore the things I read from a different perspective. I told Mother I didn't want to live on the campus.

Josie came to UK. We'd written and visited ever since our days at the boarding school and I was so excited she'd be back in town. We even had World History class together. She'd lost weight since I saw her and was taller than I was. Of course, I took after Mother, so most everybody was taller. She lived in one of the dorms and wanted me to come share a room with her, but I wanted the time to enjoy being at home with Mother and without Hunter.

"Lily, you should get away, where you can be your own person," Josie told me.

"I don't feel that comfortable with a lot of strangers," I started to explain.

Josie broke in, "What about your art? Your drawings were wonderful and now is your chance. When are you ever going to have another chance to study art and see what you can do?"

"I don't really draw any more. They were just silly kid's drawings I used to do. And even if Mother would let me major in art, which she wouldn't, UK's art department isn't one of the good ones."

"Lily, it's the best one you're in a position to go to. Please, take a course at least."

I was touched that she remembered my pictures so fondly, but I knew that I wasn't that good. The art teachers in junior high and high school didn't like my work any more than the teacher at boarding school and I quit even taking art classes the last two years of school. I couldn't copy the things they wanted copied and they just shook their heads over my work. I started out in college without a major and took all required courses.

Before long in World History I noticed a boy kept coming and sitting near us. He wore kind of funny old clothes that didn't fit too well although they were always clean and neat. He always seemed serious and frequently answered the professor's questions to the class. One day after class he came up and asked me what I thought about something the professor had talked about. I hadn't been paying attention, so I said I thought it was interesting and asked him what he thought. He told me and finished by saying, "My name is Blaine Anderson."

"I'm Lily," I said and put out my hand. He smiled and gripped my hand just a little too long.

"Lily, what a pretty name," he said. He spoke with an accent that wasn't Lexington but wasn't quite a hills accent either.

"Where are you from?" He named a small Kentucky town called Waddy. His father was a local preacher and saw that his children had enough learning that they didn't talk like the rural people around them, but traces of the hometown accent came through anyway. He asked me to see a movie the next Friday and I agreed.

"Lily, did he ask you out?" Josie waited outside the building for me.

"Yes."

"Are you going?"

"Yes."

"Oh, Lily, he's a dreamboat, but those clothes. Do you think he's somebody you should go out with?"

"You sound like Hunter. He's a preacher's son. I suppose they don't have much money." Later I found out a lot of his clothes were hand-me-downs from parishioners. He worked two jobs to help pay for school and didn't have extra for clothes. He showed up for our date wearing a nice new suit, though. He was extremely polite to Mother so she liked him right off.

I hadn't dated many boys back at Henry Clay, but I'd had a few beaus along the way. I loved to dance and a couple of the boys I went with were great dancers too.

We entered contests together and went to lots of dances. I had quite a few ribbons from winning contests all hanging around the mirror in my room. There was a small crowd of us that did a lot of things together and had such a good time. My friends weren't from the horsy set and they weren't rich like the crowd Hunter ran with, but they were the nicest people. Mother liked to have them visit because they were always polite and would help her out with things around the house. Not like Hunter's friends who came by and expected to be waited on hand and foot.

Mother had some pretty dresses made for me to dance in. My favorite had yards of fabric with giant flowers that surrounded the skirt. It was soft and fluid and moved with the dance so that I felt very graceful. If I still painted, I'd have liked to put it on a model and paint the flow of it. Somehow when a band started up my feet had a life of their own and I forgot how nervous people made me or that I didn't like to have a lot of people watching me. I felt the music from head to toe and it moved me along with it. Sometimes I liked to watch from the sidelines as the girls, with their fancy dresses of every color in the rainbow swinging and swaying, circled the room in their partners' arms. It made me think of fairy tale balls and magic and I knew just how I would draw it.

Blaine never learned to dance because his father said it was a sin. He didn't drink either. I didn't mind about the drinking because I didn't really drink. Also, I remembered I didn't like the way Daddy sounded when he'd been drinking and Hunter got meaner than ever when she got a hold of some drinks—a feat I wouldn't have thought possible. But Blaine went to movies and out for sodas and for nice long walks, so I didn't miss dancing too much.

The war had started the year before. Blaine's older brother joined up right away. Blaine wanted to sign up too, but his mother begged him not to go. She said no mother should have to send two sons to war at the same time. He was fidgety, though, about staying behind. He'd gone to school summers and only had a year-and-a-half of college left after this one, so it seemed a shame for him to leave but I figured he would.

Most of the boys seemed to have gone off to fight. In high school we used to go over to the campus sometimes for a walk. It was exciting to be there when classes changed and watch the walks fill up and everybody talking and laughing. With the war, though, it wasn't as lively. No fellas showing off for the girls or couples flirting or walking hand in hand. The classrooms were eerily filled with girls, as if King Harrod had reigned in Kentucky 18 years ago and only a few boys escaped. Some of the boys Hunter and I went to school with had already died. The battles were far away, and except for rationing and more women working, our lives stayed the same. Occasionally I thought it could not be real that such horrors went on while our days unfolded as usual. Lexington still dressed itself for fall in the finest reds and ambers and oranges and the Keeneland meet went on.

Mother never bothered to go to the races or the sales any more. She rarely accepted an invitation for one of the parties. Not even in the round of balls and dinners and all that were held four or five a day every day for a week before the Derby. Hunter blew up every now and then about how she needed those connections and why couldn't Mother do anything to help her. I didn't blame Mother. Those horse people are snooty. They only talked to people who came from certain families with money or who had certain positions in the horse business, like trainers, and all they wanted to do was gossip about what everybody else in the business was doing. They were nice to people's faces and then they ripped them apart behind their backs. Hunter and that crowd made fun of me and of my friends all the time. I wondered what kind of man Daddy was that he spent so much of his life in the midst of people like that and left us behind so he could be with them.

By Christmas, Blaine was the only boy I dated and we saw one another often. Mother and I bought some new clothes for him in the right sizes and wrapped the boxes in shiny papers with pretty ribbons wrapped around. He seemed embarrassed and for a while I thought he might not accept them, but Mother said what a tremendous pleasure it had been to shop for a handsome man again and he thanked her graciously. He'd been handsome before, but, oh my, in new clothes that fit well, he was dreamy. His eyes were of the deep, clear blue that only raven-haired people seemed to have so we got him shirts that brought out the brilliance of his eyes. He and Aunt Georgie and Hunter's friend Mimi joined us for Christmas dinner. Blaine had to keep working through the holidays so he wouldn't get home until the weekend. He and Aunt Georgie talked of a number of books they'd read and got along fine.

"Lily, you're not serious about that gawky old thing are you?" Hunter asked when everyone left.

"If you mean Blaine, he's not gawky and I'll thank you not to talk that way about him."

"Oh my God, you are serious!" she exclaimed. "Mother you're not going to let her throw herself away on this nothing man whose parents are from nowheresville are you?"

"You wouldn't know anything about a decent person like Blaine, you witch. He's an honor student and a kind person and he's worth a dozen of those stupid playboys you run around with," I retorted.

"Lily, calm down. Hunter stop baiting her. Now Blaine is a nice boy. His manners are all they should be and he's obviously bright and ambitious. His parents have clearly brought him up with good values and if Lily loves him, I think nothing else needs to be said."

"Oh, Mother, you have to be kidding. You aren't going to even try to talk some sense into her?"

"Hunter, I said that's enough. Now leave it alone. I don't want to hear anything more from you about this."

Hunter always seemed to try to tear down everything I liked, to insist that whatever I wanted wasn't worth wanting, to categorize my friends as not good enough, and to tell me that most anything that I did she did better. I felt sort of small and stupid most of the time. It was hard to talk to people because I figured no one would be interested in anything I had to say or if I said too much they'd know I wasn't very good at anything. Blaine thought I was pretty and he told me he felt proud going out with me by his side. I liked the way that made me feel.

****

"Your sister doesn't like me, does she?" asked Blaine. We sat in Gratz Park, surrounded by pre-Civil War homes, stately and gracious. The branches of fine old trees met everywhere overhead, forming an arbor to protect this little corner of history. I loved sitting there where I could turn my eyes to creations that formed in someone else's imagination so long ago. Blaine was the first beau I ever brought with me to that special place. He didn't seem to notice the magic, though. He was determined to talk.

"Oh, don't mind Hunter," I said, "she doesn't like much of anybody. Meanness is her middle name."

"Well, I'd like your family to like me." He paused a moment, then said, "Gee, your mother's swell."

"Yes, she's such fun," I agreed.

"Josie said you used to draw pictures all the time," he suddenly informed me.

"Yes, I did. I still have most of them, but they're just child's things. I haven't drawn anything much for a long time."

"So you're not gonna suddenly take off and become some kind of crazy artist on me?"

"Well, I guess not. But would it be so bad if I wanted to paint again?"

"I don't much hold with all that art business. Seems like a lot of sinners get involved and try to spread their ways to innocent people."

Since I met Blaine the world seemed to be a lot more filled with sinners than I ever realized before and a bewildering array of things he'd prefer that I not do. Blaine was very strong and had a lot of set ideas about life and how to live it. I rather admired the amount of certainty about life that his system of rules created. I watched him in wonder as he went on about the reasons why I shouldn't be an artist. I sort of wished Josie hadn't set him off on that since I didn't really have any plans to study art or even to begin drawing again.

"Lily, are you listening?" he interrupted my wandering thoughts.

"Oh, yes, Blaine."

"I said I've decided to enlist in the fall."

"You are? What about your mother?"

"Well, my folks are mad at me anyway about some things. And she just doesn't understand a man's got to do his duty."

"I see. So you'll be gone," I said faintly, shrinking against the thought of being left alone again.

"Yes. And that's what I want to talk to you about, Lily. I'd like to know if you're willing to wait for me. It would mean a lot to me if I thought you'd be here for me when I get back."

It was so unexpected. And so romantic. "Of course I'll wait for you, Blaine," I told him.

****

I went to the train station to see him off. It was a sultry June day, the sky a hazy blue, as if a cloud of steam had risen from the hot sidewalks and covered the sky. Parents, girlfriends and wives sadly hovered around nervous boys, some clinging and crying, some valiantly smiling and pretending it was an ordinary leave-taking. I blinked back tears and tried to carry on a normal conversation, but it was hard to speak and, when Blaine turned to hug me, I shed a few tears onto his shoulder before pulling myself back with a sniff and smiling a misty good bye. They shipped him off to the Pacific as soon as he finished boot camp. He wrote me often—sweet love letters I wouldn't have expected from a man so serious and righteous. I told Mother I would not go back to school again that fall. I got a job at The Bon Mot, helping to design window displays. Hunter was in her last year at college and Mother and I still lived in peace. She invited me to join her Saturday lunches with "the girls" sometimes. They often went to the Lafayette Hotel. I loved to look around the dining room where highly polished silver sparkled on top of snowy white tablecloths. From the carved plaster ceiling hung lovely chandeliers with muted light.

I missed Blaine and thought all the time about his mane of dark, shiny hair and those azure eyes. I remembered all the lovely times we had and missed having his strong arm to lean on and his certainty that he knew the formula to conquer life. Still, there were fellows left behind who liked to dance and plenty of dances to attend, so I enjoyed my last chances to let my feet race freely across the floor. I figured Blaine would never know and it couldn't really hurt just to dance.

By the time the war ended, a year later, and Blaine came home, my daydreams told me I'd found a prince. He had fought courageous battles and he would finish school with flying colors and go on to be a big success. As soon as he came home he asked me to marry him and I said yes without thinking twice. I'd be out of the house right after Hunter came back home to stay.

Chapter Nineteen

Not long after Blaine and I celebrated our sixth wedding anniversary, I began hearing Josie in my mind, asking me over and over what I thought Blaine and I had in common, being from such different worlds and all. And hearing myself telling her innocently that we both liked a lot of the same things and our different backgrounds didn't matter. I wished I had listened to her.

Blaine expected his wife to take care of everything in the house and to do it without help. I knew a little about cooking because Mother said we should at least know some basics and gave us lessons now and then but she also said she didn't want us to feel pressured to cook. Some days I wished there had been more pressure, but she came and helped me cook regularly.

"Why do you need so much help from your mother?" Blaine asked.

"Mother knows more than I do about cooking."

"What was she doing when you were growing up? It's a mother's job to teach her daughters how to run a proper household for their husbands."

Blaine seemed to always have some fault to find with the way I kept house and with my mother for not teaching me better. He never seemed to grasp that we always had a housekeeper and mother didn't have to do everything. It never occurred to me that I would have to do everything either. At first, Blaine and I were so poor and so infatuated that I didn't mind. But he'd had a good job for a couple of years by that time and he refused to let me hire anyone to help me at all. He said I didn't need help and it was too expensive. That man pinched pennies more than anyone I ever knew. Mother said Daddy was cheap but he was positively extravagant compared to Blaine.

Blaine liked the house to be spotless—not a sign that any human activity had been performed there at any time. His expectation was that the house should be immaculate every day when he came home and that I should have dinner ready within 20 minutes of his arrival. Mother offered to pay for someone to come in two days a week to clean and do some cooking for me. I was thrilled, but Blaine called her and politely declined.

"Blaine that would really help me. Why did you tell her no?"

"What would people think if I let your mother pay for something like that? A man is supposed to be able to support his own family."

"Who would know that she's paying for it?"

"I would know," he said from between clenched teeth. He could force more nastiness through closed teeth than anyone I ever saw. It was as if the teeth held back anger of a ferocity beyond imagination. He didn't actually shout but I always felt that he'd been yelling. "And it wouldn't take much for people to figure out that I can't afford it."

"You're making enough money now that no one would be surprised."

"It's your job," he said and slammed his fist down on the table. "And I expect you to do it." He had a way of cutting off an argument so I knew not to dare any further attempt at swaying him.

****

I became pregnant and then miscarried several times in the first few years of our marriage. I didn't much want a baby and I wasn't sure how much I wanted Blaine any more, so I felt fine when the doctor told me he felt it was unlikely that I'd get pregnant again and that, even if I did, I probably couldn't carry a baby to term. Not that the miscarriages weren't distressing.

The first time, I cried all the way home from the hospital and Blaine looked devastated. "Oh, honey," he kept saying "Our baby's gone. I can't believe it. I'm so sorry." He really wanted a baby and was genuinely distressed. I wasn't sure why I was crying, but even though I didn't want the baby very much it seemed incredibly sad to think about that little life being gone. I moped around for days.

I don't know why I didn't go ahead and leave the marriage while I had the chance. I didn't want to move back to Mother's house and I was pretty sure I couldn't get a job that paid enough to live in a nice place. I just sort of hoped that something would come along and get me out of there. I was dismayed, then, to find I was pregnant again not long after that sixth anniversary. And that time it just kept on going.

"Oh, Lily. This is lovely news darlin'," Mother enthused when I'd been pregnant long enough that I figured I could tell people I was having a baby.

"Yes, I guess it is."

"Oh everyone suffers a bit from nerves before their first baby. But believe me, you'll be just thrilled when you have the baby."

"I suppose." Right then I threw up all the time and felt I'd never be well again. I didn't know how I would handle a baby. Sometimes I felt I'd burst out screaming and tearing my hair from the burden of Blaine's expectations of all the cleaning and cooking I should do for him. Then I found myself expecting a little creature even more helpless than he was, who would depend on me and demand that I fulfill all its needs. Some days I felt panic stricken. It would be harder to leave Blaine once we had a child, I figured, and felt completely trapped. Then I hated the baby who kicked inside me.

"Mother, didn't you ever wonder whether you really wanted to be bothered with a baby?"

"Well, as long as I waited, obviously for many years I didn't want to have to care for children. But I decided I was ready and once I decided, I didn't question it other than the normal case of nerves about whether I'd be a good mother."

"Didn't you find it awfully wearing to have to do everything for us?"

She thought for a minute and then answered as if weighing her words carefully. "Sometimes it was a lot of work and seemed chaotic. But, I always had help of course and that made such a difference. I don't suppose Blaine will hire someone for you now?"

I just laughed.

****

When Chloe was born, Blaine and Mother were absolutely thrilled. Mother said she was perfect. Blaine immediately began to make plans for how best to mold her and see that she understood all the rules she'd need to know to live in this world. I just stared at her tiny, perfect hands and her big wise eyes and wondered if she could tell me something about how to live. Blaine told me not to be silly.

Even Hunter enjoyed Chloe. She'd been married for a few years to Mike Madigan. She landed one who fit all her requirements: rich, prominent family in Lexington and the horse world, powerful and handsome. I liked Mike though; everybody did. He took to Chloe as if she were his own. Hunter and Mike could come enjoy her and then leave without having to change diapers or warm bottles. I'd always despised Hunter for her snotty outlook, but I looked sometimes at the life she led with Mike and wondered if she was as wrong as I'd thought. They traveled and went to parties, worked together and lived in a gorgeous place with several servants. I don't think Hunter ever had to make so much as a pot of coffee, let alone to scrub a sink. Mike listened to her with interest and I never heard him cut her off or dismiss her opinions as if she had no thought worth considering. Blaine treated me pretty much the way I remembered Daddy treating Mother. I hadn't known there were other kinds of men.

As Chloe grew more responsive and then more mobile, Mother and Mike went crazy for her. She laughed at the drop of a hat and her dark eyes sparkled and shone like she came from that brighter lighter place where, as a child, I thought the fairies lived. She learned any game we taught her in a blink and enjoyed it more than anyone. Blaine was pleased that she was so smart. He already talked about her doing well in school till you'd have thought Mother raised him. Whenever I put a record on the phonograph, she cooed along and waved her hands and feet in time to the music. I thought she'd be a fine dancer but of course I didn't mention that to Blaine.

Actually, removed from the influence of his father, Blaine relaxed some of those old fashioned rules. His mother had died while he was in the Pacific. His father seemed to blame him, although his mother had had a bad heart for some time. Then his father declared us a family of infidels and told Blaine he'd disown him if he married me. Blaine was hopping mad and, of course, married me anyway. He and his father had not spoken since. "I'll never dictate that way to a child of mine," he vowed.

Much to my surprise, Blaine even joined me in attending the Episcopal church and never said a word about taking me to his church. He met a lot of prominent local people at my church and I wondered once in a while whether that was really why he went. I thought it was a shame that Chloe would never know either of her grandfathers when she actually had a chance to meet one of them. On the other hand, I didn't figure she needed to start worrying about hellfire and damnation, so I never pushed for a reconciliation.

Mother was like a different person around Chloe. She chased around with her and played games for hours. The two of them laughed till they could hardly stand and then chased around some more. Chloe had boundless energy and I worried about whether Mother was really up to that much running around but there was no reasoning with her.

"Oh darlin' we're just playing and having a good time," she said.

"Well, Mother, don't you think you should rest a little, at least?"

"Oh pooh. I'm perfectly fine. Let me enjoy playing with my grandchild while I've got her."

Then Mike would come in and start flying Chloe around and swinging her upside down and she'd squeal and screech and laugh till Blaine and I wanted to put her in a box or something. I found her exuberance very wearing.

****

- 118 -

All that was before we moved to Wisconsin. Blaine got a job with much better pay, more responsibility and far more opportunity for advancement with a large company up there and suddenly we packed up and moved. After we looked, I wanted to live in one of the Chicago suburbs south of there, near the lake. Blaine said that it was too expensive and he was damned if he was going to commute that far. So we settled in Spotswood, a dull looking town where ordinary houses, one much like the next, were lined up, one after the other.

Northerners were quite rude, I found, making fun of our accents and asking questions as though they assumed we came from some place devoid of schools or books or even sufficient connection with the outside world to be aware of movies or fashion or current events. I found it extraordinary that such very ill-mannered and ordinary people just assumed that we must be backward. And the midwestern accent was so coarse! Their ridicule touched a nerve for Blaine, who began carefully losing his accent as soon as we arrived. Personally, I found their accent to be rather stupid-sounding and much preferred the lilting warmth of a Kentucky drawl.

I'd never found it very easy to talk to people or make new friends so it was lonely for an awfully long time after we moved. I got to know a couple of my neighbors. Chloe helped too, even though she was shy. With her black hair, big brown eyes and pretty smile, people started up conversations about her. When she was really small she brightened and chattered with people, but as she grew older, she moved up against my leg or behind me. People invariably nodded and said, "Oh, shy, isn't she?" Then they bent over and tried to reassure her, frightening her even more. Eventually I found some stores with nice people who went out of their way like the shopkeepers in Lexington. No one bothered with "ma'am" or "sir" or shaking hands to say hello, but after a while I found a capacity for deep friendship and loyalty in people. I made some nice friends. There was just a different sound and rhythm up there. I missed Mother and Josie.

I especially missed Mother's willingness to take Chloe for a few hours now and then. Up there I was stuck with her all the time and it got on my nerves some days. I didn't know how I would be able to train her to do anything she should do. When she was a baby I fought with her incessantly over food. I'd try to feed her something good for her and she'd clamp her mouth shut. I'd pick her up and shake her and try again. Every meal ended in hysterics and with food all over her face and clothes and the high chair. Finally I gave up and let her eat things she liked and I just hoped she'd stay healthy. Of course I'd get the blame if she didn't.

Later she wanted to run around and shout and shriek and laugh all the time. I couldn't stand all the racket. I kept telling her she was too loud and raucous and that ladies don't make such a racket. For a while she seemed irrepressible and we had some major battles of will. Eventually, though, she settled down more.

Mother worried about raising Chloe in the north and having her turn out okay. I told her I'd try to see that Chloe learned to mind her manners but I didn't really know how much would stick when things were so different up there. Once Chloe finally quieted down and became more contained, I thought I had more hope of turning out a nice young lady of whom Mother would approve.

Chapter Twenty

Blaine, Chloe and I sat in our living room. Blaine had been lecturing for what seemed like hours. Chloe's face, guarded as ever, held a defeated expression as Blaine finished explaining all the reasons why she shouldn't study music in college. I actually thought it was a shame to let a talent like hers go to waste. When she sang, that big, irrepressible voice and spirit she had when she was little came back and mesmerized whoever happened to be listening. It was kind of nice to experience it again occasionally. But Blaine had already informed me that he would not allow Chloe to study music. So I just stared around the living room.

I had decorated it a few years before in mint green and pink. I worked with the people at the paint store for days to get a mix that gave me the exact shade of pink that I wanted for the walls. Then I searched carpet places for miles around to find the shade of green that I had in mind. I wanted a light, joyful green, not one of those institutional shades. And the time I had finding fabric for the upholstery and curtains that brought the pink of the wall and the mint of the floor together with some darker and lighter shades of each! Those were not popular colors at the time, but I'd finally created the effect I aimed for. The colors were reminiscent of a rose garden and the look was cheery. I needed the place to look happy at least. That day the room didn't seem to suit our lives at all. To our surprise, he left it up to her whether she was going to an audition for one of the schools.

I tried to remember back and figure out when Chloe became so stiff and pained. She was too lively when she was little. Blaine and I had quite a time trying to get her to quiet down and quit being so wild. We were terribly afraid she was going to turn out to be like Hunter. Sometimes she'd start laughing about something and just keep going until she couldn't stop. She really got on Blaine's nerves when she did that, especially when he'd had a bad day at work. He'd tell her to stop and sometimes she just couldn't seem to contain it.

Eventually, of course, he'd spew venom with his mouth barely open, "Chloe I told you to stop laughing and I meant it." Sometimes he even slipped his hands around her neck and pretended to choke her. I thought he frightened her too much and asked him not to do that.

"Well, Lily, if you'd ever exercise some control over that child, maybe it wouldn't come to this." That was just like him, to blame it entirely on me. Sometimes I thought it was eery how much he and Hunter had in common, for all they appeared to be such opposites.

I just asked her to quiet down or put her in her room if she kept laughing or singing or running around. "Young ladies don't run around wild and make too much noise like you do," I told her. I never knew whose tactics had more impact, but eventually she did quiet down and became easier to handle. I was pleased to have taught her so well. Somewhere along the way, though, she became more than just quiet and I wished I knew how to teach her to liven up a little, but I'd never known how to do it myself.

****

Mike's death came as a terrible shock to all of us. Much as Blaine disapproved of the horse people in general, even he liked Mike. And, though nothing was ever said, I think we all appreciated the effect his presence had on Hunter. When he died, Hunter seemed stunned for a while but then she returned to her old ways with a vengeance. Mike left her his business. Finally she was in charge of something big and she began to swagger around and tell everyone what to do worse than ever. She bullied Mother into moving in with her in no time.

"Lily, you're not around here enough to realize Mother's not as strong as she used to be. I'm afraid to leave her alone," Hunter told me.

"I've been there several times a year ever since we moved and I don't see anything wrong with her. She drives her own car, she goes out with her friends, she cooks and reads."

"That's just like you. You want to leave everything to me so you just pretend there's nothing wrong to avoid taking any responsibility."

Hunter could always find some reason why I was at fault. Mother had a rather different version of events.

"Hunter's been keeping after me to come live with her out on Mike's farm. She has to save face by saying I need it, but I'm worried about her. I think she's lonelier without Mike than she admits and I don't think she's recovering well from his death. You know I always thought the two of them drank too much, but I swear she's much worse since he died."

Hunter's insistence that Mother wasn't well enough to live alone worried me though. I told Mother she could come live with us or divide her time between the two places. But she said she didn't want to leave her doctors or the friends who were still alive. She always did like spending time with Hunter more than me.

After a while Mother told me that Hunter was charging her rent. And Hunter never stopped grousing about how she *had* to take on this burden of care and got no help from me. Seemed to me she was helping herself pretty well.

Once Mother moved out to the farm, that was where we had to visit her. I'd have been happier staying with Mother in her own house. Hunter always acted like it was a big imposition for us to stay in her house even though Flo and the maid did all the cleaning and the cooking. I tried to stay on guard to keep Hunter from getting hold of Chloe. When she had the chance, she picked on Chloe the way she'd picked on me years before. Well, except she didn't punch her in the stomach. Chloe had learned long since to try to stick close to Mother if Blaine and I were out. We took her to see our friends and always visited Aunt Georgie. Chloe was crazy about her. We were all upset when Georgie had to be put in a nursing home. I visited a few times, but it was too hard to see her so confused and helpless when she'd always been so smart and lively.

Hunter kept trying to turn Chloe into a little Hunter copy. When she could, she'd take Chloe out visiting to other farms or to the Huntsman's Club. Chloe loved the countryside around Lexington almost more than we did and she liked to see other farms, so she enjoyed those outings to an extent, but Hunter always snapped her head off at some point or told her her ears were too big or her hair was cut wrong or she should quit being so smart because men don't like it. Chloe'd get out of the car and walk in stiff and straight, her eyes filled with tears. She never wanted to let Hunter know how much she'd been hurt, but she'd cry to Mother or in her room. I wished Mother and Daddy had given my witch of a sister some good swift kicks long ago, when it still might have done some good.

I did enjoy the loveliness of Mike's farm. It was a thousand acres of blue grass, white board fences stretching uphill and down, out to the horizon. The house was one of the big old white-columned places that were popular in the last century. It was filled with the sort of dark, graceful antiques that you saw in all the big homes around Lexington. Blaine liked everything new and said the whole place was old and musty and creepy. I wouldn't want the care of a big old home like that for myself but it did feel elegant to stay there. Walking out from the house to the pastures reminded me of our farm and the days I used to spend sketching the grass and sky and trees, experimenting to capture the color of the grass or the look of the light. A lot of the time I didn't remember that I'd ever been an artist and it gave me a twinge to be reminded.

Chloe wasn't accustomed to being out in the country any more. She was afraid to go to sleep the first time we went. She wandered back to Mother's rooms after she'd been put to bed and whimpered that she was scared. Mother and I had been chatting together—a rare moment for the two of us to spend time.

"There's nothing to be scared of," I told her, "go on back to bed."

"No, there's ghosts," she said.

"There's no such things as ghosts."

"Yes there are and they're in my room." She started crying.

Mother got to her feet and put out a hand. "Grandma will walk back with you and we'll check the room and I'll tell any ghosts to go away. How will that be, darlin'?" That was all it took. I didn't remember her turning me up sweet like that when I was scared and I didn't appreciate her encouraging Chloe to be so childish.

****

I felt as if I'd been living my life by rote for years. I talked to Mother a few times about wanting to leave Blaine, but she was adamant that Chloe needed to grow up with her father in the house. Hunter and I spent most of our childhoods without a father so I don't know why she felt it was so crucial, but in the absence of her support, I couldn't find the nerve to leave.

No matter how much money Blaine made he never let me have any help. Sometimes I wished I'd kept count of how many times I scrubbed the toilets, polished the furniture, changed sheets or drove to the supermarket. Over the years, the highlight of my day became the time when Chloe came home from school. Of course, as she grew older, she had more and more activities to keep her at school or take her away again as soon as she came home. All that baby cooing and foot tapping turned into musical talent and she took piano and flute and voice lessons, sang in the school choir and played in the orchestra. She won a number of competitions and expressed interest only in music, though she was an honor student all through school. I remembered being surprised that Blaine allowed all that involvement in music but I finally gathered that he thought of it as one of the accomplishments that ladies should have. His disapproval of music as a career was so great that he seemed never to have heard Chloe express any interest in it.

I knew her dreams had to involve music. I didn't say anything to Blaine when the music conservatory catalogs began arriving shortly after he told her she needed to start choosing a college although I wasn't too happy about her choice myself. Of course it had to come out and then I watched him telling her she had to be practical and learn a skill that would earn her money although he assumed she'd get married and be taken care of by her husband. I hoped she would never marry and be turned into some man's slave.

Watching her disappointment, I wished I could tell her about the trust. Mother came to me when Chloe was about five, distressed that the terms of Daddy's will meant that she couldn't do much for Chloe. But she said she had some money put aside and she wanted to start a trust for Chloe. She figured she could keep putting in a little every month and wanted to know if I wanted to contribute. I couldn't come up with too much without arousing Blaine's suspicion and he remained adamantly opposed to having any of us take money from Mother. But I added what I could. I was amazed, as the years went by, to see how large the trust grew between interest income, income from investments the trustees made and the additions that Mother and I continued to make. Mother had a stipulation, though: Chloe would get a small income as soon as Mother died, but she wanted the trust held until Chloe turned 30. Something about wanting Chloe to be mature enough and wanting to give her the means to change her life if she didn't like what she was doing by then. I wished we could use it to let her go to music school, but Mother thought music school was a pointless endeavor ("No security in it") and refused to even ask if she could change the terms of the trust. We agreed that Chloe should not be told—if only to make sure that Hunter and Blaine never got wind of it. So I couldn't even offer her hope for the future.

Blaine got a better job offer from a company back in Lexington toward the end of Chloe's senior year in high school. She wound up deciding to go to the University of Michigan. Her college career sometimes appeared designed to send Blaine wild. She grew her hair long, refused to dress in anything but dreadful looking blue jeans, protested against the war, and dated long-haired boys. She managed to continue being an honor student, though, making it hard for him to complain. Her visits home became shorter and less frequent. I missed her, but the way she and Blaine and Hunter went at it every time she came to see us, I was glad she stayed away. She and Mother were still close but Mother disapproved of what she saw of Chloe's lifestyle and complained to me after Chloe left every time. I lived in terror that Blaine would disown Chloe for violating his stringent moral code or that she would explode one day and disappear like so many young people seemed to do in those days.

Other than worrying about Chloe, I was so relieved to be back in Lexington that, for a time, life seemed much better. We found a nice home out off the Harrodsburg Road in an area that used to be way out in the country. A lot of the old farms I remembered had been eaten up by developments like ours and the gracious lifestyle of my childhood was disappearing. But after Spotswood, life in Lexington was still one of relative refinement. I could still shop at The Bon Mot department store, though all the other shops in downtown Lexington were gone. And people were still warm and friendly and polite.

Many of my friends from school days still lived in the area and I soon picked up the old threads. Josie and I talked regularly and met for lunch often.

"Lily, why don't you take a drawing class or something?"

"Oh, I don't know. I haven't done anything like that in a long time and it would send Blaine into an uproar."

"I swear, I don't understand how you have managed to stay married to him all these years. You know I like Blaine well enough, but I always did think you all were not well suited."

"And you were right," I told her. "But by the time I realized that it had been a mistake, I got pregnant with Chloe, and then it didn't seem right to leave and raise her without a father. Now, I don't know... ."

"Well, with Chloe gone, you should certainly be able to fill some of your time with something you would enjoy. And you were such a fine artist."

After considering her suggestion, I looked into the art classes offered through the extension courses at the university and decided to begin one. At first I didn't tell Blaine and just went to class and made sure that I worked on my assignments when he wasn't around. The teacher said I was really good, much to my surprise, and encouraged me to take more. So I told Blaine one day that I had decided that I wanted to paint again. He wasn't too happy, but I just told him that I intended to do it. For a couple of hours a day, I finally felt alive again.

When we first moved back, I didn't see too much of Hunter. She stayed busy at the magazine. She'd expanded the company quite a bit, I gathered, and seemed to be always scheming to make it bigger. I couldn't imagine how she got any work done when she seemed to be drunk all the time. Then she suddenly quit working, for reasons that didn't seem all that clear. She said that she wanted to devote her time to the horse business. I remembered that she had always wanted to follow in Daddy's footsteps, but Mike's company was a bigger operation than anything she was going to do with horses and it wasn't like her to walk away from all that power. Even after she quit she stayed busy with her rich friends and didn't have much time to spend with me, which was fine. She surprised me one day by telling me that she was glad I was painting again and that she had always thought I was very talented.

Mother's eyesight was not too good. She wanted to have an operation and Hunter was dead set against it. Hunter convinced me that it was too dangerous. But then Chloe urged us to let Mother make up her own mind. Mother hadn't been allowed to drive for years and complained about not getting out and being lonely since so many of her friends had died. She wanted to be able to read and watch television and I couldn't say I blamed her. I was frightened at the thought that something might happen to her, but my small foray back into art brought me an appreciation of the value of freedom to do the things you love. When Hunter complained bitterly about Chloe's intervention, I told her that I wanted Mother to be able to spend whatever time she had left doing the things she liked to do. I had a funny idea that Hunter was terrified at the idea that Mother might not be around any more, even though she'd always bitched about Mother's so-called interference in her life.

Chapter Twenty-one

"She's got to learn to take care of herself, to take charge. She should learn to manage her money better."

"Her car needs a new transmission. I don't want her driving around in some old broken down heap that could fall apart on her in some bad neighborhood."

Blaine and I argued about Chloe regularly by the time she finished college. She went from one low-paying job to another, working for environmental groups that never had enough funding. She was making about five hundred dollars a month and I thought she must be doing a hell of a job of money management if she ate and paid her rent. I didn't want to see where she was living for that kind of money. Then her car needed repair and she asked for help. Blaine would eventually send her the money but not until he'd lectured her about being more careful with her money, taking better care of her things and growing up and getting a real job.

With Chloe gone, the main reason I thought I'd stayed with Blaine all those years no longer existed and yet I didn't make a move. It had been so long since I felt truly alive that I had lost the ability even to remember how to live life another way. I didn't know how I could make it. I hadn't really ever been in the job market except my short-lived job at The Bon Mot. I didn't feel that I could take much money away from Blaine, who had struggled so hard to get what he had and who'd driven himself relentlessly all these years to succeed. I'd started keeping wine hidden in the kitchen pantry so I could have a few glasses while Blaine was gone. Of course, I had to use mouthwash before he came in since he still disapproved of drinking. Some days I drifted in some sort of limbo where I didn't know where I was for hours. Nothing would get done and I'd be surprised when he came home. For some reason, he never said a word though. He just called for pizza or asked if I wanted to go out.

The years we'd spent together weren't all terrible. We both liked movies and musicals and eating good food. We had season tickets every year for one of the local theater companies that put on all the great musicals and we saw many of the Broadway road shows that came through Chicago. Over the years we made some nice friends in Spotswood, many through Blaine's work, some from the neighborhood. Our social life was certainly tame compared to Hunter's and included no one from the social register, but we had pleasant times and I felt more comfortable with our friends than I ever had with hers.

Often it remained pleasant, however, only because I capitulated to Blaine's opinions. He had an opinion on everything. He brooded over things and deduced and figured until he was sure he'd figured out the one and only possible answer and then asserted that answer tenaciously. He tried to be polite to other people who disagreed but he spoke to me as if I were a moron when I expressed another view. I avoided disagreeing and after a while I tried never to form an opinion of my own so I didn't have to worry about letting one slip out at an inopportune moment. Chloe, on the other hand, seemed to make a point of bringing up views that she knew would send him over the edge.

"I think drugs should be legalized," she'd announce casually.

"What on earth would possess you to think something so asinine?" Blaine would reply angrily, his jaw growing tighter and his face taut.

"Well, if drugs were legal they'd probably be less expensive and the people who want to take them could kill themselves without having to mug and murder other people to get money for a fix."

"That's as stupid as anything I've ever heard you say. Obviously drugs have to be illegal." By then his mouth appeared to be caught in an invisible vice grip and the amount of venom spewing from the small space between his lips was frightening.

"Actually, historically drugs were legal and widely used for centuries. It's relatively recent that drugs were made illegal and it seems that the crime and violence have gotten out of hand since then." She'd keep this maddeningly reasonable tone, professorial almost.

Blaine looked increasingly foolish by comparison and that just fueled his fury. "I said this is a ridiculous idea and that's final!"

Sometimes I thought it was a miracle he could get his mouth open at all for the amount of time he spent with his teeth clenched. It seemed to me she made a certain amount of sense, but I couldn't see any point in drawing his fire to me, so I kept quiet and started to clear the dishes. I'd made corn pudding and green beans with country ham—some of Chloe's favorites—but I didn't know if anyone had enjoyed the food.

I spent the first 20 years of my life trying to avoid Hunter's barbs and punches and got away from her just to spend the next 30 years trying to stay hidden from Blaine's sarcastic jibes. I began to wonder if I'd ever find a place for myself where I could just be. I didn't even have much of an idea any more what I would do. I knew I wouldn't spend my days behind the handle of a vacuum or stirring pots on the stove. I just dreamed of the freedom to draw a deep breath and let it out nice and easy and then take another and another, never sucking in and then holding on, tense and afraid that I might have set off another diatribe. In the meantime, the wine helped.

****

Mother became ill while I still hesitated, my life an ongoing question. She'd actually had a variety of minor illnesses over the years, punctuated by the headaches that always plagued her. At times I wondered if she didn't just keep developing ailments because she was bored and lonely. Her bathroom closet looked like a section at the pharmacy: an amazing array of translucent brown bottles, white or blue opaque bottles, black lettering, blue lettering, typed labels, tubes, jars, pills, ointments. When Hunter called to tell me Mother was in the hospital and the doctors thought she'd not last more than a few days I had trouble comprehending that it could be true.

Blaine and I drove to the hospital immediately. Mother was asleep when we arrived. Hunter motioned us out in the hall. She was livid, as usual, and complained that everything was up to her and I was never around when Mother needed something. Since Mother seemed fine the last time I saw her and I'd come the minute Hunter called I couldn't see where I'd failed to take part this time, but Hunter made a career out of being put upon and only grew nastier if I contradicted her, so I swallowed my defense and asked for more news of Mother.

"The doctors haven't been able to make any specific diagnosis, but her vital signs are all poor and getting worse. They just don't think, at her age, that she will pull back out of this." Her eyes misted up and she angrily blinked the tears away. "Since you've never bothered about Mother in all these years, I don't know why this would disturb you."

"That's uncalled for," Blaine told her. I had to say this for Blaine, Hunter's nasty tongue didn't phase him at all and he didn't hesitate to give her her own back.

"You. When have you ever helped? You're the one who waltzed Lily off to Wisconsin and left me to take care of Mother."

"When we moved she didn't need taking care of," Blaine said with finality. "Now, we'll go in to see your mother." He thrust the door open and motioned me inside, glaring defiantly at Hunter.

Mother's white hair was slightly yellow from not being washed recently and was frizzed out around her. She was so tiny and thin that her body barely raised a lump under the covers, giving the appearance that her shoulders and head were all that was left of her. She opened her eyes as we walked in and smiled weakly.

"Hello darlin's."

"Mother, how are you feeling?" I asked lamely.

She glanced ruefully at the tubes in her arm and muttered sadly, "Too tired to fight. I don't want to live like this."

That was the first moment that I knew she really could die. She'd always wanted to live and as she grew older told me periodically that she was afraid to die. I didn't want to believe that I heard her giving up. She lasted past those few days and went home. I went out to the farm and stayed for a couple of weeks, where I could make her tea the way she liked it and keep her company when she was awake. Chloe called often to check on her and she rallied more after those calls than any other time. She wasn't as cheery when I talked with her, but we did have some good conversations.

"I want to tell you something about being a mother," she announced one day. She'd been fading in and out and she seemed only half there but determined to talk.

"Okay, what do you want to tell me?"

"I didn't know this when you were children. Now, it seems so clear.... When you have children of your own you want to protect them from ever being hurt or suffering."

"Why, yes, I suppose that's true."

"The thing is, children are like flowers. Too much light or water or food can be just as bad as not enough care. It's a question of finding the right balance. And every kind of flower has its own needs. But the point, as a gardener, is to create the conditions for the flower to bloom. And every one is uniquely itself. You wouldn't want a rose to become a snapdragon or a hyacinth to turn into a tulip because you appreciate each one for what it is."

"I'm not sure that I understand what you're getting at," I told her, puzzling over her foray into gardening.

"Let Chloe become the kind of flower she is," she said and her eyes locked onto mine for a minute before she drifted away again.

Over the next few months, she faded slowly away. Some days she barely seemed to know who we were. One morning she closed her eyes and never opened them again. She was over 90 and it shouldn't have been such a shock, but she'd always been there. Any time I had a question I knew I could call her and she'd talk with me and finish by making me laugh at some story. At first, when Daddy died and then she went off to the nursing home, I figured she'd leave us like Daddy did and waited nervously for something to happen to her. But nothing happened and she was our mainstay. Over the years it began to seem she would always be there to talk to, help me or Chloe when we needed it and to serve as a buffer between Hunter and the rest of us. It took months for it to sink in with me that she was gone. I'd find myself with the phone in my hand, starting to dial her private number before I remembered that she couldn't answer any more, wouldn't tell any more funny stories and break up, laughing that marvelous laugh of hers.

****

When the estate settled, I found myself with much more money than I had ever expected. Hunter always said Mother was cheap and we could have afforded more, but I never took her seriously. And it wasn't as if we were rich like the Rockefellers or anything. But I slowly realized that I had plenty of money to leave Blaine and live very well without taking anything from him. It took me a while to work up the courage to tell him. I went out and found an apartment and bought some furniture for it before I finally announced that I was leaving.

Just as we started dinner one night, I spoke up. "I need to tell you something," was how I started. Pretty sorry way to start, but it wasn't an easy conversation to have.

He shrugged indifferently, "What about?"

I took a deep breath, quickly trying to decide whether to lead up to the point slowly or get right to it. Then I blurted out, "I want a divorce."

Blaine seemed stunned. "You can't mean that," he said resolutely and began to cut his meat as if that ended it.

"No, I mean it," I told him firmly.

He slammed his cutlery down and shouted, "I don't believe in divorce, and I won't have it."

I didn't know where the strength came from, but nothing in me backed down, "You don't have to want it," I informed him. "This is the 1980's and I can file for a divorce whether you want me to or not."

He suddenly deflated. "What can I do to change your mind?"

"Nothing. It's too late."

"I don't understand. I've always had a good job, provided you with nice houses."

"Do you really think that's all it takes to make a marriage work? Buying a house?"

"Of course not. But we have the same tastes... ."

I cut him off, "No, you imagined that I liked everything you liked and agreed with all your stupid opinions because you're too arrogant and pigheaded to believe that anyone could disagree with you. You never cared what I thought or what I wanted to do or that I wasn't raised to be some household slave." I grew so angry that I was spluttering, but kept on telling him the things I couldn't stand.

He stared at me in disbelief. "Who have you turned into? I would never have believed the girl I married could talk this ugly." He shoved his chair back from the table and stalked out. "File for your damn divorce," he threw over his shoulder.

The next day he asked me again what he could do to change my mind; said he'd do whatever I wanted him to to make me happy. By then I'd accumulated too much anger to forgive him. Besides, our problems came from attitudes and character traits so deeply ingrained in Blaine and differences in background and outlook so fundamental to us both that I couldn't see how any change could be made that would fix it. I'd already made my plans and, in fact, the movers arrived the next day to pick up the things I wanted to take to my new place.

I felt panicky for a while. I'd never been on my own and I didn't know about finances and things. But I found a good CPA and the fellow who'd been handling our investments for years had done a good job, so I took their advice and worked out a budget for myself that meant I spent only income. Hunter kept trying to nose in and give advice and take over managing my money, but I knew that she just wanted to get her hands on it for herself, so I told her no.

Shortly after our divorce was final, Blaine married some much younger woman. I wouldn't have thought he had it in him to get into such a whirlwind romance.

"It wasn't exactly whirlwind, Lily," Josie told me over lunch one day. She'd expanded into comfortable plumpness and still dressed with the same casual disregard for fashion that she'd always shown.

"What do you mean? How do you know about it?"

"Well, a few people have been talking. I hadn't heard anything before—I want you to know that. But since you all divorced and Blaine remarried, several people have mentioned to me that he was seen with her here and there for quite a while." I just sat transfixed. "Lily, are you all right? I didn't think it would bother you at this point."

I began to laugh. "No, no it doesn't bother me. Blaine. Who'd have figured? All this time I stayed there listening to all his moralizing, and worrying about upsetting him by leaving—and that hypocrite was running around with some bimbo. Blaine." I laughed harder. "Would you have ever in a million years thought Blaine...?"

Josie looked bewildered at first, then she thought about it and burst out laughing too.

****

When Mother's will was read, the news about Chloe's trust finally came out. Blaine was torn between anger over Chloe getting an unearned handout and pleasure that Mother had set something up for his daughter. Hunter, on the other hand, was purely and simply outraged. Her fury that anything that might have come to her went to Chloe instead flamed as hot as any temper tantrum I'd seen her throw—especially after she found out how much was in the trust.

"That was money Daddy intended for me!" she declared.

"Hunter, Daddy's estate came to both of us," I reminded her, "but the income was Mother's to use as she pleased."

Hunter cut me off, "Oh, and of course it pleased her to hand over money to that good-for-nothing daughter of yours instead of compensating me for all I've sacrificed."

"Please, you charged Mother for everything while she lived there. And I can't believe that with half of Daddy's estate added to the millions Mike left you that you actually begrudge Chloe even this small trust."

"I charged Mother? What about all those checks that went out to you and Chloe all these years? They should have taken away some of your share of the estate for all the money you took ahead of time."

From that point on she was forever bringing up the unfairness of it all and making dark references to how I'd robbed Mother. Usually she was so drunk it wasn't worth bothering to argue with her. The one disadvantage to leaving Blaine when Mother wasn't around either was that Hunter felt free to attack me any time. I heard from Chloe that she was getting ugly, drunken phone calls from her aunt, "the wicked bitch," threatening to challenge the trust.

It didn't take long before I realized that I couldn't stay in the same city as Hunter. I felt restless anyway, bored with just having get togethers with my old friends and taking art classes. Josie had been spending winters on Sanibel Island in Florida since her husband died a few years before and talked about moving down there permanently. Chloe had visited friends down there several times and said it was gorgeous. So I accepted Josie's invitation to go down and visit for a couple of weeks.

Sanibel enchanted me. The wildlife preserve was endlessly fascinating. Lush plants arrayed in every shade of green imaginable with bold flowers nestled in their midst and multihued birds flying, preening, and hunting throughout. The sunsets over the Gulf were magnificent. As I watched the pageantry of brilliant pinks and yellows, lavenders and oranges in the billowing clouds, memories of drawing and painting out on the farm and at the ocean came bubbling up and I went over to Fort Myers to buy some sketchbooks and water colors. In between painting sessions, I looked at houses, consulted with my accountant about what I could afford and bought myself a nice house on the beach.

I took my time about moving. The kitchen needed renovation and the whole place needed refurbishing. I made arrangements to get the work started and returned to Lexington to begin laying plans for the move. I decided to keep my apartment in Lexington for the time being and see whether I could afford it. I'd keep it furnished as it was and buy the sort of light and delicate pieces that seemed to belong in Florida for the new house. On one of my later trips down there to check on the progress of the house, I arranged for carpeting to be laid and brought in a painter. I had the whole place done in the pinks and greens I loved. By then those were fashionable colors and the array of choices let me fine tune each room to my exact desires. I changed the shades and the percentages of green and pink from room to room so that everything blended yet every room was distinct.

Life was quiet down there. I spent hours sketching and painting. Of course, I assumed it was just a hobby. Through Josie, I met quite a few people quickly and really enjoyed my new friends. I'd never really decided what I wanted to do with my life and by then it seemed too late to do more than salvage what I could, enjoy living with no one criticizing or getting angry. After a while, I even put some of my own pastels and watercolors on the walls.

****

Chloe started seeing a therapist. She felt her life was really in limbo. I was terribly afraid that meant she would decide that something I did had blighted her life. I wasn't sure I liked this trend for everyone to see a therapist. I supposed that if she really felt it was doing some good she should keep at it. Of course she wouldn't have listened to me if I tried to tell her she shouldn't do it. She'd have made some sarcastic remark. Actually, she reminded me of Hunter sometimes.

Not long after she started in with the therapy, I was painting down on the beach one day when a woman came along and started watching me. I didn't especially like being watched like that, but I'd learned that if you painted out on the beach you were going to have gawkers, so I tried to ignore her and just kept working.

After a while, she moved closer and said, "That's really very good."

"Thank you," I told her and kept painting.

"I don't think I've seen your work in any of the galleries around here. Are you showing your things some place else?"

"Showing them?" I laughed. "No. I just paint for myself. I don't think I'm good enough to sell them."

"You haven't sold any paintings?" She sounded incredulous. "My dear, we should talk."

"We should?" I stared at her. "Why should we?"

"Well, I own the Thorn Bird gallery over in Venice. I think this is really good. I'd like to see some of your other paintings and talk about putting a few of them in my gallery."

I was flabbergasted. After I pulled myself together enough to speak, we arranged for her to meet me back at my house in an hour. I showed her the room full of my paintings and she became very enthusiastic. She invited me to bring six of my paintings to her gallery and told me that if I liked the place, she'd show them. The next day I loaded up the paintings and drove down to Venice. It was an interesting gallery. There were other paintings with fairies and spirits and devas. She said it was all New Age or inspirational work. I hadn't known there was such a thing, but my paintings fit right in.

We discussed prices and valued each painting in line with the other paintings she was showing. I was stunned at the prices she thought I could get. I left the six paintings with her and she called the next week to tell me that three of them had already sold. She wanted me to bring more. And she thought I should put together a show.

My head was spinning. Even though my more recent art teachers had been really enthusiastic about my work, I had been so convinced that I was not very good, that I just assumed it was something that I would do for my own pleasure and nothing else. All of a sudden several thousand dollars worth of paintings sold in one week and she thought it would keep happening.

The show was a couple of months later. I mentioned it to Hunter on the phone, not making any big deal of it. Much to my surprise, she came down to visit for the show. There was a big party the day the show opened. The gallery was packed with people munching hors d'oeuvres and sipping champagne. There were critics and artists and dealers and gallery owners from all over the place and they really liked my work. Hunter turned on the charm and really worked the room for me and helped me past my shyness by leading the conversations when people came up to shake my hand and congratulate me.

"That was quite something, Lily," she told me when we got home later that night. "She really seemed to have good connections. I hadn't expected from what you told me that she'd produce such a collection of big names for you."

"I know. This all came out of the blue. I never figured that some woman who came walking up to me on the beach was this big deal gallery owner."

"It looked like she was making some sales."

"Yes, I think she was. Of course, the exhibit is for the week. So there may be a few sold by the end."

"Well, I think this is wonderful. Really, I'm so pleased."

Everything in the exhibit sold and people were asking for more. Suddenly when I wandered out to the beach or into the forest preserve to paint the things I wanted to paint, it was an act of tremendous value. I smiled to myself every time I thought about it. I thought maybe I finally understood more about why Chloe felt she had to give music a real try.

****

I talked to Hunter a little more often after that visit. I was so touched by her support for my opening. And, as the pictures kept selling she seemed genuinely pleased and proud. I noticed every time I talked to her that her speech was slurred. I stopped drinking as soon as I divorced Blaine. I hadn't realized how much it affected me until I noticed how much better I felt when I quit. Hunter had been drinking so much more for so much longer, I couldn't help but worry—especially about her liver.

We met in Chicago to go hear Chloe's band nearly a year after that. Chloe was so good I couldn't believe that Blaine and I hadn't pushed her to follow her musical interest. And I thought her boyfriend, Jamie, was great. Mike used to look at Hunter that way, but otherwise I don't know when I've seen a man look so obviously in love with a woman.

Hunter and I had a nice time shopping on Michigan Avenue and wandering through the art galleries together. She never much liked to go to galleries and museums, but she tried to really take an interest and ask me questions. It was fun. But she started drinking at breakfast every day and kept it up till we went to bed. She enjoyed hearing Chloe and meeting Jamie, but she seemed to be just going through the motions.

When I got home, I talked with Chloe about Hunter. She told me about a conversation they had when we were all in Lexington and said Hunter had been very depressed and talked about wanting to be with Mike. I tried to call Hunter more often and brought up Chloe's suggestion that she try the Betty Ford Clinic. She didn't want to hear it though.

In spite of my worry, it came as a huge shock when the call came in shortly after that, informing me that after leaving a party out in the country Hunter lost control of her car on a curve and crashed into a tree. They said that she was killed instantly and wrote it off as a drunk driving accident. I wonder how accidental it was. Suddenly I look back over the years since Mike's death and question whether she really ever recovered. She always seemed so strong and tough, so take charge, that I just felt cowed by the force of her energy. But for all the gruffness, I think she was more sensitive than any of us realized. We all wondered what the real story was behind her sudden departure from Mike's company and it did appear after that that she deteriorated.

After all the years that I loathed her and wished that I'd been an only child, I was surprised to realize that I missed her. Suddenly I just remembered the times that she stood up for me about my art or kept the other girls from being mean to me, and her support at my exhibition. If I hadn't been so afraid, if I'd tried to get to know the person behind the ornery facade, I wonder whether we could have been better friends. At any rate, I'm glad that we were closer for a little while before she died.

Virginia

Chapter Twenty-two

A couple of hours of chopping, mixing and baking wore me out and I sat, exhausted, on one of the hard kitchen chairs. I stared at my hands for a moment, trying to remember when and how they'd become so gnarled and twisted. At each joint the fingers turned a new direction as if they'd forgotten which way they grew. My nails were filed and polished as always. After so much activity the joints were red and throbbing.

I glanced around the kitchen. Hunter remodelled it when she and Mike moved into his family's house and it still shone, though the years had taken small tolls. It was one of those huge old kitchens where the cooking had once been done in a giant fireplace by an array of servants. Now cupboards and counters surrounded the room; an enormous refrigerator hummed in the corner and a large oven with a stove top of four burners and a warmer gleamed in the middle of one wall. She had a new dishwasher under the sink. So different from the kitchen in which Grandmama taught me to cook. Behind the refrigerator door sat a roast leg of lamb, resting in my special wine sauce, prepared ahead and kept perfectly fresh. Amazing.

A big old oak table stood in the middle of the room. Matching chairs surrounded it. I gazed at the big platter of warm, golden meringues that were cooling on one end of the table. Chloe loved egg kisses. Blaine and Lily were driving down with her that day and I had everything ready.

It took me a while to adjust when both my girls were married and I was alone in the house. After a while I bought what they called a ranch style home so I wouldn't have to climb so many stairs by myself. I chose a place with two extra bedrooms so the children could still come to stay. And I picked out the sweetest cat at the Humane Society. He was all black and I named him Max. Max loved to climb into my arms and nestle his head under my chin. He'd nudge my chin until I kissed the top of his head a few times and then he'd go to sleep. What a comfort he was to me.

My house was red brick with dark shutters and a big yard. A tall fence surrounded the backyard with a row of evergreens in front of it so that I had some privacy. I brought a gardener in to help me plant tulip bulbs and roses, narcissus, honeysuckle, snapdragons, mums and asters and lots of azaleas. I had a covered porch back there and could sit with my flowers around me and enjoy the colors and fragrances. Morning glories trailed luxuriantly along a trellis to the roof and hummingbirds zoomed up, nearly disappearing as they sampled the flowers. I put a patch of mint in right next to the porch so that it was easy to pick a sprig for my iced tea every day. I'd never been able to arrange everything only for my own convenience before and, once I grew accustomed to long hours alone, I relished even such small decisions as the placement of mint.

Lily married a very nice young man named Blaine. He came from a somewhat poor family although they at least had some education. He lacked polish and I don't know that I'd have chosen him for Lily as they seemed rather mismatched, but she said she loved him and I had no intention of interfering with that, so I never spoke to her about it. No one could accuse me of marrying her off for money. He was as handsome a man as I'd seen in many a day, with dimples when he smiled that could take your breath away. I could see why a girl as shy as Lily was dazzled. I just hoped she understood there was a lot more to the package than his good looks.

He was good hearted and liked to be helpful, but my, what a stiff-spined, righteous sort of man he was. A preacher's son, he had a lot of high moral values and the sort of prudish sense of right and wrong that seems to characterize the working classes. Hunter of course found him unbearable and would not hold her tongue so that I had to step in many times to prevent a major skirmish. I dreaded gatherings of the whole family for that reason.

Fortunately, Hunter married a lovely man. He was a great deal older than she was—almost as much older than her as Jack was older than me—and that worried me. She was so determined to marry someone rich that I wondered if I had somehow unwittingly given her the idea that she should. Of course I worried a great deal about money during the Depression, particularly after Miles died and I suppose I talked to the girls about it. Hunter swore I never made her feel pressured to marry a rich man, so I tried not to dwell on it. Around Mike, Hunter behaved better than she ever had—well, better than she had since her father's death. I guessed she must have heard the lessons I tried to teach her about being well-behaved and just chose to pretend that she never learned any of it, because she seemed to know what to do once she put her mind to it. Mike was always kind to Lily, who, I must admit, was terribly shy, and unfailingly cordial to Blaine whom I was sure he didn't really like. But, then, Mike was always a gentleman. His mother was a lovely woman, very charming. I used to be terribly fond of her.

****

Lily lost several babies before she finally had Chloe. The first time she was devastated. By the time Hunter and I got to the hospital, she was being discharged. They brought her out in a wheelchair and she couldn't stop crying. The times after that she never let on that it bothered her. We'd all begun to think she simply could not have a child when she suddenly had one. Mike and Hunter never talked about having children. I privately thought that Hunter was probably too self-centered to be a mother so I felt that it was probably just as well. Mike was crazy about Chloe though. Of course everyone was. That child was born with a twinkle in her eye and a chuckle on her lips. In no time you could bounce toys over her and get her to play. From the beginning she had a shock of black hair like Blaine's and her eyes were soon the same intensely dark brown as Lily's.

I felt closer to Chloe, from the day she was born, than I'd felt to anyone but Adrian and Freddie. She had this knowing look from the beginning and it seemed she already really knew me and liked me. We laughed and played for hours. Once she could toddle around, we chased around the house together and had a grand time. Hunter and Lily continually fretted that I shouldn't exert myself so much. I actually thought the two of them were jealous of that little slip of a girl.

As she grew I did wonder whether Chloe might be too rambunctious. She laughed loud and long, hollered with abandon and generally exuded life and verve irrepressibly. She was far livelier even than Hunter had been, though never ill-tempered, and I worried whether she would become just as out of control. At the same time, her laughter was infectious and she attracted people like moths to a flame.

"Lily, Chloe is a darling child, of course, but don't you think she should tone down a little, maybe?" I finally asked.

"Oh, Mother, I try to keep her more quiet. Sometimes she drives me wild with all her running around and chattering. And she really gets on Blaine's nerves. He wants her to sit still and look at books or something. I'm trying to get her to enjoy being more quiet, but she cries if I try to hold her still."

Mike kept saying we should leave her alone. But I was glad to know Lily was trying. It must have worked, because by the time she was three, Chloe was much more quiet. We still had a lot of fun when she came to visit, especially when Lily or Blaine dropped her off to spend time alone with me. Every now and then she seemed nervous to me but I decided I must be imagining things because I didn't think children that age could be nervous.

Chloe was four when Blaine got a better job in Wisconsin and they all moved north. With Chloe gone I felt lonelier than I'd ever been. Funny, she wasn't even old enough that we could really talk about things, but she brought such light into my life it was hard to see her go. She'd reached the point where she asked about everything. We'd walk in the garden and she'd put out a finger and ever so gently touch a flower and want to know its name. Her reverence for growing things was quite something. She never picked a flower without permission or even knocked petals off or broke a branch with a careless move. The same gentleness extended to Max and he'd climb into her arms and cuddle into her neck just the way he did with me.

I hated for Chloe to grow up in the north. I never did think too much of the people up there. Some of them were good hearted enough I supposed but they were careless about manners and courtesies that we in the South were always civilized enough to observe. I hoped to see Chloe come back one day and I wanted her to behave like she'd been well brought up. Lily said the northerners were rude. I knew Blaine got a much better position there and all but it distressed me to hear Lily talk about how lonely and bleak it was and she was too far away for me to really help. I called her every week though.

She complained about Blaine all the time and told me now and then that she wanted to leave. I told her no child should be left to wonder why her father didn't want to live with her any more. She clearly didn't understand, but she obeyed me, as always. Blaine was a difficult man, I knew. He worked hard and moved ahead in business but he still came from a poor family and he never seemed to become easy about money or his new position. He refused to hire any help for Lily and she worked so hard. I never gave my daughters the kind of rigorous training that Mama gave to me and Lily wasn't used to keeping house all alone.

Georgie missed Chloe and Lily too. The four of us had gone to lunch or visited often. Georgie never got over being sorry that Lily stopped sketching and painting, but the two of them stayed close. Chloe's delight in Georgie's garden and interest in all the treasures from around the world pleased her a great deal. She said it reminded her of Lily as a little girl. Georgie was some years older than I and a year or two after the children moved away I began to notice that she had more difficulty getting around. She had to stop driving and I always had to fetch her when we went out together. I tried to drop by more often and to take her things I thought she'd need. It

was nice for both of us because I enjoyed filling my time with more visits to her house.
****

When Mike died I was almost as devastated as if he'd been my own child. I'd known him since he was a boy. A couple of years after I came to Lexington, I was out at the Polo Club one day when his mother brought him out to the pool. She had his hair fixed in ringlets so he looked like a big sissy but he jumped right in and began splashing everyone as if to dispel any notion he might not be all boy. He wasn't even 60 yet and appeared to be healthy as could be when he died so suddenly.

I worried for months about Hunter. Her whole life had revolved around Mike. I'd never understood their lifestyle, but the constant travel and partying and business, all intertwined in some complicated fashion, suited Hunter to a tee. She'd by and large stopped pulling outlandish pranks by the time she began working for the Journal; under Mike's eye she minded her p's and q's. I waited for her to grieve or show some sign of pain and she did break down with me one day, but she quickly returned to the magazine and in no time began expanding the company.

The two of them drank too much, of course. At least I thought so. They had drinks at lunch and drinks at dinner and drinks all through the evening. Every now and then some rumor floated back to me about Hunter becoming too loud or staggering around or something when she drank too much. Any time I mentioned her drinking she snapped my head off and told me to mind my own business. While Mike was alive, he kept an eye on her and I had the idea he lit into her when she carried on too much. Still, as much as he drank, he couldn't very well tell her to stop drinking. I suspected he liked her to drink with him just like Miles had wanted me to join him.

After Mike died, all the boundaries and limits within which Hunter had been living disappeared in no time. Nasty remarks followed one after another as if they'd been held back and collected while she tried to please Mike all those years and then, freed by his absence, broke uncontrollably to freedom. I never saw Mike do anything openly to control her, never heard him tell her what she should or shouldn't do. I watched for that, fearful that he'd curtail her the way Jack and Miles hemmed me in—only I wasn't sure Hunter could take it. But Mike worked some kind of magic on Hunter. I watched my incorrigible daughter become a likeable young woman.

Of course, she'd always been able to be charming at will and Mike gave her all the things she always wanted. I'd noticed that her worst temper flares came whenever she felt she wasn't getting what she wanted or deserved. Even though Mike left her everything, she became dissatisfied and complained often about things not going her way or things she thought should be hers. I was troubled by her attitude toward Lily and Chloe. She was extremely jealous and decided somewhere along the way that everything her father left belonged to her.

One day when Lily and Chloe were in town visiting, Hunter dropped by and came to me in the living room, dragging a frightened Chloe with her. "Mother, I caught Chloe taking one of Daddy's silver plates out of the cabinet. I swear, she's just like her mother—always trying to get her hands on everything."

"Hunter, what on earth gets into you? You're frightening the child," I told her, and pulled Chloe to me. "I was telling her about the races and going down to the winner's circle with your father and I told her to go get one of the trophies," I explained and then informed her, "These trophies belong to me and not to you. If I chose to give one to Chloe or a stranger on the street, it would be none of your business."

"Give them away!" she spluttered. "Daddy left that estate for us, for his family, not so some preacher's son could waltz off with it."

"I might remind you that Lily and Chloe are just as much a part of Miles's family as you are," I retorted. "Furthermore, most of that estate came from my first husband, Jack, who had no reason to care if you ever saw a penny of it." I'd never said much about Jack and I probably shouldn't have brought it up then, but I admit I enjoyed the stunned expression on Hunter's face almost as much as I enjoyed rendering her speechless, for once. "No, go put on some tea and then see if Lily is awake and would like some."

"Grandma, why is Hunter so mean?" Chloe turned those brown eyes to me, opened wide in question.

"I wish I knew darlin'. I wish I knew. I don't think she means to be so ugly."

"Mommy says she was born mean."

"Here, now, let's not have that sort of talk about your Aunt Hunter," I told her, although I thought it was true and wondered how Lily, who arrived on the scene so much later, knew.

Hunter never asked any more questions about Jack and soon displayed the same possessiveness and greediness as before and used the same irrational argument about Miles, just as if she'd never heard anything to the contrary.

About six months after Mike died, she began dropping by my house and telling me how worried she was about me. I had no idea what she was talking about. I got around fine. Flo had been taking care of the house for me for several years. I owned a nice Buick and shopped or visited with friends regularly and my health was all right for my age. Soon she began talking about bringing me out to live with her. At first I fought, not at all anxious to give up the experience of freedom I'd never had. After a while, though, I began to realize that she was lonely without Mike and she needed me but didn't want to say so. That was just like Hunter to turn it around and insist that she was doing it for me.

I finally agreed to go out to the farm for a few months, if we could arrange for Flo to keep my house up. Sitting on my porch one day I suddenly changed my mind. I'd planted many of the same flowers that I'd had in my little plot back on the farm in Tennessee. Staring out at the bright blossoms, I found myself back on the farm. It was May and the bulb plants were just waning as the heliotropes, sunny twinkles, and baby's breath began to bloom. I kneeled and carefully pulled every tiny weed I saw before standing up with two big patches of dirt on the front of my old calico work dress.

All my chores were done and I hurried off to change out of the dirty dress and clean up for dinner. As Sarah finished fastening my dress there were shouts of laughter out in the yard and then a big commotion with shouts of "Oh no, look out." I twisted away from Sarah to peer out the window.

"Ahhh!" I screeched. "Look what they've done." I turned and ran down the stairs and out into the yard where a wheelbarrow was upended in the midst of my garden. A pile of dirt covered a patch of sunny twinkles. A few bedraggled daisies emerged from beneath the wheels while others laid flat and still others were upended with their roots in the air. Tommy was picking himself up from where he had pulverized some of the last hyacinths and the early roses and lavender. Bob and Charley were doubled over laughing a few feet away. When I got there they straightened up and tried to look serious.

"You did it on purpose, didn't you?" I accused.

"Ginnie, it was an accident," Charley assured me.

"There's no reason you had to be near my garden with that thing."

"We were rolling it near here on the way to the barn," Bob chimed in.

"And then you wheeled it into my garden and dumped all that dirt by accident. I'll get you all for this."

"Really, we were clowning around and we should have been more careful, but it was an accident." Tommy had been brushing dust and flower petals off his clothes with a sheepish expression on his face.

As I picked up a daisy, tiny white petals dropped slowly to the ground. "I'll get you all for this," I repeated and turned to storm back into the house before they could see me crying.

One day the next week, Mama insisted that I help her deliver the eggs. When I came back I saw the boys on their knees by my garden plot. I jumped down from the cart before it even stopped and ran over to see what they were doing. I stopped short a few feet back, swallowing wrathful words in amazement. The garden had been restored, new plants trembling in the spaces left by the wheelbarrow.

The boys stood up, shuffling their feet and grinning like they'd just won a big game. Tommy, hands shoved in his pockets, spoke up, "We, uh, felt bad about your garden. We really didn't mean to do it. So we went around town and talked to all the ladies with big gardens and offered to pay them for a few plants to transplant into your garden."

Bob cut in to say, "Mama told us which kinds of flowers to ask for and most all the ladies gave us some flowers when they heard what happened."

"Then we asked Mama to keep you away today," Charley finished.

Remembering that day, I missed my brothers. I'd never met their children or Tommy's and Bobby's wives. So many years and milestones had gone by out of my reach. With time my reasons for abandoning the boys dwindled in importance, replaced with a vague disquiet at all we'd lost. I didn't want to wake up one day wishing that I'd had more time to make my peace with my difficult daughter.

Even so, at that point I had no intention of selling my house and staying with Hunter. I assumed she'd get tired of having me around since she'd complained all her life that I interfered too much. Instead, she insisted that I sell my house and make the move permanent. I kept saying no and she became increasingly belligerent, then started calling Lily and telling her that I couldn't live on my own any more until Lily started panicking and asking what was wrong. Eventually I grew tired of fighting and agreed to the change on the condition that I have a suite of rooms upstairs to myself.

It came as a shock that I'd become so old that my daughters thought I might need looking after. The white of my hair and the twists of my fingers proved daily that I had, in fact, grown old. But in many ways I didn't feel so different from the young girl who swirled around a ballroom in Adrian's arms and naively imagined her dreams were coming true. Sixty intervening years had etched themselves on my body, but I was still me and I couldn't fathom that so much time had gone by.

＊＊＊＊

As soon as Chloe learned to write her first words, she began sending me notes. They arrived regularly, printed in uneven letters of varied sizes and, at first, not saying much, really just showing me the new words she'd learned. In a twinkling she could write sentences and she'd tell me that she loved me and missed me. I didn't know what Blaine and Lily told her about Mike but she seemed to have difficulty grasping what death meant. In her notes and on the phone, she kept asking when Mike would be coming back. "I need to talk to Uncle Mike," she'd tell me.

How I looked forward to her visits. I sent Flo to the grocery to buy Chloe's favorites and had her make egg kisses. Hunter grew more irritable a few days before a visit was to begin. Flo and I readied two guests rooms. I wanted to put some children's pictures and toys in Chloe's room but Hunter insisted that Chloe shouldn't be encouraged to be so childish and it didn't seem worth the energy to fight her. I put flowers in there, though.

When she was six, Chloe announced on arrival that she was learning how to play piano and that she wanted to be a singer when she grew up.

"Oh darlin', ladies don't get up in front of people like that," I told her.

I figured at her age she'd change her mind a number of times, so I didn't worry much about the music idea. I didn't want to dictate to her what she must do and I wanted her to have some measure of freedom as an adult to pursue some sensible career of her choice. Since Miles left my money tied up, I couldn't directly give a share to Chloe, but my income was generous and I'd saved quite a bit from the extra money I received every month. I set up a trust with the savings and arranged to add a small amount every month. I told Lily about it and she began sending small additions when she could. I insisted that Chloe had to wait until she was 30 to receive the principal. Lily fought me, arguing that the money would do her more good when she was younger toward setting her up in something she wanted to do. But I wanted to be sure that Chloe used the money wisely and that she would be old enough to protect herself from Hunter.

On every visit with her parents, Chloe wriggled out the door of the car as soon as it drove up, yelling, "Grandma," and came flying into my arms before her parents had even opened their doors. I held her tight and got ready to enjoy every minute. I collected memories every time she visited and used them to brighten some of the long hours in the many months when I did not see her. When she was older, her parents started letting her fly down to spend more time in the summers with me. With her friend Maggie, she was in and out, up and down, laughing, playing—bringing life into the place.

Chapter Twenty-three

I watched television for hours some days, a gauze patch taped over one eye and the other gazing blearily at all sorts of programs. I loved Lawrence Welk, but so many of those shows were silly. I lived most of my life without television and I always found more pleasure in reading, but after my cataract operation, I couldn't focus on a book for very long. It fascinated me that on a box in my room I could watch an orchestra and singers and dancers who performed in some faraway place. When I was a girl we wouldn't even have dreamed of wanting such a thing.

I remembered back to my girlhood on the farm. Between chores and schoolwork and hearty play outdoors, our hours stayed full and we dropped into bed early and slept long and hard. Tommy and I exchanged notes at Christmas time for many years, but when I moved out to Hunter's place I lost his address and he didn't write to me the next Christmas. He told me years ago that Jimmy died. There'd been no news of Charley for decades. He'd have been over 90 so I supposed he'd died. When I found out what Mama did and realized that I'd been the sacrifice so my brothers could have better lives, I just didn't feel part of them any more. Not one of them ever thanked me. But when I recalled attacks at the outhouse, playing soldiers and skipping stones, I felt some small measure of regret. Water under the bridge, I decided.

Chloe came in with a tablet of paper one day and asked me all kinds of questions about my family.

"Your father left? That happened back then? Why did he leave?"

"How would I know? I was just a little girl. These things happen."

Then I started telling her my brothers' names.

"You had four brothers? Where are they?"

"I don't know," I told her matter-of-factly.

"You don't know where you brothers are? How could you just lose track of your brothers?" she asked incredulously.

She exclaimed over the 10 half brothers and sisters too. I didn't feel like getting into all that. I left and when I looked back it was too late, so I could see no point in bringing it up. "That's enough questions," I told her. "You've given me the headache. Go find something else to do."

Chloe was always a sweet child, though. She never minded giving me her arm and walking as slowly as I needed and she sent me lovely notes and called me up often. She always got top grades in school and was smart about everything. Raised up there with those Yankees, she said "yeah" instead of "yes ma'am" or "yes sir" and forgot to stand up when her elders came into a room as well as other annoying lapses in manners. I told Blaine and Lily they shouldn't take her up there. She begged to come back down here to live with me and go to Carter but they wouldn't let her. I'd have been delighted to have her but I worried about how she'd get on with Hunter. It seemed the older Chloe got the more Hunter tried to change her and the angrier she became with Hunter. If she lived here it would be much more difficult to keep them separated—it was wearing enough for a few weeks in the summer.

"All that time she spends practicing voice and piano could be much better spent on trying to get ahead in some more practical way," Hunter said.

"Hunter, she loves to play and she must be talented—she's won all kinds of awards."

"You don't actually approve of her ambition to sing do you?"

"Of course not as a career, but ladies have learned to play piano and sing for generations and I don't see why she shouldn't enjoy it."

"Well, with her nose in sheet music and books all the time, she's not making connections that can help her get ahead."

"Oh, connections, phooey! Not everyone wants the life you have."

"Nonsense. Everyone wants to know rich people and one day Chloe will wake up and realize she wants it too. I just hope it won't be too late."

Hunter never had been able to understand Lily and she was just as bad about Chloe. I couldn't decide how well they understood her. They certainly saw the meanness of spirit and greediness that Hunter never saw in herself. But in their anger, I thought they missed her charm and the drive that accomplished such impressive work. Without Mike, she carried on with the magazine and expanded the company. I thought it was peculiar when she suddenly quit, but she'd always wanted to be in her daddy's business and she said she wanted to put her attention on her horses. Seemed to me her manager did everything for the horses while she went to parties and drank, but I didn't mention it, not caring to have my head snapped off.

****

"Is this where I turn Grandma?" Chloe asked one day as she drove me to the beauty parlor. We left early, but by then we were a few minutes late. It was the first summer she had a driver's license and she didn't know her way around Lexington very well. She sat tensely forward, gripping the steering wheel. My eyes had gotten so bad that I couldn't see much and the shop was in a newly built up area that was unfamiliar to me. Those new areas always seemed so barren with their little scraggly trees and plain little boxy houses. Everything looked the same.

Panic rose, as it did every time I realized that my sight would soon be gone and I cried to her, "I can't see, Chloe. I don't know where we are. Lexington has changed so... and I can't see." I looked frantically from side to side, trying to recognize something that would help her.

"It's all right, Grandma," she answered. "I'll find a phone and call for directions or something. It'll be fine." She spoke with forced brightness, trying, as always, to make me feel better.

"No. My eyes are getting worse all the time. Some days I can't read. I hate this, Chloe. I hate being old." I couldn't remember when I had cried to anyone as I cried to her that day.

"Oh, Grandma, I'm sorry. Can't the doctor do something for your eyes?"

"What could the doctor do? I'm old, Chloe. My eyes are just giving out." I squinted out the window fruitlessly and cried again as I told her, "I'm afraid I'll never see Lily's face again."

Just then she pulled into a driveway and drove back into a shopping center. "There must be a phone back in here somewhere," she said, then started laughing.

"What's so funny?" I demanded to know.

"We just pulled up to the shop," she chuckled. "We've been past this shopping center five times." She burst out laughing.

"Oh, for heaven's sake," I laughed too.

****

Hunter often gave dinner parties and cocktail parties at the house. She hired caterers and parking attendants, set Flo polishing silver and brought out the fine linen tablecloths. She never invited me to join, but I knew many of her guests and during each party one or two at a time came up to see me. I enjoyed every visit.

Most of my friends were dead or in nursing homes and I spent much of my time alone. Georgie died in the nursing home. Every time I went out to see her she was pitiful and I hadn't been in months when the news arrived that she'd died. It seemed I never managed to be there for my friends in the end. I hated those homes. Every time Hunter got mad at me she threatened to put me in one of them. I tried to assume she didn't really mean to carry through on her threat—I never thought Hunter was as mean as she seemed. Now and then, though, doubts nagged at me and I feared that she really was as bad as Lily and Chloe claimed.

Sometimes even five or six people at a time wound up in my room at her parties. I'd get to telling stories to a couple of people and we'd be laughing and a couple more would come in and stay and then more. If the party wasn't a large one, Hunter lit into me afterwards as if I forced them to come see me. I just ignored her though and enjoyed myself when I had the chance.

"Miz Harrison, how are you?" said Mimi. "Hunter was tellin' us that you had a bad fall." Mimi was one of the only close friends from Hunter's school days who remained close. Hunter ran most people off sooner or later.

"Oh, yes. It was the funniest thing," I began. "Sonny Wilson from the bank came out to bring me some papers. No one else was here when the doorbell rang, and I was upstairs. I hurried out to the staircase and hallooed to him. The big door was open and I could see him through the screen. Then, I'm not sure what happened, but my feet went out from under me all of a sudden and I began falling. I heard Sonny shriek, 'Oh my lord.' I banged into the wall and turned around and fell head first all the way downstairs."

"Oh my God. Were you hurt?"

"Well, I couldn't get up. But I looked up and saw Sonny yanking at the screen door. It was latched, of course, so he couldn't get it open. He kept repeating, 'Miz Harrison oh my lord Miz Harrison oh my lord.' Then..." I had to stop myself from laughing so I could talk, "after a while he started butting his head against the door, still shouting, 'oh my lord Miz Harrison.' It was one of the funniest sights I ever did see. Lord, I wish you all could have seen Sonny with that big bald head of his... ." I got to giggling so hard I couldn't go on.

When the others stopped chuckling, Mimi asked again if I'd been hurt. I did crack a rib. One of my shoes dragged along the wall and made a mark on the paper that Hunter was really mad about. My glasses broke and there was a little cut on my temple. At the time I thought every bone was broken and I could hardly move for days. After a while, I just remembered the sight of poor Sonny and I figured the story was worth it.

****

After the day Chloe and I got so lost I decided to check with the eye doctor one more time about my eyes. He told me several years before that I was developing cataracts and left me with the impression that not much could be done about it. I began to wonder, like Chloe, if something could keep me from losing my sight and that's when I finally pressed him until he told me about the surgery. But he didn't recommend it for me.

"Virginia, I've known you for years and I know how stubborn you can be when your mind's made up about something, but this is dangerous for someone your age."

"Dr. Hazelton, what kind of life am I going to have if I can't see? Reading and watching the television are almost my only amusements now. What do I do when I can't see well enough to do either?"

He quit fighting me after we argued back and forth for a while and gave me the number of the surgeon he'd recommended. Then I told Hunter what I planned to do. Of course, I didn't mention anything about danger. She called the doctor, though, and he pointed it out to her. Well, she ranted and railed and roped Lily into calling me. Both of them were nearly hysterical as they listed reasons why I couldn't do this. Then I gathered that they turned to Chloe and asked her to talk some sense into me. She called and just asked me what I wanted to do.

"I want to be able to see," I answered.

"Mom says it's dangerous."

"Well, I suppose it could be."

"I don't want anything to happen to you Grandma."

"I know you don't darlin'," I told her, "but I don't want to live without my sight."

"You might not live through the operation."

"There's always a risk with surgery. The doctor just said the risk is greater because of my age. He didn't say that it was likely to happen."

"Well, if you know the risks and you've made the decision, I don't see why we should influence you not to. Maybe if I talk to Mom and Hunter about how much it means to you to be able to see, they'll change their minds."

After we hung up, I heard Hunter's phone ring. I waited a while for her to have time to finish—speculating on why my granddaughter could understand so much about me that my daughters couldn't grasp—then got up and started toward her office downstairs. She was just coming in to see me. She tried one more time to convince me not to do it, but without much force and finally said, "Oh, all right, do what you want to."

I scheduled first one eye, then the other, and endured weeks of wearing a patch. The doctors ordered that I take it easy—I don't know what they imagined I'd be doing. But we did arrange for Flo to bring my meals up to my rooms so that I didn't have to climb up and down the stairs. It wasn't the exciting life I used to yearn for but I finally made my own choices about how to spend each hour of the day and that was very precious.

****

Chloe asked me to help her go to music school. Her father was adamantly against it and I didn't feel that I should interfere. I had never been easy in my own mind about the idea of her getting up in front of people to perform. Ladies didn't behave that way in my day. Still, I was glad that I could use Blaine as an excuse so that I avoided telling her that I was against her plans. She finally settled on the University of Michigan. I felt so relieved at first. Then she came to visit me during her spring holidays that first year of college.

She apparently made the arrangements with Hunter and kept it as a surprise for me. When she came bounding up the stairs I didn't recognize her. Her hair was long and straight, flying out behind her as she ran and coming to rest just a few inches above her waist. She had on the kind of blue jeans that only the field hands wore in my experience—and they were faded and had big patches at the knees. When I asked her why her mother didn't buy her some new clothes, she laughed and informed me that she had worked for months to get this pair into that condition and she wasn't about to get another pair and go through it again. She had on a big, coarse-looking flannel shirt with the tails flapping out and the ugliest shoes I ever did see—desert boots, she called them.

Hunter took the two of us out for dinner that night and, to my relief, Chloe came downstairs wearing a dress, even if it was considerably shorter than I thought it should be. Hunter had made reservations at one of the elegant restaurants she frequented, The Paddock. White linen tablecloths, waiters in white jackets and black ties and excellent food; the only sort of restaurant Hunter liked.

At first, Chloe chattered about crazy things like redistributing the wealth and such. Hunter nearly went wild, what with informing her that we are the power elite Chloe went on about and that people like us should be the ones to have the money. I thought they were both nutty as fruitcakes. The idea that we had the same kind of money and power as the people Chloe ranted about was ludicrous and I hadn't realized that Hunter had become so delusional about her position in society. I couldn't for the life of me figure out what it was that made Chloe so mad about those people.

"Both of you, hush!" I finally told them. "Chloe, have you talked to your mother? How does she seem to you?"

"She doesn't talk much any more, but I guess she's okay. She hasn't been sick or anything. Mostly every week they call and Dad gives me lectures on the importance of not doing drugs or not having sex or not participating in protests or of doing well in school.... You know how he is. I just listen and at the end of the lecture Mom asks if I'm eating okay and then they hang up."

"I wish you'd check on her Chloe. She doesn't sound quite right to me."

"What do you mean, Grandma?"

I couldn't explain it. I just felt that Lily had been depressed for a long time and something seemed off. Actually I'd long thought that Hunter was depressed too, but she just snapped at me if I tried to find out how she was really doing, so I thought I'd see what I could do for Lily. "Just check on her, please."

"All right," she finally said. "Okay, now I think you should read the dessert menu to us so we can tell if that operation really worked. What do you say?"

"I can read just fine missy," I told her, "and I'll show you when we get home. But it just so happens that Hunter had Flo make some egg kisses today and we have plenty of chocolate ice cream, so we don't need to have dessert here." Once we got home, I knew that Hunter would go off to the library and drink, but at least the two of them would be separate and I could ask Chloe to watch what she said to Hunter.

Somehow from that point on, Chloe didn't seem quite as close to me. She chatted brightly whenever she came or called and we talked about gardens and books and all sorts of things the way we always had. But I had an idea there was a lot about her life that she didn't tell me any more. Every now and then I wondered if she was angry with me for not helping her with music school. But then I looked at how she dressed and listened to what Lily told me about those hippies she was running around with and I figured they had just turned her against her family. I missed her.

Chloe

Chapter Twenty-four

Mom and Daddy put lots of books and coloring books and dolls in the back seat of our turquoise Chevrolet. It was a long drive to Kentucky and I got pretty bored usually. It seemed like it took a couple of days. After hours and hours and hours there were hills and trees and a bridge over a river, but before that there was nothing much to look at—just the road and lots of brown fields. Mom and me watched out how much we drank because Daddy didn't like us to stop and go to the bathroom.

We used to live by Grandma and I saw her all the time. She was my best friend. We played hide and seek and "You're It" and talked about things.

"Just look at that Nixon." She held out a picture in a magazine. "Isn't he disgusting looking? You should always vote democrat. Now see Kennedy? There's a man you can vote for."

"What if the other guy looks better than the democrat?" I asked.

"Well, the really important thing," she told me, "is to study the issues and vote for the person who will do the best job. Usually a democrat. Being able to vote is a great privilege. I couldn't vote when I was young. I want you to appreciate the importance of that right."

She also said land is very important because no matter what else happens, you can always eat if you have land and she told me I have to try to keep the farm in the family when I grow up. I worried sometimes about what things could happen and why we'd only be able to eat if we had land.

I sang songs for her and told her how I wanted to sing when I grew up. She said ladies don't get up on stage, but I thought she just didn't know because Doris Day and Teresa Brewer sure looked like ladies to me.

One of my crayons rolled off my book and got some color on the seat. Daddy yelled, "Can't you ever take care of anything? You don't deserve to have anything nice." Mom said she thought she could get it out with spot remover and told him to calm down. Daddy lost his temper pretty often and we tried never to make him mad. When he did I got really scared and my stomach felt all tight and funny and I could hardly breathe.

I quit coloring and after a while I got pretty bored. So I started telling knock knock jokes. After a few jokes Mom started laughing really hard. Then I quit telling jokes and just started laughing too. If I laughed enough I could get her going and she couldn't stop. That was one of my favorite things. Pretty soon I had her in stitches and then Daddy told us to shut up. Since he was already mad about the crayons, I curled up in the corner to take a nap.

I loved going to Grandma's house even more before Uncle Mike died and went away. Uncle Mike was my best friend too. He swung me around in the air and helped with the hide and seek and said all the time I was a fine little girl. It was funny, I had to watch out and be careful all the time with Mom and Daddy and they said I was spoiled and a lot of trouble, but I didn't watch out much at all with Uncle Mike and Grandma and they liked me all the time. Mom said it was because they didn't have to fool with me every day. After he went away, Grandma went to live with Hunter at Uncle Mike's house. I kept wishing Uncle Mike would come back soon so Grandma could go back to her house and we could visit her there. I prayed every night that Grandma would never die.

Even though we had to visit with Grandma at Hunter's house, I was excited to go and I threw up in the sink after breakfast. Then Mom and Daddy discussed whether I was sick and we should wait to go. They put their hands on my forehead and asked me questions and finally we got to leave.

I didn't like the new place we moved. It wasn't pretty like our real home. All the trees in our neighborhood were little bitty spindly things without enough branches to even make the right sounds when the wind blew. I kept asking Mom where the birds could live, but she just said she didn't know. She cried sometimes because people made fun of her accent. I wasn't surprised, because Grandma told me before we moved that Yankees were bad people and they came down to Tennessee and tore up her grandma's house once. They even ruined paintings. Mom made me learn our address in case I ever got lost, but I'd be afraid to tell a Yankee where I live 'cause they might rip my pictures off the refrigerator and tear them up. At first, I tried not to talk to them at all.

After I started school, Grandma always said I talked like a Yankee. I didn't mean to quit talking like Kentucky people, it just happened. I heard my teacher tell Mom that my language skills were excellent. Mom turned pink and smiled and thanked her, so I guessed that was something good. I had almost all A's in school every time. I was a little nervous about school at first, especially when Mom went off and left me with this strange Yankee lady, but then I liked Mrs. Levine pretty well and after a while I wanted to go and I hoped every day the teacher would ask me to stay to help with clean up or that I could just go to my friend Jane's house and play so I didn't have to go home right away where Mom would tell me stuff about how to behave and what young ladies must do.

Daddy checked my reports over and every time I got a B he asked me all kinds of questions about the subject and my homework and how hard I tried and told me he expected me to do better. Daddy didn't like me to ever make a mistake. Mom said my grades were fine and there was nothing wrong with a B. She never said it to Daddy though. Grandma exclaimed over what a smart child I was and told everyone we saw. Hunter just said, "Hmph." School was pretty easy and I just had fun at first learning to do all kinds of things. But after we started getting report cards and everyone started studying mine and getting excited over my grades, I got kind of scared about what would happen if I didn't get such good grades and it didn't always seem fun.

In first grade, we started learning words. I liked words and making them go together and how they sounded. As soon as I knew enough words, I wrote some poems. Grandma still had a typewriter that Mom and Hunter used in college and she set it up for me. I learned how to use it and typed lots of poems. Grandma and Daddy showed them to people and got all puffed up.

A lot of times I made up songs for the poems. They hardly ever asked me to sing one. I started taking piano lessons in first grade and sometimes I tried to make up my songs on the piano. Someday I figured I'd be able to write my songs so they looked like the pieces I played for my lessons.

I didn't know how to read or write or play piano when Uncle Mike died so he wasn't there when I wrote poems or anything. I bet he'd have liked them and he'd have liked my songs and said I should keep writing them. He told me I should find what I really wanted to do because people needed to make their dreams come true. I didn't understand him so well when he told me, but later I dreamed about writing songs and singing and I guessed that he meant that's what I should do. Everyone else said it was silly or not a good idea or not the right thing, though. Daddy said show business is very uncertain and even people who are good don't make a living at music. I knew he meant I wasn't good but I still just wanted to sing songs. I wished Uncle Mike could come hear me.

I liked to listen to sounds like the tiny rustles and taps when the wind blew through a willow and then to try to sing their song. There was a big old weeping willow out on Hunter's farm next to a pond. The willow had different songs depending on how much the wind blew or whether it was raining. In a little wind the leaves tap tap tapped. In a hard wind it sounded the way a kite sounds when it catches and the paper crackles. The pond had its own songs. Sometimes a frog or a cricket or a bird sang another song or everything sang at once. Their songs all fit together I thought. At the stables, when they brought horses in and out of their stalls, the hooves clopped on the floor and crunched the hay while the tails flecked from side to side with a whir and a faint slap. I liked the sounds on the farm better than the city ones, mostly.

****

Hunter got mad when we visited when I turned six and she asked whether I'd been taking riding lessons.

"She should have started two years ago, Lily."

"Says who?"

"All the children down here start riding before they start school."

"That's ridiculous Hunter. Only the horse people's children ride. And besides, Chloe doesn't live down here and we don't know that she ever will."

"Of course she will. This house will be hers and naturally she'll want to live here."

"That's a long way off and it surely doesn't mean that she has to start riding now."

They argued and argued and I went off where I couldn't hear because I hated the way they fought all the time. The next day Hunter took me to a stable out Versailles Road run by Mr. Sands, the riding master she said was best. Mom and I stayed six weeks that time and I had three lessons a week. I liked the horses pretty much, except from up on their backs it was such a long way down. One day the horse I was on, Goldie, decided to leave the outdoor ring and go back to the stable. We were trotting along and all of a sudden he whirled around and jumped the fence. I flew off and landed on my back. The ground was really hard and it knocked the wind out of me and Mr. Sands said, "Who told you to get off?"

"I think Goldie did," I told him. "I'm pretty sure I heard her say it."

"Scamp," he chuckled on his way to pull Goldie back. He picked me up and put me right back on. He said, "You have to get back on right away."

By the end of six weeks, Mr. Sands said I was doing very well. I could walk, trot—sitting or posting—and canter. Hunter came out to ride with me the last day. She followed along behind and told me I held my elbows out too far and I didn't keep my knees close enough or sit straight enough. She said she'd have to find a new master for me next summer because this one clearly had allowed me to get away with too much. She didn't really like anything I did very well, so I wasn't too disappointed that she didn't think I was good at riding. I liked Mr. Sands, though.

****

Daddy said Hunter was a wastrel with a lifestyle that had nothing to recommend it. He didn't like her house or her parties or the number of dresses she had and I wondered if having a big beautiful house and horses and pretty clothes made her so mean. Whatever Hunter told me I should do, Daddy said I shouldn't do. Hunter said Daddy was hopeless.

"When I think of the chances your mother could have had," she'd say and shake her head, "and then she married your father. Don't you listen to his ridiculous ideas about life. I'll introduce you to the right people. With good connections you can get ahead."

"Do they know about singing?" I asked.

"Are you still harping about that? Well, you'll change your mind a few times probably. Now, you know I don't have any children, Chloe, so you can inherit everything I have."

She brought up that inherit thing every time I said I didn't want to do something. I had lots of toys so I figured I didn't have to have whatever it was she wouldn't give me. And Daddy got mad if I did what Hunter wanted anyway.

Mostly Daddy didn't have much to do with Hunter. But when Hunter got really mean with Mom or me and wouldn't stop, after a while he'd come up to her with his mouth all tight and tell her from between his teeth that he wanted her to mind her own business or that she was greedy and self-centered. She'd stop talking and flounce off. I didn't like it when Daddy talked to me that way but I sure liked to be there when he did it to Hunter.

When Mom and Daddy went out to visit friends and Grandma was napping I stayed in the kitchen with Flo. Flo was big and warm and funny and she made egg kisses when I came to visit. The kitchen was probably as big as our living room. I could sit at the table and watch. Hunter snapped Flo's head off all the time and we liked to talk about how ornery she was. Grandma was mean to Flo too sometimes. She said you had to be careful with coloreds and carried her purse around with her while Flo cleaned her room. That hurt Flo's feelings and I couldn't understand why Grandma did it. Mom said she came from a different time. Daddy said all people are equal and that that meant I should be nice to everybody and never to act with anyone like Grandma acted with Flo. Flo was my friend and I didn't want anybody to be mean to her. She said she had to put up with it because she needed the job. She had three children. She used to bring her daughter, Sarah, who was my age, to play with me and we had great fun but Hunter didn't want me to play with her and Flo didn't bring her any more.

Once a week Flo cleaned the refrigerator. She took every single thing out and checked it. Some food she threw away. Everything she kept she wiped off. She cleaned off all the shelves with a cloth that she dipped in and out of a pail of water. I liked to hear the noise the water made when the cloth went in and then the drips when she wrung it out. She always wore a bright white uniform. I told her one day that I thought the white looked so good next to her skin that I thought white people should always wear black and black people should always wear white and she laughed and laughed. But, really, I knew it would look very nice.

After Lexington, our house always seemed really small and our neighborhood looked flat and sad. The lawns seemed lonely without the shade from the big old trees. Without many birds and frogs and things it just didn't seem very happy there.

Chapter Twenty-five

The morning was already hot and I stretched and stared out the window for a while. I could hear the birds in the big old tree outside the back windows. I never heard their song at home—a sort of long, high note and then a quick lower tone—and it always told me I was in Lexington. As I watched, a squirrel struggled up the tree with a big chunk of doughnut in his mouth, ignoring the angry squawks of the birds. The smells of bacon and coffee floated up into my room and I knew that Grandma and Hunter must be in the kitchen.

Finally, I put one lazy leg over the side of the bed and then the other and rolled up to a stand. On my way to the door, I looked over the big pink flowers on the wallpaper and grabbed a light robe, then ambled into the hall and hesitated, trying to decide which staircase to use. The back staircase, which was closer to my room, brought me right to the door of the kitchen. The front staircase was at the other end of the house. With its curving bannister and beautiful wood, it was much more grand than the other—and when no one else was around, I liked to slide down. A lot of times, I listened for Hunter's voice and picked the staircase that would keep me from running into her. It was the first full day of my visit that summer and, knowing that they were both in the kitchen, I scooted to the front and slid quickly down the bannister.

I skimmed my feet along the oriental rug that stretched down the hall, watching the familiar navy and green pattern as I passed over it. Once in the kitchen, I went to Grandma and bent down to give her a kiss.

"Good morning darlin'. I left some eggs for you on the stove and the bacon is under the paper towel. Did you sleep well?"

Before I could answer, Hunter broke in, "Mother she's old enough to fend for herself." She sat with one leg tucked up under her, reading newspapers, like she did every morning. One last corner of toast sat on her plate and a half-filled cup of coffee rested next to it.

I went on to the refrigerator to get the orange juice and stopped and made a face behind Hunter's back. Grandma pretended not to see me and said, "I just told her where things were. I declare I don't know what makes you so ornery. Just finish your breakfast and leave the child alone. Come on Chloe, pour your juice and fix your plate while everything is still warm."

While I got my breakfast, Hunter muttered about how I was spoiled and that she never had it so easy. As far as I could tell she muscled other people into doing almost everything that got done in her life so I couldn't figure how she imagined that she worked so hard. I'd never had the chance to order people around so I wondered if it was harder than it looked.

While I wondered, I started eating. Grandma put all these herbs like dill and chervil in the eggs and they were great. The bacon was crisp and perfect. I looked at Grandma's toast and remembered that she always had Rose's lime marmalade. I reached for the jar and wondered if it could get any better than that.

"What are you going to do today?"

"Maggie's mom is bringing her by to pick me up and dropping us downtown."

"Oh, it'll be so nice to see Maggie and Caroline. You must tell her mother to come in and say hello when they get here. Will you go into The Bon Mot and pick up a box of Ruth Hunt candy? I'll give you some money."

"Sure!" I loved Ruth Hunt candy and I knew that meant that Grandma and I would dip into the box every night and talk about how there were never enough chocolate dipped cream candies in a box. I took my dishes to the sink and started rinsing, but Grandma told me to go on and get ready.

"Mother, there's no reason for you to do the dishes. Let her do them," Hunter looked over her paper to command.

"Hunter, you know perfectly well that Flo will do all the dishes later. Would you stop fussing? Now Chloe, I'm going to have Flo make some egg kisses and there is chocolate ice cream, so don't you all head to the French Bauer and fill up on ice cream there."

"Wow." It kept getting better. Flo walked into the kitchen just then. "Flo. Grandma says you're going to make egg kisses. Thank you. And how are you?"

Flo beamed, asked me when I'd gotten in and told me with a grin that she had better things to do than making egg kisses. We caught up on how her children were doing and how my parents were doing and I ran upstairs to get ready. In Lexington you always had to ask about everyone in a person's family and tell them about everyone in yours at the start of your conversation. I kind of liked it.

When the doorbell rang I ran to the front stairs. I could see Maggie's tall, slender figure through the screen and raced down the stairs. I was so excited I could hardly open the latch but I got the door open and gave her a big hug. Maggie's folks owned the next farm over and we'd been playing together on my vacations since we were really little. I shouted to her mother to come on inside and say hello. I led them back to the kitchen where Grandma had put on more coffee and left them all talking while I ran upstairs to get my things.

When I got back downstairs, I could hear Maggie and her mother laughing so I knew Grandma was telling one of her stories. She told the funniest stories of anyone I knew. Mrs. Thompson put down her coffee cup as I walked in, "You ready hon? Well, Miz Harrison, thank you for the coffee. It's so nice to see you and have a little visit. But I need to drop the girls off so I can go on to my appointment. You have a nice day now." Mrs. Thompson always looked gorgeous and she had this really husky voice that I loved to listen to. She shepherded us out the door while Grandma told us to be careful.

We asked Maggie's Mom to drop us off by the public library at Gratz Park. It was a little bit of a walk from there but we loved the park. The trees met over our heads and the houses were old. Even though it was right in town, it was always peaceful there and you could hear the leaves and the birds. Once we went on a tour of the Hunt Morgan House, at the corner of the square, and heard all about how Yankees and Johnny Rebs lived next to one another around the square during the war. It must have been so exciting. After the park, we walked past Mary Todd Lincoln's father's law office. I liked having places from history all around. We didn't linger though because we only had a couple of hours and a lot of shops to cover.

We were on our preliminary search for school clothes. First we would look through all the stores and see where there were outfits we really liked. The next time we went down, we'd start trying things on. By the time I left we'd have decided which skirts and sweaters we wanted and worked on our moms to let us buy them.

Clerks in most of the stores knew Grandma and Hunter and Mom and usually they either remembered me or recognized me because we all looked alike, so everywhere we went, people asked about Mom and Dad and Grandma and all. I liked being in a place where everyone knew us. It felt so homey everywhere.

We went to all the places that carried Villager and John Meyer and Emily M and examined all the plaids and the matching sweater colors. Maggie had an eye for putting things together and I loved the things she chose. We saved The Bon Mot for last so that I wouldn't have to carry the box of candy around. The Bon Mot had been there forever and the owner, old Mr. Haslett, would always come say hello and tell me stories.

"Your mother used to come in here after school with her school bag full of books. She'd buy some little thing and announce that she wanted it delivered. Then she'd say, just as serious as could be, 'And, by the way, will you send my school bag too?'" Mr. Haslett cracked up over that every time he told me. My dad would have killed me if I ever did anything like that. But none of the stores at home delivered anyway. I liked to hear those stories about the funny things Mom and Hunter did when they were little girls.

Mr. Haslett took us upstairs and got Mrs. Orsini to wait on us. She was the one who picked out dresses for Grandma and had them sent to the house for her to look at and she always remembered me. Maggie and I felt kind of embarrassed since we knew we weren't buying anything that day, but Mrs. Orsini just nodded and said, "Of course, you need to look before your Mama comes to visit at the end of the summer." She knew I'd probably get some clothes there in the end. And I did see a plaid that I loved with a matching sweater and Maggie found knee socks to go with it too.

When it was time to meet her mother, we went back down Main Street to the tobacco shop and bought bottles of Coke to sip. It was really hot and humid by then. Grandma had asked Mrs. Thompson to let Maggie come for dinner and spend the night, so we stopped at Maggie's house and got her things before we went back to Hunter's farm.

"Mama told me to ask you to come for dinner tomorrow night so she can really see you," Maggie told me while we dropped her things off upstairs.

"Great, I'm sure Grandma will say it's okay. You know I loved that green plaid on you."

"Wasn't it pretty? That might just be the outfit to get Bobby to ask me to a dance."

"Sure," I told her. I felt a little funny because I had never been out with a boy and I didn't expect to go to any dances any time soon. We had just finished seventh grade and Maggie had already had a boyfriend who carried her books and stuff. She was pretty and bright and popular and I was amazed that she liked to spend time with me every summer.

After we had some coffee ice cream in the kitchen with Grandma, we went out to the pond to try skipping stones. Grandma told us about contests she had with her brothers and we begged her to come out and show us. It took a little persuading, but finally she laughed and came outside with us.

"I'm too old for this," she protested when we got out there. "Chloe, give me your hand and help me get down on my knees here to look for some stones." Once down, she began intently searching through the stones, picking up dozens of them and rejecting almost all. After she'd found a couple of nice smooth, flat, round ones, she showed them to us and had us start looking too. When we'd collected a little pile, she asked for a hand to get back up and had me reach down and hand her a stone. "My arthritis is so bad," she muttered and rubbed her hands. Then she turned at an angle to the pond, gripped the stone in her hand, brought her arm in front of her body and flipped it back out from the elbow, letting go of the stone with a little flourish at the end. It only skipped twice, but it was neat. She took another and the same thing happened. "It's too hot out here," she said after that. "You girls go on and practice. I'm going to go back inside."

We were keen to try to match the record. Neither one of us got more than one or two skips, though. Most of the time the stones just sank right off. After a while we worked more at getting them to splash us so we could cool off than at making them skip. Once we were good and wet, we stretched out under a big old tree while we dried off and took turns naming the pictures we saw in the clouds when we weren't trying to imagine Grandma as a little girl out skipping stones. It was hard to picture.

As soon as we got inside, Grandma told us to go upstairs and get cleaned up for dinner. Going past Hunter's bathroom, I saw that she'd been putting on make-up and left everything sitting out around the sink. Her bedroom door was closed. We hurried to wipe off the dirt from our knees and hands and ran out to the hall just as her door opened. The scent of Blue Grass filled the hall and she stepped out. With all her make-up on and wearing one of those close-fitting, flattering dresses and her three-inch slingback pumps, she really looked elegant. When she dressed up like that to go out it always felt like the world was filled with beaus and parties and exciting nights. I just stood there staring.

"Well, hello, Maggie. How nice to see you again," she said in her most charming drawl—the one she used to talk to everyone but family.

"Hello, Hunter. You look so pretty tonight!" Maggie always seemed to know the right thing to say to everyone. I tried to think of something else to add but my mind went blank.

"Yes, you look nice," I finally added lamely.

"Well, thank you girls. Now, I'm running late, as usual. You all go on down-stairs and see if you can help Mother. I'll be down in a few minutes."

Back in the kitchen, Grandma asked us to set the table and we started traipsing back and forth from the butler's pantry to the kitchen table with all the dish-es she said we would need. When we finished, I asked, "Do you think Flo could drive us to the Huntsman's Club tomorrow?"

Hunter had appeared in the doorway by that time and barked, "Flo has bet-ter things to do than haul you out there. We don't pay her good money just to wait on you when you come down here."

"Hunter, hush. *I* pay Flo and it won't take her that long to drive them out there if they want to swim. It's supposed to be hot again tomorrow. You all will be glad to be at the pool. I've been burnin' up today." Grandma glared at Hunter, whose mouth was opening to say something back. She just pinched her lips together though, said she'd be back late and stormed out.

"Thanks, Grandma."

She shook her head sadly. "I don't know what makes her act so ugly." She looked kind of far off and muttered something about Hunter reminding her of her Mama and Grandmama, then said, "Her father had a bad temper."

"Was he that mean?" I asked. I always tried to get her to tell me more about my grandfather.

"Hush and finish setting the table," she told me and turned back to the stove. In a couple of minutes she opened the oven and the kitchen filled with the aroma of her chicken in wine sauce.

"Oh, Grandma, you fixed my favorite."

"Yes, darlin'. I know you love it so. And some beans the Taylors brought over fresh from our farm and new potatoes. Oh, and Miz Taylor invited us out for tea one afternoon so you can visit the farm." I loved going to see the farm where Mom and Hunter grew up.

"I always think of it as the sweetest place in Lexington," Grandma sighed.

"You all must have had such fun while you lived there," Maggie mentioned with a little question in her voice.

"Fun? Well, I suppose we did have some fun." Grandma appeared to consider for a moment. "Yes, when the children were little and Miles was alive there were some funny times. Did I ever tell you about the time your mother threw mashed beans on Hunter's head?" Maggie and I started giggling. She had told us, but it was always nice to hear about Hunter getting plastered with baby food so we said no. As soon as we'd all fixed our plates, Grandma asked Maggie to tell her about school.

"Well, I did just fine. I was on the honor roll. And I'm going to be on the track team next year."

"How lovely. You two girls have always been so smart. I'm proud of you all. Chloe was on the honor roll too you know."

"Yes ma'am. Thank you ma'am."

We made sure to keep her talking about school and how it was when she went to school and things like that because whenever Hunter went out for the evening, for some reason Grandma started talking about every grisly crime she knew of that had happened anywhere in the area and we didn't want to hear it. We kept up all the way through the egg kisses. Grandma went on upstairs while we loaded the dishwasher.

Then we were ready to scare one another at hide and seek. I went to hide first and Maggie stayed in the kitchen where the humming and spraying and splashing of the dishwasher provided cover for me. The house was old and creaky and it was hard to be quiet enough that she couldn't hear where I went. I ran up the back stairs and made just enough noise that she could probably hear me anyway. Then I slipped to the front as quietly as I could and back down the front stairs and ducked into the dining room. There was a big old closet full of shelves in the corner and I scooted in there. It was totally dark in the dining room and I kept hearing little noises and thinking someone else was in there. Creaks seemed to move around the floor of the room as if a person were walking around on it.

I heard Maggie leave the kitchen and go upstairs where she quietly opened and shut doors in the back section of the house. It was funny to listen and know that I'd fooled her, but she was taking a long time and I wished she'd hurry up so I didn't have to stay alone in there. I thought about sneaking back upstairs, but I was too afraid to go out into the dining room alone. Finally the dining room door opened and Maggie stepped softly into the room. I let her get a little closer and then gave a yell and blasted the closet door open at the same time. Maggie jumped and screamed so suddenly that I screamed too and then we both fell over laughing.

After Maggie took a turn at hiding, we were both too nervous to keep playing the game and we went to see if Grandma was ready to watch TV in her room. We still had to work at keeping Grandma from launching into the gruesome crime catalog, but it wasn't too hard. Finally she sent us back to my room and we got ready for bed and then talked about clothes and boys till we fell asleep.

****

While we were eating breakfast the next morning Flo came in and announced that she would be going to the grocery at eleven o'clock and she would take us to the club then. "You'd better be ready," she admonished. We finished eating and ran upstairs to take our baths and collect swimsuits and towels and suntan lotion. We had said good bye to Grandma and were waiting in the kitchen on one foot and then the other by quarter to eleven.

I let Maggie sit in the front and she and Flo caught up on one another while I just watched out the windows. The ride to the club took us across the countryside, winding and turning. After we turned onto the Mill Road, the ride was so pretty it was like being in a different world. The road was so narrow that if a car came in the other direction, both cars had to put the outside wheels over the pavement to make room to pass. The road twisted and turned through rolling hills, past lovely old farm houses and under beautiful trees and finally down to the quaint old mill that now served as the club house for the Huntsman's Club.

Flo pulled into the lot by the barn across the street and turned to tell us, "Hunter told me to go in and remind Harry who you are, so it'll be all right for you to use the pool." We all climbed out of the car and across the road. While Flo went back into the kitchen to find Harry, Maggie and I waited in the main room. It was always a little dark. I looked around at the hunting prints on the walls, the big old fireplace, the slightly worn leather furniture and the faded oriental rugs that all combined somehow to feel really elegant.

As soon as Flo gave us the nod, we ran down the stairs to the dank changing room, jumped into our suits and took the outside stairs up to the pool. It was one of the lucky days when only a couple of ladies lounged by the poolside and no one else was swimming. We were free to have races to see who could stand on her hands at the bottom of the deep end the fastest and the longest and who could sit down on the bottom first and stuff. After we were tired, we stretched out on lounges for a while. The mill was in a hollow and I could lie back and look up at tree-lined bluffs that were beautiful. Crickets chirped from down by the stream and every now and then you could hear a whinny from the barn. Sometimes one of the ladies would swim for a while and the water sang a quiet little song while it lapped against the sides of the pool after she got out.

We swam some more and climbed out to the lounges again and when we got bored we headed down to the creek and walked along in the water and splashed around for a while. Then we figured it was time to buy some sodas and peanut butter crackers from the machines in the basement. There was time for one more swim before we had to go change back into our shorts and tops and wait for Flo to pick us up again. That little hollow was one of my favorite places in the whole world.

****

In Lexington, mostly my days were like those first two, swimming and shopping and hanging around with Maggie, and lots of time talking with Grandma. Sometimes she'd tell me about what it was like when Mom and Hunter were little; stories about life on the farm. She'd hardly ever talk about when she was a girl, but sometimes she'd tell some really funny story. Every once in a while on my visits, Hunter would get hold of me and try to make me do stuff she wanted me to.

One night she gave a cocktail party. I had to dress up and stand at the door and greet all the guests and introduce myself and show them where to go. Then, after everyone had arrived, I had to go out to the back lawn, where she was holding it, and try to keep an eye on people's drinks and tell their orders to the waiters. All the people were dressed in really nice clothes and the ladies had pretty jewelry. They were all involved in the horse business and talked about trainers and jockeys and what this or that owner said after a race. Eventually I got kind of bored and went up to my room. I could see down to the party and I watched for a while. Pretty soon, though, somebody saw me up there and a bunch of people looked up. I ducked back but Hunter showed up in a few minutes and was livid. "You either come downstairs and join the party or go do something else. I won't have you behaving so childishly," she yelled and wheeled around to stomp back downstairs. I wandered on to Grandma's room and told her I was in trouble with Hunter again.

"Well, you stay in here with Grandma. One of the waiters brought up a tray for me with piles of hors d'oeuvres. Come help me eat some of this." After we munched for a while, she looked up and said, "You know your aunt just wants to try to help launch you into society."

"But Grandma, I don't know anything about horses and I don't want to have to spend my whole life talking about them."

"I know darlin'. But she thinks she's doing something to help you. Can you understand that?"

"I suppose." I did know she meant well. But the more she tried to push me to be part of her world, the less I wanted anything to do with it. I didn't even talk to anyone but Maggie any more about wanting to sing or anything. I sure didn't expect anybody would help me to do what I wanted to do. It seemed to me they could at least not try to make me do things I definitely did not want to do.

Chapter Twenty-six

When I came home from school one hot September day, Mom handed me a big envelope from the California Arts Institute. I'd sent an early application with some nice recommendations and a letter from Beaux Arts, the famous music school, telling me how sorry they were that I was unable to take the place in their high school that I'd won in competition. Even though Dad never stopped telling me that music was no career, and he wouldn't let me go to the school, he let me keep taking piano and voice lessons. He thought it was a nice little hobby, I guess. This packet told me that CAI was holding auditions in Chicago in two months and that I was in if I met their standards there.

I was so excited. That was the school that offered the kinds of music training I wanted. You could work with a lot of styles besides classical and I'd been begging my teachers to let me move out of classical for years. I wanted to sing jazz and work on improvisations in piano. I created some pieces that played the sounds of the farm but my teachers didn't like them and wouldn't help me learn more about composing. My voice teacher didn't like my idol, Carmen MacRae, either. She said she couldn't understand why anyone with a nice voice like mine would want to throw it away on low brow music like that. I hated "art" songs.

California was so nice and far away. My senior year of high school all I could think about was how soon I'd be able to leave. I never did like the town we lived in that much. And in high school everything seemed to get worse. I was bored in my classes. It wasn't cool to be smart, so I was an outsider for getting good grades and reading Dickens and Hardy for fun. On top of that, the Lexington sort of way we lived was too different for the kids at school. No one else spent summers swimming at country clubs or even going out of state. You couldn't even find the kind of clothes we bought for me in Lexington in the stores in Spotswood. There was just nothing about me that fit.

I had a few friends that I spent lots of time with, but I never got invited to the dances or anything. If I joined the yearbook or the newspaper staff, I got left by myself doing all the work for my team and on picture day some person who'd never been to a meeting came and stood in front of me. At least the kids didn't go out of their way to be cruel to me. There were some kind of poor kids with funny clothes and learning problems who were teased and tricked and tormented all the time. I tried to be nice to them but you had to be careful how much time you spent talking to them or you'd get taunted too. Sometimes it happened anyway. My stomach felt tight most of the time—like at home, wondering when Dad might pop off.

I worked as a counselor's aide during home room. One day, when everyone going to homecoming was in the gym for a big lecture during home room, I was out in the hall on an errand for the counselor—I wasn't going to the dance, of course. I ran into a couple of guys from my year hanging out in the hall.

"You aren't going to home room are you?" asked one.

"I thought I would."

"Ah c'mon. You don't want to go hang out with all the ugly girls no one wanted to take to the dance do you?" Just like I wasn't right there instead of in the gym.

I guessed they figured I was just one of those ugly girls who don't matter. I already thought that I was, but I felt humiliated to have people say it. I tried always to sit in the back corner of the room and to say as little as possible so no one would notice me. So, at the beginning of the year, the teachers always thought I was one of the troublemakers. Then I'd start getting hundreds on my tests and they'd start calling on me all the time. I had a lot of trouble talking loud enough to be heard at the front of the room so I had to say the answer more than once every time, till I felt like I was shouting.

I did have some fun with my friends Ellen and Carla. Our dads arranged their carpools so that one of us got to drive to school every day. The one with the car picked up the others and then after school drove the group to the ice cream parlor or the park. None of us dated, but we all had crushes on different boys. Every now and then one of us changed boys—never having dated the first one.... One of our favorite things was to figure out where they lived and drive past each boy's house. If he was in the yard or the driveway we all screamed and whoever had the crush ducked down so he wouldn't know she'd been driving by.

Once every few weekends I'd spend the night with one or both of them or one or both would spend the night with me. We talked about boys and where we wanted to go to school. Ellen wanted to get married and read *Bride's Magazine* all the time to get ideas for her wedding. I never thought about weddings for myself and I couldn't imagine wearing one of those dresses. Carla was another honor student and wanted to be a marine biologist. We both planned to get out of Spotswood and never look back. We ate potato chips and dip and pretzels and listened to the Beatles and the Turtles and Sergio Mendes and Brasil '66. Sometimes we practiced the latest dances we'd learned from Shindig or American Bandstand. We all expected or hoped to be asked to a dance one day and we were going to be ready. Ellen actually started dating Joe senior year. He wasn't one of the boys she had had a crush on, but she fell for him and the wedding plans started featuring him as bridegroom.

The last two years of high school, I was madly in love with Allen Whitman. He was smart and sophisticated, dark and handsome. He actually said hello to me every now and then or chatted a little. But he dated Christina, one of the popular girls. Everyone arrived at school early and walked around in the halls saying hello and gossiping each morning. I lived for the days Allen passed me in the hall and said hi. Sometimes I was so nervous that I could barely smile in reply. Every now and then he tried to talk to me but I couldn't think of much to say. Carla said I was really funny and told good stories when I was with her and that I should do the same with him but I didn't know how to make myself do it. When I was really comfortable jokes just came out and other times they weren't there. Once in a while when Allen teased me I managed to say something really snappy back and he'd crack up. I couldn't figure out why he made a point of talking to me since we hadn't been friends when we were younger or anything. I prayed that it meant he planned to dump Christina for me. Preferably in time to take me to the prom. Never happened.

****

I showed Dad the letter from CAI at dinner. He smiled without turning up the corners of his mouth and said, "Well, isn't that nice," without pleasure. We ate in silence. A while after dinner, he came to my room and asked me to come down to the living room so we could all talk.

Mom was already in there, sitting alone on the couch and looking stiff and nervous; she was as small as Grandma and looked lost on the big pink couch. Dad sat in another chair and I sat in one near him where I also faced Mom. Dad did all the talking.

"You didn't tell me you were applying to music school."

I just shrugged one shoulder in response. Of course I hadn't told him. He always sounded so hurt, like he couldn't understand why I wouldn't tell a nice guy like him just anything. He'd have given me the same lecture I was about to get and told me I couldn't even write for a catalog.

"I thought we'd discussed this before."

Still I looked at him and said nothing. My stomach tightened and I could hardly breathe. I hadn't discussed. He had instructed me about what I should and shouldn't want.

"Music is a very risky business," he continued. "We could spend all this money on an education and you could try for years to break in and never make it. New York and Hollywood are flooded with people searching for a chance who never get one. Now, it's a nice talent to have. You'll enjoy being able to play and sing in your spare time. Probably you're going to get married, your husband will support you and it won't matter. But what if something happens to him? You need to be able to earn a living. It's my duty to see to it that you're prepared to take care of yourself if you need to. If you get your bachelor's degree from a good liberal arts college, you can earn a living if you need to and I'm prepared to pay for that. ..."

He went on and on but I quit listening. Mom twisted her hands in her lap but she never said a word. Dad was all worked up this time. We had to hear about nice ladies not parading themselves in front of people. Then, all of a sudden I realized he was adding a new twist.

"Well, you're old enough to make some of your own decisions. I'm not going to make any final decision since you don't even know yet if you'll be accepted. I might give you some assistance toward music school if you get in. Although I frankly would be more favorably inclined if you chose a school closer to home. I really do not approve of your going so far away, particularly to a place as full of nuts as California. But still, if you want to prepare for the audition and see whether you get accepted before you make your choice, then that's what I think you should do."

I was in shock. When I looked over at Mom she was blinking as if slightly bewildered. I don't think I really expected to be allowed to audition. I called my voice teacher the next day and asked her to think about what I should plan to sing. At my lesson that week we went over a few pieces I'd been working on and finally chose Cesar Franck's "Lied."

"Maggie, I'm gonna have a chance to audition for CAI—and my dad's gonna let me do it."

"Fantastic. Oh, that'll be so good if you can go to California. That's the program you told me about over the summer isn't it?"

"Yes. Jazz and rock... ."

"This is great. I've been accepted at a design school out there so we might even be able to see one another more often." Maggie was a terrific artist and she wanted to be a fashion designer.

"Wow. And you can design outfits for me to wear on stage."

If Dad wouldn't pay my tuition, I wasn't sure there was any point in auditioning, but I figured I should just be glad I'd been allowed to advance one step closer to "Go" and take the pass I'd been given. I started practicing, but I began having trouble with my throat. It was dry and scratchy off and on and tight. Suddenly I couldn't get the big opening I needed for the high notes. My neck was stiff and tense. Some days I could only practice for a few minutes.

While that was going on, I took the SAT and gathered catalogs for liberal arts schools so that I could get my applications in before the deadlines. I spent hours going over the courses and requirements and trying to decide what I would even want to do. I decided I'd try Transylvania since I'd always loved it and liked the idea of really living in Lexington. If I went there I guessed I'd major in history. Grinnell in Iowa looked okay and had a pretty good writing program. University of Michigan had a very good creative writing program and offered such an astonishing array of possibilities that I figured I could major in education or history and toss in some other electives and hide the fact that I was taking lots of writing courses. Dad wasn't too crazy about my second love either. I picked a couple more places to apply and began gathering materials so that I could prepare the applications after I got past the audition.

By a month before the big day, I was becoming alarmed at the problems with my voice. By then, if I practiced very long I could barely speak for a few hours afterward. Every day it grew worse. Ordinarily, I had a three octave range but it narrowed more all the time. I didn't have enough range left to hit all the notes in my piece. Every night I tossed and turned for ages before I got to sleep. Then I had nightmares where I was up in front of a whole roomful of people and opened my mouth to sing but no sound came out and everyone started laughing.

"You're gonna be great," Carla said. "You've won awards and people say you're good every time you sing for them—not that you do it very often."

"But this wasn't happening to my throat before," I told her with rising panic. "Can't you just do something about it?"

"My voice teacher gave me a gargle recipe and said I should drink hot water with fresh lemon in it. The family doctor told my mom that he thinks I'm too high strung and that she could try giving me one of her valium pills every other night before I go to bed. I don't have trouble sleeping those nights and my neck doesn't hurt as much. But my voice hasn't gotten any better. What am I going to do?"

"Chloe you just have to get into CAI. Just think of the famous teachers and the special programs. And *California*. What better place to get discovered?"

"Right. I have to. But what if I'm really not good enough? What if no band ever wants me?"

I didn't tell anyone else how scared I was about going to CAI even if I did get accepted. I did tell Grandma about the audition and that Dad wouldn't pay all my tuition if I decided to go there. I hoped that she would talk to Dad. I knew she'd never been keen about me singing. But she told me once that she'd wanted to be a teacher and sometimes she was sorry she'd been pressured not to do it, so I thought maybe she'd help me.

"Oh darlin'. I don't think I should do something that your father wouldn't like. But I suppose I could just ask the trustees whether I could take some money from the estate to help pay the tuition if it's what you really want to do."

A couple of days later Hunter called for me. "Mother just asked for permission to take some money out of the estate to help pay your tuition. The bank won't do it without approval from both your mother and me. I suppose I can assume your mother said yes. But let me tell you something, I'm not going to let you take my money out of the estate for every stupid whim you have. I know you want to get your hands on everything you can bleed. Well Mother may be an easy touch for you but I will see to it that you are stopped." Her usually nasty tone was even worse when she was drunk.

I couldn't imagine how I would find enough money to pay half my own expenses. Dad refused to let me get a part time job in high school so I didn't have savings for college. He always said he'd pay for it. By a few days before the audition I had trouble singing a single note that didn't sound forced. My head ached all the time and Mom decided to quit giving me Valium when my voice was still bad after two weeks, so the last week I couldn't sleep at all.

When the day of the audition came, I wasn't any better. The piece I'd chosen required quite a range and I was petrified. As I sat in the auditorium waiting for my turn, my throat was tighter than ever. They finally called my name and I walked up to the stage with lead feet and handed my music to the accompanist. She played the introduction and I came in on cue but my voice barely made a sound. A few more bars into the song and there was no sound at all. They let me start again, but halfway through I signalled that I wanted to stop. They didn't have to tell me that I didn't get in.

My teacher had driven me down to the city and played my accompaniment. On the way home she kept clicking her tongue against the roof of her mouth sadly and shaking her head. I didn't want to cry in front of her, so I sat really still, holding my whole body tight to keep anything from getting out. I stared really hard at the lane in front of us, like I was fascinated by the view of flat cement. Still, I kept having to blink away tears.

"Well, dear," she finally said, "this was a shame. But it happens sometimes. I'm sure your throat will be fine for other auditions."

"My dad won't pay for me to go to music school anyway," I had to whisper to keep holding all that crying in. "So I don't think I'll set up any more auditions."

That night I hid my head under the pillows and sobbed until I knew for sure that music was not going to be my life. Then I felt a little relieved that I wouldn't have to figure out how to pay all that tuition money.
****

Grandma decided she wanted the cataracts taken off her eyes that year. Hunter didn't want her to do it. I thought Hunter wanted Grandma helpless so that she could be even more of a martyr about "having to take care of Mother" while Mom and I just spent our days having a gay old time. Eventually I told Hunter and Mom how scared Grandma was about being blind and that I thought she should have the operation if she wanted to. Hunter said I obviously didn't really care what happened to Grandma, but she quit fighting. Grandma was so excited once she could see again.

I received acceptances from all the colleges I applied to and chose Michigan. I thought Ann Arbor was really charming when I went up for my interview and I liked the idea of a school so big that no one would especially notice me. On graduation day, when other kids were crying and clinging to one another, I couldn't stop smiling and saying, "I get to leave! I get to leave!" Carla and I chanted it and danced a little jig.

Chapter Twenty-seven

I was living in Boston the year Grandma became ill. After I graduated from Michigan, I stayed in Ann Arbor for a couple of years, working for the neighborhood technology group that some of us helped to start after the Viet Nam war de-escalated. The war was winding down when I got to college and the big protests had already happened. I was kind of scared about being at a school where there were a lot of protests because students had been killed at Kent State and a couple of other places before I started. I didn't have an opinion, really, about the war or the protests, then. My dad was furious about the protestors. But the idea that I could be shot by the National Guard just walking to class bothered me.

When I got to school, though, I started hearing a lot of things I'd never heard before. After listening to some of the professors who spoke at anti-war rallies, I began reading and taking classes that could help answer some of my questions. All of a sudden it seemed that the things my family always taught me to believe about my country weren't true. At first I assumed that anyone who really believed this was the land of opportunity would be as mad as I was when they got the true facts. When I tried to talk to my dad, though, I found out I was wrong.

"Dad, did you know that most of the boys going to Viet Nam are poor and non-white?"

"Well, no."

"The only reason we're there is so a bunch of rich guys in the Council on Foreign Relations can keep access to the resources... ."

"Nonsense. You're listening to a bunch of nut cases."

"Dad, the guy's who's done the work on the CFR has a Ph.D. from Northwestern."

"Well, some nuts get through every school."

"Rich people need this war and poor people are dying."

"Stop being ridiculous. I don't want to hear you've been out protesting."

So I didn't tell him about the protests. His hypocrisy became one with all the shocking discoveries of distortions and untruths that fanned the flames of anger for me and for my friends and inspired us to believe that we could change the world and that, in part, it was our responsibility to build a new order. Most of the protests were pretty small compared to the sixties, except when they mined the harbor at Hai Phong. Even though there wasn't as much going on, we were intense about the issues. Most of my friends were really into politics and worked on McGovern's campaign. I became more interested in environmental issues. That was when I started recycling and using a kerosene lamp. All those summers on Hunter's farm gave me such an appreciation for greenness and open spaces filled with songs of nature, I just felt I had to help.

I wasn't comfortable with public speaking, so I didn't act as spokesperson for any of the groups I helped. But I turned out to be pretty good at running an office and really good at writing pamphlets and newsletters. When we went after a grant for the neighborhood technology project, we included a salary for me to manage. It wasn't very much money, but it was more than the budget Dad kept me on in college. My college roommate, Lisa, stayed on for a two-year MFA program so we kept our apartment and my expenses stayed the same. The extra money felt luxurious.

Lisa and I met during orientation week freshmen year. I looked at her and just knew I'd like her. She was tall and blonde and willowy, with huge brown eyes, like a fawn's. I figured anyone so lovely wouldn't be interested in me, but she came right up and started talking and we were inseparable after that. We met Terry and his friend Bruce in the student union that first week. We all became great friends and stayed tight even when one or more of us dated someone. We leafletted together and went to teach-ins and fundraising concerts besides smoking pot and going to films. Lisa was the daughter of a St. Louis jazz drummer and Terry had been a drummer for a jazz band in high school. They introduced me to a lot of music I'd not heard before. I tried to sing for them once. They said it was good but I could hear that my throat was still tight and kind of strangled the notes and I knew from their lack of enthusiasm that they were merely being polite. I didn't tell them I used to think I'd be a singer.

We got the apartment our sophomore year and decorated with print spreads from India that covered the furniture Lisa's mother gave us, beads hanging cross the door into the living room, a mobile of white doves, and posters with sayings like Thoreau's "different drummer". The Moody Blues, It's a Beautiful Day and Bonnie Raitt blasted on the stereo when we weren't playing Carmen or Don Ellis or Rahsaan Roland Kirk. Various boyfriends came and went but we were always there for each other. Feminism swept through and we caught the determination to be independent career women, which worked well, since all the guys needed to be free to go west and find themselves and "commitment" was an unspeakable word.

There were days I watched Terry, with his dark frizzy hair in that sort of white guy's Afro that was in then, big mustache and laughing eyes, and wondered how my adored friend could be one of those creatures. When I checked him out with his girlfriends, they'd tell me about things he did just like the guys I dated, though. I tried to get him to explain to me once how it was that we were all regular people being friends in one setting and then he turned into an alien when he was with his girlfriends. He said we were the ones who turned into aliens and we wound up all throwing popcorn at one another till we were so convulsed our sides ached.

Those were wonderful years. Finally I had lots of friends. Being smart was normal at Michigan. Plus, there was something about the time, the way we pulled together and worked for causes we believed in that created an aura of being one big happy family—better than our real families. We studied hard and put in time on our pamphlets and protests but always found time for big parties where we danced to "One More Saturday Night" and "Brown Sugar" and talked politics and gossiped for hours. I hated to see it end, but since I still roomed with Lisa and worked with a lot of the same folks on the project, it didn't seem so different.

When a group in Boston asked me to come set up their new neighborhood technology project, I decided it was time to move on. Although the rooftop greenhouse projects never took off, we had expanded our efforts by trying to promote the neighborhood technology idea. I thought the greenhouse thing was super and would still catch on one day. The idea was to put greenhouses on top of city apartment buildings and to grow fresh fruits and vegetables for nearby residents. By using solar energy properly, the greenhouses helped to heat the building without relying on big power supplies that guzzled resources while at the same time providing fresh food without wasting further resources in transit. The neighborhood technology program involved helping neighborhoods to design and execute plans for local projects that could save electricity, help the environment or produce small-scale power. I liked being part of something that could really help the earth.

Lisa was finishing her degree and planning to move to Chicago to marry Terry, who had a job on the *Chicago Daily News*. They fell in love after Terry left to get his master's in journalism at Northwestern. He came back to visit us whenever he could and next thing we knew, they were crazy about one another. Once it happened it seemed so natural it was hard to believe that they hadn't been together while we were all still in school.

I really didn't enjoy that year in Boston, but I talked to Lisa and Terry at least once a week and Maggie every couple of weeks and that really helped me get through it.

****

Grandma was ill through a lot of that time, so I headed to Lexington for long weekends whenever I could. My dad had gotten a new job back there before I left for college, so Mom was out at the farm with Grandma a lot. Even though it was upsetting to see Grandma so ill, it was a relief to get away and back to the kindly warmth of Lexington. I always thought of Grandma as lively and full of fun even though she was kind of frail and had those headaches all the time. In those last months she was listless and it was hard to get her to laugh. She fretted about Mom—kept saying she didn't think Mom was doing very well and that she wasn't sure she'd done the right thing. It was never clear what she meant by that. Then she worried that once she was gone, Mom would quit talking to Hunter. I figured that was probably true. Since Grandma had turned out to have all those brothers she didn't talk to, I couldn't see why she cared.

Towards the end, sometimes she was really out of it. Then at some point she became very peaceful and light and seemed to be communing more with some other world than with ours. One day she started talking to someone named Adrian, telling him she hadn't known. After a while she cried and just kept saying, "I didn't know." Then she muttered about Santa Fe and being the teacher. When she came around more and I asked her who Adrian was, she just said he was someone she knew a long time ago. But I saw her eyes light up at the sound of his name.

Once she told me she wished she could have done more for me. "I wanted to help give you the freedom to make some of your own choices," she said. "Try to live your own life."

She stared off into some faraway place for a minute, then continued, "We should have helped you with your music. I wanted my children to be allowed to choose their own lives, but then I found myself discouraging choices that frightened me just like my mama did. Now I can't think why I did it. All those worries." She grabbed my hand and looked intently at me. "There isn't any need to worry, Chloe. Do what's in your heart."

Then she began sighing and telling someone, "They call me Miz Harrison or

Mother. Sometimes people call me Virginia. But I was always Ginnie. I'm Ginnie, you know. Freddie knew."

"Grandma, who was Freddie?" I asked, wondering whether there had been yet another mystery man in her youth. But she had drifted off to sleep.

****

The guy I dated in Boston was pretty much like most of the guys I dated. His name was Ron, he had long frizzy hair and wore the uniform of blue work shirts and faded jeans that we all wore. He worked for another environmental group that put some funds in on one of our rooftop greenhouse projects. The primary focus of his life was the preservation of the environment. He was impatient with anyone who didn't recycle and avoid taking store sacks, who turned the heat above 55 degrees and failed to use a wood stove or who bought a new instead of a second-hand car. Like most environmentalists, his standards were rigid and you couldn't be a part of his group unless you displayed the right attitudes and behaviors. They prided themselves on having rejected their parents' values and rules and become free. I privately thought they'd just changed one set of limiting rules for another. I was always in a pivotal position because I had the right credentials but I would never buy the whole party line. But, I'd long since learned to be good at keeping my mouth shut about the things that would make other people angry and the skill served me well enough to allow me to remain in the heart of the movement.

Ron and I saw one another once or twice a week unless he thought I was too involved in other things, then he saw me more often. If I got used to it and started expecting to see him more, he'd suddenly disappear for days at a time. I was absolutely wrapped up in him. As with most of the men I dated, my instinct at the beginning was that he was trouble, but as he kept asking me out and telling me he wanted to make love to me, I convinced myself that this time it would work out. Through all his push/pull, here/not here tactics I told myself he really loved me and made up excuses for him.

"Chloe, he just didn't call you for a week? I'm sorry, there's no excuse for that. If he cared about you he wouldn't disappear because you offered to give him a key to your place."

"Oh, Lisa, you just don't understand him. I pushed him too hard is all."

"You told him you loved him and he left you alone and miserable."

"Well, I could have called him. Maybe he's wondering why I'm not calling."

"Chloe, get real. Terry's getting pretty mad, hearing how this guy's treating you."

We had some version of that conversation about most of the guys I dated, sooner or later. Week after week, I'd dredge up every little incident or word or look that supported my claim that he really loved me until the growing pain and the mounting evidence to the contrary could no longer be denied and then I'd break it off bitterly and Lisa or Maggie would get a series of tearful phone calls in which I excoriated the latest jerk and questioned whether I would ever find someone.

About the time I'd reached that turning point with Ron, I received an offer to work for a branch of a national environmental organization in Portland, Oregon. So I took the job and told him I'd be leaving. When he surprised me by suddenly deciding that he should think about going with me, I knew it was just his wanting-what-he-

can't-have syndrome and didn't say much when he brought it up. Predictably, he decided a few weeks before I left that he had to stay in Boston and that he couldn't stand the pain of staying together when I was leaving. Where did I find them?
****

Grandma died as soon as I got to Portland and I flew back for the funeral. Maggie couldn't come in from New York, where she got a job after design school in California, but she called and cried with me. Grandma and I weren't as close in the last few years as we had been. She didn't really understand or approve of my work and she said I dressed like a ragamuffin. I tried to keep her happy by just talking about things I did that she'd enjoy hearing about, but it was a strain. When she died, though, I felt like there was a hole in my life that would never be filled. I always knew she loved me no matter what and nobody else but Uncle Mike had made me feel that way. When the will was read, it turned out she created a trust for me. I was so touched. I thought everything had been tied up by my grandfather's will and hadn't expected anything. She instructed that I couldn't have the money until I turned 30, but there was a small income until then. Hunter pitched a fit when that part came out. There was a private letter from Grandma to me, telling me that the trust wasn't as much as she'd have liked to give but she hoped it would help to make me happy. She also said that Mom contributed to the trust too but I shouldn't let Dad or Hunter know that or they'd be angry with her. I couldn't believe it. I was so sad about Grandma that I couldn't focus on the trust, especially since it wouldn't affect me much for a few years.

I helped go through some boxes she'd kept in the closets up in her room and in the secretary at which she always sat to write her bills and letters. There was a little packet of notes and dried corsages wrapped in ribbon. The notes were from that guy Adrian and it sounded to me like he was a lot more than just some guy. Mom said her first husband's name was Jack and she'd never heard anything about this Adrian. Hunter said she thought they'd run into an old friend named Adrian on a train once but she didn't remember anything about him. His letters were charming and so filled with love for Grandma. I was dying to know the story. I could have fallen in love with him for his letters. There were some letters from Grandpa too. He must have been a dead bore.

We also found a whole trunk full of embroidered linens. I recognized some patterns from linens Grandma used all the time and I knew she had done the needle-work. "Wow," I asked over dinner, "did somebody close her in a room for a year with a thread and a needle and tell her she had to cross-stitch non-stop? There's more needlework than I can imagine one person doing!"

Hunter choked up, "She did such lovely work. You shouldn't make fun of it."

"I don't know when she did so much. She had already done most of it when I was a little bit of a thing," Mom said matter-of-factly.

"How about that guy Adrian? Do you think that was her first big love or something?"

"Ha! I can't imagine Mother having a big love," said Hunter with one of her abrupt changes of mood. "She was a repressed Victorian type if ever there was one."

"She sure inspired him to write some unrestrained gushing."

Mom faded away as her defenses went up and she just murmured, "There's a lot I guess we'll just never know now. We should have taken more interest while she was alive."

The next day I found a box full of sketches and pastels and watercolors that were dreamy and beautiful. Hunter said Mom did them. Mom wouldn't say any more than that that was a long time ago. I could tell she was pleased that Grandma had kept so many of them. I thought they were good and told her it was a shame she'd stopped.

"Why don't you just get some pastels and take a class or something?"

"I said I don't want to do it any more."

"But it would be such a nice way to fill more of your time... ."

"Leave me alone, Chloe!"

****

At first I found Portland really beautiful and was pleased to be there. It was late summer and the skies were an unrelenting bright blue. The mountains were clear in the distance—Mt. Hood, with its pointed peak, and Mt. St. Helen, looking like the top of a giant vanilla ice cream cone, to the north. Before long, though, I was glad that I'd just taken a one year contract. The rains started about a month after I moved. It was grey and drizzly for 20, 25 days in a row, then the sun would shine for a day and then it was grey again for a few weeks. Horrible.

People were really exclusive about hiking, camping and backpacking, organic gardening and self-sufficiency. They went on and on about how many miles they hiked with how many pounds in their packs. After a while, I thought if one more person talked to me about the best order of packing a backpack—like where to put the beef jerky and other equally scintillating details—I'd just start screaming and not stop. Several people told me I was too obviously urban and intellectual which I found interesting since my year in Boston was the only time I'd lived in a big city. Except for my years in Ann Arbor, it seemed like I'd never fit anywhere.

The project was interesting and the people I worked with were nice, but I put out feelers and was pleased to get an offer in Chicago with another environmental project. The pay was low, like all those jobs, but I knew I could get by on it. Mt. St. Helen's blew up before I left and the ash was everywhere. It took all the finish off the old red Volvo I picked up after I moved out there. Seemed like a good time to leave.

Lisa and Terry still lived in Chicago. Terry worked for the *Sun Times* since the *Daily News* folded and Lisa was doing illustrations for books. A few other friends from Michigan were in the area, so I figured it would be more comfortable. Every time I moved to a new place I hoped to be able to find a niche, but somehow I always wound up uncomfortable, awkwardly groping for a way to connect, but just not knowing how to relate to people.

Chapter Twenty-eight

On my thirtieth birthday, Mom presented me with the trust papers and told me I could renew the trust or the trustees would wind it up and I could do what I wanted with it. I hadn't expected it to be nearly as big as it was. I decided to dissolve it and used Mom's investment counselors to invest it and set it up to get the income. Then I really thought about what I wanted, since I knew that was what Grandma was trying to let me do. I really believed in my environmental work, but I kind of fell into it after giving up on music. If I were really honest with myself, I had to admit that I didn't actually like the work. It was more of a compromise—a way to earn a living that my conscience could live with if I couldn't do what I really wanted to do. My voice had never come back. I did well in creative writing for a while but then my imagination kind of dried up just like my voice had. I couldn't see any other way to make money. Suddenly I had enough money to do whatever I wanted without having to win Dad or Hunter over and I was more than slightly overwhelmed.

****

Mom left Dad not long after Grandma died. At first I was shocked because she'd never said anything about being that unhappy and I just assumed that she didn't mind all his rules and regulations about everything we did. Then she moved into her own place and all of a sudden there were all these hints of whimsy and brightness around her that I hadn't seen in her before. She'd left all the furniture with Dad and bought all new pieces—all delicate and airy. She came to Chicago to comb the galleries around Michigan Avenue and purchased some wild paintings. I'd never known her to have such energy.

Then, her first winter alone she went down to Sanibel, Florida with a friend and the next thing I knew she'd bought a house on the beach. Hunter called me up to convince me that Mom was going to throw away all her money if we didn't do something.

"Chloe, that money should be yours, but mark my words it will all be gone."

"That money belongs to her and if she chooses to spend it all that's up to her."

"I'm telling you, Chloe, that money needs to go into a trust... ."

"Hunter, the money is hers and it is giving her the freedom to do the things she wants to do for the first time in her life. Now, she has a CPA who's helping her and she consults with him before she spends any large amounts. He's not going to let her run through everything."

"Well, if you don't care anything about your mother, I wash my hands of you," she shouted and hung up. And *she* thinks Mom is nuts.

Mom had been off on her own a few years when I found myself with the option of choosing a new direction if I wanted it. Mom was back painting and sketching. She insisted it was just for fun, a hobby, and that she had no intention of trying to sell any of her work.

****

I figured that if I chose to study music I'd better plan on being able to earn some money with it. I didn't want to depend only on the trust income and never do anything else, like Hunter. I never understood why she decided to quit running the magazine. If I quit my job, I wasn't sure I could ever go back to the organizational work I'd been doing. I had a talent for it, but I actually despised the orderliness of it, the constant rational process of figuring out the best arrangements of personnel and income. The clear, logical writing required for pamphlets and newsletters afforded me no sense of creative accomplishment either. I didn't really notice how uncomfortable I'd become until I abruptly found myself free to quit.

Frankly, I had grown increasingly tired of the self-righteous elitism of the people with whom I worked. There was never enough funding to pay very much to secretaries or other staff, but everyone was expected to work outrageously long hours and put up with being snapped at. It was proof of devotion to the cause and being part of the group meant constantly proving that devotion. Sometimes it seemed to me that people in the liberal/left were really good at caring deeply about faceless masses in far away places but lacked the capacity to care for the people standing right next to them. I began to watch myself in action and didn't like what I saw.

I'd risen to a place of honor a couple of years before by consenting to be one of a group that planned to be arrested at the South African Consulate. Some lawyers with the Free South Africa movement wanted to create a forum for publicity on the situation in South Africa and to set a precedent for using the necessity defense to justify that form of protest. It was a cause to which I felt deeply committed and I didn't hesitate to volunteer for the assignment. Pretty ironic, considering my family's history and some of the attitudes I'd seen as a child. Fortunately, after a week-long media circus at the courthouse, the defense was accepted and we got off. Boy, Dad and Hunter were beside themselves over the whole thing. Mostly they were worried about what people would think. In my crowd, people thought it was great, but I wasn't as thrilled as I'd expected to be on achieving elevated status.

My neck stayed so stiff I could hardly turn my head and my head ached sometimes for days at a time. I tossed and turned most nights until three or four in the morning and I had to get up at six-thirty to get ready for work. Whenever we had a fundraiser I had a few especially bad weeks. I usually had to coordinate everything, which felt like a lot of pressure. Even worse, I was expected to show up and chat with people and be a salesperson for the group. I remembered all the times Hunter made me greet people at the door of her parties or hissed, "Get out there and mingle," when she took me somewhere. The next morning she'd complain to Grandma that she didn't think she could take me any place because I acted like a post and it was embarrassing. I had more in common with the guests at our fundraisers, but I always felt like I was about 14 and someone was going to come tell me to stop acting like a piece of wood. I tried to avoid parties when I could because I generally wound up going home in tears, after an evening spent wandering around in search of a familiar face to attach myself to; isolated, awkward and, ultimately, never belonging.

****

"Chloe, have you made any decisions yet about what to do with the money?"

Lisa and Terry had just fed me spinach lasagne and we were polishing off the Merlot I brought them. A big pot of French roast brewed in the background and the ginger mousse I made for dessert was still hidden in the refrigerator.

"Yea, kiddo. You gonna make some changes?" Terry chimed in.

"I haven't decided everything. I dissolved the trust and invested the money. And I reached one conclusion." I smiled over at them.

"What is it?" "C'mon. What're you gonna do?" They both demanded.

"I'm going to find a new apartment. Up here near you." Lisa and Terry lived in a great old apartment in Evanston. The floors were hardwood, in gorgeous condition, and the door and window frames were all mahogany. Lisa had found some wonderful antiques in oak and mixed them with newer solid oak pieces so that everything seemed to fit. I'd lived in small, crummy old places for years, decorated with whatever dredge I found at the Salvation Army in each new town.

"Fabulous. Evanston?"

"Well, I'm going to look in Evanston and Rogers Park. I've been studying the ads in the Reader and it appears I can probably get a better place for the same money in Rogers Park. But I'd prefer Evanston." I fell in love with Evanston the first time I saw it. The stately homes on tree-lined streets reminded me of Lexington. And I loved to sit on the beaches or walk the paths by the lake on Northwestern's campus.

"How much do you plan to spend?"

"I think I can go $300 more than I'm paying now."

"Oh you should be able to find a good place for that. We'll ask around."

"You could get a really exquisite place if you thought you could add another $100," Lisa told me.

"I could, except I haven't decided what to do about my job or school. At this level, I figured I could cut back to half time and pay tuition at the Chicago Conservatory if that's my choice and still keep my new place. And, if I wait a few months to change, I can afford to buy some new furniture. So, I want you to go antique hunting up in Richmond with me."

Thanks to Terry, I got a beautiful apartment in an old Victorian that had been split into three flats. The owner knew Terry and liked to choose his tenants personally and based in part on whether he thought they'd really love his flats. We met and liked one another and signed a lease. He didn't charge the going rate so I got more than I expected for the price I wanted to pay. The kitchen was newly remodelled, the hardwood recently refinished and the bathroom had been modernized. The living room had bay windows and there was a big dining room, plus a tiny extra bedroom that I turned into a study. Lisa and I started making weekly excursions and had collected some big old oak pieces by the time I moved in. Mom bought me a set of dishes that I picked out. It was the first time I ever had a place that looked like it belonged to a grown up. I even had original artwork—I sneaked out one of Mom's childhood watercolors, Maggie gave me some full color design drawings she'd made and Lisa had given me a couple of her paintings over the years. For weeks I came home every day and walked from room to room, trailing my fingers across tables and chair backs, gazing at all the lovely things in each room, noticing that everything matched, everything was in good condition. I didn't feel like a grown up though.

****

My housewarming party was about six weeks after I moved in. That was the night I finally made my choice. I invited lots of people from "the movement" and Lisa and Terry and the writers and artists I met through them. The latter were lively and interesting and enthusiastic about my new place. They agreed with our politics but they didn't talk about it incessantly nor did they judge people by some rigid set of standards for political correctness. I watched the politicos milling around in angst, all caught up over the latest crises in the legislature, South Africa, the rain forest.... I didn't want to be bothered any more. It wasn't that the issues lacked meaning for me, I was simply no longer interested in living up to the requirement that my life revolve around nothing else.

I lost count of the vaguely disapproving remarks about how elegant my new place was, how expensive the furniture looked. Others tried to ferret out how I afforded this change and said, "Ohhh," with just the faintest hint of distaste when they heard "inheritance." By the end of the evening I wanted to scream, "How dare you come to my home and judge me—and it's none of your fucking business how much money I have."

That Monday I made an appointment with the admissions director at the Chicago Conservatory to discuss becoming a part-time student the next term. They were pleased with my credentials, told me they accepted quite a few students who had taken time off from music studies and scheduled an appointment for me to play piano for a couple of the instructors. I found a place to practice and polished up a Chopin prelude I'd always liked. I played well but they gave me the impression they'd have taken me anyway.

As soon as I knew I could enroll at the Conservatory I put in my request to cut back to half-time. They weren't happy and it was clear that I was no longer considered "PC" but we worked out splitting my position and I began training my other half.

Dad was really angry when I told him. "I thought you'd given up on all that nonsense," he growled. Even over the phone I knew his jaw was jammed shut. Mom said Hunter wanted to know if I was ever going to grow up. As usual Mom expressed no personal opinion.

The choice made, the arrangements completed, I faced the greatest battle when I actually began attending classes. In every class I felt that I was the only student who'd never studied theory or had ear training. My teachers had all been oriented to actual practice only. It was possible at the school to study mainly jazz and modern music but my training had all been classical and it seemed I knew less than anyone there. Furthermore, I'd planned to slide from piano to voice once I was in, and signed up with a vocal coach, but my tight throat quickly became apparent and was of great concern to my teacher. In the one place I'd thought I'd really belong, I felt just as alienated and alone as I did everywhere else.

Day by day my tolerance for my job decreased. The man who ran the organization was a pompous ass and I'd never liked him, but when I was full-time and a favorite of the board, he rarely interfered with me. He became much more intrusive once I cut back— several times a week he'd invade my office to tell me what he wanted me to do differently. He'd lean back in his chair with his arms behind his head and big old sweat stains showing. He wasn't the only one though. Everyone seemed to question my loyalty and willingness to do a good job. Suddenly the petty bureaucratic processes I'd previously managed to ignore pervaded every activity. No matter what I did, someone proffered an alternative that might be better and I had to defend every decision. I started throwing up before going to work a couple of times a week. I slept no more than I had before and my nights were spent alternating between replaying outrageous office interchanges and creating nightmarish visions of flawed performances before laughing audiences.

The chance to practice again at first beckoned enticingly and I planned a rigorous schedule in the practice rooms. Some days I could barely force a note past the steel cords that surrounded my neck, though, and my instructor soon cautioned me to take it easy on the practice until he could figure out how to reduce the strain. The transition to jazz on the piano, where I'd always relied on a piece of music with a precise key and time signature, proved to be more of a challenge than I anticipated.

Something in me began distracting me from practice. I would decide to go to practice at three, say, and I'd get in the car and start driving. Suddenly it would be four and I'd have run some errands and found myself cruising along trying to remember why it was I'd come out to begin with. Consciously, no decision to skip practice or study was ever made—I simply drifted into another activity as if sleepwalking. Having started out feeling behind, the gap between my skills and those of the other students seemed to widen daily. I became more than usually inept at socializing with my classmates as I imagined they saw me as pathetically unskilled and minimally talented.

By finals time at the end of my first semester I'd lost 15 pounds and the circles under my eyes rivalled a raccoon's. I managed to get through the finals and even got better grades than I expected, but during the break I went in to ask the dean whether I could withdraw and come back later. With his help, I filed papers that gave me an indefinite leave status and went home to take stock. All through that period I called Lisa and Terry and a handful of other close friends several times a week to complain and panic. No suggestion that anyone made seemed workable to me. The more they offered possible solutions that were unacceptable to me, the more boxed in I felt.

I continued half-time at the project, but by then I loathed everything about it. The pompous ass escalated into open hostilities, making increasingly ridiculous demands for me to report to him on everything. His florid face appeared in my office four or five times every morning, in each case to register a complaint, though I was doing the same job I'd always done in the same way I'd always done it. He'd put similar pressures on the man who held the other half of my job until he quit shortly before I dropped out of school. I never mentioned that I could be available full time again.

Over the next couple of months, I looked at my financial picture and realized that, thanks to the impecunious style of financial management Dad taught me, I had budgeted myself quite a bit below my means and, with no school tuition to pay, that I could afford to live on the investment income alone. I gave notice the next week. I let my family think I still had the job, but I indicated that I'd taken a leave from school so that I could catch up.

****

Initially, relief was the overwhelming sensation at being rid of both the job and the studies; I'd worked and/or studied long hours ever since I went to Michigan and I luxuriated in vast unfilled hours in which I could read and listen to music. I still tossed and turned through much of the night, but, once I finally sank into uneasy sleep, I could stay asleep into the morning so that I wasn't quite as exhausted as I had been. Pleasure in my newly acquired freedom shifted downward gradually, almost imperceptibly, into depression. I had no idea what to do with my life. The only work I'd ever done had become an anathema to me and the only dream I'd ever had for myself clearly had been a child's fantasy, never to be realized. Some days I lounged around in my robe all day. Hours flew by while I read novels or immersed myself in reruns on TV—anything to avoid the silent spaces in which unanswerable questions arose and melancholy reflections on futility filled my thoughts. The panicky phone calls to every friend who would listen multiplied.

My friends compiled endless lists of possibilities to present to me and I carefully explained why each one was fatally flawed, proving by the end of every conversation that there was nothing I could do. My last relationship had gone the way of all the others so I couldn't even hold out the time-honored hope that I might be rescued by marriage. I began researching methods of suicide and pondered which I would choose. It wasn't exactly a serious pursuit although I found comfort in the knowledge of a means of escape and some mornings I cried when I woke up and found I hadn't died in the night.

Lisa and Terry called and announced they were bringing dinner one evening and arrived with a selection of dishes from my favorite Indian restaurant. We chatted inconsequentially over chicken masala and aloo mutter. As the eating wound down and rice-flecked plates sat amongst empty white cartons on the coffee table, Terry and Lisa shot one another a look before Lisa began talking.

"Chloe, we're pretty worried about you. And, uh, we wanted to talk with you about our therapist. You know we've both been seeing a therapist off and on the last couple of years and it has really helped and ... we were wondering if you'd ever considered consulting someone—you know, professionally."

I swallowed and found I had difficulty raising my eyes. That was actually the third time in a week that a friend suggested therapy for me. I'd already been thinking about it.

"Kiddo, we don't want to upset you or make you feel bad," Terry added, "but you've been so nervous and so down... ."

"It's okay, you're right. You're not even the first ones to bring it up," I told them. "And, actually, I've been considering whether to ask you more about your therapist. I've been intrigued by what you've told me about using meditation and regression and all. So ... I'd like her name and number."

Chapter Twenty-nine

"Okay, tell me about your reality with men. Did you think about your patterns this week? Kirsten looked over at me and smiled from where she sat, cross-legged, in her big overstuffed chair. A wild array of red curls was piled on top of her head and big hoops of gold hung from her ears. She had her office set up like a living room, with a couch and a couple of matching chairs, an oriental rug, and wind chimes softly toning outside the window. Sounds of flowing water and chirping birds emanated from a tape player in the corner.

"Yes, I thought a lot about it." I hesitated, as usual, before the plunge into revealing my insights.

"And?"

"And there've been a few patterns. One is that all the men I've dated have been commitment phobic. A second is that I turn into this dependent, clinging woman and start trying to make the guy want to stay; to be the one who finally tames him."

"How have these commitment phobic men responded?"

"They break it off. Or start pulling mean stunts until I break it off. So, I pick these guys who don't want to get married and I behave in the one way that's most likely to ensure that they won't want to be with me at all."

"What do you believe will happen to your life and your work if you get married?"

I squirmed as we touched into the heart of the matter. "I'm afraid that I won't be able to do anything I want to do, especially playing music."

"Chloe, what do the women in your family believe about men?"

I stopped and closed my eyes, remembering the answers to that question that had been floating into my consciousness all week. "They believe that men turn their wives into slaves. That men don't let women do what they want to do with their lives. That women need men to take care of them, so they should find a stable husband to marry and not worry about whether they really love him."

"Okay, important stuff. So you're caught in a place where you'd like to be married but you believe you can't have both a husband and the career that you also want."

"So I wind up sabotaging both because as soon as I start to achieve one, then I believe I lose the other." I felt the shiver of excitement that went through me each time I understood another part of the puzzle.

"Exactly. Now the part I want to explore is the fact that your beliefs about relationships have become one more in the network of beliefs that hold you back from letting yourself pursue your music. For next week, I want you to think about the mother figures in your family again and tell me everything they taught you to believe about success and womanhood, about careers for women, about careers in art, about creating a life that's what you want. Now, before we explore that a little further, I want you to tell me how your practice with the new meditation went and how the Rolfing is going. Any progress on your neck?"

Kirsten introduced me to a whole new world concept that, for me, brought a sense of meaning and order to the world for the first time. Terry and Lisa were excited about the new perspective she'd taught them and the three of us chatted enthusiastically all the time. The core principal of Kirsten's work was that each person creates her own reality with her beliefs. She taught me that I could take any situation in my life and then look inward to explore the beliefs that created that reality. It was amazing for me to start uncovering the things I really believed about life—all these sentences that Mom, Dad, Hunter and Grandma repeated incessantly began floating into my awareness and I began to see how much I had taken in of their fears and beliefs. Lisa, Terry and I talked regularly and in depth about the discoveries we were making.

"All of a sudden I'm looking at how I've always had these low paying jobs and stretched every dollar and now I hear my Dad saying, 'There are only so many dollars to go around,' and Mom saying 'Waste not want not.' Or my Grandmother fretting over whether the trustees would manage her money well enough and talking about holding onto the land so we can plant potatoes and have food when our money is wiped out... ."

"Oh, I know. And I've been thinking about how I've never really let my art take off. There was like this attitude that there's a big price to pay to have financial security and working at something you love isn't an option. Making a living has to be this unpleasant process," Lisa added.

"Exactly. You're never supposed to make money doing something you want to do. And my parents always disapproved of people who made 'too much' money—like they called Hunter and her friends 'wastrels'."

Terry nodded his head vehemently, "Right. So you can't do what you want and if you're halfway successful at anything you should feel guilty and whatever you have, you have to worry all the time that it can be taken away."

We talked for hours like that, each of us learning from the others' insights. But identifying belief systems was just part of the work. Kirsten taught me to meditate and gave me tips on learning to hear my inner wisdom and create a new belief system from my heart. "You can think about your world and how you want it to be, visualize it as you want it to be, and, if you've cleared any contrary beliefs, it will become what you envision," she'd tell me. She pressed me to sign on for the 10 sessions of Rolfing and to try massage and acupuncture, explaining that the body reflects whatever is out of balance in the mind or spirit.

My body had become one giant mass of tense muscles and my neck was in constant pain. According to Kirsten, all those twists and knots represented emotions and feelings that had been repressed. The total tension represented the restriction of my spirit, expressing the degree to which I had subverted my own personality and desires and talents in order to conform to the family rules as I perceived them. As the various practitioners worked on me, the shape of my body changed and I began to experience a freedom of movement and a sensation of lightness that I didn't remember ever feeling. My headaches pretty much disappeared and I began to be able to sleep at night. Once I finally could sleep, I felt totally exhausted. My voice was still tight and restricted and my neck remained something of a trouble spot, though with all the bodywork I had regained much more range of motion and no longer experienced constant pain. Some days I felt like I'd waked up in a different body.

And it did all work together. The more my body loosened up, the more my thinking seemed to relax. I used to get upset about every little thing that happened but I noticed after a while that I stayed pretty relaxed and I'd see myself laugh at things that would have sent me into a tailspin before. And the more I let go of the system of beliefs that had been holding my life in check, the more the bodyworkers were able to realign my body and release knotted muscles.

****

"Nonsense, why would you need therapy? Aside from the fact that you refuse to make something of yourself, you're perfectly normal," was Hunter's instant response when I told her I was seeing a therapist. "It's a waste of the money Mother left you. What is this with your generation and the self-centered need to focus all your attention on yourselves?" She was on her third drink since we'd been seated for lunch in her favorite restaurant—one of those white tablecloth, deep red carpeting places with overly attentive waiters.

"Well, things got pretty bad for me for a while there. I wasn't sleeping or eating and my head ached all the time."

"Oh, pooh. Everybody has a nervous spell once in a while and doesn't sleep. You just get on with it."

"So why did you quit working for the magazine?"

"We're not talking about me, but I decided to put more time into building a first class stable of race horses."

I didn't mention that I'd rarely seen her contribute anything much to that enterprise except pains in the necks of her employees. She seemed to feel the comment in the air, though, and her eyes misted over.

"I haven't accomplished much in my life—at least not compared to what I wanted to do. If I could have some of my opportunities back, I might do things differently. I tried to give you opportunities, you know." She shook her head ever so slightly from side to side and gazed unseeingly down at the table. I was so amazed that Hunter would ever make such an admission that I couldn't think of a thing to say. I wondered how many drinks she had before she came to lunch.

Suddenly the moment of candor vanished and she snapped upright, an ornery gleam in her eye. "Mother gave you an opportunity that she never gave Lily or me. All I can say is I'm glad she doesn't know how you're throwing it away."

I wondered for the umpteenth time what possessed me to consent to these occasional weekends in Lexington. When it wasn't Hunter, it was my dad. He told me therapy was for crazy people and forbade me to go on with it. I asked him what he figured his leverage was since I was well over 30 and had my own income. He told me I wouldn't be welcome in his house any more and I said "Fine," and left.

****

"Have you been thinking about what your 'mother figures' believed about success and women's lives?"

"Yes. I have."

"And, what have you come up with?"

"Well, I don't think my mom and my grandmother really believed women could be successful on their own. In fact, they didn't believe women should try. Hunter believed in trying, but I don't know if she really believed it was okay to succeed. She went pretty far—although that had a lot to do with Uncle Mike—and then she quit."

"How do you think she'd feel about it if you were to succeed?"

I closed my eyes and searched inside for an answer. The one that popped up a minute later surprised me. "She never wanted me to be more successful than she was—or even to come close. She wanted to be the star."

"Okay, we've already realized that you tried to conform to your parents' expectations because, on some level, you sensed their vulnerability and felt a need to protect them. What did you feel about Hunter?"

Again I went inward and asked the question. "Wow. She was almost more vulnerable than they were. I felt responsible for her too. It was like I was afraid they'd all fall apart if I disappointed them."

"Now add in your father. What did he believe about success?"

"He believed that if you worked really hard you were entitled to some success. Really, when I think about it, all of them connected success with money."

"How did they feel about people being successful at things they're good at or that make them happy?"

"Whoa! Not cool!" I was beginning to feel that thrill that came with insight and I started talking faster and waving my hands more as I grew more excited. "First of all, if you're good at something, then usually doing it comes easily and the only things worth having or doing take struggle and hard work. It's not worth anything if it comes easily." I thought for a second, "Wow, so almost by definition any special talent you're born with isn't worth doing."

Kirsten nodded agreement and I continued, "My dad and my aunt think it's like a sin to even want to be happy. Dad thinks you decide a career based on where the high salaries are no matter what you might want to do. Hunter thinks you can enjoy your work as long as what you want is to be at the top of some prominent business but nothing else is worth doing. Mom and Grandma believed in opting for stability—provided by men—over trying to live their dreams."

"How does it make you feel to realize that they all tried to teach you that you couldn't do what you wanted with your life?"

She was always trying to lead me back to the feeling. Even as long forgotten parts of my body regained sensation, I remained numb and drew a blank when she asked me to feel. I stared at her and shrugged, "I don't know. I guess I feel disappointed that they taught me such limiting things."

"A little disappointment? Is that really all you feel as you sit here too paralyzed to pursue the career you want?"

"Well, more than disappointment. Kind of upset, I guess."

"Chloe, don't you feel even a little angry? They were supposed to teach you how to be yourself in the world, not to take your dreams away and show you how to match some prototype of life they created out of their own fears. Now I want you to think about all these beliefs we've discussed the last few weeks. You had a right to expect that you, the real you, the essential you, would be loved unconditionally by your family. It was their job to help you unfold according to your nature, not to bind you in so that you couldn't find any way to survive as yourself. Try again to do a release session."

It wasn't the first time she asked me to try. The idea was to pile up lots of pillows and do some "charge up" breathing that she taught me, while thinking about the system of beliefs my family had taught me, then to take a Styrofoam bat she gave me and release the emotions I'd called up by yelling and bashing the pillows. I managed to work up a small amount of anger the first couple of times, but mostly I cried. She said that was fine, that I'd reached the pain and the anger was underneath that. I hated those sessions. Even alone in my apartment, I felt like a fool sitting and staring at a pile of inert pillows, trying to pretend that they were my family and that I was furious with them.

I didn't realize at first how totally I had frozen in response to her last questions, but at the same time that I looked up and found those dark green eyes staring thoughtfully at me I became conscious that I was holding my breath and my shoulders were creeping up to the vicinity of my ears.

"Are you sure that neither of your parents was an alcoholic?"

She'd asked me before. "Well, I know my father isn't. It's against his religion, so he doesn't drink at all. But I did think about it after you brought it up. My aunt drinks a lot. And I remember a few things my grandmother mentioned about my grandfather—I think he drank a lot. And, I'm not sure about it, but there was a spell when Grandma told me she was worried about Mom. It was long after I left home, but I had a funny feeling sometimes when I talked to her that she'd been drinking. She never did before then. While I lived with them, there was never any alcohol in the house."

"Okay, that would explain it."

"Explain what?" I asked warily.

"You exhibit a lot of the behaviors of an adult child of alcoholic parents."

"Such as?"

"The inability to feel your feelings, the sense of being different and an outsider, the strong family loyalty, the devotion to choosing the path that will most please other people while abandoning your own goals and wishes. All those behaviors that we keep addressing are typical ACOA behaviors. And if there is a history of alcohol abuse in your family, it wouldn't be surprising that you would exhibit those behaviors even though neither of your parents drank when you were a child. It doesn't really change the treatment I want to pursue with you, but you might find it useful to read a little on the subject. I think you'll be able to identify some of your behavior patterns."

****

Ironically, around the time Kirsten and I worked on success issues, Mom was "discovered." She was sitting out on the beach painting one day and some woman who ran an art gallery watched her work and got really excited. Mom used light in really interesting ways in her pictures and she tended to tuck little wood nymphs and fairies here and there in them. The woman said they were wonderful examples of "New Age" inspirational art and bought a few for her gallery. The paintings sold quickly and the woman asked for more.

"Mom, that's pretty amazing. How does it feel to be selling all these paintings all of a sudden?"

"Surprising. I never expected to make any money from my art, let alone to be making quite an income for it."

"I think it's exciting. As soon as you started doing the one thing you loved to do most, success came and found you. That's the way it's supposed to work." I'd come to believe that the best way to success was to be able to follow your heart, but I hadn't known any major examples that proved the maxim.

"Well, it was just a fluke. This kind of thing doesn't usually happen. Is that something that therapist told you?" she asked uneasily.

"Well, she introduced me to the concept, but I ran into it other places and developed my own feeling about it."

"Well, I don't understand why you feel you want this therapy. I hope nothing I ever did caused some kind of harm."

Her biggest fear from the day I started therapy was that I might blame her for something. I tried to explain that the memories you bring up are your own perceptions of what happened at the time and that the important thing is your interpretation of what happened and the beliefs you formed based on your perceptions so that blame wasn't an issue. But she didn't really get it.

Chapter Thirty

When I returned to the Conservatory, I was still working hard with Kirsten, but my life had already changed amazingly. I walked into the school feeling that I belonged there. In fact, I felt pretty comfortable everywhere I went. It had been a long process, one small step at a time. Sometimes a new insight immediately led to a new behavior, sometimes I worked around many aspects of an issue, like fear of success, before I saw any sign of impact in my everyday life.

The school was in an old building and I had thought of it as kind of dingy and depressing, but it seemed brighter than I remembered it and I noticed how highly polished the old floors and bannisters were kept. I walked down the halls feeling relaxed and friendly and looked at people directly—and many of them said hello. Starting conversations was still not one of my greater skills, but other people just began talking to me everywhere I went and I discovered a talent for keeping the conversation going. Even though a few years had passed, a few students who were enrolled at the school on my first attempt were still there. Some did not recognize me. Others were surprised when I smiled and said hello. Suddenly I belonged. It was so amazing to feel like I was part of the world, connected to people.

Invitations to jam with fellow students became frequent. I was shy about going at first, still unsure of the caliber of my talent. Once I finally tried, though, it was fun. The range of skill levels represented varied widely and I soon learned to avoid the groups that considered themselves superior and met to show off and one-up each other. Many graduates played in bands throughout the Chicago music scene and my network began to extend to some of those more established musicians.

Lisa and Terry loved club hopping, so the three of us began regular outings to hear jazz and blues around the city, especially on Lincoln Avenue where we could take in several clubs in one night, from the smoky little bar, Orphans, to the Bulls, with its cavern atmosphere and red-checked tablecloths. Traditional jazz, Latin jazz, modern jazz, acoustic or electric blues, rock and roll—we drank it all in. Often we encountered students from the school or were joined between sets by musicians I'd met along the way. Every now and then someone asked me to sit in but my new found courage did not extend to public performance and I refused. I was so happy just to be at the school, making friends and allowing myself to try.

In the old days when I went to the clubs it felt so different. I loved to hear the music and feel its immediacy in the intimate setting. I watched the musicians carefully and wondered how they found the courage to get up there. I developed an occasional crush on some musician whose music I particularly admired. But I never wanted to date him. It was more like I wanted to be him—some kind of vicarious way to experience being a musician. After I went back to music school, it never happened again. Naturally, I ran into some of those guys in my new life and at first I felt a twinge of initial embarrassment. But then it occurred to me that they probably never knew I'd wanted to suck the musician essence from their veins.

****

"Okay. I'm glad that things are going so much better. You know I'm delighted that you're back in music school. But you're still struggling to release the last of the tension from your body, you can't bring yourself to perform in public and you don't want to try dating again because you're not sure about whether you can handle a serious relationship. So, are you ready to talk about doing the emotional release work?" Kirsten sounded firm.

I wriggled uncomfortably. I knew that we couldn't accomplish much more without that work. I gave her a half-hearted smile and told her I was willing to have a go at it.

"Great. Now, before we start next week, there's some work I want you to do." She reached into her desk and pulled out a big set of stapled pages. "These are lists of negative beliefs. I want you to make a list of your mother's beliefs, then your father's. Since you've done a lot of work on beliefs, this should be a pretty easy job. This is just going to be a more comprehensive list than you've made. Will you have time this week?"

"Oh, sure. I can do this."

"Great. Then we'll be ready to start next week."

I enjoyed working on figuring out my belief systems and bringing to light the many beliefs I held unconsciously, so I was glad to find time to sit down with the list. One night I showed it to Lisa and Terry and the three of us really got into shouting out the admonitions we heard all the time as children.

"Oh, don't take chances," Lisa commanded.

Terry threw in, "Don't trust anyone outside the family and be wary of anyone you don't know."

Lisa hung her head and whined, "Never let anyone see that you're angry."

"Hey, never let anyone see that you feel anything," Terry growled.

"Do as I wish or I will not love you," I told them, mock seriously. After a while we were jumping around, pointing fingers at one another and trying to outshout one another, "Realize you can never be good enough ... Avoid success ... Know how to do everything without asking for directions..."

Finally we settled back down on the couch together and sipped some wine. Terry stared out into space and spoke for all of us when he said, "You know, this was fun. But the sad thing is the three of us really believed all that crap and it's hurt us."

"Yea," I said, "it makes me kind of mad."

****

"Ready?"

I wanted to smack the perky smile off Kirsten's face, but I forced myself to smile back and said, "You bet."

She got up and opened a door off to the side. I'd never known where it led. She waved me into a small room with padding on the walls and floor. There were lots of pillows piled up in one corner and in another, on a stand, was a big, round inflated figure that reminded me of a cartoon Bozo, with a big Styrofoam bat lying next to it. I felt frozen in the center of the room.

Kirsten just started right in. "First we're going to do the charge-ups to get your energy moving and bring the emotions to the surface. I'll do them with you and then you're going to go with whatever emotion comes up. You can kick or pound on a pile of pillows, scream or cry, or bash the guy in the corner with the bat. Any questions?"

"No," I said weakly. "I think I understand."

Kirsten started the charge-ups and pretty soon we were both jumping up and down, making weird noises, shaking around. I felt like an idiot. We did it for a while and stopped.

"What are you feeling, Chloe?"

I thought for a moment and shrugged, "Winded."

"Let's do some more. Now think about those beliefs you worked with this week while you're charging."

That time when we finished, I dropped to my knees and started to cry.

"That's good. Go with it Chloe." She set up some pillows for me to curl up on and brought a box of Kleenex. When the crying faded, she placed one hand over my solar plexus and put a little pressure on. "From here, Chloe. Come on, let it out." Suddenly I began sobbing. "That's right. Cry it all out. This is the place to do it." Every time I slowed down she pressed her hand in again—it was like she pressed right on the place where some emotion was held and a jolt of energy popped it to the surface. After a while, she said, "Don't stop crying. But talk to me while you cry. Tell me what you're seeing or remembering."

"My mother didn't want to have a baby," I sobbed first, then jumped into another experience, "They didn't want me to be myself. They were always telling me to be different. Nothing I ever did was right except to get good grades." I could barely sob out the words.

At the end of the session, Kirsten was encouraging, "That was a good start. You moved into it faster than I thought you might. I think all this pain is covering a lot of anger. But we haven't gotten out all the pain. Give me a call if anything comes up this week and you need some help. You may find that more emotions keep coming up."

She was right. Several nights that week I found myself sobbing over some memory or something on TV that touched a chord in me and set me off. I never realized before how stunted and repressed I felt by all the rules and regulations, all the decorum I was supposed to observe. Much as I had dreaded that part of the work, I actually felt a deep sense of relief each time I cried. I could almost literally feel a space open up in my body. I began to feel even more relief from the tension in my muscles.

My meditations became deeper and I began to receive remarkable insights and information that were like guide posts for my life. I had this clear vision of myself as a very small child, only this child was bright and vivacious, energetic, full of life and extremely extroverted. Suddenly I understood how far off I had gone from the person I started out to be, how much I had buried of myself in order to satisfy my family. That original, essential child, I could feel, had the capacity to do everything I wanted to do and would have been doing it already if she'd been supported and nurtured.

"How could they not have liked her?" I found myself wondering in growing pain and anger.

The next week, I began to sob almost as soon as we started the charge-ups. The sobs quickly turned to howls and screams. "Where are you Chloe?"

"In a room."

"Can you see who's there?"

"Mom and Daddy." A child's voice that seemed unrelated to me came out.

"And what's happening?"

I started to see something and then it faded. I gasped and sucked in my breath.

"Chloe, who's taking your breath away?"

I started crying again and shrank away from her.

"Come on Chloe. Don't disappear on me. Nothing is going to happen to you here. You need to remember. This was when you learned to disappear. Do you want to stay hidden the rest of your life?"

"No."

"Then relax for a second. Breathe with me. Now, slowly move back into that room."

I started sobbing again.

"What's happening?"

"It's Daddy."

"What's he doing?"

"He's trying to strangle me." The sobs began turning to screams again and I began to writhe around.

"Why, Chloe?"

I struggled through the sobs and screams to keep myself in the picture and to see and feel what was happening. "I laughed too much. He wanted to kill me for laughing too much."

"Was anyone else there?"

"I think Mom and Hunter. They all wanted to kill me... why did they want to kill me?" Finally I just screamed and yelled out in pain at feeling abandoned and betrayed. For the first time I really knew how it had felt to be that loving, happy child as she came to realize that nothing about her was acceptable to the people she loved. I kept reliving the hands around my neck.

Then I began to see unfamiliar scenes. A small young woman in a long ball gown with a bustle, dancing with a tall blonde man who left her in the middle of a dance. A little girl with an easel, painting a picture, when a cranky woman came in and turned the easel over and took the paints away. A young woman watched some soldiers knock an old man down. Another little girl was angry because she thought her mother didn't want her. All these scenes flickered in and out in the midst of my memories of being choked and feeling that they all wanted to destroy the essence of me.

Through it all, I screamed and cried. My body seemed to be responding to directions from some place other than my brain. My fists pounded the pillows with a vengeance. My head twisted from side to side. My heels crashed into a pillow as my legs kicked at a furious pace. Somewhere in the back of my mind I took it in that I was out of control for the first time in my life but I had moved to some place beyond self-consciousness and the screaming and writhing just went on.

When the screams finally faded back to sobs, Kirsten said, "You were little then and he could overpower you. But none of them can do that now." Suddenly she grabbed some pillows and threw them on me, then jumped on top, pinning me down and reaching for my throat. The pillows were heavy and Kirsten was six feet tall, big boned and built on very sturdy lines, so I felt truly trapped. "Your father's going to try to choke you again. What are you going to do this time?"

Under the weight of Kirsten and the pillows, I felt panicky and helpless. "I can't move," I whined.

"Is that it? Are you going to let him choke the life out of you? You're just going to lie back and let him do it?"

"No." I began to squirm.

"C'mon. Is that the best you can do? Tell 'em you're mad."

"I'm mad," I yelled. "I hate you!"

"Fight, Chloe. Don't let them win this time."

I began to struggle. Every time I got an arm or a foot free, she piled a pillow over it and pressed down again. I cried and kicked and yelled and poked and she stayed right with me. Finally I was livid with hatred and anger and focused all my strength on one last push with my arms and legs and whole body that sent Kirsten and the pillows flying.

Kirsten jumped up right away and started clapping. "You did it Chloe. You did it. Do you understand this? You've taken control in this moment and pushed out the past so that in the now you can be yourself. How do you feel?"

"Like a huge weight just lifted," I grinned and winked at her. Actually I felt like a balloon that had been sitting around for about a week. After I stayed still for a couple of minutes, I turned my head from side to side and there were a couple of pops. Suddenly warmth and energy started pouring through my neck. "My neck is free."

Over the next weeks I worked through the pain and the tears and eventually uncovered a lot of anger. Anger at Mom for all her rules about being a lady and following the norm. Anger at my dad for being so rigid and unyielding. Anger at Hunter for trying to make me into somebody else, anger at myself for listening to them. Angry that I'd spent my life feeling that I had no right to be alive. I bashed that bat of Kirsten's into piles of pillows so hard and so long that pieces of Styrofoam began to fly and I had to ask her for another bat and then another.

I was startled one day in the midst of a frenzied session to realize that I'd have beaten the crap out of anyone who came in and crossed me at that moment and that I actually had a capacity to be really violent and even enjoy it. Kirsten told me that everyone has that capacity within them and that it is part of our oneness that each of us contains all possibilities but that I didn't need to worry that I would actually do it.

My massage therapist began exclaiming over the changes in my body and getting previously resistant muscles to release. People started telling me how great I looked and when I gazed in the mirror I saw a relaxed and happy face that seemed to belong to a stranger.

Chapter Thirty-one

The day my neck loosened my life changed on so many levels, not the least of which was the end of the pain that had been constant for years. The personality changes were subtle and unfolded one after the other. Every now and then I would watch myself cracking jokes in class or unselfconsciously experimenting musically in front of other students or calmly insisting upon service to my satisfaction in some store and think, "Who is this woman? I never would have done that before."

"Oh, Chloe, it's like a miracle," Maggie spoke in awed tones. "You sound so completely different. Strong and confident. You used to sort of swallow most of your sound so your voice was tiny. And then to hear your enthusiasm for what you're doing and your assumption that you'll keep moving ahead. Really. It makes me want to call once a week just to drink in the good vibes."

"Wow, it's so great to have other people tell me how much shifting they see in me because I lose track." Maggie lived in New York and had been designing for a specialty boutique for a few years. We still saw one another occasionally while visiting our families in Lexington but most of the time the phone was our only connection. Friends who saw me or talked to me after a long absence often commented on the tremendous difference in me and, on reflection, I could recognize the degree of change they saw, but for me each new shading followed so smoothly from the one before that I wasn't always conscious of just how different I was.

Even Lisa and Terry noticed changes now and then. "You don't complain all the time any more."

"Terry," Lisa gave him a shocked look.

I just laughed. "It's okay. It's true, I used to complain all the time. Now I feel good about my life and I know that if I'm not happy about something the place to look is inside myself. The whole world looks different, now."

"You look different too," Lisa added. "You stand tall and straight and your face is so relaxed instead of tight and defended and worried."

The change that most dramatically affected my life was my singing voice. After the tension in my neck disappeared my ability to sing came back with a clarity and range beyond anything I ever remembered hearing from myself before. In my voice classes everyone suddenly sat up and listened. I found it very exciting to sing in front of a room full of people and to realize that they were enthralled.

My voice teacher, Avery, was blown away and launched an intensive training program in the styles of jazz I'd been begging to learn. Finally my voice was free enough to slide from note to note and move lightly over minor thirds and tough melodic changes. After a few months Avery started inviting me to sit in with him and some local musicians he played with off and on. By the end of the school year he told me that he had some friends in a hot band that needed a vocalist and he thought I'd be just what they needed.

That created a serious dilemma because I was more than a couple of years shy of a degree. If the band offered me the gig and I accepted I'd need to quit school because the band travelled around the Midwest quite a bit and often played five or six nights a week. On the one hand, I worried about quitting school and whether I had quit too many things, whether I'd be sorry one day that I didn't have the degree in music. On the other hand, a couple of the guys had been in bands with hit records years before and supposedly this group was attracting interest from several record companies. It was the kind of shot I'd wished for all my life and it seemed foolish to throw it away. Underneath it all I was unbelievably excited, partly because this was exactly what I'd started visualizing about what I wanted to do when I finished school. I just hadn't expected to draw what I asked for so quickly.

All my friends thought I should go for it. "I can't believe this is even a question." Terry shook his head in disbelief.

Lisa chimed in, "This is a fabulous opportunity, Chloe. Really. What is the music degree going to get you that is any better than this? Besides, why do you have to decide before you've even auditioned?"

"I know, you're right. The degree just gives me more back-up for teaching music if all else fails. But if I'm a working musician, no one will care about anything but whether I'm good. And I guess I could just audition and then see if I even have a decision to make." For some reason I still waffled back and forth about what to do.

Kirsten helped me begin to tip the balance. "Isn't that your family talking on this quitter thing?"

"Well, I suppose it might be."

"C'mon. What do you imagine they're going to say when you tell them? And don't tell me you haven't imagined what it would be like to lay this one on them."

"You're right. For me it's a dream. My friends think I should do it. And I can just hear Hunter now."

"Okay, this is the point where you decide whether you're going to live your own life. You have to be able to follow your dream whether or not your folks like it or they'll control you all your life. When you started therapy, you wanted to free yourself to do exactly this. Is this still what you want to do?"

"I think so. Sometimes I wonder if I'm just hanging onto a kid's fantasy and really don't know what dream is mine in the here and now."

"Well, that's a question only you can answer. I can tell you that when you talk about music you sound like a person who knows her life's purpose."

I kept thinking and thinking about it, weighing pros and cons. Finally one day when I laid it all out to Lisa one more time, she frowned slightly and tossed a speculative glance my way before asking, "How do you feel when you sing?"

My mouth opened and shut a time or two before I told her with some surprise, "You know, I've never paid attention."

After she left, I put on some of my favorite songs, stretched out on my big striped couch and paid attention to my whole body while I listened. Then I sang along with some other favorites and stopped to close my eyes and take in everything I could feel in and around myself from head to toe. I found I was part of the music, connected with something larger than myself. I wasn't really aware of my body any more—at least not as something separate. Instead it belonged to a pulsating force that came from inside me yet surrounded me and was part of everything. When I stopped, I was at peace, energized, expanded! Any question I might have felt about whether I'd been born to play music was laid to rest. I was left with a profound sense of knowing who I was in a way I never had before.

Then I just had to decide how to pursue my life as a musician. I knew I might have another shot at a band at some later point but I finally chose to grab the opportunity that had been put right in my hands. This time I went to my audition and got the gig. I was a back-up vocalist for a working band and I'd get to do some leads.

****

"Well, we might have known you wouldn't finish music school. One of these days, Chloe, you're going to have to grow up and decide what to do with your life." Hunter and Mom and I were having lunch together. Mom and I tried to coordinate our visits to Lexington because we could handle Hunter better as a team.

"I did make a decision. When I went to music school I wanted to become a singer and now I've accepted a fabulous job as a singer." I spoke in measured tones, trying not to panic nor to betray the rising fury I felt over the way she talked to me.

"Oh, if you imagine this is really going to lead to anything you're a bigger fool than I thought," she shot back with disdain.

"I think it sounds like a good opportunity," Mom said quietly. Hunter and I both turned to stare. Once Mom started selling all those paintings something in her seemed to change. She was still kind of reticent, like she was always hidden behind herself, but she'd speak up with real conviction now and then. That was the first time I'd heard her defend me against Hunter.

"I swear, neither one of you has ever had a drop of common sense."

"Mom is making all kinds of money from her painting," I shot back. "What can you say you've produced lately? I'm trying to do something with my life. And I think bringing music to people is important work. I haven't seen you do anything but party for years." I shocked myself with that one, but I was wound up and ready to keep going.

"How dare you talk to me like that?" she almost hollered.

"How dare *I*? How dare you? You've talked to both of us that way all our lives. Well let me tell you something Hunter. I can't speak for Mom, but I'm going to tell you here and now you may not speak to me that way any more. The next time you do, I'll walk out and we'll never talk again."

"Lily, are you going to let your daughter speak to me this way?"

"It's about time someone did," Mom said. "I'll throw my two cents in. I don't like it when you talk to me that way either. Chloe and I have made different choices and we have different lifestyles than you do. Not worse than, not less than, just different than. We're entitled to make those choices without being belittled by you. So don't do it to me again either."

Hunter started to stand up, then seemed to think better of it and sat back down again. She glared at us in silence for quite a while. Mom and I just stared back at her—and grinned at one another every now and then. "Well, since you obviously don't want to hear anything else I have to say, I'm going to go on home," she finally said with what I'm sure she imagined was a great deal of dignity.

She was pretty drunk by then and staggered on the way out of the restaurant. I followed to make sure she didn't get in her car. The restaurant, where she was a regular, had, as usual, called a cab to wait for her. Mom followed me out to the farm, but we just left her car and didn't go in. I'd never seen her quite so bad. The next day, she called and wanted to get together and acted as though nothing had happened. Over the next few days of the visit I realized that she'd reached the point where she basically drank all day long and stayed plastered all the time.

On the last day, I finally spoke up, "Hunter, your drinking has gotten way out of hand."

"Who are you to criticize anything about the way I live?" she snapped.

"I'm not criticizing. I'm worried. You can't keep on this way. It's going to kill you."

"And what difference would that make?" she asked. I noticed that her eyes, already bloodshot and slightly damp with bleariness, filled with tears. "At least I could be with Mike again."

"Oh, Hunter. Come on. Mike would be the last person to want to hear you talking like that. And don't tell me I couldn't know, because I remember Mike. He was the one person who tried to teach me to follow my dreams."

"You remember that?"

"Yes. He believed in having dreams and making them come true so you could get the most out of life. I can't believe he'd like you to drown yourself in booze and die young because you gave up. Don't you think he'll know what you've done?"

"I don't know. I suppose if he still exists up there, he might be able to see me."

"Is this what you want him to see? You slurring your speech and not making any sense, barely able to walk half the time and talking about wanting to die?"

She started crying. "I can't do anything about it. I don't know how to stop. And if I checked into one of those clinics people would talk."

"Oh, please. What difference does it really make if they talk? Besides, all the best people seem to check in and out of the Betty Ford clinic at the drop of a hat."

"Movie people," she said with a dismissive wave of her hand.

"Well, they're pretty rich and famous. And some major political figures have been there. You could make a splash in a whole new crowd." I could see that I'd gotten her attention; the wheels were turning somewhere in the middle of that semi-pickled brain.

"I'll think about it."

It wasn't until the plane ride back to Chicago that I realized that I was going home to begin the life I'd always wanted, that I'd just lived through announcing that fact to my family—and I actually laid down the law with my aunt and then told her what I thought she should do with her life! When I got home I just put my bags down and jumped in the car and drove to Lisa and Terry's. I was jumping up and down in the hall when they opened the door, squealing, "I did it! I did it!"

"Did what?" I heard as I jumped past them through the door.

I executed a little dance around their glass coffee table and past the Shaker rocker while I announced, "I told Hunter off about everything. About not making nasty remarks to me any more, about her drinking too much. Everything. And I didn't back down. And I didn't shake too badly while I did it either."

"You're kidding! Congratulations!"

"I think this calls for a toast," Terry called over his shoulder on his way down the long hall to their kitchen.

I poured out every detail of the confrontation while we sipped sparkling cider and munched on the cinnamon doughnuts that Terry conjured up. They were a duly appreciative audience. Each of us, I think, always felt delighted by the others' breakthroughs because every victory reassured us that the new path we were trying really worked.

****

I arrived early for my audition with the band. Someone in the group was friends with a club owner who let them practice in the afternoon, when the club was closed. I went in through the back, as instructed. From the bar, I could hear someone playing in the main room. I noticed how strange the long mirror over the bar looked without the reflections of dozens of heads. And how lonely the bar stools seemed without a lot of butts parked on them. I moved as quietly as I could to the door between the rooms and stayed there listening. I'd never heard the song before but I felt as if the person who wrote it had taken the lyrics and the melody from some place in my soul.

When he finished I walked into the room and toward the stage. The tables, usually nearly hidden by the people gathered around them, revealed their many battle scars. The chairs stood around them forlornly, as if just waiting for the time when occupants had rearranged them to face the stage and the music had begun. One guy sat alone on a stool, a guitar cradled in his hands. When he saw me he stood and I could see that he was very tall and slender. His hair was blonde and nearly brushed the tops of his shoulders. His eyes were large, so dark they were almost black, very pure and open. When he looked at me I'd have sworn I saw lights flash out from behind his eyes. The next second, from out of nowhere, I thought, "Oh my God, I've waited for this man all my life. This is him. This is it." Then I thought, "Geez, it's been too long since I had a date." Except, I remembered, it hadn't been all that long.

He just stood there staring for a minute, then said, "You must be Chloe. I'm Jamie Hudson. Avery says you're just what we need. And I don't know if he mentioned it, but you've actually jammed with a couple of guys in the band. They told me not to line up any other auditions until I heard you."

I could hardly tear my gaze from him and I was more than a little nonplused to hear all that praise. "Well, I don't know about harmony so much. I don't have a lot of experience... I, uh, loved that song you were practicing. I haven't heard it before."

"It's one of my new ones." He kept gazing at me and then staring down to where his hand strummed lightly, soundlessly, just beyond the strings of his guitar. "Well, uh, let me just hear you first on your own so I can get an idea of your style and range and then we'll see what you can do on harmony."

In my first few weeks with the band we stuck to professional business. Although my attraction to him only grew, I was too nervous about whether I could make it singing back-up to let myself think about Jamie personally. Once I settled in more, and realized that I had more aptitude for harmony than I thought, I allowed myself to pay more attention to him. That was when I realized that he was also quietly paying attention to me. Sometimes a few of us from the band went out for coffee after practice. Jamie and I started saying yes every time someone brought up coffee and then we'd manage to sit next to each other. It was nice because it gave us a chance to get to know one another without pressure. That was a whole new behavior for me—I'd always jumped in with both feet right off the bat and then realized after I got to know the guy that I shouldn't have been there in the first place. After a while the two of us started having coffee alone on the days when no one else went.

"I don't know what I think about most of the political issues any more. I mean, once I was sure I knew how to define the problems and what all the answers were. I worked for all these environmental groups and spent my spare time helping other causes. Now I'm not so sure any more." It was the first time I'd told anyone my growing doubts.

"That's how I've been feeling. I'm not so sure some of the things we won over the years were really victories. I mean, would you really call welfare a success? Or do you think it has helped to try to terrify people into environmental consciousness?"

"Exactly. My sense is that we've been looking at every situation with our minds and not our hearts and that we can never find good solutions until we add heart." I paused and reflected a moment on the array of coffees listed on the board over the counter. "I don't know how to do that. But now I feel like I wouldn't presume to push any program unless I did know how to do it."

"That's just what I've been thinking."

Our conversations seemed to go that way most of the time. Sometimes we even finished one another's sentences. A lot of the songs he wrote touched the same place in me I felt when I heard that first one. Jamie liked to talk with me about serious things and he always took me seriously. He was sensitive and not afraid to be indecisive yet there was a real strength in him.

I laughingly asked him one day, "How'd you get to be so together?"

He smiled ruefully and cocked one eyebrow while he confided, "A lot of therapy and a good spiritual teacher."

"Really, you too?"

"Yea. Me. I was 19 when Foxglove had its first hit. A pretty immature 19. I didn't handle success well. In three years I wrote some big hits, made a lot of money, got married, started writing bad songs and showing up for gigs stoned out of my mind, threw away the money, and lost the recording contract. A couple of years later my wife left me. I came back here and played with a series of small time bands—when I was straight enough to play—and worked part-time jobs and watched my life go downhill. Finally one day a friend of mine pressured me to go talk to her shrink. I went and something clicked. I wanted another chance to go for the brass ring and to do it right the second time around. It took a long time and a lot of rough work to get this far... ."

"I know about that."

"What do you mean?"

"After *my* friends pushed me to their therapist, I spent a couple of years exploring issues and figuring out what I really believed before I could even bring myself to make a real commitment to music school. What did you mean about the spiritual teacher?"

"Well, my therapist turned me on to some new ideas and I started exploring more on my own. I wound up getting interested in the Hawaiian philosophy of Huna, found a good teacher and began studying with him. It's made a big difference for me."

"Huna. What's the philosophy about?"

"There's a lot to it, but the basis is really that people create their own realities with their thoughts and beliefs."

"You're kidding! That's the main principle that Kirsten—my therapist—has taught me. Just that one concept has changed my life around. Is there more to it?"

"Well, you can go very deeply into it, but the principles are quite simple, really. Like the idea that there aren't any limits to what you can create with your imagination. I mean, that sounds pretty easy, but when you really think about it, there's a lot to it. None of the physical laws or rules and regulations that we think of as limiting us have any real power to set boundaries."

"For instance?"

"Hmm. Take food. People tend to think that there are rules about their bodies, or biology, that are immutable, and that includes the idea that there are good foods and bad foods, foods that heal the body and foods that cause disease. It's amazing how many people who believe they create their own lives still believe that there are food rules that limit them. But really, you make the decision how any given food will affect your body by the beliefs you hold."

"You're not just talking about conscious beliefs then, are you? Because all kinds of people get ill from eating things that they don't consciously think are bad."

"No, the most important beliefs are often the unconscious ones and, let's face it, in this country we have some crazy beliefs about food."

"I'd really like to learn more about Huna. Would you mind spending some time teaching me about it?" The question just popped out and then it occurred to me that I had just been more forward than I'd ever been before. My stomach created a little throbbing knot and yet I also realized that it felt good to just ask naturally for what I wanted.

Pleasure spread slowly up his face, from the corners of his mouth pulling his chin up tightly to the gleam in his eyes. "Sure, I'd be happy to." He bit his upper lip thoughtfully and gazed into his cappucino as if expecting the foam to create a message. "In fact, we could start with one important idea now. It's called blessing. The idea is that everything you bless increases or multiplies. So if you say a prayer of thanks and blessing every time something happens that you like or appreciate, then you increase the incidences or amounts of that thing in your life."

"So, since I really love cappucino and I love having a quiet place like this to sit and have one, I should say, 'Thank you, universe, for providing me with this cappucino and this café'?"

"Right." He reached out and took my hands. "Let's do it together." He closed his eyes lightly while I repeated my prayer. Then they flickered open as I added, "And thank you for good company."

****

"This guy is great, Chloe. I don't get why you're holding back," Lisa admonished me after she and Terry had met Jamie and I for coffee a couple of times.

"Really, Chloe. He's all right," Terry agreed.

"Well, I know he's terrific. I'm just afraid to shake things up from where they are now. And what if he just likes me in a friendly sort of way?"

"I wish you could see how the two of you look at one another," began Lisa.

Terry cut in, "I have no qualms in telling you, if this guy isn't in love with you, I know nothing about the topic."

Lisa grinned, "And believe me, he knows plenty about the topic."

"You really think he looks at me like he loves me?" They both picked up pillows from the couch and lobbed them at me.

I don't know exactly when it was that I realized that my first reaction to Jamie had been absolutely right, but I did realize it and felt myself growing more in love by the day. I wasn't sure what he felt. Obviously we were close. And the things he taught me added a dimension to the work I'd been doing with Kirsten that made the world seem miraculous to me. I experimented all the time with the degree to which I could be the creator of my life.

But when it came to Jamie, I was afraid to push for more. I didn't know if I'd handle it any better this time than I ever had and I didn't want to jeopardize our friendship or my position in the band. When I thought about it I felt my muscles stiffen and realized that I was holding my breath.

I hadn't worked up the courage to do anything about it when Jamie drove me home one night after a gig and asked if he could come in and talk to me. He moved uneasily around the apartment while I put on a pot of decaf. When I returned to the living room he sat down near me on the couch and stared at his hands.

"What did you want to talk to me about, Jamie?"

"Now that it's time to start, it seems kind of crazy," he muttered, still staring down as he clutched his hands together and pulled them apart.

I reached over and took one hand in mine. "Try me."

He looked intently into my eyes and finally blurted out, "Would you think I was nuts if I told you that that first day when you walked into the club and looked up at me I thought, 'Oh my God, that's her. I've waited all my life for this woman'?"

I could have swooned. Instead, never taking my eyes off his, I slipped my arms around his shoulders. "Well, if you're nuts, then I'm nuts too," I whispered just before my lips met his.

Chapter Thirty-two

While my life was moving forward into new realms, the world of my childhood was changing. I didn't really notice for a while. Then one day Mom sent me a clipping from the Lexington paper telling about the closing of The Bon Mot. There were color pictures of the store and old Mr. Haslett. I collapsed on the couch in tears.

The Bon Mot had been the last of the old stores left downtown. All the other shops where Maggie and I had spent so many summer hours had long since closed, but I could still go to The Bon Mot whenever I visited. As long as it was still there, Lexington maintained something of the aura it had held for me. The last link, the store where Grandma had shopped before the first World War, where Mom had begged to have her books sent home, where we'd all bought clothes and candy and perfume, was gone.

I pictured Main Street the way it had become: the blank storefronts, the empty sidewalks. Floods of memories flew through my mind and I realized that Maggie and I could never cruise the shops again, that old family friends wouldn't stop to say hello to me because they died a long time ago, and many buildings I remembered no longer existed. The city I had adored from my earliest memories slipped away over the years until the place I knew had vanished just as thoroughly as if an earthquake or a bomb or something had levelled it. I felt the loss as if all the deaths and closings and vanishings had occurred at once and it took me days to stop grieving for what I could not get back. I wondered what it had been like for Grandma to watch the incredible changes that took place in her lifetime.

A couple of weeks later, Mom and Hunter came to town to see me, hear the band and meet Jamie—not necessarily in that order. We arranged for the four of us to have dinner one night before we played at a club that Jamie and I decided was nice enough for Hunter's finicky tastes. We picked an expensive restaurant to try to put her in a good humor before she came to hear the band. Jamie's family was pretty well to do and he'd had all the social graces lessons, so he pulled back chairs, opened doors, poured wine for the rest of us and was generally charming. I could tell Mom liked him.

"Aren't you going to have some wine, Jamie?" Hunter asked. I stiffened, remembering that Hunter never liked it when other people refused to drink with her.

"No, I don't drink."

"Oh, come on, we'll have fun."

"Sorry. I had a problem with drugs and alcohol when I was younger and I don't ever drink or get high now."

I watched her closely to see whether she was really taking this in, hoping that she would ask him some serious questions about how he'd stopped, but she just took a quick swig of Merlot and subsided from the conversation for a while. The rest of us kept on chattering inconsequentially. She eventually joined in and the tension passed.

After a while she started up again, though. "Jamie," she asked as uniformed waiters cleared the entrees, "is this music business the only thing you do?"

He swallowed a smile, "Why, yes, it is."

"You don't have a degree in business or something you can use when you're too old to play in one of these bands?"

"No, my first band took off my second year in college and I dropped out and never went back. Music is what I do."

"Hmph," said Hunter.

Jamie very sweetly made out a set list that night that let me sing more leads than usual. We put the two visitors at a table right up front and the rest of the place was jammed. I really had to work at blocking them out of my consciousness at first so that I wasn't too nervous, but I thought in the end we were particularly hot. By the time we'd played a couple of songs, I was always so into the music and the rhythm that, for once, I kind of forgot myself and just became a voice. Like I turned into pure music energy or something. I loved it.

I went alone to meet Mom and Hunter for breakfast the next morning.

"Well, I must admit you sing very well," Hunter owned.

Mom gushed, "I thought you were simply wonderful. The whole band. The audience went wild over y'all. It was quite something. And Jamie is just as attractive as he can be."

"I admit that he's good looking. His manners are fine. I can see why you're infatuated with him. And there's a sort of obvious mystique about him being a musician. But really, Chloe, you could do better."

"I don't think there's any such thing as a man better for me than Jamie." I stared at her with as much defiance as I could muster and hoped that she was receiving the signal that she was about to cross that line I'd drawn months before.

"Hmph."

It wasn't that long after their visit that Mom called me one day in tears.

"Chloe, I have some really bad news," she sobbed. My heart started pounding and I started asking her to tell me what but for a minute she cried so hard she couldn't say anything I could understand. Finally she pulled together enough to say, "Hunter's dead," before she broke down again.

I just sat there, listening to her cry and too stunned to speak. Eventually she managed to tell me that there'd been an accident and that she was flying to Lexington that night. I joined her the next day at Hunter's farm. The house felt empty and eerie. In every room I remembered some incident or conversation with Grandma or Hunter that had happened there. If a house could mourn, that one was doing it. I spent a long time in Hunter's study, where she'd told me how sad she was and that she wanted to be with Mike. I'd been so caught up with Jamie and the band that I didn't really check up on her as much as I probably should have. And I hadn't realized until much later that she'd never told Mom anything about how she was feeling. I'd assumed that Mom knew and would have been talking to her. Hunter was always so strong, I guess I didn't take it in that she could be that despondent. The police might have deemed this an accident, but I had an uneasy feeling she drove that Jaguar into the tree on purpose.

I went down to the tow lot to get Hunter's things out of the car. I couldn't believe how badly smashed in the front end was—the car must have been about three feet shorter. There was a small hole in the windshield with a complex web of cracks spreading out from it. I tried not to look at all the blood on the driver's side while I pulled out her purse, and the miscellaneous books and papers. When I noticed the brochure from the Betty Ford Center, I sat down right there in the dirt and cried. Suddenly I felt how lonely she must have been, how fragile and sensitive underneath all that bluster. How could we not have seen it? How could we have let her go downhill so far without doing anything to stop it?

Mom and I didn't talk much then, just enough that I knew she was feeling some of the same things. Mostly Mom was like a zombie as we went through the funeral and the reading of the will. Hunter had changed it the week before she died. Mom got half of the estate and she left me her half of my grandfather's farm and all her stock in Mike's company. I knew we'd all been resolving some of our problems with one another and apparently Hunter felt we'd done well enough that she changed her mind about the will, but I felt undeserving. I could have, should have done so much more.

****

After Hunter's death, I really wanted to get away and, in the midst of a frantic schedule of club dates, Jamie and I managed to cancel a few dates and to keep from booking anything new for two weeks. We spent a week in Paris, first. I barely noticed the city for the first few days and cried every time we got back to our room. At first, Jamie just stayed with me, let me be morose, held me when I cried and was generally wonderful. Then he suggested one day that I should really try to experience a little of Paris and hinted that he wouldn't mind enjoying it more. So, I pulled myself together and we spent the last few days running from park to museum to monument, walking by the Seine and sipping "café crème" at little round tables on the sidewalk.

Next we headed to the Riviera. Jamie and I wrote our first song together there. So far removed from my ordinary life, I managed to stop thinking obsessively about Hunter. At Foundation Maeght, I enjoyed wandering in the museum, but it was outside that I became mesmerized by Pol-Bury's fountain. As the sculpture moved and sent water cascading down into the pool, it sang a beautiful song. The fountain had a number of moveable chrome pipes that extended in different directions from a central core. It looked like it could be a creature that would walk into the bar from Star Wars. You could hear the water sliding down one of the pipes at a time, in one long note followed by a series of splashes as the water hit the pool. Little squeaks emanated from the pipes as they moved. Jamie, who had lingered in the Chagall chapel, found me sitting on a little stone bench, transfixed by the fountain. He sat down and threw his arms around me, planting a kiss under my ear.

I whispered, "Listen," and snuggled into him. He watched the fountain for a while and then closed his eyes to hear. "Do you hear the song?" I asked. In a minute we both began simultaneously to hum along—the same song.

Then he quietly instructed me, "Okay, try this Huna exercise. Close your eyes and go inside. Create a dream body. Send it into the fountain so that you can become the fountain, feel what it's like to be the fountain, hear the sound as the fountain hears it. And I'll join you."

I recognized that the exercise dealt in part with the idea that everything is connected, or one, and obediently closed my eyes. I visualized a dream version of myself that could see and hear and feel and sent it into the fountain. In a moment, I could feel Jamie join me there. The experience of the fountain's song immediately deepened for me. Each sound was sharper and I became aware of more nuances to the sound.

"Stay there," Jamie murmured, and began to hum again. I soon joined him and realized that the original melody was still at the center but our song had become more complex.

Once we'd gotten the melody, Jamie said, "Okay, you keep going with that," and he started doing percussion. After a while we realized that people were carefully walking in a wide circle around us, except a few admirers who stood back listening. When we stopped, one fellow threw a five franc piece at our feet. I smiled to myself when I realized that a couple of years before I'd never have had the courage to allow myself that wonderful experience. The world seemed to offer me new and wonderful adventures all the time and the new me jumped at opportunities I'd have recoiled from before—and had the time of her life.

When we finished, we sat in silence for a while, both saying prayers of thanks for the clear azure sky, the cool shade of the trees, the inspiration of the artists whose creations surrounded us and for the fountain and its song.

Making love with Jamie had been special, deep and profound, from the beginning. Every time we went beyond just physical pleasure and into realms of joy and expansion. The night we wrote our first song together, making love became a mystical union. As Jamie moved gently inside me, I lost all sense of separateness, unable to identify where I stopped and he began. We were one and in that night "ecstasy" took on new meaning.

Lying next to him the next morning, I noticed that my cheeks felt wet and reached up to wipe away tears that had fallen unconsciously. "Jamie, something happened," I murmured and raised myself on one elbow, from which vantage point I could see pools forming in the corners of his eyes, "I had this dream."

"I know," he said, "it was like cosmic. For a minute I felt like I saw the whole universe, and..."

"And we were both seeing the universe at once..." I added.

"Like we were one."

"I never knew two people could be so connected or..."

"Experience more profound bliss together than separately?" he finished.
****

Before that day, I hadn't really tried to write a song since I was a little girl. I remembered listening to the sounds on Hunter's farm and singing along. I had been hearing the songs around me again for a while, but it didn't occur to me to do anything with them. After we came back from France, Jamie and I continued to collaborate and I wrote a few songs on my own. For a while, I'd been visualizing myself sitting at a piano and writing songs, not sure how I wanted that to work out—and before long I started writing songs. When I could see a result like that, I found the process of creating my life amazing.

Between practices, gigs, travel time and our personal relationship, Jamie and I were rarely apart. I still wasn't sure that I knew how to handle a relationship. I regularly became aware that I had no role model for being truly intimate with another person and sometimes I felt like I was driving in the dark on a road that wasn't on the map or that I had landed on a distant star and had to learn how to relate to Pleiadeans. I worried that we spent too much time together and that Jamie would grow tired of me. To my amazement and delight, though, we grew closer and our connection became deeper. Our fights became occasions for both of us to learn about what it really means to create harmony between two people. Well, once we calmed down, anyway.

The band was doing well. We packed every club we played around Chicago and travelled around the Midwest and, occasionally, beyond. Some of the clubs were pretty small and funky, but we drew a lot of enthusiasm wherever we played. I basked in the warm energy that surrounded us every time a crowd of admirers came to hear us. A small, local label called 'Gator had sent people to hear us a few times and they finally signed the band a little over a year after I joined. My life had become so much like my dreams that I wondered sometimes if I were really awake. We were in the midst of cutting the album when Jamie offered me so much more that I began to panic.

"I saw Len Forest—you know, from Windjam—a few days ago. 'Gator's interested in signing them too except the company wants the band to get a new lead vocalist. I told him you'd be perfect for the spot. He was really excited and said if you're interested, you've got it."

"But, Jamie, what about your band? What about the record?" I jerked my head up to look at him. "What about us? You don't want me around any more?"

"Whoa. Where did that come from? Remember me, the guy who loves you? C'mon." He slid his chair back from the table and motioned me into his lap. After I settled in, he went on, "It's a great opportunity for you. You're a lead singer and this is a great shot. If I were just looking out for myself, I'd want to keep you in the band. You're not going to be easy to replace. And I want you with me. But I'm pretty sure 'Gator will sign Windjam if you're the vocalist—they love Len's tunes and all their comments about you have been great. You deserve this, Chloe."

Suddenly anger flared through my whole body. I leapt to my feet and whirled around to face him. "Don't pressure me to do what you want me to do," I snarled.

"Who's pressuring? I just told you I don't really want to lose you but this is such a great opportunity that I wouldn't stand in the way."

"Yeah, right." I snapped. "The way you're putting it makes it obvious that this is what you want me to do."

He opened his mouth to respond in kind, then closed it and stared at me for a minute. "What is this really about?" he asked.

I didn't know why I was so angry. But I couldn't cool down that fast. So I glowered at him and shrugged my shoulders.

"Come on Chloe, talk to me. I know that I haven't said anything that should have made you this angry with me. Are you making me your Dad again?"

We'd already discovered on other occasions that every now and then I reacted violently to statements or situations where Jamie suddenly reminded me of my Dad or said something my Dad might have said. "Well, I guess I do kind of look for any time you might be trying to tell me what to do," I admitted. But there was more to it.

Windjam's style was that sort of New Age rock/jazz sound that had become popular. The vocals suited my voice better than any other music and I had been hearing the likes of Julia Fordham and Barbara Long of Hiroshima and feeling like my time in music had arrived. Jamie's band leaned a little more towards rock, and singing backup limited me anyway. It would be a giant step forward for my career. And I was afraid about that. "But it's also that this feels like such a huge decision. It scares me and I guess I just need some time to let it sink in." Finally I came back to the big one. "And what about us Jamie? We'll be touring separately and working different schedules."

"I know. I'm trying not to think about that part. But we can work it out. I'm sure we can. If the records work for both of us we may be able to form our own band or do some separate projects together later or something. I just don't want you to throw away the best break you may ever get. Remember, 'now' is the moment of power. Don't let fears from the past or about the future stop you."

I waved to stop him. "I need to think. Please don't make this a philosophy lesson. How much time do I have?"

"Well, you wouldn't make the switch until we finish recording. But he'll need to know pretty soon. You'll have to talk to him and find out how soon he wants an answer. While you're thinking about that, there's something else I want you to think about." Then he asked me to marry him.

I was thrilled for a minute and then my stomach tightened. "Oh, Jamie, I can't tell you how much this means to me," I stammered, "but I'm feeling overwhelmed. This is all too much for me to take in and decisions that are too big for me to make all at once. Can you understand that?"

Shock crossed his face before he swallowed and nodded lamely. "I guess I can see that it's a lot to take in. I just thought, well, it seemed like this was clearly where we were headed. Are you still mad at me for bringing up the new gig?"

The hurt and bewilderment in his face pierced my heart, but, although I could reassure him that I really wasn't angry with him, I could not give him an answer that night.

****

"Oh, Kirsten, I feel absolutely panic stricken. I don't know what's the matter with me. I thought I'd finally changed and I wouldn't do this stuff any more. Jamie is really upset. He said he doesn't want to see me outside of work until I make up my mind. And I still haven't gotten everything about Hunter sorted out. Without Jamie around I keep feeling bad about her."

"First things first," she ordered. "You are not doing things the way you did them before. You're aware that you're feeling panic stricken and frightened. Not that long ago, you'd have been tense and nervous but you would not have been able to tell me what you were feeling. You also would have become totally reactive and you'd have done something wild to resolve the situation one way or another so you could get away from it. Instead, you're here, talking to me and trying to figure out how to go through this and come out on the other side without having destroyed anything. That's a whole new way of handling it. So don't be so hard on yourself. You've accomplished a lot."

I straightened up a little from the miserable slouch in which I'd placed myself when I sat down. "I guess you're right, this is different. Do you really think I can salvage this?"

"It isn't even at a point where 'salvage' is a word that is appropriate. Don't forget that energy follows attention—if your attention is focused on negative outcomes, that's where your energy is going to head." Kirsten had gotten interested in Huna after I talked to her about Jamie, and now she occasionally handed me one of the principles. "Now, tell me again how you feel about Jamie's love."

"Like I've said before, it feels almost preordained and I absolutely trust that he loves me—like I've never felt anyone loved me."

"What would it do to that trust if Jamie said he didn't want to make any more of a commitment to you than what you have now?"

"Oh, my. I guess it would shake my faith a little."

"Okay, I just want you to see what it means to you to feel that you can trust in his love—and maybe you can also understand Jamie's perspective and why he's reacted by withdrawing. Now, I want to come back to this, but first let's talk about Hunter. Why are you having such a hard time letting her go?"

"I don't know. She was such a big part of my life. And she was so big. Not in the size sense; she just, well, filled up a room. When she was there I felt insignificant and when she had something she wanted me to do I felt there was no room for me to have another opinion. I just spent all my time trying to keep her from getting control of me, trying to keep her power from taking me over. I don't know if I ever really saw her."

"What she chose to show you about herself was her power. Why do you feel that you should have known more?"

"Did I see what she chose for me to see or did I see only the part that fit my projections? I guess I feel like I should have been able to stop at some point and talk to her and find out what else she was. There had to be some reason she felt such a need to drink. If she were really as powerful as I thought she was she wouldn't have needed the booze to get through the day."

"You were a little girl through most of the time you knew her. She might not have been purposefully displaying herself as powerful, but from what you've told me, she certainly did make a point of concealing her vulnerability. Do you really think it was your job to understand what made her an alcoholic?"

"Maybe not as a little girl, but I've been grown for a lot of years now. I haven't seen her as often, but I knew she was drinking. Mom knew she was drinking. Since she wouldn't do anything, shouldn't we have done something? Signed her into rehab or something?"

"Do you really think that one person can force another to stop drinking?"

"No, I suppose not. But, if you see that someone is going over the edge, shouldn't you at least try?"

"Didn't you suggest to her that she try a clinic?"

"Yes. But maybe we should have gotten a court order and made her go in or something."

"If you'd forced her to quit, you know she probably would have gone back to it. The result probably would have been the same. Would you really feel better if she'd died in that accident but you knew that once you had had her committed against her will?"

"I don't know. I might feel better if I knew I'd tried to help her. But, when you put it that way, I'm not so sure."

"Is there any other reason you feel guilty?"

I didn't answer for a minute, struggling about admitting my failure. "I kept putting off really straightening things out with her. You know, always thinking there was time. She was so alone at the end. And she died before I could tell her that I loved her. Without knowing that I felt like she was the one who gave me a model for having the power to get out there and make things happen."

"Do you think she has to be alive for you to tell her how you feel?"

I stopped and stared at her. "No... no I don't. I believe that her spirit still exists and is aware of us."

"Why don't you think about saying some prayers and asking for her soul to hear you?"

"Yeah, that's a good idea. I'll try that."

"Good. Try it this week and we'll talk about how it went. So, now let's stop and look at what's going on with you about this marriage thing and see what beliefs may be operating here. First let's think about Jamie. I want you to go inside and ask how your mom and aunt and grandmother felt about the kind of love that you and Jamie have."

I obediently closed my eyes and delved in. After a few moments I opened my eyes, "None of them really believe that it's possible to find a love like Jamie and I have and make it work. What I felt was that none of them want to believe that it's possible to have and keep a relationship with this kind of depth because then their choices would have been wrong. Except maybe Hunter. I think she really loved Mike, but he died, so she didn't get to keep it. I think she felt like men just leave you. Anyway, it feels like a betrayal for me to say yes to this." I still had trouble talking about Hunter, especially in the context of ferreting out her faults.

"Okay. Now, how do they all feel about happiness in relationships and in work?"

It took me a little longer. "They believe you only get occasional moments of being happy. But mostly life is hard and a struggle and it isn't right somehow to get what you want in relationships or work."

"So if you're happy, what have you done with the family rules?"

"Broken them. Betrayed my family."

"I know you've gone into this before, but how do they feel about people being successful at what they want to do?"

"It's not OK. I think my mom has changed on that since her art became successful, but that's not what she taught me. So, another betrayal of family patterns."

"How do they feel about women getting up on stage and singing?"

"It's not what *ladies* do. Another betrayal."

"Okay, now we know what they thought about a lot of these things before and you've addressed most of these beliefs. But now we're looking at an underlying configuration. Are you seeing this?"

"Well, I feel some sort of responsibility to follow all their rules, like they're counting on me and I'm betraying them if I don't live by their codes."

"How does that make you feel?"

"Angry."

"Okay. We're going to go in and bash out some of that anger. But first I want to bring up your grandmother. You notice I threw her in today. We haven't really ever dealt with her very much."

"I guess I always felt so close to her and so much more supported by her than the others I didn't think of her as someone who hindered me. But I could feel the thread today—the way her attitudes influenced Mom and Hunter and then they influenced me. And I knew a lot of what she believed about the world."

"Are you ready to let yourself feel angry with her?"

"Well, you showed me with the rest of my family that it's not really about being mad at the person or blaming the person, just my childhood perceptions, so I guess I can do the same thing with my grandmother."

Actually it was a little harder to swing that bat and imagine that the figure was Grandma at first. But Kirsten fanned the flames until I could do it. "She doesn't think you should have Jamie's love, Chloe, what are you going to tell her? How about that chance to sing lead? She doesn't want you to do it. Are you going to let her stop you?" Before long I was yelling and bashing and crying at Grandma and then, one more time, at Mom and Dad and Hunter.

****

After emotional release work, Kirsten had me connect in meditation with whomever I'd been yelling at and get in touch with their reasons and how they'd gone off track from who they started out to be. I'd seen that Mom had started with this great sense of magic that came out in her art. And that Hunter had all this charisma and power. And Dad had been this fun-loving little boy. Now I saw that Grandma was always funny but she also had this adventurous tomboy aspect. I felt sad to realize how much they all gave up because of the family rules.

Then it was time to work on forgiving my images of them while insisting on breaking the ties to them and taking my own path. I made my decisions about Jamie and the band and felt that I needed to complete something more with Grandma. So, after conferring with Kirsten, I wrote a letter to her and took it down to the beach early one morning to read it to her.

Dear Grandma,

There are some things I need to talk to you about and so I'm going to hope that somehow you can hear what's in this letter.

I've been making some big decisions lately and I'm not sure whether you would really like them. Actually, that advice you gave me about not being afraid to live my own life my own way helped me a lot. I don't know if I'd even be in the position to mull over these great opportunities if you hadn't given me that encouragement. And the trust fund made a big difference. I was able to get therapy and go to music school and live in a nice place. If you meant what you said there at the end, I think you'll be excited for me.

I'm in love with this terrific man. His name is Jamie. He's a musician and he writes the most beautiful songs. You never seemed to think too much of musicians, but I understand the music in him. His hair is a little longer than you like, but I love the way it curves down below his neck. Well, I think he's very handsome, but what is more important, he understands me better than anyone ever has. We have this deep connection between us—it's hard to explain, but with him I've felt places deeper in my heart than I knew my heart had. Which is not to say we don't push each other's buttons and have some pretty good fights, because we do, but we also have a commitment to working things out.

We're both trying to live our lives according to a very different philosophy than what we were raised with—and that's important to both of us. Because of him and the changes we're making together, I've learned more about what it means to really love people than I ever knew.

The thing is, he asked me to marry him. And I've had a hard time saying yes. I have this feeling you didn't have this kind of love with Grandpa and I don't want you to feel bad about the choices you made. But I'm going to tell Jamie that I'll marry him. I hope that doesn't upset you but whether it does or it doesn't I'm still going to marry him. I think you only find a love like this once in a lifetime and I'm not going to lose it.

I also have a chance to be lead vocalist for a band that is about to land a recording contract. I always felt like no one in the family, including you, wanted me to sing or could even love the part of me that lived for music. I gave it up and tried to bury it and it was a long struggle to bring myself to the place where I have an offer like this. I'm already singing in front of people—I know, you think ladies don't do that. But I do it and I'm not a bad person because of it. It's my dream, Grandma. And this is my chance to go about as far with it as anyone can hope to go. I've learned that power comes from within—external forces don't make my life, I do.

I don't think you lived your dream. I wish I knew what it was. It's so hard for me to believe I never asked and you never told me. I felt closer to you than to anyone in the family and there is so much I don't know. From the things you told me on my last visits, though, I'm pretty sure that you gave up what you wanted for your life and that you ended up sorry that you had. So I hope you'll be glad to hear that I said yes to the band too. I chose to live my dream. I start after I finish recording with Jamie's band—oh, yeah, by the way, there's already a CD coming out that I'm on.

Mom's living down in Florida and selling paintings almost as fast as she can finish them. And she got a contract with a greeting card company that is reproducing her paintings on their cards. She's been happier since the divorce. But I always feel like there's a lot more in her than she lets any of us see. Still, ever since she went back to her art and it took off, she's been stronger. She actually reached the point where she told Hunter where to get off sometimes! Well, before Hunter died. Mom and I stood up to her one day and told her that if she got nasty with us ever again we wouldn't talk to her any more. Oddly enough, she really tried after that.

Speaking of Hunter, I'm really sorry, Grandma. I hope you aren't too disappointed that Mom and I didn't help her more, understand her better. I keep thinking that we could have stopped it. I've been hoping that she's found you and Mike and that she finally isn't lonely any more.

I miss you Grandma. I remember how you used to tell such funny stories and we'd laugh until our sides hurt. And how you stood up for me when Hunter or Mom pushed too hard. I don't think I ever thanked you for all the fun and the love and the coffee ice cream breaks. In therapy sometimes I felt like you and Uncle Mike saved me—if it weren't for the oases of support I had with the two of you, I don't know whether I'd have found the strength in me to pull through. Thanks Grandma.

Of course I never knew Grandpa and you didn't talk a lot about him. But I have the feeling that the love of your life was that guy Adrian and not my grandfather. So, I keep hoping that you and Adrian are cavorting around the universe together on some happy adventure. That's how I like to think of you.

Love,
Chloe

I slipped out that morning when it was still dark after calling Jamie and asking him to meet me on the beach in an hour. I was almost surprised that he agreed to see me. We'd only seen one another at practices and recording sessions, at which he was coolly civil, barely looking at me and not saying anything unrelated to the work at hand. As I arrived on the beach, the first streaks of pink were beginning to appear over the lake. When I finished reading, tears were pouring down my cheeks and I just sat there, watching the sun begin to stretch a bright orange path across the water toward me. It flashed through my mind that Grandma would like that.

Then I went inside and asked to connect with Hunter. When I had a sense of her presence, I began, inwardly, to tell her the things I'd never told her. Once I felt I'd said all that needed to be said, I just prayed for her. I finally experienced some sense of peacefulness about her sudden death, though I knew it would take a long time before I worked it all through. After a couple of minutes, I heard footsteps in the sand behind me and turned around just as Jamie sank down beside me.

"Okay, I'm here. What is it you want to talk to me about that couldn't wait until a decent hour?" He looked a little anxious and he didn't touch me.

I turned and wrapped my legs around him, planting my hands on his shoulders. "I'm ready to give you an answer." He stiffened a little, but didn't back away.

"Great. I think. At least, I mean, depending on the answer... ."

"Yes. My answer is YES!" I threw my head back and announced, "I will marry you Jamie!" I wrapped my hands behind his neck and kissed him.

He still didn't look too thrilled. "You really scared me, you know," he told me.

"I know. And I can't tell you how sorry I am. I just had some things to work through."

"What made up your mind? I mean, how can I be sure you're not going to back off again?"

"A lot of things. Not wanting to live without love the way my mom and grandmother did. Kirsten did some emotional release work with me that really helped. And we talked about the principle that loving someone means being happy with them. That panic and anxiety aren't about love, they're about old things. She asked me to look inside from a place where the past didn't influence me and to feel whether being with you made me happy. It did. It does." I hesitated before adding the final piece. "Then, that night I had this deep meditation and all of a sudden there was this voice from deep inside that said, 'This is your chance to break the family pattern and create a new one. Take it.' And it was so profound. There was more, but that was the big thing. I just knew that it was finally okay for me to say yes to being happy. And I won't change my mind."

He fell over backwards and stretched out, staring up at the sky while he pondered this. Then, a smile slowly grew, he pulled me over on top of him and started rolling. The sand was cool and soft enough to cushion us on our ride. A little short of the water's edge, he jumped up and spread his hands to the sun.

"She said yes. She's going to marry me!" he shouted.

I jumped in front of him and spread my arms out. "He's going to marry me!" I shouted and felt simultaneously afraid and more exhilarated than I'd ever felt before.

Epilogue

"A toast to Chloe's first performance. May it be the first of many!" Lisa raised her glass and Terry, Jamie and I put ours up to tap hers. We were celebrating in the new apartment Jamie and I were sharing. Most of the living room furniture was mine, but a few of Jamie's things were in there. They didn't exactly match, but it all sort of blended, my oak tables and his walnut-trimmed chairs.... The largest flat in my building had opened up just when we decided to get married and we were able to get it before it had ever been advertised. For the most part, ever since I landed the audition with his band, whatever I pictured for the next logical step seemed to appear soon thereafter.

"Absolutely," I added. "I loved it."

"You were great," Terry enthused. "I mean I knew you were good, but I haven't really heard you do that much as the vocalist before. Wow. I'm impressed."

"Thanks. I can't tell you how great I feel!"

"Well, tell us anyway, hon," Jamie demanded.

"It was like this moment I always dreamed about. But for so many years it seemed impossible to imagine that I would ever really be in the position to do it. And then, there I was, standing at center stage, knowing that I was the focus of attention. I mean, the rest of the band is fabulous and absolutely necessary and their solos are wonderful and all, but I'm the singer, the one people pay the most attention to. And instead of feeling self-conscious or worried that I didn't belong there, I was eating it up. And, there was this moment when I felt the energy of the crowd and I knew they were with me. It's like being swept along on this wave... I loved it. I don't know what else to say, I just loved it."

"I wish you could have seen her ahead of time," Jamie smirked and rubbed a hand up and down my back. "She had me by the collar backstage going, 'Oh my god, I don't think I can do this!'"

Lisa and Terry cracked up. "Did you really?"

"Maybe I was a little nervous," I allowed. "Actually I was a little nervous through the first couple of songs. But once I'd made it through those and my voice came out okay and the audience liked the numbers, I was into it. And it kept feeling more exciting to me as the night went on."

"You should be excited, Chloe, really." Lisa shook her head and smiled over at me. "When I think back over all the years... I didn't even know you wanted to sing at first. And when you did, once or twice, you sure didn't sound like this."

"Yeah, I remember that," Terry added. "And I remember when you first tried to go back to music school and dropped out. How depressed you were. You were questioning whether music was even what you really wanted to do."

"I don't think you ever told me that," Jamie turned to me in surprise. He leaned over and kissed me. "Well, I'm glad you changed your mind. We wouldn't have met...."

Things had not been quite the same with us since my hesitation over his marriage proposal. Having worked so hard to understand what it meant to me, I was more in love with him than ever. But I could always feel him holding back a little, being less open to me than he was before. We talked about it every now and then. All he could tell me was that he'd had this huge faith and openness about me—so much so that it had never occurred to him that I would say anything but a resounding yes when he proposed. It came as such a shock when I took so long to think about it that it took away some of that faith. He still loved me, but now I had to hold the faith that one day we would get back the depth we once had. He'd always been there for me when I had doubts and I figured it was my turn to be there for him. Fortunately there was still enough love that we both wanted to get married.

"Speaking of the two of you meeting, have you set a date yet?" Lisa asked.

"Well, we can have a week off in three months if each of our bands can clear one club date. We'll know next week if we can do it then. Otherwise, we haven't decided whether to go ahead or wait for a time when we can have a honeymoon right away."

"Oh, this is so exciting," exclaimed Lisa, squeezing Terry's knee.

Jamie threw his arms around me, spilling a little of that bubbling cider in his enthusiasm. "Yes, it is exciting." He started to kiss me and got my ear as I whipped my head around to add, "Yes, very exciting."

I was glad that Jamie got along so well with Lisa and Terry. Among the three of them, I felt supported and loved the way I wished I'd been able to feel when I was growing up. Jamie and I were a few weeks into our new schedule since I'd started rehearsing with the new band. I felt a little lost at first, not seeing him as much as I had. But sometimes I also sort of guiltily enjoyed having a little more space for myself than I'd been having. We made a deal that we would put aside some time every day that we were both in town that would be just for us. So far that was going well, but, of course, it was pretty new.

The phone rang in the midst of our celebration.

"Hi, Chloe, it's Mom. Well, how did it go last night?"

"It went great!"

"Yes? Oh, I'm so pleased." Mom sounded really enthusiastic. "Did you have a big crowd?"

"The place was packed. The band did some good promo and Jamie made announcements at his last few gigs. Standing room only."

"Sounds marvelous," she said. "So you're still planning to marry Jamie?"

I had scooted over and settled between his knees to lean back on his chest. I moved to the side and grinned up at him, "Yes, I'm still planning to marry Jamie. We're trying to get a date set when we can both take a little time off."

"Is your schedule so busy then?" she asked.

"Yes, Windjam had already been booked all around town with their old vocalist, so we're playing a few nights every week."

"Well, that's great. Really."

"Yes. I'm so glad that.everything is working out so well for you." Mom really sounded like she meant it.

"Well, listen, some friends are here and I really should get back to them. But I'm so glad you called to hear about last night. It was a big success I think. You'll have to come up to hear the band."

"Yes, that would be nice."

After I hung up, the phone rang again.

"Chloe, it's Maggie."

"Hi! How are you?"

"Great. I wanted to hear about last night and to find out whether you all have set a date so I can figure out a schedule for designing and making your dress."

I caught her up on all the news while the others chatted softly in the background. As soon as I hung up, the doorbell rang and Kirsten waltzed in when I opened it, hair as wild as ever and a bottle of sparkling cider in hand.

"Sorry I couldn't make it earlier," she apologized as she handed me the bottle. "I thought just a little bubbly would be in order. We were so impressed last night, Chloe." She brought several friends to my debut. "When I think about the amount of change in you since the day I first saw you. What a transformation! I feel so successful." She slapped her hands together and threw her head back, laughing.

I drifted back through the past and examined the woman I had been as though she were a stranger, so far removed did I feel from the life I had been living then. I saw myself, shy and awkward, shrinking to the back of the room to avoid contact with people, hunched and sullen. I remembered tossing and turning with such tightness and pain in my neck that I thought I couldn't bear it. Amazing to think that I had been that person.

"I'd like to propose another toast," Jamie recalled me from my reverie. We all grabbed our glasses, and poured the cider.

"Okay, what do you want to toast?" I asked.

"I want to offer a toast to living your dreams and to finding true love."

Five glasses shot upward and bubbles sprayed into the air.